AGENTS OF FORTUNE

MARISOL'S WINDOW

JEFFREY TODD EVANS

Agents Of Fortune
©2020, Jeffrey Todd Evans

Inevitechpress@gmail.com

All rights reserved. This book or any portion thereof may not be reproduced or used in any manner whatsoever without the express written permission of the publisher except for the use of brief quotations in a book review.

Any references to historical events, real people, or real places are used fictitiously. Names, characters, and places are products of the author's imagination.

ISBN: 978-1-09833-130-6
ISBN eBook: 978-1-09833-131-3

Acknowledgment

This book would not be possible without the inspiration, guidance, and editing skills of Scot Andrews of Barcelona, Spain. I would also like to thank my Mom for her faith in me. My Uncle Ernest and his wife Barbara Kolowrat for having belief in this project. Additionally, I would like to thank David Brown at invisibleinkediting for his manuscript advice. Lastly, I want to thank my sister Christy Milliken for her "back to reality" beta-reading insights.

"I can pluck a nobody from Nowheresville and make them special."

"I don't think you can."

"Care to wager?"

"Since we're old friends, how about one-tenth of your power against one-tenth of my realm?"

"Make it one percent"

"Agreed."

—Algeronian epigram

CHAPTER 1

They say I killed billions, but come on; that's an awfully big number. I suppose the truth is out there somewhere, existing between the cracks and crevices that sometimes form when fiction and reality converge. And by the way, if you're reading this right now, you're a part of that truth. So try not to be too judgmental and remember, things were different back then. History needed a villain; how else could it justify its very existence?

Perhaps I should start at the beginning. I was an average baby, born after two older siblings and ahead of two younger. By the time I reached ten years of age, I lagged behind most of my contemporaries in both size and achievement. At twenty, I dropped out of college and silenced the irritating noise of the world by observing it from the backyard of a shack I lived in. By the age of thirty, I remained unmarried, unremarkable, and inebriated. By the time forty had come and gone, I'd retired from the human race altogether. Then, on my fiftieth birthday, something remarkable happened: I got a second chance.

My name is Seth Bridges and this is my story.

It was April 19, 2010. I was power snaking an overhead waste line at the Dunes Bluff Motel and had just received a complimentary shit shower, courtesy of a sewer line's cross-threaded cover plate, when my phone vibrated. I turned the snake off, removed my gloves and pulled out my phone.

"What."

"Hey. I need you to head over to Bay View Motel and swap out the coils on that hot-water heater in the tens building. They're full up for the weekend and it's an emergency. There's fifty bucks in it if you get them to commit to a new install. And answer the damn phone when I call. It's a company phone; that's what it's for."

"Yeah, about that. You can have the phone back. I quit."

"Goddammit Seth, not this crap again. We both know you don't have a choice. Listen, we'll talk about this later. But for now, I need you to wrap up what you're doing, head over to the Bay View, and get them to buy a new unit. OK?"

I dropped the phone into the watery mess of human excrement at my feet, stripped off my coveralls, and headed over to my truck. After picking up some supplies at Perry's Liquors, I drove down Provincetown Massachusetts' section of Route 6 and pulled into the Herring Cove Beach parking lot.

It was early in the tourist season and thankfully, the beach was relatively empty: some dog walkers and a few people eating their lunch and enjoying the day. I smelled like crap and my headache from binge-drinking the night before was demanding attention. After downing a nip of vodka and a whole can of Budweiser, I lit a smoke and stared at the ocean.

I don't have a choice. Really? Sounds like noise to me. I flicked on the radio, then pulled the .38 revolver from under the seat and laid it on my lap. A human-interest story spilled out of the truck's torn speakers: An old geezer on his deathbed was boasting that the only regret he'd ever had, in his entire life, was not proposing to his *lovely* wife sooner. "A day, an hour, or even another second," he went on.

What an idiot, I thought. Ninety-six years on this planet and his only regret is not having another day with his wife? What, your life was so perfect you can't think of one thing you'd change? That's pushing it, don't yeah think? You never stole anything you didn't need to? You never told lies to prop yourself up? No regrets about being hurt by someone? Oh, or better yet, you don't regret hurting other people, because what, you're a goddamn fucking saint and you love your dead wife? Bullshit. They'd have been better off doing a story on Alzheimer's. The talk-show pablum and yesterday's drink had bile rising in my gullet.

That's about the time I saw her—down aways, along the shore. She was barefoot, wore a long white summer dress, and was skirting the line between sand and sea. And in a town populated with lovesick lesbians, hornymoes, and hip-happy hippies, she was anything but ordinary. I couldn't make out her face through the sand-pitted windshield, but there was something about her, something that seemed so—right. I used the rule of thirds along with the truck's windshield to frame her and the beach.

"Not bad," I said to myself. Then I drank another nip, changed the station, and wondered if I knew her.

An encore broadcast of Art Bell's paranormal talk show *Coast to Coast* rattled out of the dashboard speakers. Today's topic: the end of the world as prophesied by the Mayan calendar. The callers sounded convinced the end was near. Hell, I thought: wasn't the world always ending for somebody, somewhere? I rested my chin on the top of the steering wheel and imagined a fiery asteroid streaking across the sky—smashing into the ocean.

"Tell you what," I said to God through the windshield, "send one of those suckers down here right now. Go ahead and use me as a target. I dare you... Yeah, that's what I thought, wuss."

On the radio, the lyrics to the show's bumper music, "(Don't) Fear the Reaper" by Blue Oyster Cult, theorized about the number of people that die every day. They had it at forty thousand, but the song was thirty years old. I quickly calculated, due to population growth and other reasons, that the number should have been around 100,001. I downed another nip and put the barrel of the .38 into my mouth.

Everything faded into nothingness. And then, I was a kid again, back in my childhood home.

CHAPTER 2

McCarran International Airport, Las Vegas
January 28, 1980

Eight interesting years later, I arrived in Las Vegas. I was eighteen, had fifty-eight years of life knowledge under my belt, had just graduated from high school—for the second time—and was ready to exploit my good fortune and wait for further instructions. I walked down the jetway, past the slot machines and wide-eyed tourists, and over to the baggage claim.

"Yo, Bridges, see you made it in one piece."

Colton Hill, an ex-classmate from Tabor Academy, waved to me from the gate. A mutual friend had arranged for him to pick me up, and hopefully, help get me settled.

"Hey, Colton." I offered a handshake. "Thanks for the lift."

"Yeah, sure. Whatever." He ignored my extended hand and flicked his cigarette to the floor. "Come on, grab your crap."

He drove me to the outskirts of the city and into an area of Las Vegas that public servants, cabbies, and anyone carrying items more valuable than a pair of Nike's probably avoided. Our conversation was limited to Colton's deficient view of the world, his contempt for his incarcerated dad and, as he so eloquently put it, "gay fucking preppies." Probably still embarrassed that he got expelled for smoking in his dorm room.

He pulled up to a squad of overstuffed garbage barrels and jammed the car into park. "I live in the back. You can crash on the couch."

As we walked up his driveway, past a burnt-out Lincoln Continental resting on cement blocks, he slapped me on the back. "I hope you like gooks, coons, and spics, because the neighborhood's crawling with them. It's a fucking zoo around here. Goddamn hebes aren't far behind. But hey, a guy like you..." He loomed over me. "Christov said you had cash. How much you got?"

His breath stank of ass, his mind of misery.

"I'm out of here." I turned and walked back down the driveway.

"Hey preppy," he yelled. "You owe me money for the ride."

I dropped my suitcase, pulled up my shirt and exposed the hundred grand taped to my waist—cash I'd amassed betting long odds against old money.

"Here it is," I said. "Come and get it."

At five ten and one hundred fifty pounds, I didn't cut much of a threat, but I hated bullies, and this guy knew I'd spent most of my free time at school training in the sweet sciences of boxing, Greco wrestling, and a whole complement of martial arts.

Time traveling does have its benefits.

He scrunched his face and yelled, "Fuck you, jerk-off." Then, jabbing his thumb into his chest, he hollered, "I run Vegas. Understand? I *run* Vegas."

I pulled a twenty from my billfold, crumpled it up, tossed it in his direction, then headed toward the Strip.

After a mile or so, the temperature dropped rapidly and the skies closed in with black cloud walls. Somehow, I'd stumbled into one of those micro-bursts the weathermen occasionally speak of. Howling wind cratered rain into my face. And, as if that wasn't bad enough, pebble-sized hail began to pelt me. I crouched next to a postal drop box and took cover under my suitcase. Surprisingly, a cat had taken shelter under the drop box too. I rubbed its chin and said, "Hey, buddy." It purred.

I spotted a cab, flagged it down and got into the back seat.

"That's some nasty weather we're having," said the driver. "You just get into town? Where you headed?"

The redheaded cabbie was fortyish, had a thick, bold crust around her mannerisms, and looked a little like the pop-star Bette Midler.

"Jeez," I said over the swooshing of the cab's wipers. "That came out of nowhere. Does this kind of thing happen a lot around here?"

"Not really. I was going to ask if you brought it with you."

"Ahh, I don't think so... Well, thanks for stopping. I'm looking for a motel. Something near the Strip, nothing special, low profile."

"Know just the place." She zeroed the meter. "Name's Dextron. Most folks call me Dex. So... what the hell are you doing out here in Shitsville, in the middle of a tornado no less?"

"Yeah, well, it's a long story."

Twenty minutes later she pulled up to the lobby of the Starlite Motel. "This is the place, kid. Here's my card."

I thanked her with a twenty and checked into the Starlite Motel—room #5. The place had a worn shag carpet, funky floor-length purple drapes, a puffy flower-patterned bed cover, and, on the wall, opposite the bed, a velvet painting of Elvis. A black-and-white television and a small refrigerator crowded the top of a dresser. A small occasional table and two chairs were jammed into a corner. The air conditioner clamored and clunked, which wasn't so bad because the noise helped isolate the room from the outside world. The power cord to the bed's Magic-Fingers coin meter had been cut, maid service was every other day, and for ninety bucks a week, I had a new home.

I called my mom to let her know I'd arrived safe and sound, then unpacked my suitcase: clothes, toiletries, a bottle of whiskey, a family photograph taken last Christmas at my grandparent's farm, a journal I'd started eight years ago, and a book on the legendary Japanese swordsman Miyamoto Musashi—a gift from my Budo instructor, Master Poe.

I was tired from the long trip, and the meal on the plane had left me hungry, but still, I was here, exactly where I wanted to be.

The storm from earlier had returned, but I felt safe from the thunder and rain inside this old motel room—surely it had withstood worse. I drank a few shots of whiskey, then went to bed and thought about my plans for the next day: secure my cash, get some decent clothes, and get ready to place some bets on the upcoming Winter Olympics in Lake Placid.

I closed my eyes and fondly remembered Jim Craig, the goalie for the US hockey team, skating around the Olympic ice rink, draped in the American flag. Craig and the rest of the ragtag squad of US Olympic hockey hopefuls would go on to win the gold. Their victory against the USSR would be called the Miracle on Ice.

My first night in Vegas was unsettled: strange surroundings, loud noises, and a recurring dream had me tossing and turning all night. I had named the dream The City of The Dead, and whenever I had it, I couldn't help but think there was a message in it.

It was an upsetting dream: thousands of putrefying human corpses lay scattered about a decaying city landscape. A few hundred yards in front of me, on a parkway, a house-sized dredge hovered between two decrepit skyscrapers. The dredge had spider-like robotic arms that were busy inhaling, chewing, and unceremoniously spitting fermented bodies into its hold. People-juice drained from the machine's belly as a compactor pressed the remains further into its gut. A loudspeaker, mounted atop its cabin, broadcast: "Bring out your dead. Bring out your dead."

And every time I was there, I tripped on a sidewalk cornerstone, dropped to my knees, and wretched out the contents of my stomach. Then, while gasping for air—and admiring a horde of maggots attempting to animate the remains of a nearby cadaver—I would look up. Two blocks down, a pack of sturdy-looking survivor dogs gathered under a statue of a man holding a book. Their eyes keyed in on my movements. The largest dog spun around in a circle and wagged its tail, like it was happy to see me.

That was my recurring dream.

CHAPTER 3

In the morning, I deposited thirty grand into a checking account at the nearby Vegas Trust Bank, then headed down Las Vegas Boulevard in search of a tailor who could sharpen up my image. Back in my previous timeline, I'd seen a series of commercials for Allstate Insurance. They had featured a sharp-dressed guy called Mayhem. That guy wore the best-looking suit I'd ever seen. The single-breasted black jacket was snug and was complemented by a dark, low-cut vest, a starch-white collared shirt, and a charcoal tie with a slim diagonal white stripe. That was the look I wanted.

I spotted a sign across the street: Mung's Suits, Wen Nguyen Proprietor.

As I opened the door, new linen in the presence of Old World craftsmanship filled my senses.

"You need suit," said the man hustling over from behind the counter. "I make you look like Cary Grant."

I looked around the crowded but well-organized shop. "Alright. Sounds good to me."

After he took my measurements, I ordered five custom-fitted Mayhem suits and two pairs of shoes. Wen assured me that one suit would be ready by tomorrow, although it would take five days for the remaining four. I left a deposit and made a quick left into the barbershop next door—which was owned by Wen's brother Win.

After my cut, I ambled over to a Middle-Eastern food cart, aptly named Mohamed's Middle Eastern Food Cart, and ordered a falafel wrap.

"You are new, yes?" said the cook as he worked the grill.

"Yeah, just got in town. I'm Seth. How's it going?"

"It is going very well, thank you. I am Mohamed. This is my cart. I serve the freshest and most delicious food on the Strip."

With a name like that, I just had to bust his chops and ask, "Hey Mohamed, do you believe in God?"

He paused, looked at me with a face that indicated offense, and handed me my food. "Eat, my friend; your question, it will cease its importance."

He was right; the food trumped all thoughts of God and faith. I ordered a second serving.

After lunch, I hailed a cab. "Sands Casino, please," I said as I got into the back.

The driver stank of dirty socks, cigarettes, and a liberal slathering of Hai Karate aftershave lotion—the latter of which was battling a cloud of Pig-Pen-squiggly-lines that enveloped him. Stinky Driver released the emergency brake with a loud *clunk*, and as he drove, he used hand signals for turns.

"How's it going?" he asked.

I looked up at the rearview mirror and saw the eyes of a tweaker on the wrong side of a meth binge. "Good, good. You?"

"I'm Dings. I can get you anything you need. Anything."

"Just the ride for now, thanks."

At the Sands Casino, the cabbie turned, handed me a card, and said, "You need anything, call me."

I paid the fare and gave the driver an equal tip.

CHAPTER 4

The Sands Casino was glorious: with its lights, sounds, and hustle, it was everything I'd imagined. I stashed 20k in an in-house safe deposit box; then, after downing a frosty beer, I walked past an aging security guard, placed a hand on the staircase's brass rail, and went down to the sportsbook: a place where dog races, horse races, football, and almost every other sport were worshiped with sacrifices of money, faith, and family.

I snagged an abandoned newspaper and took a seat at a booth. News was needed to awaken old pathways in my memory. It was one thing to have lived this timeline before, and another remembering the details of *what* exactly had happened and *when*—specificity was what I was looking for.

It was in the sports section of the *Las Vegas Times* that I found it. In two weeks the 1980 Winter Olympics would begin. As I was tearing out the hockey schedule, I noticed an article below. It was an announcement for an upcoming middleweight title fight: *World Middleweight Boxing Champion Vito Antuofermo will defend his WBA and WBC titles against #1 ranked challenger, Marvelous Marvin Hagler. The bout will be contested at Caesars Palace on 1/02//80.*

Holy fuck, I thought. That was tomorrow. How had I missed this? My heart raced. I put the paper down and calmed myself.

I was never a big sports fan, although I have to admit, Marvin and his fights were different; he was a local hero back in Brockton, Massachusetts, and I held onto the rounds he fought as if they were my own. Marvelous Marvin was arguably the best middleweight boxer ever: his arm length was an anomaly, his ambidextrous style allowed him to control the ring with either a left or right-handed jab, and his right cross was powerful enough to end the careers of most of his challengers. Years after he retired—in my past timeline—I would stay up late at night, drinking and watching his fights on YouTube. Hell, one time I saw him in person. I'd snuck into a post-fight press conference at the Boston Garden. Marvin's people were clearing out the dressing room, and a disabled fan, grasping a pen with a palsied hand, stumbled over to the champ. And just as he got close, he tripped and fell. I rushed over and helped the fan get to his feet. Marvin joined in on the assist and welcomed the unfortunate soul. After Marvin signed the disabled fan's fight card, he turned to me and shook my hand. That was when I knew Marvelous Marvin Hagler was a true champion—worthy of my admiration.

According to my memory, Marvin was supposed to lose this fight in a controversial fifteen-round draw.

I went to the betting window and asked about the odds in this weekend's middleweight championship fight.

"Antuofermo is a 4:1 dog," said a skinny guy behind the window.

"Can I place a bet on the winner and round?"

"Well, if you're referring to a propositional wager, I can get those odds for yeh. But uhh"—he slicked back his hair—"what kind of money are we talking here?"

"I've got forty grand."

"Alright. Just give me a few minutes. Why don't you take a seat; I'll find you when I've got those numbers."

Ten minutes later he came over and handed me a notepad along with a pen. "Sir, my supervisor would like you to write down the exact bet."

Never bet against your heart: that's what my old friend Mike the Bookie used to say. Sorry Mike, but your advice didn't apply in this world.

I wrote: *Vito Antuofermo will retain his title in a fifteen-round draw. Wager: $40,000.* I handed the pad back. The skinny guy gave it a glance, offered a nod, then pigeon-toed back to his cage.

I looked around the casino and wondered if my action would affect the outcome of this closely decided boxing match. Back in prep school, I'd made smaller bets—mostly with my classmates' rich dads—and I hadn't been able to discern any worldly changes. I suppose I was an authority on such things, being a time traveler and all, but most of what I know about this sort of stuff comes from the movies, and they all seem to agree that changing the past leads to disastrous results. But I wasn't really changing anything; more like I was benefiting from it. Yeah, I was benefiting from the past. Nothing wrong with that.

"Excuse me, sir."

"Yes?"

I looked up and saw an interdimensional monster—or at least what I thought one would look like.

Panic oozed from the reptilian part of my brain. Was it here to kill me? Adrenaline shot into my veins. No. It was wearing an employee name tag. He worked here.

"Hi," he said. "My name is Adamit Lee. I'm the cage supervisor. If you could just follow me back to the window, we can get this bet wrapped up."

My God, I thought. This guy was a frigging beast. "Sure," I said, nodding. "No problem."

He was huge: six foot seven, a good three hundred fifty pounds. A scar ran diagonally from the corner of his forehead to the underside of his chin, and his hands were the size of old-time baseball gloves.

He brought me into a side room. "We can offer you 6:1. You might do better at some of the other casinos, but it's fair odds."

Without further comment, I handed the monster four 10k bundles. He smiled, then gave me a receipt and a pair of general-seating tickets for the fight.

I made a wobbly dash for the exit—with the help of Paranoid, a friend of mine who liked to show up when things got sketchy. Then I stumbled down Las Vegas Boulevard.

I hurried back to my motel room and drew the curtains tight. After pouring myself a whiskey and downing it, I thought, shit, that sportsbook guy had looked scary. I drank another shot, lay down on the bed, and once again tried to figure out how grateful I should be: I was alive, and from what I could gather, living in an alternate reality that took place a lifetime ago. Maybe I was still dying, back in my other world, and this reality existed within the expansion of time occurring between the last beats of my heart. A funky-ass reincarnation system like that seemed plausible enough to go on indefinitely. Just then, the phone rang. Paranoid, who had decided to stick around, crossed his arms and shook his head as if he knew something was up.

"Hello?"

CHAPTER 5

"Hi Seth, it's Mom."

"Oh, hey Mom, how's everything?"

"Not so good. I have bad news. Grandpa, he ahh, he died yesterday."

"Oh..."

"The doctors said he went quickly, so... there's that."

"Jeez, Mom, I'm sorry. Are you OK?"

"Oh, I'll be alright."

"When is the service?"

"Well, there are plans that need to be made... I know you two were close."

"Mom, he was your dad; what about you? Are you going to be alright?"

"Yes, yes. I'll be fine. I have to make some calls; you take care, Seth."

"You too, Mom."

I had known this day would come—but now?

I thought he had lived a few years longer.

Grandpa had been born in Czechoslovakia in 1898. He had fought in three wars—the first one from the back of a horse. A man among men, he was an actual count from a family of aristocrats that had been around since the fourteenth century. He had owned forests, industries, palaces, and castles before the Nazis confiscated it all. His unwillingness to bend to Hitler's tyranny had seen him buying passage for his family and himself on the SS *America*. They had landed at Ellis Island, New York. Eventually, they had made their way to Western Massachusetts and bought a dairy farm for 250 pieces of gold.

I had a few more whiskeys, entered some notes into my journal, then hit the hay. Right before I fell asleep, I glanced down at the glass's crumpled sanitary wrapper: someone had drawn a drunken smiley face on it. And for the slightest part of a moment, I swore it winked at me.

That night I had my recurring dream again, only this time it was lucid, immersive, and things had changed: as I was staring at the pack of dogs under the statue of a man holding a book, like I normally did, a wall-like invisible wave washed over the place and it became alive again—well, half-alive. Someone had removed the bodies, cleared the streets, and the pack of dogs no longer waited under the statue of the man holding a book. There was a slight breeze, and above me the sun grappled with cloud cover. Here and there, dust devils dervished with clumps of migrating trash. Up ahead, just past a hub of crumbling buildings, dark cloud banks gathered—as if they were preparing to wall-in the metropolis.

Just as I was admiring the details of my own dream, a rudimentary Heads Up Display appeared in my mind. That's pretty cool, I thought. The HUD indicated the city was San Francisco and the year was 1995, five years after the Soul Breaker virus had run its course. Hm... Soul Breaker Virus, that's a cool name. Nice one, Seth.

I stood and tried to jump up and float—a test I'd developed to determine if I was in a dream or not. Nope couldn't float; this was not a dream. Probably a vision of some type. But wasn't I asleep? A hovering, box-shaped van pulled alongside me and whooshed open its doors. Inside, leathery human skeletons lay crumpled-up on the floorboards. An electronic voice said, "Thank you for choosing Bezos Peoples Transport."

I waved it off. "No thanks, I'm good."

The zombie cab sputtered away like a cartoon mash-up of a *Jetsons* car stuck in a *Scooby Doo* ghost town. Up ahead, the statue of the man holding a book was, on occasion, moving like an idle character in a video game. I jogged the block and a half between us, looked up at the twelve-foot bronze, and said, "Hey! Is somebody in there?"

He lowered his book—which I recognized as the Bible—stooped slightly and said, "Greetings, traveler. Welcome to the fair and humble city of San Francisco. I'm an animatronic representation of our recently deceased mayor: the most honorable and enlightened Reverend James Warren Jones. The time is 10:00 a.m., and all is well. Can I help you with directions to a restaurant, a nightclub or bar, a museum, a sexual encounter—or perhaps you're in need of spiritual guidance?"

"Where are the dogs that used to hang out here?" I asked.

The animatronic Jim Jones pondered my question for a moment before performing a Nazi-style hand salute. "Heil Ted," he said, then pointed to a five-story building that held a large vertical arrow pointing down to a neon sign that blinked out: Kaczynski's Doomerville Lounge & Surgical Saloon.

"Thanks," I said. "And lay off the Kool-Aid; you're starting to look a little rusty." Just as I turned to cross the street, I noticed somebody had sloppily painted "Heidi Was Here" onto the base of the statue.

A half-block down, I caught my reflection in a dirty, cracked storefront window.

"Oh shit."

I was old again. I had a scraggly, greying beard, an old New England Patriots tee-shirt was wrapped around my head like a turban, and I was wearing a faded one-piece striped jumper. In the reflection, a dinner-plate-sized flying saucer was silently hovering a yard behind my head. The drone bore an uncanny resemblance to the *Jupiter 2* from the TV series *Lost in Space*. I turned around quickly and swiped at it a few times, but like a dog playing a game, it was too fast to catch. I headed over to the giant arrow with the *Jupiter 2* in tow.

Kaczynski's Doomerville Lounge & Surgical Saloon was sandwiched between two dilapidated storefronts. It had mottled spray-on siding and a boarded-up window protected by rusty steel bars. Amazed at my mind's capacity for creating such a scenario, I went inside for more.

The place was dark and smelled of musty zombies—if there was such a smell. Celtic dirge music drifted innocuously in the background. A half dozen ugly people—probably descendants of the *Village People*, or at the very least, escapees from the Island of Doctor Moreau—sat on red stools tucked in close to the bar. Cool: a seedy club in a post-apocalyptic San Franciscan slum. I should remember all of this, I thought, and write it in my journal.

I sidled up to the bar, tossed a few smiles at the other patrons, then looked down at the electronic menu embedded into the bar. As I ordered a cold beer, a Chiron scrolled a news-vert along the bottom of the screen: *Eugenicist Doctor Octavius Sun Taziu, from the New Caltech territory, has submitted his final plans to repopulate the planet.*

"Octavius? Hmm...?"

"Are you talking to me?" The bartender draped a small towel over his shoulder. "You must be talking to me." He came closer, groaning out pieces of mental anguish along the way. Then he stood before me. "You got something to say, honey, you just go ahead and say it."

Dear God. The dim overhead lighting revealed a visually disturbing bar-keep of mixed gender. They, he, or she stood around six-five and was wearing a sleeveless plaid shirt that showcased toned biceps and grotesquely swollen, Dolly-Parton-sized breasts. He batted his Tammy Faye eyelashes, nodded at the electronic menu, and said in a deep, cigarette-damaged voice, "Menu's dead tech. Died with the dog people. Just a stream of news-verts now—pretty, though. So, tell me, friend. What's a nice girl like you doing in a place like this?"

Nearby, two booze-sodden barfly queens, who were nursing dildo-shaped steins of beer, snickered. A third, who appeared to have constructed a bathhouse-sailor personality around his Tom Selleck mustache, pulled a wet, stubby cigar butt away from his mouth long enough to jeer, "Yeah, what's a nice girl like you doing in a place like this? Heh, heh, heh."

Where in my mind had these guys come from? I looked around the bar, then at the barkeep, and said, "Since you're all figments of my imagination, and I'd like to keep my buzz on, I'll take a beer and a shot of rum. Please."

The bar-keep tossed me a friendly nod, motioned me closer, and said, "I need to scan your PIC." Behind him, a cockroach the size of an anemic lab-rat scampered along an empty display shelf. My HUD flashed: *PIC. Personal Identification Chip, used for transaction facilitation. Location: underside of right wrist. Caution! All subjects in the immediate vicinity are exhibiting high levels of deception.* I held out my right wrist.

A pink laser beam shot out of a small lens embedded between the barkeeper's eyes.

"Says your BlockChain is empty."

I looked closer at the gender-phobe's face and could see botched surgery scars underneath his smudged mascara. Damn, I thought, Snake Plissken would love this place.

"Listen, buddy," I said, "this is my dream, and you'll give me whatever I want."

The bar-keep placed the drinks in front of me and said, "Hail Ted."

The peanut gallery saluted with their right arms and said, "Hail Ted."

I dropped the shot of rum into my mug of beer, said, "Yeah, whatever," and gulped the entire drink down.

The bar-keep motioned to someone in the back. A few guys wheeled out a cage that contained a red mastiff. The bar-keep leaned back, crossed his arms, and said, "Got to admit, I didn't think it would be this easy."

My vision blurred and I became woozy. I heard giggling and wondered if Tasmanian devils could get worked up enough to have sex with giant cockroaches. My consciousness faded as a trapdoor opened up beneath my stool. Shit, I thought. They're shanghaiing me. I slid down a chute and I was back in my bed at the Starlight Motel.

CHAPTER 6

I fumbled for the clock-radio and looked at the time. Fuck, was I thirsty. I was still debating with my morning hangover and jotting the new version my recurring dream down when I heard someone knocking at the door. "Hold on," I said, slipping into my slacks. It was the maid. "Oh, hello"—I read her name tag—"Marisol. C'mon in; I was just leaving. Marisol. Huh, that's a beautiful name."

"Thank you, sir. I clean now?"

She was young, attractive, probably nineteen or twenty, and she reminded me of that woman on the beach so many years before. "That'd be great," I said. "You do wonders with this old room. You know what?" I pulled a fifty from my billfold and gave it to her.

"Muchas gracias!" she said with a big smile.

"Housekeeping is a difficult job; you deserve it." I stepped into my shoes, threw on a sweater, and headed over to a nearby restaurant called the Tumblin' Dice Diner—a meal that would go down as the best I'd ever eaten.

It wasn't the crisp golden exterior of the hash browns or the over-hard eggs, nor was it the side order of perfectly ripe melon, or even the fresh-squeezed orange juice, all of which had been served up by a competent waitress, no—it was the fact that I was here and on course, doing exactly what I was supposed to be doing: fulfilling my part of an unspoken bargain, the bargain that had given me a second chance to redeem my squandered first.

I was adding a little cream to my third cup of coffee when it hit me: at first, it was the swirls in the coffee that expanded, and then the booth, then the diner wobbled, then the whole world began to pitch and yaw, this way and that, like an unbalanced washing machine thumping out of control. Suddenly, I was transported back to the City of the Dead 2.0 and that omnicidal heat-wave of a wall appeared in the distance.

How the hell could this be happening? I was in a diner. I'd just had a perfect breakfast. If I didn't end up stuck here, I would work this out, maybe see a doctor or something. The heat wave of a wall passed over the dystopian landscape and renewed it, bringing forth life, vibrancy, and commerce. There were tens of thousands of people all alive and going about their day. Then, the wall returned, leaving a path of death and destruction in its wake. This scenario kept looping over and over until I was able to shake myself out of it and back into the diner.

What the fuck? First I'd dreamed about it, then it happened while I was awake? I'd once read about grand mal seizures... but this?

I collected my bearings, paid the tab, and after stocking up on some motel-living essentials at a nearby store, I went to Mung's and changed into my new Mayhem suit. After saying "good riddance" to my jeans, I stuffed them into the store's trash bin, walked outside, gave the sky two enthusiastic middle fingers, and railed, "How do you like me now, motherfuckers?"

I had lunch at Mohamed's Middle Eastern Food Cart, then went back to my motel room and unpacked and relaxed for a bit. Marvelous Marvin's fight was scheduled for 9:00 p.m. at Caesars Palace's outdoor stadium, three hours from now. I took a shower, got dressed, and headed down Las Vegas Boulevard.

Caesars was teeming with excitement. Electricity flowed through people as if they were Tesla coils at a Tesla coil factory reunion. If casinos could get hangovers, this place was going to have a doozy in the morning. I had two hours to kill, so I played some poker—one of the few things in my previous timeline that I had been moderately successful at.

I went to a table with a buy-in of five-thousand dollars—a level I'd never played before. Everyone at the table seemed nice enough, and I was enjoying myself—that was until my last hand: I'd been in weak, or what some people call first position, when I bet the pot with two black aces in the hole. The next four players folded. The small and big blind called as did a fat Chinese player who was on the button: last position. The flop was a seven, nine, and jack of diamonds. The fat Chinese player had shouted, "I best spider in box. I da Gamble. I all in!"

Yeah, that's right; he had called himself the Gamble. What a stupid name. I wasn't even sure if the name was grammatically correct. The dealer reprimanded him for betting out of turn and the action was back to me. I checked. The small and big blind checked—I guess we were curious what the loud-mouth was up to. For the second time, the fat Chinese guy who called himself the Gamble yelled, "I all in, muvfucks!"

He was either bluffing or on a draw to a straight, a flush, or straight flush. The action was to me and my pocket aces. I was playing small-ball poker, and the bet was pushing the limits of my faith.

Just then, the waiter delivered my drink order. "Your Captain Morgan's, sir," he said, then leaned in and whispered, "fold."

It seemed appropriate at the time, so I said, "Fold," and mucked my cards.

Then, the Gamble guy jumped up and screamed, "Why you no call with aces, Sefco? What your problem? This game bullshit. I have strait flush. I win!"

The pit boss went over to the Gamble and said something like, "Sir, this is your only warning: finish the hand quietly or leave the casino."

Then the Gamble said, "Oh, dealer need help, call the big man over. You all no understand, I da Gamble. I Octavius 3 of 8. I best spider in box!"

That's right, he had also referred to himself as Octavius 3 of 8. Another stupid name. That's about the time the pit boss waved security over and had him removed.

After that, I collected my winnings, made my way over to Caesars' outdoor arena, bought a few beers, and found my seat. The undercard fights had just finished and Marvin was making his way into the ring when suddenly I was hit with another one of those washing-machine-thumping out-of-control lucid dream episodes:

I was transported back to the City of the Dead 2.0. Back to Kaczynski's Doomerville Lounge & Surgical Saloon. As I opened my eyes, I remembered they had shanghaied me and that I had slid down a chute. I tried to move but couldn't because I was dressed in rigid overalls, and I was firmly stuck to a Velcro wall, or something like it.

"You really did it this time," said a voice to my left.

I turned, squeaked my eyes to the left, and saw a middle-aged Black man who was also stuck to the wall.

He looked familiar but I couldn't place him. "Hey," I said. "How's it going? Do I know you?"

"Uhm... Yes, and no. You will, in the future."

For some reason I said, "I think I've done something so bad I can't remember it."

"Relax, brother-man; you're in a vision. We discussed all of this last night at Piggy's. You know, I get captured, you get captured, we rescue the dog, then you teach these commies a lesson and save the universe. Man, this chicken or the egg shit is difficult when it's moving in both directions."

"Did you just say Chicken of the Sea?"

"No. What I said was chicken or the egg, you know, vision Shifter déjà vu. Now hush. Everything is in place, just like we planned. Oh yeah, the suit's release combo is shoulder tap, SOS, you know, dot-dot-dot, dash-dash-dash, dot-dot-dot. And don't forget to come back for me. I got that gig on the Amundsen colony."

Just then, as some goons in sharkskin zoot suits showed up and were hauling me off on a floating hand truck, the heat-wave of a wall returned and a cosmic bungee cord pulled me back to the outdoor stadium at Caesars Palace.

CHAPTER 7

The fight was over and everyone was leaving.

"Hey, buddy... you OK?"

As I looked up at a security guard, I tried to remember the details of my very real and very lucid dream.

"What happened?" I asked. "The fight. Why is everyone leaving?"

"It's all over, bub. C'mon, time to go home."

As I got to my feet, I knocked over my beer—spilling it onto the guard's shoes.

"Alright, that's it, buster," he said, grabbing me by the back of my collar and dragging me into the aisle.

"Ahh... sorry about that. Hey! Just hold on a second, will you? I'm not drunk; I have a sleeping disorder."

"Well," he said, as he released his hold. "You seem OK. You know, my wife gave me those shoes for our 35th."

"Here." I peeled a $100 from my billfold. "Will this cover the damage?"

"Sure, that'll do."

I handed him the bill. "Now tell me, how did the fight end?"

"The fight! *Pff*... The fix was in. A draw, in a championship fight? C'mon! Bastards stole it from Marvin. Let me ask you something. How do you fight an iron-jawed caveman whose body is made of, ahh, stone?"

"You use a gun," I said. "Now, how did the fight end?"

"The Caveman took it in a fifteen-round draw."

"Yes!"

I left the stadium and headed over to the Sands Casino. Forty grand, I thought, at 6:1... that's two hundred and forty grand. Hmm, not bad for a few days' work.

The big scary-looking guy from the other day was working the window at the sportsbook. What was his name again? Oh yeah, Lee, Adamit Lee. How could I forget? He gave me a nod.

"Hello, Mr. Bridges. I take it your night is going well?" I was surprised the Frankensteinian figure had remembered my name, so I placed my betting receipt under the window without comment. He glanced at the receipt, looked up, and pointed to his left. "Could you go through that door past the last window and wait for me?"

The door opened into a small alcove. I sat on a red-cushioned bench. Two minutes later, Mr. Giganotosaurus Lee came over carrying a casino money bag filled with bundled stacks of one-hundred-dollar bills. "Mr. Bridges, the Sands has extended to you a two-hundred-thousand-dollar line of credit and complimentary use of our suites." His dulcet voice belied his terrifying presence.

"Oh," I said. "That's, ahh, very generous."

"Do you need a security escort?"

"Yeah, sure, I'm just going to my deposit box."

He nodded and said, "It just so happens I'm free. I'll walk you there myself."

I felt safe walking next to this guy. In all my years I couldn't remember anyone that could have challenged him. At my in-house deposit box, I kept a few bundles of cash and stashed the rest.

"How did you know?" asked Mr. Lee. "The fight. How did you know it would end in a split decision?"

I shrugged. "Lucky guess."

He nodded, but I didn't think he believed me. "Hey," he said. "My sister and a few friends are going out for drinks. You should join us. It'll be fun."

"Now?"

"Well, my shift is over and the night is still young. Come on, you'll have a good time."

Paranoid appeared and shrugged, as if to say he had no idea what was going on.

"That's cool," I said. "Lead on."

CHAPTER 8

We went through an employees-only door and descended into the brick and steel underpinnings of an addiction factory, past kitchens and loading docks, and through a labyrinth of corridors until we ended up outside, standing in front of two large doors that held back the pulsing rhythms of live music. Adamit nodded at the bouncers who, after a quick frisking, waved us through—into the real Vegas underground.

The place was happening. Neon-colored laser lights flashed about the writhing bodies that packed the dance floor. Half-naked chicks danced in cages. Cocaine, pot, and expensive-looking bottles of champagne were flaunted without discernment. Up front, on a stage, a bare-bones bar band was cranking out Chicago's hit song "Make Me Smile."

"What the hell is this place?" I asked.

Adamit gave me a friendly pat on the back, leaned down, and said, "This is Purgatorium. Can I get you a drink?"

"I'll take a shot of rum please... and a beer."

The band had a three-piece horn section and, surprisingly, were up to the challenge of such an ambitious cover tune. The next song was "25 or 6 to 4." Another Chicago tune? I took a closer look. Wait, it *was* Chicago. But it wasn't the glitzy overproduced orchestra I'd seen on their album covers. No, it was a stripped-down version of the band, and they were grungy and brilliant.

"What do you think?" Adamit asked, handing me my drinks.

A blonde, blue-eyed beauty holding a glass of wine came over, laid a hand on Adamit's shoulder, and said, "Brother, you must introduce me to this lad. He isn't by any chance...?"

Had she just said *brother*?

"Mr. Bridges," said Adamit. The acoustics were so good he didn't have to yell to be heard over the music. "May I present my sister, Miss Katya Lee."

She gave me a brief visual appraisal then held her hand out. I thought she wanted me to kiss it, so I set my drinks down and kissed it. Despite her casino uniform, she had the look of a 1940s Lauren Bacall. She was easy on the eyes, and her smile—or rather, the slight upward curve of her lips—was no doubt the inspiration of untold heartache. I tried to age her—guess what she would look like in twenty years—but still, I could find no fault with her beauty.

"Please," I said, "call me Seth. You know, you two don't look—"

"We're twins," she said. "There's been speculation about our father, or fathers, but I don't heed such jibber-jabber. Though I must say, Mr. Bridges, it is a pleasure to make your acquaintance. A true pleasure."

"The pleasure is all mine," I said, trying to match her speech pattern.

"Take it easy on him, sis," Adamit said. "It's his first time."

"I'll do no such thing." She took a sip of her wine and locked her eyes onto mine.

Just then, a good-looking, well-built guy who looked like he'd just stepped off the beaches of Maui came over and gave her an enthusiastic kiss on the cheek. "Is this him?" he asked.

"Yessiree," she replied.

He gave me a broad, friendly smile and said, "Dean Forest."

"Seth Bridges," I said, shaking his hand.

"Well, well, well," he said, "if this doesn't beat all." He looked over at Adamit and said, "Can I show him around?"

Adamit nodded and said, "He's all yours."

Dean draped his arm around my shoulders and brought me over to a booth with three geishas in it. They had white-painted faces, floral kimonos, pinned up hair, and appeared to be genuine.

"This is Yoshimi and her two sisters, Asuka and Izumi," Dean said. "They're triplets. Cool, right?" One of the geishas poured out some powder. "Pink Peruvian," Dean said. "Cleanest shit on the planet."

The second geisha smiled submissively, while the third politely cut some lines. Yeah, this was cool: a legendary band, geishas, alcohol, and a mound of cocaine. I shrugged my shoulders and dove into the deep end.

Most of these people seemed to know one another, and at some point, our party merged with the rest of the club. The music, booze, and blow lightened my load. I danced haphazardly with the rhythms of the club and its patrons. When I took a break at a partially occupied table, a shot glass was slammed down before me and green liquid was poured into it. I remember people chanting, "Drink, Shifter, drink!"

I obliged and that was when my lights began to flicker.

Somebody was lifting me up. It was the blond woman. Wait, what was her name again? Kat-woman, KitKat, Yo-Yo Ma?

"Come on, Mr. Bridges," she said. "Time to leave."

She walked me outside and tucked me into a car. The city slurred past the window like a disco-ball sailing through a lagoon of fancied-up human excrement. When the car stopped moving, I managed to open the door and vomit.

"What's going on?" I mumbled at the pavement.

The blonde woman led me past a doorway and over to a couch. She laid a blanket over me. "You've had too much fun, Mr. Bridges. Now go to sleep."

I did as I was told.

CHAPTER 9

Tweet-tweet-tweet. I removed the blanket that covered my face and sussed the situation: I was on a couch in somebody's living room. Kitchen sounds filtered in from nearby. How the hell had I gotten here? Outside, a bird re-tweeted a pattern. Had I hurt anyone? I groped for my billfold—still there. I grabbed my suit coat from the top of the couch and checked the pockets. The bundles of cash were still there, as were my keys.

The blonde woman from the club came over and offered a warm smile. "Oh, look who's up. It's Mr. Sleepy Head." She set a glass of water on a coffee table. "I'm Katya; we met last night."

My hangover only amplified her attractiveness.

"Do you know," she said, "I can get a man to do anything I want him to? That is, except for the one thing I need him to do. Can you guess what that *one thing* is?"

I played it safe. "No."

"Well, Jumping Jehoshaphat. I simply cannot get a man to make me fall in love with him. And I so desperately want to know what love is."

I sat up and took a sip of water. "You're not missing anything."

"Come again," she said.

"I was just saying... Maybe you haven't found the right man."

"I suppose, but jeepers creepers." She gave me a grin. "How long does a girl have to look?" She handed me a newspaper ad. "Do you know anything about this?"

I gave it a look:

One Million Dollar $ REWARD $ For Information On Sethco T Destroyer.
Call 702-555-0404 $ REWARD $ To Collect.

"For the last three months," she said, "that ad has been running every Sunday in the Personals section of the *Las Vegas Sun*."

Just then, Adamit walked in and said, "Morning." He set a pot of fresh brew and some cups on the coffee table, then sat opposite me—on a custom-built oversized chair. "Do you remember last night?" he asked.

"Not really," I said, shaking the cobwebs from my brain. "One minute I was having a great time and then… it all went blurry, and I ended up here."

"Do you remember what you drank?"

"I had a few shots of rum, a few beers, then… someone poured green liquid into a glass and a bunch of people egged me on to drink it."

"How many of those green drinks did you have?" Katya asked.

"Three or four. But now that you mention it, that's where my memory ends. Did I cause a problem? Was I drugged?"

"No," Adamit said. "You didn't cause a problem. But I should've warned you. Sometimes newcomers to Purgatorium are welcomed with Teater juice: the green stuff you drank. It's like absinthe, only stronger." He poured me a cup of coffee. "You were never in any real danger. I kept an eye on you the whole time."

I took a sip of coffee. "Hey, are you two really brother and sister? She doesn't—"

"She certainly does," said a voice from the hall. Just then, two dwarfs or little people, one woman and one man, entered the kitchen. "How ya feeling, Mr. Bridges?" asked the woman.

I vaguely remembered them—had I met them last night?

"Mr. Bridges," Adamit said, "it is my great pleasure to introduce to you my darling sister, Rebekah, and my dear brother, Jacob."

I shook their hands. "Please," I said. "Call me Seth. Uh-oh… could someone tell me where the bathroom is? I think I'm about to have an accident."

Rebekah pointed down the hall and said, "Second door on the left."

"Thank you, Rebekah."

"Call me Becky. Everyone else does."

I jumped up, ran down the hall, and barely made it to the toilet as my gut expelled the poisonous remains of an evening spent in Purgatorium. After freshening up, I returned to the living room and quieted their muted laughter by performing a mock curtsy and saying, "Thank you, thank you very much," in my best Elvis impersonation.

"So, Seth," Adamit said, "what's your story?"

I could have told him my story, but he'd probably have thought I was messing with him and bashed me with that sledgehammer of a fist. I sat on the couch next to Rebekah and asked, "Are you guys really related? You all look so… different."

"Like I told you last night," Adamit said, "Katya's my twin. Becky and Jacob, they're our step-siblings. Years ago, when Katya and I were just kids, we were in a plane crash, here in Vegas. We were the sole survivors. Our birth parents were on that plane. After that, a local orphanage took us in until the Lees were kind enough to adopt us. Mom and Pop Lee... they were the salt of the earth."

Katya interrupted Adamit and said, "They fell in love working the soundstage for *The Wizard of Oz*. Can you believe that? I think it's beautiful."

"Heck," said Adamit. "Pop Lee even pinch-hit one time for the St. Louis Browns. I loved that man. We all loved him, and we loved Mom Lee even more. Unfortunately,"—he gave Becky and Jacob a nod—"we lost them last year to Little People's disease. So yeah, we're different, but we're family."

Jacob, who was sitting in a small, customized chair next to Adamit, said, "My brother just wants to know who you are, where you're from? It's not a difficult question."

I took a sip of coffee. Hm... They wanted some background info, nothing serious. No need for time-traveling escapades. I was torn between spilling my guts or puking them into my lap.

"Seth," Adamit said before I could get a word out, "We believe *you* are the one we have been waiting for."

"Me? Hah, you got the wrong guy. Believe me when I tell you, nobody waits for me—nobody. And if this has something to do with that reward money, you got the wrong guy. My name is Seth, Seth Bridges, not Sethco the... Discombobulator thingy."

Katya looked into my eyes and asked, "What are you doing in Las Vegas?"

"I'm here to win enough money," I said, "so I can build a spaceship and leave Earth before it's too late." I had no idea why I said that. It felt like someone else's words. Plus, I didn't know how to build a spaceship.

"Too late for what?" asked Becky.

"I... I don't know?"

Adamit gave me an understanding look and said, "Mr. Bridges, we want you to know you are not alone."

"Guys"—I set my cup down and stood up—"this is getting weird. I had a great time and everything last night, but I think I should leave now."

"Don't be a silly prickly pear," Katya said, placing her hand on mine. "Brother is trying to tell you something important. Now sit."

I was compelled to do as she said.

Katya gave Adamit a glance, then looked at me and asked, "How old do you think we are?"

I bought some time with a few sips of coffee and tried to figure out their angle.

Katya looked directly into my eyes. "Adamit and I were born in Willoughby, Ohio, in the year 1877. How old are you?"

The room started to wobble—sparkly and curving. Great, I was having another episode. Wait... had she just said she was born in 1877? In Willoughby? Wasn't that a town from a *Twilight Zone* episode?

CHAPTER 10

I was flung into that shiny unbalanced washing machine that had been taking hold of me lately, and then I was in a futuristic laboratory of some sort.

My arms were shiny and metal, like a robot's. A man in a blood-stained lab coat stared at me wide-eyed. A squadron of surprised commandos aimed their rifle-like weapons at me. Off to the side, a dozen, recently-decapitated soldiers were haphazardly stacked in a pile. The floor was freshly painted in blood. In the center of the lab a large cylindrical glass tank, filled with pink liquid, contained a child in repose. An old lady floated around on a throne and screamed, "It's him. He's here. Kill him! Kill him now!"

The episode was brief and, thankfully, I was returned to the Lees' living room.

"Wake up, Seth," Adamit said. "Come on. Wake up."

"Err... ah... Hey," I said.

Katya placed a wet napkin across my forehead. "Should we take him to the hospital?"

"No hospitals," I said, waving her off. "I'm OK. Sometimes I pass out—low blood pressure. I'm fine. Really." I sat up and looked at Katya. "Wait... did you say you were born in *1877*?"

She used the napkin to wipe some drool from the corner of my mouth. "Yes, Seth, I did. And according to my math, that makes brother and I... one-hundred and thirty-three years old. So, how old are you?"

"Fifty-eight," I said without hesitation.

She got up, hugged Adamit, and shrieked, "You were right, brother. You were right!" Then she repeatedly kissed my face. "Seth, you're one of us... you're a Shifter. This is pos-i-tive-ly momentous. We must celebrate!"

I looked around at the Lees and thought, Shifter? Wasn't that what they had been chanting last night when I was drinking those green shots?

"What the hell is a Shifter?" I asked.

"We're involuntary time travelers," said Adamit. "Our purpose is to serve our creator: the Progenitor."

"Whoa... hold on. You guys went back in time too?"

"Katya and I did," said Adamit. "Becky and Jacob are, unfortunately, Short-Timers; that's what we call normal people."

After a pot of coffee and a delicious breakfast served up by Becky, we were talking like long-lost family members. I'd told them my real story, but had only learned a fraction of their eventful lives. From what I could gather, the first time they had shifted, like me, was when they had turned fifty years old. They had gone back in time forty years and ended up returning to their family farm and childhood. The next time they turned fifty—for the second time—they were thrust fifty years into the future, once again as children.

My mind struggled to understand the rules: start out as a regular person, and when you turned fifty years old, you went back in time to when you were ten years old, and repeated that timeline. When you turned fifty for the second time, you shifted a half-a-century into the future.

"So, Seth," Katya said. "That means in thirty-two years you will shift into the year 2060—you'll be a 100-year-old kid. Oh, and it doesn't stop there. It continues: the whole process repeats itself over and over again."

"Huh..." I said. "So how many Shifters are there? And why the hell are you guys working service jobs in a casino?"

"There are approximately," Adamit said, "one thousand of us scattered around the globe at any given moment. The older Shifters tell us that our purpose is to advance technology. There is an ongoing debate concerning this subject, but we'll save that for another day." He adjusted his posture and continued. "We're not immortal—we can die like anyone else. In the beginning—on your first shift—you repeat your previous timeline. On your second fiftieth birthday, you're fast-forwarded fifty years into the future, young again in a new world. The pattern will continue until you are dead or nine-hundred-some odd years pass—whatever comes first."

"That's twelve good lifetimes," said Katya. "Fourteen years ago,"—she fanned her arms out—"on our second fiftieth birthday, we woke up to this... confoundingly amazing world. And things don't necessarily get easier because you're older, wiser. We have bills to pay and problems just like everyone else. Plus, work helps pass the time until we are called to serve our purpose."

"Hey," Jacob said. "Don't forget to tell him you guys all have gifts—"

"Hold on," I said, "what do you mean by purpose? And who is *calling* you to serve it?"

Adamit glanced at Katya and said, "There is an alien who became stranded here on Earth a long, long time ago. She wants us to help her develop the technology that will take her back home. She is the Progenitor: she created us."

"An alien?" I said. "Really?"

This was crazy talk. I thought about my old prep-school roommate Pablo and his simple dream of becoming a backup goalie on the school's hockey team. Maybe I could go back to my parent's house and live in the cellar. I could farm mushrooms and order out for food, or, better yet, I could buy an old submarine and live under the ocean, raise seahorses and sell them to pet shops or something.

Adamit got up and slowly paced around the living room. "As Shifters, we all have gifts: unique abilities that help with our purpose. Katya can push a mind to her will. I can intimidate people with hallucinations of their deepest fears. Some Shifters can influence luck or even the roll of the dice. Point is, we all have gifts, including you. Would you care to enlighten us on yours?" He sat down. "Your seizures, Seth. What are they?"

I looked around the table. "You guys don't have seizures?"

"No Seth, we don't."

Katya caught my attention and asked, "What is your gift?"

I blurted, "I can see glimpses of the future—by going there, into the future, and being a part of it. I think it's an early warning system—premonitions helping me be prepared for when specific events actually happen."

Paranoid jumped out from behind Katya, pointed at her, and mouthed the words, "She, Katya, can push your thoughts. I know this because she just did it to you." Then, he clasped his hands behind his back, and began to pace behind Adamit.

"So," Jacob said. "Earlier you mentioned something about building a spaceship before it's too late. You want to expand?"

"I don't know why I said that. Really. I've been having these dreams about the end of the world being caused by a pandemic called the Soul Breaker Virus. I just thought they were dreams. But earlier, when I passed out, I think I was in the future. It was a laboratory and there were dead guards and... there was this boy in a glass tank, and a crazy old lady flying around on a throne. I mean, your guess is as good as mine."

Adamit asked, "Do you have a lot of these dreams?"

"They've been ramping up ever since I arrived; that was a few days ago. Hey, does this mean I can't make bets anymore?"

"No," said Adamit. "That's what Vegas is for. Eventually they'll catch on and ban you, or the timeline will get screwy. Best to get it while you can."

"Do you have a girlfriend?" asked Katya.

"Here we go," said Adamit. "Please excuse my sister; she's on a quest."

"No, it's OK," I said. "I don't have a girlfriend. Kinda gave up on them years ago, but I'm honored you'd ask."

"Delightful," she said. "I love a challenge."

"So, ahh... I guess I should head back to my motel and digest all of this. We should stay in touch, right?"

"Sounds like a plan," said Adamit. "I'll give you a ride."

Becky hugged me around my waist. "Sure was nice to meet you, Mr. Bridges. Sorry—I mean Seth."

Jacob shook my hand. "You're a good man, Mr. Bridges. Stay your course."

Katya gave me a peck on the cheek.

CHAPTER 11

"Nice truck," I said as Adamit led me to his faded red Toyota Land Cruiser. "I used to have one just like it, except it was blue."

"You live near the Strip?" he asked, easing the truck onto Spring Mountain Road.

"Yeah, Starlite Motel on Flamingo. Hey, that thing back there, when Katya Obi-Wan Kenobied me. Is that considered cheating in the Shifter world?"

"What? Pushing? No. Our gifts are meant to be used. Why? Do you like her?"

"Well, sure. Who wouldn't?"

"Shifters are attracted to other Shifters. My sister wants to fall in love, but her gift makes it very difficult—maybe even impossible. A word of caution may be in order here: protect your heart when you're around my sister."

"Sure, no problem." As we got near the Starlite Motel, I pointed at Mohamed's Middle Eastern Food Cart and said, "Could you drop me off here? I want to grab some food. You hungry?"

"I have to get to work. You take care of yourself, Mr. Bridges."

As I went up to the food cart, Mohamed bellowed, "How are you, my friend?"

"I'm alright. Thanks. What's new in your world?"

"My wife, she thinks I work too much, and my sister, she still needs a man. Have you found yourself a woman?"

"Well... I'm kinda—"

"I am sorry, friend; I do not mean to be intrusive. Here"—he handed me a small box—"my sister has made a wonderful ba'lawa, best tasting dessert you will ever eat. Please—Kali, that is her name—she would be honored if you would accept some—no charge."

"Thank you, Mohamed. It looks delicious. Tell Kali I appreciate her efforts." After downing a falafel wrap, I began footing it back to my motel.

Just as I was passing the last corner before the Starlite, a guy jabbed a knife into my rib cage and, in a decent Clint Eastwood growl, said, "Give me your money or I'll kill yeh dead."

Time seemed to slow a bit, so I took the opportunity to remember my Budo instructor Master Poe. He was a middle-aged Polish man who had worked in a Chinese restaurant, as a pot-washer, near my old boarding school. He had professed to be the only non-Chinese person to have been raised in a Shaolin temple, and that the TV show *Kung-Fu* was based on a stolen diary he had written while growing up in the temple. As I cracked a smile at Master Poe's penchant for bold fabrications, adrenaline and a quote from the master himself took hold of me: *When taken by surprise, retake the element.*

"Please..." I feigned, careful not to over-act. "I have money; you can have it. Just don't hurt me."

How had this low-life snuck up on me? I'd have to be more vigilant of my surroundings in the future. I turned my suit pockets inside-out and let the ba'lawa and two cash bundles fall to the sidewalk.

"Just take it," I said in my best wussy voice. "It's all yours."

As the knife left my side, I dropped into a crouch, pivoted left, and in a smooth, well-practiced motion, I snatched up the robber's right arm, Aikido style, then slammed it down—backward across my knee. His elbow broke with a muffled *crack,* and the knife hit the concrete with a *ting.* I retrieved my money and ba'lawa, stood up and gave the guy a kick to one of his kidneys. It was then that I realized my would-be assailant was Colton: my misery-mongering former classmate that had picked me up at the airport. "Oh, hey Colton. What's up?"

"Hey man," he screamed. "You broke my arm! You can't go around breaking people's arms."

I pushed his head down with my foot. "Oh, you rob me, and now you tell me how to behave?"

"Fuck you, man, just get me some help."

"There you go again, telling me what to do." I delivered another kick, but harder this time, and to his liver. "The name is Bridges. Mr. Bridges to you."

A morning robbery on a moderately busy street corner seemed out of place. Why here? Why now? A group of onlookers murmured with approval. Three blocks down, a plume of blue smoke rose from the rear quarter panel of a dented yellow cab. It was the same cab and smelly driver who had picked me up a few days ago. I pulled out my billfold, removed the card the loser cabbie had given me, and read: *Dings Mulligan, Las Vegas Taxi Cab Co-operative.* Was he behind this? I needed confirmation. I bent down and grabbed a handful of Colton's hair. "Who put you up to this?"

"Nobody!" he yelled.

Police sirens doppled in the distance—I needed answers. I placed my knee under his good elbow, locked-up his arm, and started to crank it backward: in effect, threatening to break it.

"Aaah! Stop, stop. I give!" Colton screamed. Pain tears trickled down his face. "It was some guy named Dings. He said you'd be here with lots of money. Said you were loaded. We were gonna split it 50/50."

Just then, a black-cherry Rolls Royce pulled up to the curb. The driver rolled down the heavily tinted drivers-side window, nodded at me, and said, "Get in."

CHAPTER 12

The driver of the Rolls was an Asian woman. She gave me a threatening look and said, "I am Kogo. You get in. No talk."

My *get-the fuck-outta-here* alarms went off. "What if I don't want to?"

"You have small choice. You must obey."

In the time it took for me to look around for an alternative course of action, she exited the Rolls and stood before me. She smelled like honeysuckle and looked like a pack of unopened razor blades that had just stepped off a Quentin Tarantino movie set.

Metro was making its way around the corner when she opened the back door of the Rolls. I noticed her hand was tattooed blood red, and her pinky finger appeared to have been severed off just above its first knuckle. Probably Yakuza punishment for not having a dick or something.

"Is this your car?" I asked.

"No. Car employer property." She looked down the street at the advancing police cars. "Let us go. Now."

"Is that where we're going?" I asked as I got into the back of the car. "To see your employer?" She gave me an amused snort. "Yes, now we go to see Master Willhammer."

Paranoid sat next to me and shrugged. I cranked down the window and watched the buildings of Vegas gloss past in a neon-pink blur. Maybe this place wasn't so bad, I thought. Truth be told, Vegas amplified most of the things that made us human. Perhaps I should start a committee to advocate changing the name from Las Vegas to Virtue City. Yeah, Virtue City would be a more appropriate name for this town...

At the Stardust Casino, Kogo pulled into a private entrance, and we went inside.

"Sethco," she said, as we entered an elevator. "No sudden movements. This you understand?"

"Yeah, got it. And the name is Seth, not Sethco."

Four Uzi-toting guards greeted us when the elevator doors slid open. The room was dark, except for a thirty-foot long, illuminated carpeted path that led to a desk. A pale-faced man sat behind it. On each side of the desk sat a living gargoyle.

The pale-faced man waved me forward. As I got closer, I recognized the gargoyles to be hyenas. They were restrained with spiked collars buckled to thick-silver chains embedded into the floor. The beasts chomped at the air—probably searching for fear molecules, or perhaps the scent of a Slim Jim.

Additional bodyguards emerged from the shadows and clicked the safeties on their firearms. The pale-faced man behind the desk wore a pinstriped double-breasted gangster suit, white gloves, and he looked like a Hollywood version of Howard Hughes—mustache and all.

"Mr. Bridges," he said as if we were old acquaintances. "Please... have a seat."

My heart raced. I calmed myself with one of Master Poe's ninja breathing techniques and prepared for the unexpected. Scantily clad people emerged from just beyond the shadow-line. They placed a comfortable-looking chair in front of the pale-faced man's desk, then gestured I sit.

Fuck it. Might as well get on with it.

As I sat in the chair, both hyenas began to laugh at me, or at least it sounded that way. I visualized ripping out their windpipes. And as if they could read my mind, the beasts assumed an attack stance.

"*La!*" said the man behind the desk. The hyenas let out a brief whine, then heeled to a sitting position. The shadow people brought out a small pedestal table and placed it to my left. They poured a small amount of dark liquid into an antique-looking shot glass, set it on the table, then withdrew into the shadows.

"Mr. Bridges," said the man behind the desk, "would it be acceptable if I called you Seth?"

"Whatever. Why am I here?"

He cast a practiced smile at me. "Let's talk."

I leaned back in my chair. "Sure. What's on your mind, mister...?"

He adjusted his seated position as if he had hemorrhoids. "The Mormons, the US government, and the Short-Timers call me Mr. Hughes, but Willhammer is my true name—Cyrus Willhammer. I'm the Constable around here—for Shifters, that is. You're new, so I thought we'd have an informal get-together. And because the world is busy spinning, I'll get to the point. Do you know who you are, what you are?"

"What's it to you?"

"Oh, ho, ho, did you hear that, children?" He looked around at the expressionless faces of his security staff. "We have an obdurate in the room. My boy, I've killed for far less, so please consider your next words more carefully. I have a question for you, and be assured I will know if you are being truthful or not. My asking of this question is merely an opportunity for you to correct your recent insolence. Now, tell me, Mr. Bridges, what is your gift?"

I had always suffered from a fear of people and their desire to entangle themselves into my life, but this guy...

"What's the deal with your mustache? You look ridiculous."

"Seize him!" demanded Willhammer as he got up and came towards me. Four goons rushed out from behind the shadow-line and held me down onto the chair. Then, Willhammer removed the glove on his right hand, and a woman, outfitted as an Egyptian slave girl, misted it with a spray bottle. Willhammer nodded, and two of the goons held my mouth open, while another poured the liquid from the shot glass into my mouth. Willhammer bent down, looked me in the eyes, and said, "It's neophytes like yourself that task me so. Do you think my job is easy?"

While trying not to choke on the liquid, I surmised its ingredients to be a combination of ball sweat, vaginal juice, and liquefied bacon bits. "What's with the pig swill?" I asked after swallowing the last of the drink.

Willhammer placed his misted hand on my forehead, and I was transported straight into my recurring, wobbly-washing-machine episode generator.

I found myself in an Italian sports car; it was snowing, and I was in the middle of a four-way traffic light. There was a .38 caliber handgun in my lap. Willhammer stood on a nearby sidewalk. I eased through the traffic light, wondering what the fuck was about to happen, when suddenly a tractor-trailer bore down on me broadside—its horn was blasting. There was a Chinese-looking guy behind the truck's steering wheel. I recognized him as the man I had played poker with while waiting for the Hagler fight to begin. I stomped the accelerator. Traction was limited, and there was nothing I could do to prevent the forces of premonition and kinetic energy from colliding. I heard screeching tires and crunching metal, and then, ever so briefly, I floated above the wreck and looked down at my own demise.

Then I was back in Willhammer's lair. "He's already dead," Willhammer shouted as he removed his hand from my forehead. "Remove this null from my presence. Immediately."

The goons dragged me into the elevator and handed me off to Kogo, who was waiting for me inside.

I was dizzy and my legs were unsteady. "That's one hell of a master you got," I said. "So what's next? You gonna kill me? Huh, doesn't matter." I was feeling loopy from Cyrus's swine swill and actually felt safe with Kogo. "Hey," I said, "have you ever wondered how many times a person can die?"

She snorted out a laugh, then pushed the down button. Once she had escorted me outside, she turned and headed back in.

"Hold up," I said. "Are you just going to leave me here?"

"Yes," she said. "I leave you now. You are killer of untold people. You very bad person."

"Me? I'm a bad person? You just kidnapped me. And you work for, ah... a lunatic psychic vampire."

CHAPTER 13

I was hoofing it down Las Vegas Boulevard, and wondering why I was a killer of *untold people* and why the hell some fat Chinese guy would want to run me over with a truck.

As I replayed the poker game in my head, I remembered the fat Chinese guy was a jerk, and he had referred to himself as Octavius 3 of 8. He said he was *the best spider in box*, whatever the hell that meant, and he had to be removed from the table for causing a scene. Now that I thought about it, the waiter who had brought me my drink and told me to *fold* was Dean, the guy with the three geishas from Club Purgatorium.

Did this Gamble guy, who referred to himself in the third and fourth person, want to kill me because I had folded aces? How had he known my pocket-cards, and why had he *and* Kogo called me Sethco? And why had Dean told me to fold? None of it made sense. I was tempted to hop on the next plane home.

"Whaddya know!" I turned and saw Dex, the cabbie I'd met on my first day in town. She pulled her taxi over. "It's the Tornado kid. You sticking to it?"

I nodded and got in the cab. "Yeah... I guess?"

"So, where we headed today?"

"This city is too big. I need a car." I thought about my recent demise and decided to face my premonitions head on. "You know where I could buy a green Italian sports car?"

"If you're serious," she said, "I can take you over to Premier Imports West. They've got a nice selection."

I checked my pockets to see if my bundles of cash were there—which they were. "Sounds good to me."

At the dealership, Dex handed me a round business card. "Listen, kid, if you ever need anything, anything at all, these people can get it; call 'em. Well, if there's nothing else, I'll see you around." I gave her a wave and looked at the card.

JERICHO SIMS

"If it exists, we can get it."

555-867-5309

I slipped the card into my pocket and took a stroll through the high-end European car lot. Just as I was taking a liking to a mint green Maserati, the same car that had been in my vision at Willhammers', a middle-aged salesman in a tan polyester leisure suit introduced himself as Carmine.

"Seth Bridges," I said, shaking his hand.

"She's a real beauty, this one," he said with a smile. "A 1970 Maserati Ghibli SS: one owner, twenty-seven thousand miles, smoothest-driving car on the lot. You have a good eye, son, a really good eye."

Oh God, the bullshit was already underfoot. My old friend Joann had worked a used-car lot for years—she had explained to me the tricks of the used-car trade, and the best way around them: never show interest in the car you like, pretend to like some other car, start the paperwork, make a low-ball offer, then get up and leave when the offer cannot be accepted. While the salesman pleads for compromise, ask offhandedly for the price of the car you really want. The salesman, now frustrated, will relent to your offer. This information was all good in theory, but I didn't want to play games. The sticker price was $15,500. I crouched down and inspected the car's undercarriage. No rust, just surface corrosion.

"So," I said, "what's the story on this car?"

"Well, it was imported from Italy nine years ago by its previous owner, who, I may add, was killed by a five-iron embedded in his temple—compliments of his now-incarcerated third wife. We picked it up last week at an estate auction."

"Could you pop the hood?" The motor had no visible oil leaks and appeared to be all original. Some duct work on the air filter seemed askew, but overall, it looked like it had been well cared for. "Can we go for a test drive?"

"Let me get the keys." Two minutes later he tossed them to me.

I pulled onto the street and mashed the accelerator. My head snapped back, and adrenaline shot into my gut. Carmine braced himself with the dash and said, "Three hundred and twenty-five horsepower V-8," loud enough to be heard over the well-tuned growl of the motor. "Italian horses, mind you."

I checked the rear-view mirror for smoke—she was clear. The interior was more elegant than any car I'd ever been in. The handling was firm and free of telltale vibrations, and it was equipped with factory air.

After the test drive, we went to the sales office. "Carmine," I said, "if you can hook me up with insurance and registration, and not rip me off, I'll pay cash today."

Thirty minutes later I pulled out of the dealership in my new-to-me 1970 Maserati Ghibli SS Coupe.

I flicked the car's radio on. A preacher blathered on about the lost souls of the condemned. I downshifted, switched the station to a Top 40, then slid my fingers across the mahogany dashboard. Nice. I avoided as many four-way stoplights as possible and bought a load of basic food necessities at a nearby Green Valley Grocery store. After picking up two cases of beer and a full complement of top-shelf booze at Fanny's Liquors, I stopped off at Wen's, picked up my four remaining Mayhem suits, then went back to my room at the Starlite Motel.

CHAPTER 14

I unpacked my supplies, took a shower, and went to bed. Then, as I drifted off, something hijacked my dreams and injected my consciousness into a vision of the future.

I was a kid again, seated on a white padded bench in a kitchen-sized white modular room. It must have been a dream, I remember thinking, or maybe it was a vision? I wasn't sure.

The far wall was clear as glass, and beyond the glass were stars. Was this some sort of spaceship dream? My stomach felt queasy. I stood and tried to jump up and float to determine if I was dreaming or not. Nope, couldn't float. For a moment, I wondered if artificial gravity could affect my dream test, then decided I wasn't capable of making such a determination. I looked around for a moment, then went over to the transparent wall and saw, among other things, a purple planet.

"Lovely, isn't it?" said a voice that sounded like Morgan Freeman's. Which of course startled me. "It's called Varuka 5," the voice continued, "the last of the supply-dock planets in the sector. Please, Mr. Bridges, if you would, have a seat. Can you access your Cog-Link?"

"Cog-Link? How did I get here?" My voice sounded funny. Probably because I was a kid.

"End-point Quantum Synaptics. Very complicated stuff. Try to burp, that will activate your Cog-Link and save us all some time."

"What is this place? Where am I?"

"I was hoping to avoid this, but... you are on the *Alda Maru*, and, additionally, you are at a weigh station of sorts, an enthropomorphic node where time and gravity are perfectly in tune within the remnants of a nonlocality quantum string vibration."

"Ahh, that," I said as I sat down and attempted to burp. A holographic display floated in my mind and served as a screen for a documentary-style presentation. Like a 3D movie, images and sounds enveloped my peripherals.

Morgan narrated: "By 1996, the Soul Breaker Virus, originating from TorwardAll's life-extension drug for dogs and commonly known as Puppy Pox, had reduced the human population by ninety-eight percent—"

"Wait," I said. "What year is it right now? On this ship. What year is it?"

"That is a difficult question. There are many variables, but suffice it to say the relative Earth-time year designation for you, at this moment, is 2060 AD. Now, I must insist, no further interruptions. Our time is limited."

Fuck, I thought. That's what Katya had said: that on my second *fiftieth* birthday I would shift fifty years into the future.

"Let's see..." continued the voice of Morgan Freeman, "here we are. The pandemic ushered in the Silent Fall, which was followed by thirty years of hope and despair. Oh, and as an aside, before you get any ideas, believe me when I tell you, your attempts to stop the Soul Breaker Virus will fail, just as they have always failed. You cannot stop it. OK, where was I? Oh, yes. Eventually, two groups emerged. The larger of these two groups were the Kaczynski: a loose amalgam of nomadic tribes comprised of Ted Kaczynski Manifesto devotees. They worshiped anti-technological belief constructs, shunned modern medicine as well as labor-saving devices, and preached that the virus was nature's wrath for the fungus that is Man. The smaller group, known as the Modern Cause, was composed of agnostic technocrats that formed around collegiate hubs. They were technologically progressive and believed it was their responsibility to save Man from extinction. And with no moral debates or conflicts to hold them back, that's exactly what they did. They leaped past the tenets of natural selection and developed stronger, age-defying, disease-resistant humans—pushing the boundaries of human evolution outward. Eventually, they created the Surrogates: human-like machines that were used for mundane tasks.

"At some point—nobody knows exactly when—Hei Jiankui, a registered Modern Cause scientist, placed a cloned, Modern Cause brain into a surrogate chassis and unceremoniously ushered in the Dawn Of the Artificials: a hybrid of humanity and robotics. These Artificials, commonly referred to as ARTs, were first used for protection against rare but violent Kaczynski incursions. Eventually, the ARTs were mass-produced to perform such tasks as food collection and general maintenance; some were even used as personal assistants and companions. As the ARTs grew in number, so did their advanced cognitive awareness. It was a busy time, filled with unconstrained technological expansion; so busy, nobody thought it was their responsibility to rein in the ARTs' human aspirations. Ten years after the ARTs were summoned into being, they took control of the Earth.

"Right then, let's see here... oh yes, this is the good part. Mind Corp, in conjunction with ART Command, developed consciousness-only time travel. They called it TSQEC, short for Tachyon Stream Quantum Entanglement Comb. Many historians have speculated this technology, categorized as Dark-Science, was responsible for the creation of the ARTs as well as their subsequent rise to power. Some of these historians speculated the ARTs employed the Sethco Bootstrap Strategy and used TSQEC to go back in time and create themselves—similar to what you're doing right now."

"Oh," I said, "is that what I'm doing right now? I thought I was just going to bed and getting some sleep."

"No, Mr. Bridges, you are doing much more than sleeping. You have the unique ability to project your mind into the future. I know this because shortly after creating me, you told me so. I also know that your mind is currently in such a state. This mind-projecting ability places you in a position to monitor the Nothingness, an unfortunate byproduct of the TSQEC and a threat to everything of human origin. You, Mr. Bridges, will navigate Man around the Nothingness and into perpetuity. Do you believe in free will?"

"I don't know what my belief system has to do with the price of tea in China, or in India, but I'm quite certain I don't control the universe, the Nothingness, or my dick for that matter. And you should know that because, apparently, I made you." My squeaky-sounding, ten-year-old outburst surprised me.

"You are wrong," said Morgan. "Are you aware ninety-nine-point-nine percent of all species that have lived on Earth have gone extinct? You and I both know Man will eventually succumb to such overwhelming odds. Mr. Bridges, you possess the ability to change those odds—for Man, that is. That leads us to the rub. You have to trade the lives of 4.3 billion people to do it."

"What are you talking about?" I said.

"You have a choice. You can let the human species continue as is, fumbling about until they eventually cede to atrophy, or you can change the inevitable by delivering them into the cosmos, where they will travel, and evolve, and gain a foothold in every region of the universe and live for a million years."

"Why do you think Man will become extinct? Do you have any proof?"

"History will support my assertion as well as an algorithm that proves Man will not survive long enough to develop interstellar travel."

I looked out, past the glass wall and into space. "Can't we do both?"

"No: it's like mixing oil and vinegar. Eventually they will separate. And that's the problem; it's why we're here. Doing both is in your nature. You have tried doing both so many times they are tired of explaining it to you. So now they send me to explain it to you. One of these times you'll get it right. I know this because I exist, and they exist."

"OK, I'll bite. Who are they?"

"They are you. You are they. Now, I will give you the 132nd variation of a message they believe will unlock your true nature: Ahem... Seth Bridges, you must allow the Soul Breaker Virus to infect the planet. Do not interfere with its intendment. Mankind's existence depends on the virus's synthesis. Space is your salvation, your destiny. Do not be swayed from its grasp. Save yourself, Mr. Bridges: ride the Pandemic out in space and humanity will follow. The Pandemic begins in seven years. Verification code Exon. End Message. Oh, you'd better hold on to something, we've got incoming."

"Wait." I said, "Exon is my dog. What does she have to do with this?" Through the ship's viewport, I saw lasers flashing.

Klaxons sounded.

The ship shuddered.

Metal screamed as it tore; sparks bounced off the walls.

Pain.

A woman cradled my head and asked, "What is your damage?"

Shrapnel had slashed away parts of her face, exposing a polished metal skull. She looked familiar. Wait—it was Kogo. Didn't she work for Willhammer? Was she a secret-agent-guardian robot sent here to protect me?

"Lieutenant," shouted a voice from the room's passageway. "Timelock is confirmed. This is it!"

Robot Kogo carried me to an array of escape pods.

Thrusters ejected our pod into space.

Gravity pinned my bloodied face against a porthole.

"Señor," billowed another voice, reverberating throughout the escape pod—almost as if it were coming from space itself. "Señor—"

CHAPTER 15

I opened my eyes and saw Marisol. I was back in my motel room, and she was holding a cardboard box in her hands. "This thing arrive for you at front desk," she said. "I bring to you. This is OK?"

"What time is it?"

"Time is the morning." She set the package on the counter. "You would want I come back later for room cleaning?"

"Hold on." I grabbed some cash from the top of the credenza and handed her a twenty. "Thanks for bringing it over. And this"—I gave her a fifty—"is for doing such a great job with the room. I'm not sure if I introduced myself when we first met. I'm Seth."

"I am Marisol. You are happy with room cleaning?"

"It's perfect, thanks to you. Housekeeping is a difficult job."

"I work hard for my family."

"Are they here, in America?"

"I am alone, but I am to see them soon."

"Are they in Mexico?"

"No, señor. Algeron."

"Algeron? Where's that? I'm not sure I've heard of—"

"Guatemala. I Mayan, work hard, save money."

"Of course you do. You should be very proud of yourself."

"Sí, Mr. Seth, thank you."

"Listen, Marisol, my room is fine; it doesn't need cleaning today. Maybe tomorrow, OK?"

"Sí, tomorrow."

Just as she left, I grabbed my journal and wrote down my dream. I figured it might be my Shifter gift. I wrote it all down: Morgan, Cog-Links, Soul Breaker Virus, Artificials, the collapse of the human population, and, most importantly, how Morgan had said space was my salvation.

As I reviewed my notes, I realized I was in need of psychiatric help. Maybe all of this was some sort of mental breakdown. Maybe I wasn't even here. I filled a glass halfway up with rum, topped it off with orange juice, and drank it down. I poured another one, started feeling a little better about my situation, and came up with a plan: put on my shoes, go out, get a few cooked meals at Mohamed's, come back here and figure stuff out. It wasn't much of a plan, but it was all I could muster at the moment. I got dressed and headed out.

"Hey Mohamed, do you think we're ready to travel to the stars?" I asked as he prepped my meals.

"You and your questions, they will be the death of me," he said, assembling my meal. "I ask you, my friend, why go to the stars when I have the best couscous right here, right now?"

I thanked him, stepped aside, and watched him serve other customers. He was happy. The universe, its wonders and the billions of galaxies that it contained, had no apparent influence on Mohamed's gregarious attitude. He knew his place and it brought him peace. Purpose, existence—did I have it all wrong? Maybe I could go back home and marry Linda Hanshaw. I had gone to the prom with her. We could get married, have kids: give them cool names like Sylvia and Arnue. I could be a stay-at-home dad. I'd show them how to play baseball and teach them about life, and we could all live happily ever after... Huh. I gave Mohamed a half-hearted wave, then went back to my room.

CHAPTER 16

Mohamed was right about his couscous; I doubted they would have anything as good as it in space. I once read an article that said your sense of taste becomes compromised in space. With the help of another rum and OJ, I began to pace around the room and put things into perspective.

First of all, I wasn't crazy. Facts supported that. Fact one, I'd had a vision of the future—that was what I was going to call them from now on: visions. Fact two, eight years ago, on my fiftieth birthday, I had traveled forty years backwards in time. Fact three, Katya and Adamit also claimed to have traveled in time. Fact four, the Soul Breaker Virus is coming in seven years, and I am either going to stop it or detour around it in space.

I suppose I could attempt to save the world's population... But come on, Seth, you spent your entire life not caring for people. Now all of a sudden you care? I bet the Nothingness was that omniscient wall I sometimes saw in my visions. Morgan said I can save our species by navigating around it and allowing the world's population to expire prematurely. That should be easy, right? The problem was... I did care about people. I always had. It was just when they got too close that it became overwhelming. Maybe I cared too much.

So, Seth, what are you going to do: save a generation of people, or the entire species?

Who was kidding who? I was no superhero... a competent plumber and a drunk, yes—but superhero, a saver of Man? No. Let's just say if I could prevent the Soul Breaker Virus from taking hold, I'd still have to worry about things like wars, financial meltdowns, not to mention famines and the like. The real problem with all of it was mankind itself. It has a dark side, and as long as that was true, I'd never be able to stop bad things from happening. I supposed, if I was king of the world and used Draconian measures to control the populace, I could stop the Virus and a majority of man-made disasters; but fuck, there was so much randomness involved... It was impossible. And anyway, everyone dies, right? It was just a matter of time.

What if I were to focus my efforts and go into space? I would need things: money, engineers, and craftsmen, and a place to build whatever I was supposed to build to get into space. What was I going to do, build a space station? A base on the moon would be nice. Probably need a spaceship first, so I could get there. And it wasn't like I was really doing anything important at the moment. And I had wasted my other life. If I doubled up on my bets, I could get a few million to get things rolling. I'd need an office, personnel, a machine shop... Yeah, I knew about that kind of stuff. I'd been doing it all my life.

I lay back on the bed and thought about that robot lady. Someone, before the explosion, had called her lieutenant; and yet here she was in Vegas, calling herself Kogo.

I propped a pillow under my head and thought about the day I'd been given a second chance: I'd driven to the beach, and there had been that girl in a long white dress, walking along the shoreline. Then, I had heard glass shatter, and I had fallen down a tunnel, or at least my mind had.

That fucking tunnel was scary. The scariest thing that had ever happened to me. I couldn't do anything to stop the fall; everything became useless. As I fell, I thought of the very worst thing that could happen and realized it paled in comparison to what was happening to me at that very moment. It was like a panic attack happening inside a mental breakdown. All controls were vacant—except one: in my mind's eye, I focused on the girl I'd seen on the beach. I brought her forth, in my mind, and studied her: the linen of her clean white dress, the curve of her smile, the way the water swirled around her feet, her hair rustled by the wind, everything.

Then, by the grace of God, my fall had ended, and I found myself in a safe place, on a bed, in a dark room. And I remembered wondering if I was late for work. I flung the cover aside, swung my feet to the floor, took a few steps, and tripped on something hairy. It let out a whelp. Then, a voice from another part of the room said, "Go back to bed, Seth. We still got a few minutes."

After that, I crawled back through the darkness on somebody else's little knees, found the bed, got under the covers, and remained still. And then something cold and wet nudged my hand. Then it woofed and licked my face.

"Exon!" I said as I wrapped my arms around the best doggone dog in the world. Then I remembered thinking, how the hell could I be four feet tall and holding a dog that died thirty years ago?

After that my oldest brother Mark smacked me in the face with a pillow, and my Mom said, "Breakfast is on the table. Let's go, boys,"

I looked at my other brother, Casey. He gave me a stuck-eyed sleepy nod.

"Come on," he said as he shifted his feet onto the floor. "Get dressed. Remember what Mrs. Washington says; 'Today is the first day of the rest of your life.'"

Then, on the way to the bathroom, I bumped into my dad. He wore a suit and tie. I looked up. He walked right past me—obtuse as ever. After that, I went to the kitchen and took a seat in my old chair, next to the twins, Gabriel and Gabrielle, who were enthusiastically swirling food around on the trays of their high-chairs. Dad held out a newspaper and flipped the page. "Mark, Casey, Seth, I want the lawn mowed and the edges clipped before I get home. And don't forget to vacuum the house—the entire house—and take out the trash. Do the trash first."

There we were, living the 1970s version of the American Dream... Then the phone rang and Mom said something like, "Heavens, who could be calling?" Then she rushed over and answered it. "Yes," she said. "OK. Hold on. Seth, it's for you, honey." She put her palm over the mouthpiece as she told me, "Tell them it's impolite to call so early."

"Hello?" I said.

"Hey, Seth, how's breakfast?" The voice was thin and sounded like it had been recorded on an old-time gramophone. "Mom's cooking," he continued. "Mm, so good."

"Who's this?"

He said, "It's me—you. Listen up. It's time for you to get your act together. Call Grandpa K and tell him it's time to change the future. He is going to send you to boarding school. It'll be fun, I promise. While you're there, you need to brush up on your math skills. Also, you need to enroll in the wrestling team—try to get some boxing in too. You need to know how to fight. After you graduate, you're going to go to Las Vegas to await further instructions. You got it?"

"No," I said. "I don't."

Then he; or rather, future me, said, "You will. This is your second chance. Now, get out there and try to enjoy yourself this time around."

Then I made some wise-ass comment like, "Enjoy myself? I enjoy myself."

Future me said, "Call Grandpa. We'll talk again."

The phone made some *clicking* sounds and a computer-voiced operator came on the line and said something like, "Iampod8, Chronospool trace receipt 001, Sethco time derivative unknown." Then there was a *click* and a dial tone.

I shook the memory, grabbed the bottle of rum from the motel's nightstand, held it up to the Velvet Elvis painting in such a way that Elvis's head sat atop the bottle, and said, "Yeah, enjoy yourself."

Ring, ring, ring. Oh, shit, who the fuck was that?

"Hello."

"Hello, Seth, it's Mom. How are you?"

"Hey, Mom, I'm good. I was just thinking about you. How's everything there?"

"Oh... did I call at a bad time?" she asked. "I'm not too sure of the time difference."

"No, no. Is everything alright?"

"Yes, it's just that you haven't called in a few days and—"

"Jeez, I'm sorry, Mom. Things are so busy around here. I'll call you more often. I promise."

We talked for the next half hour, catching up on Grandpa passing and other family matters. My oldest brother Mark had achieved Navy SEAL status. Casey was doing well with his theology studies at Brigham Young—paid for by Grandpa. Dad wanted the twins, which still had the run of the house, to attend Tabor Academy, but Mom would not hear of it. Toward the end of the call, she asked, "Did you receive the box from Grandpa?"

"Hold on." I got up and looked at the return address on the package Marisol had dropped off. It was from Grandpa's estate. "Yeah, I got it. Haven't opened it yet though. Do you know anything about it?"

"Well, he treasured that box. Nikola Tesla gave it to him for safekeeping. Your grandfather and Mr. Tesla were lifelong friends. That charlatan Edison and a bunch of people from the government wanted the box. Dad kept it in the safe behind the old clock on the mantel. We—I mean us kids—were sworn to secrecy and only allowed to touch it once. You should probably take care of it. And don't forget to call."

"OK, Mom, I will. Bye now, take care. Oh, wait. Mom, how's Exon doing?"

"...I'm sorry, Seth. I didn't know how to tell you... We had to put her down yesterday. It was time."

"Did she suffer... you know, at the end?"

"No, not at all."

"Did you stay with her... when they gave her the shot?"

"Yes. She was peaceful... like going to sleep."

"I should've been there! She would have been there for me—"

"Now, now. We all knew when we got her she wouldn't live forever. Some things just can't be changed." In the background, I heard my dad say, "Give me the phone."

"Seth," he said. "Since you've chosen *not* to attend college, I think it's time you get your head out of the clouds. You should settle down and take a position at the family business. You'll have to start at an entry level, just like I did, but you'll learn the value of hard work. And who knows—someday you and your brothers could be running the place."

I couldn't help but laugh. "Yeah, about that... Dad, I have a job, and I'm fine right where I am."

"That's ridiculous. Come home, son. It's good, decent work; it provided for our family and paid for your schooling... Have you been drinking?"

"Yes, I've been drinking, and it was Grandpa that paid for my schooling. Listen, Dad, I'm not going to argue with you. I have a job, and that's it. Sorry."

"What exactly do you do out there, anyway?"

"I'm going to build an aerospace company."

"Are you caught up in that hippy-dippy drug scene? Is that it, son?"

"Bye, Dad." I hung up the phone.

CHAPTER 17

Exon was dead? I put on my suit coat, grabbed my walking-around gear, then drove to the Sands and ordered a beer at the casino's Landing Lounge. The activity on the floor seemed normal enough: slot machines clanged alongside shouts of luck and misfortune. Everything appeared to be in its proper place, but something was askew, like someone had shifted the universe over a smidge and upgraded it with new configurations.

This was the second time Exon had died without me at her side.

Then, out of nowhere, sitting on the stool next to me, I saw Lonely. His head was lowered, and he was innocuously sipping at a glass of red wine through a yellow flexible straw. Born of past regrets and tailored from fear of the future, Lonely seemed superfluous in the here and now. He was a harbinger of self-destruction, a reconciliation of my past I'd yet to deal with. He'd hung out at my shack in my previous timeline—it was mostly on weekends, and he'd even had his own chair in the backyard. Towards the end, he'd never left. He just hung out, sitting in that chair, drinking and smoking. He was a good listener, and he didn't complain. But one thing was certain: the longer he stuck around, the worse things would get.

"Were you there for Exon?" I asked, not bothering to look him in the eyes.

He barely raised an eyebrow. Fuck, I thought. I'm screwing up timelines. Lonely had never met Exon. He had started hanging around after Exon died, when I began working for my family's stupid fucking plumbing business.

"What are you gonna do," I said, getting into his face, "hide all the sharp objects?"

He looked at my left wrist, then casually resumed sucking wine through his straw.

"Hey," I said. "You should mind your own damn business." I wanted to smack him, but we both knew how cruel that would be. "Listen, it's like I told you before. I haven't got time for you anymore. OK? Everything here is fine, hunky-dory. I'm sure there are tons of people out there that would love your company. Why don't you go help them?"

He ignored me and attempted to light a cigarette with a Bugs Bunny Pez dispenser. I felt my foundations of hope began to weaken, crumble.

Wait, I thought. All I had to do was keep busy. That had always worked before. I chugged down my beer, gave Lonely a mocking salute, and said, "Adios, amigo."

When I got to my car, he was in the passenger seat, quietly sipping at a can of Pabst Blue Ribbon through his straw. He followed me into my motel room and watched me fill a tall glass with ice and some Captain Morgan's rum. After pouring himself a drink and sticking his straw in it, he stepped over to the window and stared out at the world.

"Hey," I said, "What do you want from me?" He turned, then nodded at the package from my grandfather.

I ripped through the shipping cardboard, removed the packing material, and lifted out an ornately engraved, five-by-seven-inch silver box and a letter that explained the box was my inheritance—a gift from Grandpa. I returned my attention to the box. The lid was adorned with Greek symbols, locked tight, and had no visible latch or keyhole. Best I could figure, the symbols spelled out *Illumina Pandoron*. Nikola Tesla had given this to Grandpa?

I estimated the price of silver was about four dollars an ounce, downed another drink, then held the box in my hands. It was unusually heavy for its size. I looked over at Lonely. He was smiling. That was odd, because he never smiled.

Just then, my fingers tripped a latch, which opened the lid and revealed a red velvet interior. An emerald-green ball that resembled a trackball for a computer was centered halfway deep into the base. When I touched the ball, a twelve-by-twelve-inch, multi-colored holographic display materialized before me.

I jerked back in surprise. When I returned my finger to the ball, groupings of odd symbols and pictographs floated before me. I rotated the trackball, which moved a holographic cursor, and stopped at the word *English*. Nothing. I tried it again, but this time, when the cursor reached the word, I pressed the trackball down. There was a slight *click,* and the display converted over to English. The box was an advanced computer. My mind raced. These things didn't exist yet. Fuck! Not even the government had this kind of technology! Grandpa, you sly old dog.

I rotated the trackball and a display of options was presented. I studied the hologram for a few minutes before I realized what I was looking at. It was a timeline of man's technological existence, past, present, and *future!*

I closed the lid and held the Box close to my chest. Fuck! The future in a box? I propped a chair under the room's door handle, closed the curtains, and looked around for a hiding place. I ended up slitting an opening in the bed's box-spring and stashing the Box inside. Then, under the watchful eyes of Paranoid, I retrieved the Box and opened it up again. Fuck, I thought, am I back in Crazyville? No, I was a time traveler with a box that contained the future. It wasn't a bad thing, just a dangerous thing. I had to be careful.

My journey into the fantastic world of future technology was, at the very least, incredible. The information was presented in technical terms—most of it far beyond my comprehension. The data was endless and contained, among other things, systems and procedures for collecting antimatter from solar flares, plans for things like pulse weapons, terraforming accelerators, stellar-drive engines, cold-plasma shields, ram-force dark-energy converters, gravitational wave accelerators, and anti-time particle injectors for non-linear space travel—whatever they were.

Four hours later, I, along with Paranoid, Lonely, and Captain Morgan, had decided that going to the stars would be best for everyone involved. Tomorrow, I'd drive over to Caltech and hire an engineer.

I threw a bottle at Lonely's shadow and went to bed.

Goodnight, Exon.

CHAPTER 18

Las Vegas, Happy Time Motel, Room #21
January 31, 1980

Octavius 3 grumbled about in a seldom-used section of the Gamble's brain. It was secure from the cluttered thoughts of his host and quiet enough to admire the pleasant pictures he had imagined onto the walls of his new home. These images and barriers helped to ward off Mr. Gamble's dream people, who at night roamed around, uninvited and reckless, scaring him without cause or warning.

He wished he were anywhere but in this guy's head. This guy was fat and old and stupid and icky. When they went outside, Octavius 3 saw people talking and enjoying each other's company. Outside, some of the people even held hands; much different than at the lab, where everyone lived in fear of the soldiers and the old lady, who called herself Aunt Mun. Outside, people his size ran around in all manners: some shrieked, some laughed, and some whispered together in confidence. According to Mr. Gamble, that's what kids did: run around and have fun.

"Fun?" he had once asked Mr. Gamble. "What is it to have fun?"

As Octavius 3 remembered Mr. Gamble's explanation of fun, he added some pictures of fun to the walls. He was proud of his pictures. He remembered how proud he'd felt when they'd told him he was the direct descendant of the great and wondrous Emperor Octavius Sun Taizu, divine leader of the Taizu Empire. They had said he, Octavius 3, was special, that his family had been dishonored by defeat, and that it was his duty to restore his family's name. What family, he had thought: that old lady who flies around in a chair and yells at Doctor Heisenberg and Galahad? That was a stupid family. During attainment conditioning, they'd said he was to right history by going back in time and killing some bad guy called Sethco the Destroyer. This, they had said, would prevent the Five-Minute War and restore his family's honor.

That was stupid, Octavius had thought. If he was so special, how come there were a bunch of kids that looked exactly like him back at the lab? What if he didn't want to kill anybody? What were they going to do, send someone to kill him? Probably one of the other versions of himself. Now, in the stillness, he turned his attention to a blanket he had found: a smelly blanket that was soft, warm, and comforting. It was a blanket that refused to leave his side.

"I've been here two months," he said to the blanket. "I do not feel proud. I do not think I can take much more. Do you think they could send me someplace where it is better? What will become of me if I fail? What will become of me if I succeed? What then? Can you answer me?"

Octavius 3 reached into the gobbledygook of the Gamble's mind, grabbed a bundle of pain nerves, and said, "Mr. Gamble?"

"Stop that," said the Gamble. "Stop it!"

"Why does this blanket smell?"

"I'm sorry, Moon-boy, there's nothing I can do. It just does. It used to be mine—when I was little."

"Mr. Gamble, take me downstairs to the payphone. We have to report in."

"Can I wear my bra?" asked the Gamble. "You know, underneath?"

"Yes... but why? Those are for females."

In the lobby of the Happy Time Motel, they called a local number, connected with Acme Voice Mail & Message Service Storage System, and left a chronospool message for the company's only client: Mun Sun Taizu.

"Your Highness, arrived 8/5/79 Las Vegas. Placed reward ad in Las Vegas Sun personals, per mission objectives. Contact with target established 2/1/80, at Sands Casino Las Vegas. Forward reward money via sequential lottery digits for time segment. Proceeding with honorable dictate. Your loyal descendant, Octavius 3."

As Octavius 3 hung up the phone, he visualized his message traveling over telephone wires, across the country, and eventually ending up in the East Tower on the Manhattan side of the Brooklyn Bridge. He remembered how his cloned brother, Octavius 1, had gone back in time during the construction of the bridge and had a four-by-eight-foot climate-controlled vault installed to Mun's specifications. Octavius 3 tried to imagine the vault's interior and the small table that held a custom-built Kazuo Hashimoto answering machine, and how succeeding generations of the Roebling family maintained and transferred all incoming messages, tape-and-all, to the Wells Fargo Bank of New York. Octavius 3 imagined how his message would be placed in a safe deposit vault, and how each year, for the next eighty years, all messages and recording devices would be transferred to current technology storage devices until they were eventually spun into the internal Heads Up Display of Mun Sun Taizu.

CHAPTER 19

When I woke up, it was morning. Something had changed. Sure, I had a headache and a dry mouth, but now the suicidal machinations of my previous lifetime seemed ridiculous, and for the first time I could remember, I actually looked forward to what the day had in store for me.

I packed an overnight bag, grabbed Grandpa's Box, and just as I opened the door, I saw Marisol. She was armed with a spray bottle and a bundle of linen.

"Good morning, Marisol. It's nice to see you. I'm heading out; the room's all yours."

She set the spray bottle and the bundle of linens on the table. "Buenos días, Mr. Seth. How you are today?"

"Oh, I'm fine, thanks."

"Where you go now?" she said as she began to strip the bed.

"Well, I got this crazy idea that I'm going to build a spaceship, and then maybe build a space station, or even a base on the moon." I doubted she could comprehend what I was saying, but it felt good to actually say it out loud.

"I build many things in Guatemala. Maybe someday you see these things."

"You build things? That's great. You know, when I was younger, I used to invent all kinds of things. I would write them down, and sometimes I would even build them, and then, I don't know. It's like, life would get in the way and—"

"You are still young, yes?"

Fuck, Seth, watch what you say. Keep things simple. "Yeah, it's hard to explain."

Just then, she snapped a clean sheet in the air, and as it floated down onto the mattress, time stopped long enough for her to weave a campaign of parachuting smiles into my heart. My eighteen-year-old body transmitted lascivious thoughts to dormant sections of my mind. Then, out of nowhere, Love, my greatest nemesis, appeared. He was behind her, jumping up and down, waving his arms around like an excited contestant on a game show. I reminded myself that she was too young for an old fogey like me. Fuck, I thought. I needed a cup of coffee or something. I cleared my throat.

"Well, best I get to building things. You take care, Marisol." I got tripped up on a pile of used towels, stumbled forward, and planted an awkward kiss on her cheek. "Sorry," I said, and headed out.

As I got in my car and stashed my gear, I realized I wasn't alone. Lonely was in the front passenger seat, solemn as ever, while Paranoid and Love were in the backseat, goofing around like excited kids about to go on a family road trip.

"Alright guys," I said, "this isn't going to work."

I drove deep into the desert on a road that was sparsely traveled: just wannabe gamblers flush with green, and an equal amount of cash-strapped ex-gamblers heading home. I found a quiet side road, powered down, turned to Lonely, and said, "Hey buddy, I'm sorry, but this is the end of the line. You've been a good friend, but I'm OK now. And thanks. Couldn't have done it without you."

He removed the chewed-up straw from his mouth, tucked it behind his ear, and got out of the car. He gave me a reassuring smile and headed out into the desert.

Paranoid climbed into the front seat and gave me a questioning shoulder shrug. I knew exactly what he was thinking: I needed a gun. I remembered the gun store we had passed on our way out here. We watched Lonely walk into the desert for a few minutes and then drove to the gun store.

"Morning son," said the lady behind the glass-topped counter of the Second Amendment Gun Emporium & Shooting Range. She was slightly overweight, fortyish, and could have won beauty pageants in her youth.

"What can I do you for on this fine day?" she said.

"Well ma'am, I'm looking for a—"

"Please, everyone around here calls me Babe."

"OK... *Babe*," I said as I looked around the store. "I'd like to buy a snub-nosed .38. A policeman's special, I think it's called. And I'll need a couple hundred rounds of ammo and a shoulder holster to go with it."

She grabbed a revolver from the inside of the glass counter, four boxes of ammo from the shelf above the register, a nylon shoulder holster from a nearby display rung, and laid them all out on a cushioned section of the countertop.

"You got it. By the way, it's called a chief's special, made by Smith & Wesson—three-inch barrel, five rounds, easily concealed." She held her arms up like she was being robbed, reached back between her shoulder blades and produced a similar revolver. "Carry one myself. Is this gonna be cash or credit?"

After I signed some paperwork and paid her cash, she said, "For a hundred bucks, you can go out back and shoot a fifty caliber for five seconds."

"How about sixty seconds? What would that cost?"

"Well, that'll be the whole nine yards... I reckon that'll cost... fifteen hundred."

"I'll give you twelve."

"Mister"—she hammered her fist on the counter top and pointed at me—"Sold American!"

She took my money, put it somewhere safe, then came back with a hand truck loaded with green ammo cases. "Follow me," she said with a smile and a directional nod.

The shooting-range was strewn with spent shell casings, rotting hay stands, and old paper targets that flitted in the wind. Babe set the machine gun and tripod atop an earthen mound. Downrange, targets were paced off at twenty-five, fifty, and one-hundred-yard increments. I straddled the ground, adjusted my hearing protectors, and grasped the weapon's dual handles.

"You're clear, mister," Babe yelled, giving me the thumbs-up signal.

I squeezed the trigger.

Bullets rained forth like angry hornets on a mission from God.

Adrenaline coursed through my body.

The barrel glowed red.

Paranoid, who had been following Babe around, gave me a nod and disappeared into the ether.

As I got into my car, Love, who was still sitting in the back seat, slowly crawled into the front passenger seat. He tilted his head, gave me his best puppy-dog eyes, a smile, and a nod that said, "Do you want to talk about it?"

"Yeah, I do," I said out loud. "The last four times you showed up it all went to shit: everything. And stop with the puppy eyes cause it ain't gonna work this time. But—and this is a real big but—if it does work out, it's gonna be on my terms, not yours. So right now, I need you out." I gestured my thumb toward the door. "Out," I yelled.

He faked a sad face, rolled down the window, and crawled onto the roof. I pulled onto the main road and floored the Maserati. Love hung on, laughed, and occasionally lowered his head over the windshield and made goofy faces at me. I hit him a few times with the windshield-washer spray, and eventually I was able to get him to release his grip and fly away. Thank God, I thought. That guy is trouble with a capital T.

CHAPTER 20

I found the Interstate and drove west to Caltech. I was hoping to drum up some talent for my aerospace venture by posting job offers on a few school bulletin boards or even in the school's newspaper. Maybe I could meet someone that knew someone?

Two hours later, in Barstow, I pulled into a service area for a break. I fueled up, checked the engine's oil level, then had lunch. To my surprise, the food and service were so good I found myself mentally composing a review for TripAdvisor.Com. As I paid my tab, I asked the cashier for directions to Caltech. She wasn't sure, but a coworker, who had a son at the school, helped out and gave me a detailed map.

I got back on the Interstate and turned up the radio. A promotion for tonight's Who concert at Ohio's Riverfront Coliseum aired. I remembered Roger Schinble, a childhood friend from my first timeline, who had attended the concert. He'd had both his arms broken during a stampede of concertgoers who mistook the band's soundcheck for the start of the show. *Should I warn him?* I thought. But I didn't have his number. I could call the information operator. They would have the number. Probably cause another scene. "There goes Seth and his stories again." Same old crap. You try to help someone and you get ridiculed for it. How many times had they laughed at me or said, "That was a lucky guess, Seth." Or, "Don't think you're smarter than the rest of us, because you're not."

Thing is, you can't prove something would have happened after you've prevented it from occurring. Screw it, he's already there anyhow. I changed the radio channel: Willie Nelson was plucking out a simple but sweet guitar solo in his rendition of Irving Berlin's song "Blue Skies." The Maserati's sound system sounded good at one-half volume.

I followed a series of local road signs to the school and pulled into the campus parking lot. Just as I was getting ready to shut my car down, somebody with a bracelet-laden forearm rapped their knuckles on my door. An awkward-looking girl wearing a floppy hat and an ensemble of wannabe hippy-dippy clothes raised an eyebrow and smiled at me.

I rolled down the window and said, "Hi, there."

Her floppy hat fluttered, like it wanted to fly off and seek out a more stable perch. "You here for the penis party?" she asked.

"I don't think so?"

"Come on, I'm doing a report for the *Free Speech Gazette*. I need you to sneak me into the party. You know, like Woodward and Bernstein. So are you going to help me out or what?"

"Sure," I said. "What's your story about?"

"Fraternal male dominance in the scientific community."

After shutting down my car, I stashed my gun in my bag, then pulled some clothes out and covered the bag itself. "Do you like science?" I said as I got out and locked the car.

"Not really. The men are dorky, and it's boring."

I followed her up a flight of stairs and over to a loud party. "This story is going to win me a Pulitzer," said the floppy-hatted journalist. "Can you smell the testosterone?"

In the center of the room, a tiny-eared, snake-faced goon was beating the crap out of someone half his size. Fuck it. It seemed like a fine opportunity to finesse some Budo training in a real-world environment. I ditched Floppy Hat and jumped into the scuffle. After securing a front-side guillotine choke-hold on the goon, I dropped backward and tightened my hold, increasing the blood pressure in his cranium and forcing his autonomic-nervous system to implement last-ditch, life-saving protocol: unconsciousness. By the time I'd extracted myself from his limp body, the snake-faced goon had woken up, assumed a wobbling fighting stance and mumbled, "Fuck you, cheater. Fight me like a man."

Before his buddies could dissuade him from further action, I sent him stumbling backward with a straight-on Hikuta punch to his face. The goon was carried out. The other fighter guy, who was checking his skull for lumps and blood, got in my face and yelled, "What the fuck, man? I probably broke two of his knuckles with the back of my head. I was about to kick his ass!" The five-foot-eight fire-plug of muscle reminded me of the Bruce Willis character from the movie "Unbreakable."

"Sorry about that," I said. "It's just that... I thought he was a bully or something."

"Well, I didn't need your help, but thanks anyway." He stuck his hand out. "I'm Crash. Not my real name, just what people call me."

"Yeah, cool," I said, shaking his hand. "I'm Seth."

As we walked over to a kitchen alcove, some partiers congratulated us for sending the obnoxious drunk back to wherever he had come from. Crash poured us both a shot of whiskey.

"Haven't seen you around. You a student?"

I downed the shot. "No... you?"

"Yeah, physics... theoretical physics to be precise."

"Nice. So... what were you guys fighting about?"

"Fucker said Heinlein was gay."

"You got into a fight over that? Huh... You ever read his book *Friday*? It sounded a little—"

"No, not that kind of gay. Said he was gay like... irrelevant gay, like Heinlein didn't matter or something." He wiggled air-quotes near his ears. "And I quote, 'Heinlein couldn't hold a candle to Verne, Wells, or Shelley.'"

"Oh, well, those *are* some fighting words. Do you think he meant Mary Shelley or the poet guy?"

"I'm not sure, but I was about to Waldo his ass until you, well, you know... Hey, what's with the suit? You look a little young to be a spook. You in training?"

"No, I'm an independent agent, and I am recruiting."

"Cool. Wanna smoke some primo?"

CHAPTER 21

We headed a few doors down the hallway, over to Crash's dorm room.

"Spark it up," he said, handing me a lighter and a crazy-ass bong that could have been a prop in a Ridley Scott sci-fi movie. "This shit is the bomb."

"Who's your buddy?" I said, pointing to a hamster in a cage who was busy running in place on a rattling exercise wheel.

"Oh," said Crash, as he bent down and peeked into the wire cage. "That's Burt. Burt Reynolds. The ladies love him, but he has a nasty habit of biting people."

I sucked in a hit. "You said you study theoretical physics; does that include things like alternate universes and time travel?"

He grabbed a couple of beers from a small fridge, handed me one, and sat down on a couch. "We tweak mathematical models and theories, and we disprove old paradigms and develop ways to prove new ones. It's sort of like religion. John Q Public has big questions; so, we put on our priestly lab coats, grab a kernel of data, convince our peers to buy into whatever mumbo jumbo we are working on, and blammo, we got a working theory. Alternate universes and time travel are included in our discipline, but it's not something we're supposed to spend a lot of time on. Makes us look like… ah, you know, nerds."

As I joined him on the couch, he repacked the bong and took a hit. "Personally," he continued, "I love that shit. I'll tell you what though, it cracks me up whenever people say that, if they could go back in time, they would kill Hitler or save Kennedy. It's such a fantasy. They don't get it. It won't work."

"Why not?"

"Traveling back in time doesn't give you superpowers. And you would need them to deal with the huge number of variables that would prevent you from achieving such a goal. You couple that with all the disastrous ramifications that come with messing with the past… It's a real can of worms. Think about it. Could *you* really go back in time and kill somebody? I mean you, not a hypothetical you"—he poked me in the shoulder—"but actually *you*. Could you do it? Which Hitler are you going to kill? The cute little baby Hitler, the struggling art-student Hitler, or the Nazi-leader Hitler that is protected by layers and layers of bodyguards?"

"Well," I said. "Now that you put it that way, I'm not so—"

"The chances of your success would be pretty slim," he said in an I've-got-a-big-bong-hit-in-my-lungs voice. He blew a plume of blue smoke at the ceiling. "Do you have a weapon? Do you know how to use it? Do you speak flawless German? Oh yeah, you're working on the assumption it was Hitler who caused WW2, but what if it was the system of governance itself, adapting to the parameters programmed by the collective conscience of its creators? Someone else will fill the void you create when you kill Hitler? And what if this new person actually succeeds in dominating the planet?"

"I take it you've thought about this before?"

"Let's say you killed Hitler and saved millions. What have you accomplished? Most of the people you saved are probably dead by now—or dying in nursing homes. Oh, and by the way, now that you've fucked with the past, what are the chances of your parents meeting and conceiving you at the exact moment that resulted in your creation? Hm... how about zero? You, I, and the billions of others on this planet, we'd become Zamani: unremembered ghosts. And, if you had never lived, how could you go back in time and kill Hitler? By killing Hitler, you kill yourself. So the real question is: are you willing to sacrifice your life, this world, and all the people in it for a world that never existed? I sure as shit ain't."

"Huh, when you put it that way—"

Ring-ring. Ring-ring. Crash answered the phone, said a few words, then held it out. "It's for you."

"Hello?" I heard a few clicks and some static. As the weed crested in my brain, a thin, distant-sounding voice said, "Hey, I need you to listen very carefully."

"Who is this?"

"It's me."

"Me who?"

"Me, future-you, that's who. Now listen up. That guy you're with, Crash, he's your new engineer; hire him. Also, when you get back to Vegas, hire Adamit and his family."

"—Sir," said a voice in the background, "they've taken one of our emissaries."

"Hey bud, gotta fly. Things to blow up."

There was a stark *click,* then a computer-voiced operator said, "Iampod8, Chronospool trace receipt 002, Sethco time derivative unknown." *Click*—dial tone.

I hung up. "Hey, you got any more of that whiskey?"

Crash handed me a half-full bottle. "Who was it?"

I took a swig. "It was me... calling myself from the future."

"Huh, that's some trippy shit right there. What'd you tell yourself?"

"Hey, how would you like to work for me? I'm starting an aerospace company over in Vegas: we're launching satellites, building spaceships, space stations, that sort of thing. It pays $500 a week, plus benefits. You interested?"

He took a bong hit, closed his eyes, exhaled a plume of blue smoke, and said, "Sure, why not? I'll have enough credits to graduate in a week. When do I start?"

By the time we finished the bottle of whiskey, I'd learned that Crash had a dual major in electrical engineering and theoretical physics. He had been expelled from MIT for blowing up a lab while demonstrating the existence *and* origin of the overlooked "bang" part of the Big Bang Theory. And, from what I could gather, he had a problem with authority and needed to quell the synaptic storms in his brain with alcohol and weed.

CHAPTER 22

In the morning, I had another vision, and, like a memory lost long ago, it seemed very real.

I and my dead shipmates were in a cave. We had been attacked by the Phage, which according to my Cog-Link, were an intergalactic, migrating horde of five-legged, skyscraper-sized Bucky-Ball looking viruses whose sole purpose was replication. I, unlike my crew, was an Artificial and was self-sufficient in most environments, including the cold vacuum of space, as well as the poisonous atmosphere of the planetoid we were currently stranded on.

As shrieks from far away found their way in and echoed off the cave walls, I had my Cog-Link play back the previous few minutes on my Vid-Cord: I saw my team huddled-up in this ghastly cave. They were cold, defeated, and scared. They had a minute of air left before their spacesuits' automatic DAS (Direct Anti Suffer) valves provided a quick, painless death.

"Commodore," whispered Comm Officer Sally Tighzon, her dying face captured by my recording unit, "you remember Peter? Did I ever tell you about our plans? We were going to get married, have kids, and buy a home on Pangea. We were going to grow ancient together. Will you tell him I love him?"

I heard my recorded voice say, "Of course I will, Sally. Of course I will."

Then, the synced *clicks* of twelve DAS valves rang out like miniature guillotines.

I watched myself compose a report:

PON PON, PON PON. ART COMMAND/Musashi/

SporeNet, Sat relay—priority 1

Commodore Seth Bridges. Final Report:

Unknown planetoid, Mel's Hole Well, Cryptkey Galaxy.

During scheduled testing of our Heinlein 3 Boiler Drives, we were hit by a hyperwave of dark energy, which cast us into an unknown region of the Cryptkey Galaxy. The area *was Phage active, and as we autodeceled from gallop, we were attacked. We engaged Phage, were overwhelmed, became disabled, and crashed on a nearby planetoid. The crew—now expired—fought with valor, but succumbed to the planet and the Phage. I, acting Commander Seth Bridges, hereby posthumously promote the following crew members: Ensign Squeaky Bradford, Sergeant Skip Zana, Gunner Jamalocule "Chello" Jones, Chief Engineer R. Eldrick, Flight Surgeon Tommy "Doc" Rhodes, Com Officer First Class Sally Tighzon, Navigator Brian "Hugger" Hugles, Scientific Advisor Anthony Prokoper, Temperologist Ray Nollins, Psyop specialist Quickso Doomerville, Magi 1st Class Eddie "Zen" Rittenhouser, and our youngest officer, Private Octavius 8 Taizu. This promotion is one pay grade forward. Will return to ART Command when possible—FIND ME, KOGO—End message**

I shut off the vid-cord and made the sign of the cross—just in time to observe the cave and my vision dissolving into dust.

Someone was kicking my leg. "Hey, Suit-Man, let's get some lunch."

It was Crash. I was back at Caltech. His words stung my brain. My mouth tasted like a cat had crapped in it. My god—my crew. They all died. Damn, I thought. What a horrible way to die. I wanted to go back to sleep and save them. Poor bastards, stuck in that cave for eternity. I couldn't get them out of my mind. I grabbed a nearby pen and wrote it all down.

"What are you doing?" asked Crash. "They're gonna close soon."

"Hold on," I said. "Give me a second." Wait—before the cave, had I called myself last night? Yes, I had. I wrote that down too, then looked over at Crash and said, "Is there a cat around here?"

"No, just Burt. And he doesn't get out much because of, you know, his biting problem. Take this." He handed me a glass of water and a shot of liquor. "C'mon, let's get some grub."

We grabbed some food at the school cafeteria and sat next to a table of talkative female students. I kept my mouth shut while Crash engaged them in his own brand of social intercourse.

"Ladies," he said, "do you believe Nietzsche was right, or do you think he may have erred in his summations?"

They ignored him and resumed a collective cackle among themselves.

"Hey," I said to Crash. "Last night I offered you a job: you still interested?"

"Yeah. I also remember you offered me five hundred dollars a week and you already hired me."

"Oh... so when do you graduate?"

"I told you last night: I need a week to wrap things up here. Is that alright?"

"Yeah, of course." I counted out fifteen hundred dollars and handed it to him. "Here's your signing bonus. I'm not sure how much I told you last night, but our company has proprietary technology that is, well... advanced."

"And I told you last night, that shit's got my name written all over it." He stood up and yelled, "Woohoo, I'm going to space, you Podunk dirt farmers!"

I hushed him down and said, "It's just an R&D company but—you stick with me, I'll get you into space." I wrote down my address and phone number and gave it to him. "Call me when you get into Vegas. I got to get back now. See you in a week."

As I got into my car, Floppy Hat the Moonbat came over and said, "You get what you need?"

I smiled. "Yes, I did. Thank you. How about yourself? Did you get a story?"

She mimed the act of giving three simultaneous sex acts that involved her hands and mouth and said, "I sure did. Yeehaw!"

CHAPTER 23

An hour outside of Vegas, I pulled off the road, stabbed a few sections of newspaper onto the spines of a dead cactus, and began to get acquainted with my .38. After firing forty rounds, I felt confident my previous target-shooting abilities had returned.

I chased puffy clouds back to the city, looking for a food joint along the way. At a rise, I slowed to let a rattlesnake cross the road. For a moment, I fancied myself an existential shaman, traipsing through a few of the meatier chapters of a Carlos Castaneda novel. Perhaps appreciating puffy clouds and slowing down to let snakes cross the road could appease the gods of fate?

I was getting hungry, so on the outskirts of town, I parked in front of a club called the Circle of Willis Lounge and went inside. As I paused to let my eyes adjust to the low lighting, the club's heating system blew forth a breeze replete with yesterday's whiskey, today's cigarettes, and mummified rats from who knew when. To my right, Stevie Wonder's "Superstition" spilled out of an ancient jukebox's tired speakers. Even in the dim lighting, it was unmistakable—this was a Black club for Black people.

I sidled up to the bar, ordered a beer, and asked the guy on the stool next to me if I could buy him one. "Why, yes you can, my white brother. Thank yeh kindly."

"Bartender," I said, "could you make that two beers? And a menu, please."

The bartender slid two frosty mugs of beer at us, then a bowl of goldfish crackers, and said, "Kitchen's closed."

My bar-mate took one of the mugs, tilted it, and took a few gulps. "My name is James."

He seemed friendly enough for a man whose face appeared to have been forged by years of misfortune. Wait, I'd seen this guy before... He kinda looked like that guy from the vision I had of San Francisco. He had been stuck on the wall next to me, in that cell. "Nice to meet you. I'm Seth. You from around here? You look familiar?"

He gave me a scowl. "Hell no," he said loudly. "I ain't from around here. They make me live here, but that ain't forever. This place is evil, pure evil. They say my strings are dirty, want me to change 'um. I ain't gonna do it. Can't do it. That's where the funk is."

"Strings? Are you a musician or something?"

He pounded his fist on the bar, caught the attention of the other patrons, and shouted, "I'm James Jamerson, motherfucker. I put the funk in the Funk Brothers."

My heart quickened. Years ago, in my previous timeline, I'd read a book about him called *Standing in the Shadows of Motown*. He was a musical genius, a master of time and syncopation. He had played on hundreds of hit songs during the 60s and 70s and was arguably the most artistic bass player ever recorded. I remembered reading how he got paid shit, maybe thirty dollars a recording session, and then had died broke and disillusioned.

"See this"—he curled his right index finger up and stuck it in my face—"this is the real hook that made them songs sell. Got it slammed in the door of a '46 DeSoto when I was a kid, never set right. So yes, my finger's bent and my neck is warped, but brother, let me tell you something; I ain't never, ever, ever gonna change those strings lessin' they break."

Just then, I noticed his facial muscles relax and his pupils contract. He leaned in close and in a low and sober voice said, "You know those visions of the future you have? The ones when you're actually there?"

"How'd you—"

"It's OK, Mr. Bridges; I'm a Shifter, like you, only my visions are of the past. I'm a use-to-be agent for the Artificials. Currently, I'm in an induced vision at ART Command. It's a research facility on the planet Legion. Our window is short, so I'll be brief. You're in extreme danger. There has been a series of time breaks. The most recent will have you assassinated within the next seven minutes. I'm here to change that." He removed a new bass-string package from the inside of his coat. "Quickly, exchange the rounds in your weapon for these."

"What the...?" I looked around the bar. "Is everyone in this town a damn Shifter?"

"I fix broken time, Mr. Bridges. And if you don't do as I say, you, me, and everyone else in our future will cease to exist."

"Oh. Well, why didn't you say that in the first place? What are they?" I asked, exchanging the rounds in my .38 with the shells from the package.

"Self-targeting plasma fléchettes: point and shoot, easy peasy."

I noticed in addition to the rounds, the package still contained new bass strings. "Do you still play bass...? In the future?"

"Occasionally, but not as much as I'd like."

"So, how's it going to happen... my assassination?"

He pulled a well-polished pocket watch from the inside of his coat, glanced at it, then looked up at me. "It has been an honor, Mr. Chairman. Oh, yes—Heidi sends her love."

His facial muscles tightened up and he yelled, "Fuck that cracker-ass West Coast Sound."

He put a cigarette in his mouth, offered me one, then fumbled with his lighter. I steadied his hand while he lit our cigarettes. He gave me an angry, "*Pfft*," shook his head, and said, "Homogenized bubblegum. Change my strings for *that*?"

I gave him a shrug. "Motown would be nothing without you."

He took a deep drag of his smoke, put his hand on his forehead, exhaled from the side of his mouth, and said, "Those are some mighty kind words. Thank you."

CHAPTER 24

I headed outside—the .38 in my hand. The wind had picked up, and snowflakes swirled within its lift. Damn, I'd had no idea it snowed around here. I snuffed my cigarette out on the pavement, got in my car, and pulled away. Paranoid rode shotgun.

James' ominous warning had me worried. As I turned the heater on and eased through a four-way traffic light, I heard Paranoid scream. Suddenly, a tractor-trailer bore down on me broadside—its horn blasting. A pudgy-faced Chinese man was behind the wheel: the Gamble. I stomped the accelerator. Traction was limited. I heard rubber screech and metal crumple. Fortunately, I was wobbled straight into the unbalanced-washing-machine-vortex vision generator.

I found myself in deep space, tumbling over and over, and alone. Crap, was I dead? Was this heaven or some version of the afterlife? Cog-Link filled in the blanks: I was an Artificial. And currently, my body was a de facto spaceship—my mind its captain, my brain its cargo. My hands were missing, as were my feet: absorbed and converted into the energy needed to keep my fleshy brain safe in this -400-degree vacuum. I remembered the swarming Phage attack and how my crew had died in that ghastly cave on that godforsaken planetoid. I remembered how I was able to piece together an improvised space board by fastening an anti-gravity drive from the wreckage to a salvaged plank of titanium; and how I was able to clear the planetoid's signal-blocking konomagnetic gravity field and broadcast an SOS. Cog-Link indicated I had been out here for three years and forty-nine days, all of it spent conserving energy, chronicling the past, and identifying vision-point junctures. Junctures like this one. I also remembered I'd just been run over by a truck.

—Wait, there, it was a ship. I zoomed in on the hull markings: *Willhammer Salvage & Rescue*.

"Chairman Architect, this is Musashi. Do you copy?"

"I copy," I replied through my Cog-Link.

"Roger. Prepare for intake."

"Understood." I made a mental note as the tractor beam winched me into the belly of the ship. Once inside, Musashi gave me a salute, then leaned down and said, "It is good to see you, chairman. Everything is as it should be."

"Kogo, you found me."

"Yes. I followed the crypt-mail instructions to the letter."

She kissed me with her synthetic lips, then whirled to her crew of ARTs. "Corpsmen, bring him to the med lab, put him in the Hawking Chamber. Commander Dextron, emergency warp-bubble protocols. Proceed at full gallop to ART Command on Legion."

"Kogo," I said.

"Yes, chairman."

"Tell use-to-be agent James Jamerson—his plan failed. I died at the Circle of Willis Lounge."

"Understood, chairman."

CHAPTER 25

I was driving back to Vegas, chasing puffy clouds and looking for a place to eat. I'd just fired a few dozen rounds through my .38 and felt confident my previous target-shooting abilities had returned.

At a rise, I slowed to let two rattlesnakes cross the road. I thought, Carlos Castaneda would love this scene. Suddenly, a heat wave of a wall blocked my way. It was the same wall from my visions. I didn't have time to stop, so I had to drive right through it. As I entered the foggy mess, déjà vu flooded my senses. Then, as it cleared, I saw a man emerge from behind a large cactus. He wore a backpack, and he began to wave his arms frantically. I pulled over to see if he was alright.

He got into the passenger seat.

"We'll have to try this again Mr. Bridges."

"Do I know you?" I asked. "You look familiar."

"I'm a Shifter, like you, only my visions are of the past. I'm a use-to-be agent for the Artificials. Currently, I'm in an induced vision, in an ART command research facility on the planet Legion. Our window is short, so I'll be brief. You're in extreme danger. There has been a series of time breaks. The most recent will have you assassinated within the next ten minutes. I'm here to change that. I've put a tremendous amount of effort into this, so, if you could, just do what I say."

"Hhhh... OK."

He pulled out a pocket watch, looked at it, and said, "Drive." Ten seconds later, he pressed one of the watch's buttons, then pointed at an upcoming casino billboard. "Park behind that sign."

I backed into the area behind the sign and got out. My passenger had already gotten out and was opening his backpack when he said, "I'm sorry, chairman, but this is going to be violent. Are you prepared—mentally, that is?"

"Have we met before?"

"I'm James Jamerson, from Detroit, Michigan. I play the—"

"You're a Funk Brother. Man... I love your stuff. The whole chromatic-syncopated-approach-note technique."

"Mr. Bridges, we have to eliminate the threat to your existence. Otherwise, we are all dead. Do you understand?"

"Sure. Kill the bad guy, live to see tomorrow. Got it."

"Give me your revolver." He exchanged the rounds with some special future-tech ammo. "These are untraceable. We'll force the Gamble—that's this guy's name—off the road; then you're going to shoot him five times." He handed the revolver back. "After that, you're going to drive back to Vegas and not dwell on what you've done." He removed a heavy-duty collapsible spike strip from the backpack and walked across the road.

"You think you could give me a music lesson some time?"

"Focus, chairman. They're on their way."

"Wait, you said there was only the Gamble guy."

"Here they come. Are you ready?"

I ducked behind the sign. "Yeah. I'm ready."

A semi stormed at us. James tossed the spike strip across the road. The truck jackknifed as the two front tires burst. The truck slid to a stop.

"Now, chairman," James yelled.

I ran over to the cabin of the semi and pointed my .38 at the driver. It was the fat Chinese guy I'd played poker with a week back. He'd cut his head on something and was bleeding.

He looked at me and said, "You are the Destroyer?"

"No," I said. "I'm Seth Bridges. Why are you trying to kill me?"

"I am Octavius 3. For us to live, you must die."

"Who is us?" I asked.

"Fire your weapon," said James as he jogged over.

I looked at James. "Are you sure about this?"

"Time is brutal and unforgiving, Mr. Chairman." He took the gun from my hand and fired into the face of the Gamble. "There is no room for doubt."

We hurried back to my car and drove on.

"I'm thirsty," James said. "Pull over here." I did as he said and stopped at a place called The Circle of Willis Lounge. James got out of the car.

"You just killed a man," I said.

"That's one way of looking at it, but there are other ways. You need to believe in those other ways. The future depends on it." Then, he gave me an odd look and said, "Who the fuck are you?"

CHAPTER 26

The ride back to my motel was filled with thoughts of butterflies, tornadoes, James Jamerson, and the Gamble's dead face. With the sun fading and my stomach grumbling, I stopped by Mohamed's Middle Eastern Food Cart for a meal to go.

"Greetings, my friend," Mohamed bellowed with his arms open wide. "How are you?"

"I'm OK. What about you? How've you been?"

"It has been a long day, but I am well. How can I help you?"

"Well," I blurted, "I was wondering, what happens to us... you know... after we die?"

"Why must you task me? Are we not friends?" He turned to a small altar near the flat-top grill and blew out a religious-looking candle. "That flame—did you see how I gave it death? My friend, it does not remember its dance, or its heat, or how it lit the darkness." He relit the candle. "Aha! Look... the flame, it is alive again. Perhaps I am a fire god or some other deity, but believe me"—he turned and faced me—"The answers to the questions you seek are within yourself. *Fahum*?"

"Sorry about that. I was just... well, you seem like a prophet to me."

"You are a good person. Do not waste time on the one thing you will never remember."

I ordered two dinner plates and drove back to my room.

After eating my meal, I stashed the Box in the hide I'd made under the mattress, and went to bed. Tomorrow I would rent an office and look for a lawyer to get my aerospace venture off the ground.

Goodnight Exon.

CHAPTER 27

And then, as if on cue, I was wobbled into a futuristic medical bay. The robotic version of Kogo was there. She wore no garments, and her skin appeared to be fashioned from pliable chromed metal. She fixed an understanding smile at me.

"Isn't it wonderful?" she said. "Destiny, just as you foretold."

Some other chromed robot people gave me anesthesia that had me floating above myself. I saw automated arms remove the top of my metal head. Then, the arms removed my brain and placed it into a new, metal, human-like skull. Sometime later—it could have been hours or days—I woke up on a padded table, under an immense transparent dome.

"Welcome back," said robot Kogo. "How do you feel?"

I opened and closed my fists. I felt strong—robot strong. I saw my reflection in Kogo's polished metal skin. I was like her: an Artificial.

"Please," she said, "if you could come to a seated position, proprioception needs calibration. Yes, that's good. Now stand. Good. Can you access weapons?"

I looked at her. "I'm not certain."

"Like this," she said, flicking her wrist upward, Spiderman style.

I mimicked her actions. Molten bolts of plasma flew out from the underside of my wrist and exploded into the far wall. My Cog-Link indicated they were practice rounds.

"Good," she continued. "Now, can you engage your shield?"

As I thought about a shield, one enveloped me.

"Excellent!" she said. "Now, I need you to jump."

I squatted, leaped 13.63 meters upward, and touched a patch of condensation at the top of the dome. Funny I should know such precise information, but I did. I landed deftly on my feet and asked in a voice that sounded like my own, "Where are we?"

"Sir, equalization needs to be calibrated prior to inquiry." She slapped me.

"Hey, what was—"

"Are you angry?"

"Well, yeah, a little."

"Good. It's an emotional secretion test. You passed."

"Are you Musashi?" I had no idea why I asked that.

"It is important that we finish the calibration immediately after Awakening."

Cog-Link indicated she was indeed Musashi—Lieutenant Kogo Musashi. I went to the edge of the dome and looked out. It was fantastic—amidst green fields and clear rivers, large, good-looking, metallic-skinned people strolled around the facility. "Where am I? Who am I?"

"Sir, this is ART Command. You are 0001—the Chairman Architect. We serve through your grace."

Then there was music. I knew that voice... Stevie Nicks.

CHAPTER 28

Fleetwood Mac's "Rhiannon" played from the bedside clock radio. It was morning, and I was in my bed at the Starlite Motel. I wrote down my vision of Art Command, took a shower, and headed out. The sun was up and shining, but still, it was winter and there was a chill in the air. I recalled seeing a sign for a real estate office and drove to it.

As I walked into Vegas Light Realty, a young lady who resembled Cybill Shepherd looked up at me from behind her desk.

"Hello," she said. "Can I help you?"

"Seth Bridges. I'm looking to rent some office space. Is that something you guys do?"

"I should hope so. I'm Margie Ledoue by the way." We shook hands. "Do you have an idea of square footage?"

"Hmm." I thought of Crash and how he might need a place to stay when he got here. "Medium size, I guess. Two rooms if possible... with a full bath."

"City ordinances do not allow for full baths in commercial office space, but I have grandfathered office suites available in the building next door. We can pop over there right now if you'd like."

"Oh, that's convenient?"

"No, it's not what you think. These are old apartments converted into offices. They have private entrances, baths, kitchens, and are very reasonable at three hundred dollars a month."

"Alright. Let's go have a look at these offices of yours, but show me the best you have first."

She showed me one of the rentals. The place was run down and smelled musty. It wasn't perfect, but it fit my needs, and I had to start somewhere.

"I'll take it. What's the deal with the utilities?"

"Well, the water and electric are included in the rent." She handed me a small card. "Call this number for phone service."

"Could you help me out with that."

"I suppose, but I'm not your secretary. OK?"

"Thanks, and please, call me Seth. One more thing—do you know any good lawyers or CPA types that could help me with a business I'm starting?"

"Well, my brother Bruce is a corporate lawyer at a local firm—they're expensive."

"Could you arrange a meeting for me?"

"I can do that."

"Thanks. One more thing, could you give me a few minutes with the place?"

"Sure, I'll get the paperwork ready."

I took stock of the new office. The windows were dirty and needed curtains. The linoleum in the bathroom was peeling, and the corroded plumbing gave me second thoughts. Both bedrooms were currently supporting colonies of mold and fungus. The main room and the kitchen shared similar fates of neglect. I found a black marker in a kitchen drawer and wrote what was needed on the wall: *Paint—three colors, in all rooms. New carpet, new furniture, new kitchen...*

I figured ten grand would cover the remodel, then went back to Margie's office and filled out the paperwork. As Margie handed me the keys, I asked, "You think you could help me out remodeling my office? I'll give you two grand."

"What's your budget?"

"Whatever it costs, plus your fee. I wrote what was needed on the kitchen wall. You interested?"

"Sure, but maybe we should go look at that wall."

"Can't, too busy. Tell you what," I said, counting out some cash, "here's $12,500: ten thousand for the remodel plus $2,500 for you. Just go ahead and get it done ASAP."

"You got it."

As I was leaving, I saw a beat-up yellow Marathon cab that was stuck in traffic. I ran over and got in the back.

The cab stunk of cigarettes, alcohol, and vomit. The cabbie looked at me and yelled, "Hey man, I'm off duty." He coughed up some phlegm, then swallowed it. "Get out."

It was Dings, the guy who partnered up with Colton to rob me. "Hey buddy," I said. "I've been looking for you."

"Me?"

I pulled out my .38, cocked it, and put it to the back of his head. "Pull over." As he pulled to the curb, I said, "Did anyone ever tell you that you look just like Dustin Hoffman?"

"Yeah... What? What's going on? I don't even know you, mister."

"Yeah, you do. The name's Bridges, Seth Bridges. You gave me a ride the other day; then, you and Colton tried to rob me. Sound familiar?"

"Oh, right. I remember now. But it was his idea, not mine. Plus you broke his arm. So, that makes us, ahh, you know, copacetic. Right?" He turned around and exposed a row of gappy popcorn teeth. "Hey. You related to Sethco?"

Fucking Sethco again. "Listen, Dings, this is your only warning: stay the fuck out of my business. Got it?"

"Yeah, sure. Stay out of your business."

"You know any good pizza places around here?'

"Yeah, Vinny's New York Style Pizza. Two blocks down on the right. Tell Vinny that Dings sent you."

"You know Vinny well?

"Yeah, we go way back."

"Remember what I said."

I got out of the cab, walked back to my car, and drove to Vinny's New York Style Pizza.

After ordering a few slices, I asked the cashier if Vinny was around. A middle-aged man of Italian descent—who was fussing around with the drawer mechanism of a nearby cash register—looked up and said, "I'm Vinny. Can I help you?"

"Oh, hey. I was hoping you could give me some info on a guy named Dings. He kinda tried to rob me the other day. Should I be concerned?" I slipped a hundred into his shirt pocket.

He let out a laugh. "Dings? Are you kidding me? His luck is so bad, he makes unlucky people look like winners. He actually believes all of his losses are being *banked* and are going to be paid back to him in the future—tenfold. He's harmless. But he's got addiction problems. By the way, if you ever need a loan or more information: I'm your guy."

"Thanks. I'm Seth, by the way."

"Nice to meet you, Seth."

I shook his hand and left.

CHAPTER 29

I went to the Sands, looking to hire Adamit as well as his family. He wasn't around, so I went over to Purgatorium to look for him there. Two human gorillas, shoehorned into ill-fitting monkey-suits, blocked the way in.

"Members only," one of them said.

"Hey, uh," I said, "I'm looking for Adamit. You know, the really big guy, scar across his face. He's got a sister, Katya; she's really pretty. Have they been around today?"

"Wait here."

A few minutes later Adamit came out.

"Hey, Seth. Where've you been? We were all worried about you." He looked at the guards. "It's OK. He's with me."

I controlled my fear and reminded myself he was a friend. "Hey, Adamit. How's it going?"

"Good. Come on, we're having a birthday party for Becky."

"Well," I said as he escorted me inside, "I was wondering if you and your family might be interested—"

An alarm sounded as we went inside. Security pinned me to the wall and removed my .38 from its holster.

"Sorry fellas," Adamit said, intervening. "That's my fault. I haven't explained the rules to him."

After putting my revolver in a lock box, one of the security guards said, "You can get it back when you leave." He handed me some papers and said, "These are the rules and a form for membership, and this"—he gave me a ticket—"is a receipt for your firearm. Now, go enjoy yourself."

The club was half full: maybe a hundred people. As Adamit ushered me to his table, Katya jumped up and smothered me with kisses.

"You rascal. We've all been so very concerned about you. Brother said you were fine, but I was still worried." She pinched my cheek. "You're so cute; I don't know what I would do if something happened to you." She gave me a squinty-eyed queerish look. "You know, you look more like Monet every day. Claude Monet, that is, but...

under the right conditions, like right now, there is a fair amount of Renoir in your eyes. You should watch that—it could get you into trouble."

Dean and his three geishas were there, as well as Becky, Jacob, and a bunch of other people I sort of recognized.

Katya straightened out my tie and said, "It's Becky's birthday!"

I turned to Becky. "Happy Birthday, Becky. Sorry, I didn't bring a gift..."

She hugged me tightly. "Don't you fret, you're here now. That's the best present a person can give."

Dean stood on a chair, held his glass high, and cheered, "To Becky. Happy birthday!"

The room roared, "Happy birthday, Becky!"

Dean hopped off the chair, slapped my shoulder, and said, "Good to see you, man, How's it hanging?"

A distorted guitar salvo caught our attention. Fucking A! It was Thin Lizzy on stage, laying down a tight version of their song "Jailbreak." As if on cue, Becky's party guests stormed the dance floor, pulling me along with them.

Jacob appeared to be partial to Yoshimi, the tallest of the geisha triplets. Adamit, who was dancing with two punk-rocker hotties, nudged me gently with one elbow and said, "Looking good, Seth, looking good."

I gave him a smile and two thumbs up. Funny—he didn't look intimidating when he was dancing. He seemed like a normal guy, just having a good time.

A few hours later, as the party was breaking up, Adamit came over and said, "If you can, come by the Sands tomorrow. I'll help you fill out that membership petition. Better yet, meet me here, tomorrow at five. There's a monthly club meeting. We'll get you signed right up."

"Thanks. Sounds like a plan."

"Oh, bring ten grand with you; it's the membership fee."

"Kinda steep, isn't it?"

He shrugged. Just then, Katya came over, kissed me, and said, "I'm sorry, Seth, it's not going to work."

"What's not going to work?"

"You know, us. I've tried, but there's just no *vroom*. You understand."

"Yeah, I guess, but come on, Katya. Did you really try? We just met each other." At first, I thought she was just kidding around, but she wasn't. She was serious.

"True," she said, "but you have to understand. I need to find love. And I don't want to waste time."

I thought of the impromptu kiss I'd given to Marisol, and how soft her cheek had been. "Alright, Katya. I wish you the best of luck and I release you from the bonds of my affection."

She gave me another kiss and said, "Thank you. I knew you would understand." Then, she left.

Dean came over and invited me to his table. "So, brother man," he said as we sat down, "how's it going?"

The triplets poured us beer, lit a joint, and cut out some cocaine. Izumi asked me, "You like?"

"Yes," I said, rolling up a hundred-dollar bill, "I likee like!"

We drank, smoked, and snorted too much, but we were happy. After a while—and after retrieving my .38—we left the club, skipped arm-and-arm down Las Vegas Boulevard, and headed over to Dean's place.

CHAPTER 30

Dean lived in the heart of downtown, on the top floor of a swanky high-rise apartment building. The front half of his place looked over the city and was modeled after the command bridge of the Starship Enterprise—a fictional spacecraft from the *Star Trek* franchise. This particular bridge was from a TV show that would not be produced for another eight years. He had even installed a beveled floor-to-ceiling glass viewport that cantilevered out over the side of the building.

"Nice," I said. "I take it you like *Star Trek*."

He took two frosty Heinekens from a simulated replicator and handed me one. "Designed and built everything from memory. Well, almost everything."

Izumi plucked soothing notes from a traditional Japanese zither-like stringed instrument. Asuka accompanied her with a flute-like instrument of similar origin. Yoshimi stood off to the side, patiently waiting for cues to serve up any needs we might have. Dean insisted that I sit in the captain's chair. He sat next to me in the Number-One chair.

It came as no surprise when he said, "I can see five minutes into the future."

"Wow!" I said. "Bet they just love you at the gaming tables."

He chuckled. "Yeah, well, I'm banned from gambling in Vegas *and* Reno, but... I did manage to sock away a tidy sum before they caught on." He lit a joint, took a hit, and passed it to me. "I own this building and a few more just like it."

"And yet you wait tables?"

"Yeah, why not? I like it. Plus, I get to meet Ferris-Bueller-looking sparks like you."

I took a hit. "Do me a favor, would you?" I passed the joint back. "Remind me never to doubt you, or for that matter play poker with you."

He took a pull on the joint and exhaled a plume of blue smoke. "My life before... man, it was like I was living in a brain fog, couldn't see what was really important. What we got here... this is special. This is who we really are, who we were meant to be. Do you believe in the theory of multiple universes?"

"Yeah, I do. Plus, I just hired a guy who knows all about that stuff. You want to hear something weird? Sometimes, when I'm having a screwed-up day, stressful, that sort of thing, I get glimpses of other lives I could have lived. People, places, things I would have done."

I didn't know why I was telling Dean about something so intimate and personal. But I was, so I continued, "It's almost like a small part of me exists in the choice I thought about making but didn't. Like thousands of possible versions of myself are out there living their lives, doing the things I would have done if I'd chosen differently. Sometimes I see new people or new places, and I get this feeling, like, *hey I know you*, or, *I used to live here*. They call out to me. Almost like I should be somewhere else, but there's no door, or way to get there... They haunt me."

"I know what you mean, brother. I'm quite certain we're in one of those universes right now. But don't be frightened—it's fucking great!"

"What's with the geishas," I asked in a hushed voice. "Do you, you know...?"

"Nah," he said with a dismissive wave of his hand. "Lost my jewels a few years back at a dentist's office. A freak accident: radiation exposure. I'll get 'em back on the flip side. Have to admit, though, it's quite liberating. You should try it one shift. Anyway, this is the girls' preferred lifestyle—their art, if you will. Right girls?" They smiled back. "Picked them up through a cultural exchange program, and they never went home. Crazy about American pop culture. I provide the financial resources they require, and they take care of me—geisha style." Just as he waggled his empty beer, Yoshimi replaced it with a full one.

"So," I said, "what'd you do before—you know, before all of this shifting? I mean, you are a Shifter? Right?"

He let out a snort. "Yes, Seth, I'm a Shifter."

He paused for a bit, drank a few gulps of beer, then said, "Ever hear of Global Cross?"

"Yeah. Didn't they hardwire the planet with underwater cables or something, then go belly up after installing the final link?"

"Yup, that was me. Thought I was making the world a better place. Talk about hubris."

"Hold on," I said. "Didn't the internet make the world a better place?"

"I suppose it did, for some. But like all new technology, it was used by the few to gain and maintain an advantage over the many. And then there was the noise: opinion directing algorithms, manipulating the electronic collective conscience of a world full of isolated individuals. People so desperate to believe in something they'll believe in anything. Compassion, identity, freedoms—everything became malleable, less meaningful. Instead of bridging cultural divides, the internet deepened them. Although I do have to admit, refereeing became more accountable."

"Refereeing?"

"You know—politicians, cops, and the like. They finally had to explain their non-objective decisions." He took a sip of beer and continued, "I built Global Cross because I thought it was my purpose to lay the pipe, the rudimentary pathways for a future Human-Brain-Cloud Interface." He let out a sad chuckle. "Then, someone on Wall Street shorted us at a vulnerable moment, and bankrupted us right into obscurity. I said fuck it; I did my part... After that, I spent five years kicking around in Japan. Then around 2008, I decided to try my hand at sailing around the world—solo. Two months in, I got caught in a typhoon. Boat got all smashed-up and sank. But I survived: rescued by a mermaid, of all things."

"A mermaid?"

"Yeah, yeah, I know. But it's the truth." He offered up a smile so genuine, its honesty caught me off guard. "So anyway, there I was, barely keeping my head above the surface, sucking in water with every breath, the waves getting higher and higher—then, there she was, holding the trailing line of the sailboat's life raft. Now that I think about it, she was more like a water angel... Anyway, I managed to crawl into the raft, and when I tried to thank her, she was gone. I drifted around for the next six days until a Chinese freighter plowed me under. Then, I woke up as a kid again, back at my parent's house. That was ten years ago."

"Fuck..." I said. "That's a story right there. Wow! Wait... she rescued you and then you what, sank and drowned?"

"Hey man, this is a crazy world we live in. So, what about you? What'd you do before Vegas?"

"Me? Nothing so grand. I worked in my family's plumbing business. It's weird because, as a kid, people would ask me what I wanted to do when I grew up and... I didn't have a clue. But I knew that I never wanted to be a cog in someone else's machine. Strangely enough, that's exactly what I did: traded all my hopes and dreams for the security of a nine to five—made sure people had hot and clean water, and I directed the pitch of human waste to flow downhill." I took a swig of beer. "I became a Miserable, you know—put on your boots every morning, go to work, go home, get drunk, go to bed; then, get up in the morning and do it all over again. Huh, barely had enough money to do that. Hated it, every goddamn second of every soul-sucking minute of every boring hour that made up the squandered, unremarkable decades of my life."

"Whoa, that there is a whole lot of hate. You do know that can't be good for you."

I shrugged. "Yeah, I know. But what's even worse, what really got me... was the tedium of life itself. The drip, drip, drip, like a venereal disease. The drinking helped." I lifted my beer and took a swallow. "So, ahh, what's it like when you do your thing?"

"My thing?"

"You know, the whole five minutes into the future. What's that like?"

"Oh, right. Well, you ever see that movie *Groundhog Day?* Bill Murray played a TV reporter that kept waking up every morning on the same day?

"Sure."

"Well, it's a bit like that, only five minutes, and I can control it." He scrunched up his face like he urgently needed to use the toilet, brought his fists to his temples, then relaxed and smiled at me. "By the way, you should tie your shoelace before your next piss."

I tied up the lace. "So what would've happened if I didn't tie it?"

"You would've tripped, no biggie."

"What would you say if I offered you a job?"

He laughed. "I'd say I've already accepted your offer." We clinked our beers together, got up, went to the curved window, and looked out at the neon spectacle that was Sin City.

CHAPTER 31

Yoshimi called me a cab. And once I'd made it back to my motel room, I closed the drapes, fell backward onto my bed, and dropped into a dream.

...I was flying, Superman style; the lights of Vegas twinkled beneath me. I headed east, out over the plains, past the Continental Divide—toward New England and home. I hung a dog-leg right around Boston's Prudential Building and took a break on the roof of my old school, Berklee College of Music. I smiled. What was I thinking? I sucked as a musician back then and I still suck now. I waved to a few students below, then headed toward Cape Cod Bay. But then, out of nowhere, a bank of dark clouds forced me lower. I had to avoid buildings and power lines. Eventually, heavy fog grounded me.

I was walking towards some calliope music that was in the air, and just up ahead, a circus tent sat shrouded in mist. I went over, lifted the tent's skirt, and snuck in. The first thing I saw was a fortune teller. She was seated at a card table that displayed a crystal ball. She offered me a disarming smile.

As I looked around, I noticed the tent contained three performance rings, and in the center of the largest ring was a roped-off hole in the ground. The hole was five feet across and lined with what looked like shiny metalized rubber. An odd collection of people formed a line that led to the edge of the shiny hole. The more notable of these people included: an Inuit dressed in sealskin, a nearly naked Masai warrior who held a spear off to his side, a Vietnam-era American G.I., a Gandhi-looking fellow, a Gemini-era astronaut with his helmet still on, and, at the front of the line, a hunched-up little old lady that looked like Mother Teresa.

A circus ringmaster, complete with top hat and curlicue mustache, unclipped the rope that cordoned off the hole. He ushered the old lady that looked like Mother Teresa to the edge and nodded approvingly as she jumped in. A plume of glowing embers shot upwards. A floodlight lit up the stands, where seals and monkeys clapped on cue. Four elephants trumpeted as the ringleader clipped the rope closed.

"What are they doing?" I asked the fortune teller. "Where does that hole go?"

She looked up and waved me closer. "Young man, are you willing to sacrifice four and a half billion people to guarantee the survival of your species?"

"I haven't decided."

"That hole—it's God's toilet, and it's where we go when he's finished with us."

"Is he around?"

"God?" She shook her head. "He jumped in just after he dug it."

CHAPTER 32

It was late in the morning when I woke. I took a taxi to Purgatorium, picked up my car, then had breakfast at the Tumblin' Dice Diner. The meal was delicious and satisfying, but I couldn't get Grandpa's Box out of my mind. Paranoid had gone ahead and superimposed his image on the ten-dollar bill I'd paid my breakfast tab with. The Box worried me. It wasn't safe. I wasn't safe. How do I make things safe? I'd need a new place to live, somewhere secure, and somewhere that had a place I could put the Box into.

I bought some tools at a nearby hardware store and hurried back to my room. After pushing the dresser to the side, I cut through the carpet, pried up a loose flooring plank and made a hide. I put the Box inside. And, as I was pushing the dresser back in place, I heard, "Ooo... lo siento. I think you out."

I turned and saw Marisol. She stood at the foot of the bed, smiling.

"Oh, hey, Marisol." I said as I shook the bed frame. "This bed frame is so noisy. I thought I'd tighten it up. How are you?"

"Muy bien," she said with a smile.

I put on my suit jacket, holstered my gun, grabbed my cash and keys. I needed to get out of there before I did something I would regret—like kissing her again. "Well, I've got to head out. It was really nice to see you again."

She began to empty the trash containers. "Where you go now, Mr. Bridges?"

"Ahh... I'm joining a club."

"What is this glub?"

"Hmm... Well, it's a place where people get together to eat and drink, that sort of thing. And it's *club*, not glub. Thing is," I said in a lame, Robin Williams, Mork from Ork impression, "I'm not so sure I want to join a club that would have me as a member."

She let out a laugh. "Bueno. *Mork & Mindy.*" She tilted her head sideways a few times and said, "Na-nu, na-nu. He land on planet in egg."

"Heh, he did, didn't he?" Nice one, Seth.

"Sí, glub is good. I also have glub. Someday you take me your glub, and I take you my glub."

"Marisol, I would love to take you to my club, but let me join up first. OK?"

"Sí, then I take you to my glub."

"Sounds like we have a bargain."

As I headed for the door, she blocked the way and looked into my eyes. When I eased past her, our bodies touched, and that was it: I was hooked.

I drove to Vegas Light Realty. Love rode shotgun. I tried to push Marisol from my mind, but it was useless. The more I tried to convince myself that she would be a hindrance to my plans, the more it seemed like she was the right choice. Fuck, I thought: I had to hire people, get a new place to live, join a club, start a company, get mankind into space, and now I've got Love sitting next to me.

"I got no time for you," I said loudly. "My docket is full. You want me to be like everyone else, that's it. Right? Like crabs in a bucket. Just when one crawls to the top of the bucket, the other crabs pull it back in. We can't have him get away, oh no. We all have to die in this miserable stinking bucket together. That's just how it's done. We don't know why, but that's how we do it here in Crab Bucket City." I turned to Love. "Well, Mr. Love Crab, I've got a species to save, and I think that's slightly more important than what you've got planned for me. So, stop wasting my time. Got it!"

Love stared at me with vacant eyes and then started to pick his nose.

I parked my car in a spot reserved for Vegas Light Realty and went inside. Love stayed behind. I think I had been a bit harsh with him.

"Well, hello, Mr. Bridges," Margie said from behind her desk. "How's everything on this wonderful day?"

"Meh," I said, sitting in the chair to the side of her desk. "So, did you get a chance to talk to your brother?"

Two boys holding toy balsa-wood planes came running in from an adjoining room. "Boys," Margie said, "say hello to Mr. Bridges."

They stopped, looked up at me, and simultaneously said, "Hello."

"This is Matty and Brucey," Margie said.

I shook their hands, palmed a quarter from each one of their ears, and handed it to them. "Gee, thanks, mister," said Brucey, the taller boy. The younger boy Matty jumped up and down on one foot and tapped the side of his head in an attempt to knock out any remaining ear-quarters.

"Yours?" I asked.

"I wish. They're my brother's. I have them for the afternoon. OK, boys, Aunt Margie has some business to attend to."

They ran off with their wooden planes held high—engine noises vibrating from their lips.

"So, my brother Bruce would like to meet with you at his office, tomorrow morning at nine." She handed me a slip of paper. "Here's the address and your new telephone number. Oh, I've got news. I talked to my uncle Frank yesterday. He's a homebuilder and in between jobs right now. I told him you needed your office renovated and… Well, he's got his whole crew over there right now. They've gutted the place, followed your instructions, and should be done in a day or two."

"I'm so glad I met you, Margie. Thank you."

"My pleasure, Mr. Bridges."

"Please, call me Seth. Listen, ahh, I'm looking for a place to live: something safe, lots of security, that sort of thing. Do you have anything like that?"

"Well, you're in luck," she said, batting her eyelashes flirtatiously. "I'm looking for something secure myself."

"I'm serious, Margie, this is important. I need a place, a safe place."

She winced and her body stiffened. "I have a new listing on the North Side. I could arrange a showing for tomorrow?"

"OK, I'll come over after my meeting with your brother."

"Perfect. Tomorrow around ten?"

The boys ran by, mouthing machine-gun sounds into the toy planes' imaginary guns.

CHAPTER 33

I drove over to the sportsbook at Caesars Palace and gave the man behind the cage window a nod. He was six feet tall, had a Buddha-sized belly, a ruddy face, and sported a blueish-grey ponytail on the back of his sizable head. His name tag read: Cagey. That's an appropriate name, I thought.

"Are you guys taking action on the Olympics—hockey?"

"I'm not sure. Let me get my supervisor."

The cage boss came over. He was outfitted in a brown suit and a 1970s cop mustache.

"What can I do for you, son?" he said in a Cajun accent. His name tag read, *Ronamario Anastasio*.

"Well, sir. I want to bet on the Olympic hockey games."

He pondered my question for a moment, glanced at Cagey, and said, "The problem is the Commies are the favorites, and we don't take bets against America. It makes us look, well... un-American?"

"What if I only bet on the Americans? Would you take my action then?"

He stroked his mustache. "What kind of money are we talking here?"

"I got fifty grand that says the Americans will take home hockey gold."

"That's a lot of juice, kid. You jerking me around?"

"No. No jerking, I just want to place bets with you."

"Come back in a few days; I'll have a line for you. Hey, you want any action on tonight's Knicks game?"

"No, I'm good."

It was three in the afternoon when I went to the Landing Lounge at the Sands Casino.

"Brother Sethco, how's it hanging?"

I looked up. It was Dean in his waiter's uniform. Sethco again? He had probably read that ad in the Sunday-paper personals? "Hey Dean," I said. "How's it going?"

"Spectacular. Great time last night, huh?"

"Yeah, it was."

"What can I get for you?"

"Let's see here... I'd like a big salad, and a.... Hey Dean, a second ago you called me Sethco. Why?"

"Sorry about that, boss. Slip of the tongue. Your order will be right up."

As I ate, my thoughts alternated between Grandpa's Box and Marisol. Damn, she was hot, and her skin was so soft. It wasn't like she was model beautiful—she was more like the real deal—nothing needed to be added or subtracted. I should write that down, I thought. Or better yet, spend a shift being a writer. An autobiography could be my first book—definitely. When Dean came back with my order, he said, "So, when do we start?"

"Soon. I'm recruiting Adamit and his family, so it shouldn't be too long. And, Dean—thanks for joining up: it means a lot to me."

He put on a serious face and gave me the Vulcan live-long-and-prosper hand sign. "Thank you, boss."

At a quarter to five, I took twenty grand from my safe deposit box and headed over to Purgatorium. On a whim, I stopped at a roulette table and placed a ten-thousand-dollar bet on red—a 46% chance of doubling my money. As the ball dropped on red, an eerie voice called out to me from across the table. "Hey, mistah, can you buy me a drink?"

It was a girl. Her hair was snow white and disheveled, and her sparkly overzealous mini-dress fought with her man-lure makeup for attention. Although her eyes were hidden behind dark sunglasses, she looked like an Albino. And it was hard to discern her age: eighteen? Twenty-eight? The poor girl was looking for a handhold—anything would suffice. I collected my winnings, then turned to the unfortunate creature.

"Here," I said, handing her a thousand-dollar chip. "Get yourself a good meal, maybe some new clothes."

She kept her head low and fidgeted with the chip. "Thanks, mistah. That's awfully kind of you."

I offered her an understanding nod and headed toward the stairwell. I didn't know why I handed her a thousand-dollar chip. It had seemed like an appropriate response at the moment.

"Hey, mistah," she called out.

I turned and watched as she trudged over to me. She reached out, smoothed the front of my suit, and said in perfect trailer-park drawl, "I'll remember you; you can bet on that."

Then, she lowered her knock-off Ray Bans. I was caught off guard by her overwhelmingly mesmerizing argon-purple eyes.

CHAPTER 34

At Purgatorium, I saw Adamit talking with a few of the club's doormen. He gave me a nod. "You ready?"

"Sure. I guess so. What's the deal with the ten grand?"

"I'll explain inside."

After exchanging my .38 for a receipt, we went inside and ordered a drink at the bar.

"Nice place, right?" Adamit asked rhetorically.

"Yeah, it's great."

"That ten grand you're about to fork over is your membership fee. It pays for security costs associated with day-to-day operations. This"—he looked around—"is no ordinary club. The walls and ceilings are constructed of three-foot-thick reinforced concrete. Twice a day it's swept by bomb-sniffing dogs. There's a bunker that will support one-hundred people for three months. The whole place is monitored by closed-circuit TV. Seth, we're anathema to the world. People will always want us dead. And you can never be too careful."

"We're ready," bellowed a voice from an adjoining hallway. "You can come in now."

There were twenty people in the room. Most were seated in cushioned chairs that faced forward in a theater formation. Upfront was a long, modern conference table. A boy handed us itineraries, and we took our seats.

I nudged Adamit. "What's the story with the kid?"

"That's Roald Amundsen. He shifted here last month, from the Antarctic."

"Aha."

Five people emerged from the wings and took their respective seats behind the conference table. I immediately recognized the person in the middle chair. It was the lost girl I'd just given a thousand-dollar chip to. She had changed clothes and now wore a black and red skin-tight leather jumpsuit. With her ghost-white hair and purple eyes, she appeared to be a villainess ripped from the pages of a graphic novel. She banged a gavel down three times. "This meeting will now come to order."

I elbowed Adamit. "Hey, do you know her?"

"That's Penelope," he whispered. "She's an Old."

"An Old?"

"Yes, a very old Shifter. Now hush."

What the hell kind of name was Penelope? She acknowledged me with a teasing wink, then started the meeting.

"Thank you all for coming. As an aside, you're all invited to a very special musical event in the main room at the conclusion of this meeting. Alright, let us begin. The first order of business: sightings of the Progenitor."

The room grew lively with a debate. A European emissary said there had been no recent sightings or reports of the Progenitor in all of Europe, while most of the attendees swore she was here, in Vegas, and something of great importance was occurring. After twenty minutes of speculation, the matter was tabled. We sat quietly as routine matters were decided upon. When it was time for statements and petitions, Adamit rose from his chair.

"My name is Adamit Lee. I request a membership petition for Seth Bridges. He is on his first shift."

"Are there any objections to the Petition?" Penelope asked.

Adamit swept the room with the eyes of an executioner.

Penelope banged the gavel. "Let the record state, there are no objections. Seth Bridges, please rise and tell us why we should accept you as a member."

Fuck! I wasn't prepared for questions. I thought all I had to do is give them ten grand, and I was in. All of a sudden, the room started to wobble; and once again I was sucked into that unbalanced-washing-machine-vision generator.

Then I was somewhere else, and I was wearing a spacesuit.

"C'mon!" said someone over the suit's comm channel. It was Dean, and he was shaking my shoulders. "Let's go. The solar flares are about to hit!"

What the...? I gazed past Dean and took in the giant blue marble that was Earth. I was on the moon. My spacesuit felt clumpy and tight.

"Snap out of it," Dean said. "We've got to go. Now!"

We hop-skipped, moon-motion style, toward an entrance at the base of a nearby crater. A door-lock allowed us entry, then quickly sealed us in. Dean removed his life-pack, then helped me with mine.

"What's wrong with you?" he said, lightly shoving my shoulder. "You could've been zapped out there. Protocols and procedures brother. No second chances on this rock."

I was dumbfounded by the spectacularity of the moment. "What year is it?"

"Shit," he said, shaking his head. "I should've known it. You're back on Earth, aren't you? In a vision. I don't know how your brain compensates for this crap. C'mon, follow me."

He led me into the next airlock. Mists of go-vapor and ozone removed contagion from our bodies. We dressed in white Moon-Man coveralls, and then Dean opened the third and last of the airlocks.

"Welcome to Moonbase Virgil," he said. "And welcome to the new and improved 1989."

It was glorious: a working moonbase. The interior of the base was the size and shape of a medium-sized domed arena—and it was busy. Dozens and dozens of people, most of them looked to be indigenous people from Central America, scurried about on Segway-type vehicles that flew.

A man with a slight paunch and a receding hairline glided alongside us and said, "The hydrogen donkeys are on the fritz again, plus there's some sort of harmonic feedback coming from the solar fields. What do you think, Seth? Time for that gas shunt upgrade?"

It was Crash. I gave him a hug. "Hey, buddy! It's... This, it's all fantastic. We did it!" He gave me a nod, entered some commands into a wrist-mounted keyboard, then scooted away on his glider.

"Boss, we have problems."

I turned. It was Jacob. He wore a powered exoskeleton chassis and was now almost as big and scary looking as his brother.

"Radio chatter," he said. "The Puppy Pox, it's begun. Reports have been coming in all afternoon. Started in Chicago, spreading outward to both coasts—just like you predicted. France, England, Germany, they're also reporting unexplained deaths, lots of them. And on top of that, the Globalists are en route; they're gonna try to take the base. I'm certain of it. They still believe we have the cure. With your permission, I'm activating the HOGS defense grid."

Like having a memory inside a dream, I remembered that the Box had described a vaccine made from horseshoe crab blood, and how it had taken only twenty-six days, once the word got out, to harvest the crabs into extinction. I looked past Jacob's robotic shoulders and saw a well-dressed man that looked like Nat King Cole, in an office. He nodded at me respectfully, then returned to his desk.

"Jacob," I said. "Where's Adamit and your sisters?"

"The grid, boss—what about the grid?"

"What grid?"

"HOGS You know, the Hand of God Slayers defense grid."

"Yes! Get it running... and quarantine the base, and check our vaccination supply."

Becky—who also wore a powered exoskeleton—came over and said, "Your parents want you to stop by their pod for dinner tonight."

"My parents?"

"Seth... oh my God! Is this the time you told me about? Are you in a vision? Is your body back in Vegas right now?"

Fuck... My mind began to oscillate between Las Vegas and where I was at the moment. The moonbase thundered with low-frequency vibrations. It grew louder, and louder, like someone playing a tape recorder at a slow speed.

Becky called out, "Can you tell my past-self—it's OK to love Izumi?"

CHAPTER 35

In an instant, I was back at the club, on a bench in Purgatorium's main room. Adamit was rousing me. His voice was far away, but then it was close. "You're in," he said. "Now cough up the dough and we can make it official."

"How's he doing?" asked Penelope, her purplish albino eyes staring into mine.

"He'll be fine," Adamit said, helping me sit up. "Just needs a good strong drink."

"I'm OK," I said, handing her the ten grand.

She brushed a kiss across my cheek and left.

Adamit nodded at her as she walked away. "Stay away from that one. She's in league with Cyrus."

"Let's get out of here," I said. "I need some fresh air."

Just then, the devil himself, Cyrus Effing Willhammer, took to the stage with his two hyenas. The animals seemed agitated and each of them required two handlers with opposing chain leashes to keep them at heel.

"Ladies and gentlemen," Cyrus billowed. "It is my great pleasure to present to you the one and only Madame Deux Vox Fantastico."

Two dangerous-looking tuxedo-clad men ushered a plump, middle-aged woman to the center of the stage. She looked like a tragedy gussied-up in a blue chiffon. I nudged Adamit. He held up one finger, shook his head, then had me sit back down.

The guys working the lights adjusted their controls to complement the woman and the three musicians behind her: a guitarist, a piano player, and a cellist. Madame Deux Vox Fantastico began to whisper hauntingly erotic tones. The tones segued into bright tortured wails. The hairs on the back of my neck stood up. Adamit nodded with anticipation.

It took a few moments before I realized that two separate voices were coming out of her mouth. I knew Tibetan throat singers were capable of two simultaneous notes, but this was something different: her tones were independent of each other, in pitch, phrasing, *and* volume. The band began to perform Pink Floyd's "Wish You Were Here," and she began to sing.

It wasn't her ability to sing with two independent voices, but rather the musicality of these voices that struck me as incredible. Precious buried memories from places I'd been to and places I'd never been to surfaced and became entwined in her tones, evoking feelings of both grief and ecstasy. I wasn't the only one: all around me, gasps of amazement competed with murmurs of disbelief. We remained transfixed and flabbergasted as Madame Deux Vox Fantastico transformed Purgatorium into a realm reserved for the gods. I prayed the song would never end. Then, as she pushed the song's final notes through her larynxes, some high-pressure bulbs in the spotlights shattered, as did glassware on tables.

The anomalous singer bowed three times and was escorted off the stage by her handlers. Adamit dabbed at his eyes with a napkin, brushed glass from his lap, then stood and clapped to an empty stage. I followed his cue, as did the rest of the club's occupants. I didn't want the performance to slip from my mind, but like a dream so often does, it began to dissolve under the complexity of its own structure.

I left the club without a word, drove to my motel room, and wrote it all down in my journal. Everything: my time on the moonbase, hydrogen donkeys, horseshoe crabs, HOGS defense grids, floating scooters, and that Becky loved Izumi. I tried to write about Madame Fantastico, but I couldn't—or rather, I lacked the skills needed to put into words how she made me feel. With my nerves in check, I retrieved Grandpa's Box from the hide and began another excursion into its secrets.

Two hours later, I found an area on anti-gravity. The section contained mathematical equations and a schematic that described a gravity opposition device. I wrote the equations down, returned the Box to its hide, and lay down on the bed.

There were no frontiers left on Earth, I thought. No room for trailblazers, malcontents, or those who didn't fit into the normal tenets of society. Those who would be exterminated by well-meaning dictators for having soft hands or wearing eyeglasses, or those who would dare to come up with better ways to do things. Yet around us, just out of reach, was the rest of the universe where there was room enough for all: billions and billions of galaxies. Trillions of planets. Grandpa had given me the Box, and I was pretty sure he had known what he was doing.

Goodnight Exon…

CHAPTER 36

Octavius 4, who was gagged and strapped down onto a gurney, looked over at his Great Aunt Mun Sun Taizu. She was in that flying chair of hers, studying the lines in her face. There was no doubt, Octavius 4 thought, she was waiting for incoming chronospool messages. She was agitated. She was always agitated. That is a bad way to live. Oh, she was moving, inputting commands. Something must have changed. Her eyes were scanning her HUD. It must have been a message from my brothers in the past.

Octavius 4's neck hurt from all this looking.

"Contact has been made!" Mun screamed. "Flush it, doctor, and continue with the next. Now!"

"They're children, Your Highness," said Doctor Heisenberg. "The one in the tank is Octavius 3."

He was a nice man, thought Octavius 4. Mr. Galahad was nice too. He cleaned up the lab and talked to me when no one was around. Mr. Galahad said that Doctor Heisenberg used to be a great man. Galahad said Doctor Heisenberg had made shameful life choices, and because of those choices, he was now a prisoner here in the lab. He also said that Mun and Doctor Heisenberg were working on the dark side of science.

Octavius 4 thought he was about to go into that tank and be sent back in time, or drown. There was that lesson that dealt with the drowning of a man, and how it was an acceptable form of assassination. The trainers said going back in time would not hurt. But how would they know? They are just stupid old bad people.

"Doctor," Mun said as the guards drew their sabers. "My patience is running short. Is this concern worth losing your head over?"

Oh no, this was really it, thought Octavius 4.

"Flush the body," said Mun, "and enter the forecast into the stream, doctor. Now!"

Octavius 4 watched as Doctor Heisenberg shook his head, then opened the valve that flushed the lifeless body of his brother Octavius 3 into the Be-Gone Bin. The tank automatically began to refill itself with a pink colloidal solution. One of the guards was coming over. It was Captain Tighzon, the commanding officer. He was waiting for Mun to be distracted. He wanted to tell the doctor something.

Now, captain, Octavius 4 thought. Mun was going back to her HUD.

"Please, doctor," Octavius 4 overheard Captain Tighzon say. "This life is difficult, but we have lives, families... We want to exist."

Doctor Heisenberg was nodding. That must have been good, thought Octavius 4. Maybe he could live and not go in that tank.

"No, wait. What are you doing?" Octavius 4 struggled to say as the doctor slipped him into the tank.

Octavius 4 fought against inhaling the liquid. He realized the gag over his mouth was not designed to keep him quiet, rather, it was to prevent him from closing his mouth in the tank. As he panicked and ran out of air, he began to inhale the liquid. Octavius 4 felt himself dying.

Right before he lost consciousness, he felt the machine sneeze his mind into deep space. Far into space, so far into space that he could actually *feel* the gravity well of the galaxy's most massive black hole stretch him out, over billions of kilometers, pulling him toward its event horizon—a place, he was once told, where everything that had humanly happened, resided in a state of suspended chronological order. Octavius 4 felt nothing as he was forced to merge with his target host, Blec of the Outo clan of North Africa, 300,000 BC.

Octavius 4 opened the eyes of his host Blec. He breathed in the thick oxygenated air. He looked down. His body was broad, hairy and muscled. He stood up and surveyed the lush landscape. Something was wrong, he thought. Very wrong!

Nearby, a small group of similar-looking people were seated on their haunches. They looked up at him quizzically.

"I am Octavius 4, defender of the realm," he said. "Your assistance is needed in a matter of great importance."

They ignored his words. One of the men from the group came over and slapped Octavius 4 on the side of his head. Octavius 4 stood up. The man moved to hit him again, but Octavius 4, who had been trained in many types of martial arts, blocked the strike and returned one of his own. This went on repeatedly, with all the men in the clan, until Octavius 4 was installed as their new leader.

He had much to offer.

CHAPTER 37

As I woke to the familiar surroundings of my motel room, I felt confident enough to believe that Man's malfunctions were, in fact, his greatest attributes. I had a huge breakfast at the Tumblin' Dice Dinner, then drove to the lawyer's office to meet up with Bruce.

"Pleased to meet you, Mr. Bridges," he said, shaking my hand vigorously. "What can we do for you today?"

I explained that I wanted to form a corporation, call it InEvitech, and that I needed it done ASAP.

"That's an interesting name," he said. "What does it mean, InEvitech?"

"Well, it's like, a word for stuff that will eventually be created... the inevitable direction of tomorrow's technology."

"Hum, that's pretty good."

We filled out some paperwork and I handed him ten grand.

He put his hand on my shoulder, walked me to the door, and said, "Consider it done."

Then I was off to meet up with Margie at her office.

"...I'm fine," I said to her. "Just met with your brother. He seems like a capable guy."

"He is. So are you ready to look at that apartment?"

"Ready and willing."

I got in my car and followed her to Fort Banks, a recently built, five-story gated apartment complex. She led me past the doorman, through the lobby of polished brass and chrome, and into an elevator of similar origin. She pushed the button for the top floor. A few moments later, we walked down a beige, plush carpeted hallway to apartment #10.

She entered a code into the door's electronic lock, and after a *click,* faced me and said, "Well, Mr. Bridges, this is the place. You'll be happy to know the building is empty—an Arab prince or his holding company has the building tied up in legal limbo. The bank seized this particular apartment and would like to lease it or sell it. And so"—she opened the door—"here we are."

The apartment was furnished, had two bedrooms, two baths, a dining room and kitchen, and a large living room. It took up half of the building's top floor and had impressive views of Vegas on one side, and the desert on the other. More importantly, the master bedroom had an oven-sized safe.

"Is this secure enough for you?" Margie said, in a tone that was all business.

Paranoid, who had elected himself as my security consultant, stood behind her and nodded with satisfaction.

"Hey, Margie," I said. "Yesterday, back at your office, what I said—about you wanting a secure place. It was rude and uncalled-for. You've been very kind to me... I'm sorry. I was a jerk."

She crossed her arms, looked up at the ceiling, and exhaled a heavy sigh. "OK."

"You're the best, Margie. The best. And this place... I'll take it." I held out my hand. "When can I move in?"

She shook my hand. "It's three thousand a month, plus a security deposit and last month's rent. There's some paperwork we have to fill out, but you should be able to move in tomorrow."

After we filled out the necessary forms, I got into my car and headed over to the Sands. Paranoid rode shotgun. On the way over, I grabbed lunch at Mohamed's food cart. Ahmed, Mohamed's cousin, was working the grill. He told me Mohamed was home in bed with the flu. A hard-working man like that would have to be pretty sick not to show up for work. I'd come back tomorrow and get an update on his condition.

CHAPTER 38

Adamit was behind the sportsbook cage, going about his job, when I interrupted. I needed him to work for me. He was better than a thousand average people. He was the God of Fucking Intimidation—a god I'd be needing sooner rather than later.

"Hey, bud," I said. "Got a minute?"

"Sure. What's up?"

"I was just wondering if I could buy you dinner sometime? I've got a business offer for your consideration."

"Christ on a crapper!" he said, shaking his head. "Took you long enough. We're free tomorrow."

"We?"

"You know—Katya, Jacob, Becky."

Wow, I thought. This is turning out better than I expected. "Do you think they could make it on such short notice?"

He leaned in. "I'm sure of it."

"That's great. Let me get back to you on the specifics."

I found a payphone in the lobby. From my billfold, I removed the round business card Dex had given me and dialed the number. On the second ring, a pleasant-sounding male voice said, "Jericho Sims. What can we get for you today Mr. Bridges?"

"Ahh... good afternoon." How the hell did they know it was me? "I need some help with dinner arrangements—for tomorrow. Is that something you guys do?"

"Of course, it would be our pleasure. How many people will be in your party?"

"Ahh... five." I thought of Marisol, and how it would be nice to invite her. "Maybe six."

"Understood. Could you hold a moment?"

"Yeah, sure."

In the background I could hear people talking, papers being shuffled, and sounds of things getting done. A minute later, the man with the pleasant-sounding voice said, "You have a seven o'clock reservation tomorrow at Le Bistro Le Boli. It's a private restaurant located on the top floor of the MGM Grand. Will there be anything else I can get for you today?"

"Yeah, could you tell me your name? And who do I pay?"

"My apologies, Mr. Bridges. I'm Stanley E. Pinknie, but please, call me S. E. And as far as your bill is concerned, it's being paid through the Las Vegas Player's Complementary Network."

"Really? Wow... thanks."

"Appreciations are not necessary; your needs *are* our business."

A stark click ended the connection. I went back to Adamit's window.

"Tomorrow, seven o'clock, Le Bistro Le Boli at the MGM Grand. I'll meet you in the lobby."

He shot me a smile and a big two thumbs up. This was great, I thought. I could have Adamit run security, Katya could head up sales, front-of-house stuff, or flat out run the company. Jacob and Becky could do something. I trusted them; that was all that really mattered. I'd need more money, that was for sure. Fuck, what should I do in the meantime? I could pack my stuff up, take another look into the Box, drink, or go invite Marisol to tomorrow's dinner.

By the time I got back to my room, Marisol, along with the other maids, had left for the day. I poured a strong drink and began packing. Five minutes later, I finished and poured another drink. An hour and three drinks later, I was beginning to see things in double vision. That's when someone knocked on the door.

"Hey, Seth. You in there?"

I opened the door and faced Crash, my hire from Caltech. I gave him a hug, something I don't like people to do to me. Shit, I was drunk. Play it cool, Seth—I didn't want to fuck this up.

"Hey Crash, come on in. When did you get into town?"

"Just now."

"Want a drink?"

"Sure."

I poured him a drink and handed it to him. "It's good to see you, man. You ready to start our aerospace company?"

"I guess so. What kind of drink is this?"

"Whiskey, I believe."

He looked around the cramped quarters. "Jesus Christ, Seth, you're living in a fucking dive, and you're drunk?"

"Eh, I had a long day. Hey, you wanna go see the office? You got a car?"

"Yeah, it's outside. Why? Do *you* have a car? I'm starting to think the only thing you really got is a rich uncle and an active imagination. You know what? Fuck it. I'm outta here!"

"Hey! Where are you going?"

"Fuck man. I believed in you," he said, wheeling for the door. "You tricked me. This whole thing is a joke. I passed on a job offer from JPL to come here. You've heard of them—Jet Propulsion Laboratories? You know, the big guys? For what? Seth's hey-let's-get-drunk-and-jerk-each-other-off fantasy motel?"

Things were spiraling out of control, but sure as shit, I wasn't going to let my first hire quit on me. Besides, he'd said something no one ever told me before: he *believed in me*. I launched myself onto his back, locked my legs around the front of his waist, wedged the inner crook of my left elbow under his chin, locked it up with my right arm, and choked him out.

He woke up swinging wildly at phantoms in the room. With no attackers to hit, he sat down and asked, "What happened?"

I put my hands up, in a cautionary manner, and handed him a thousand dollars. "Does this cover your travel expenses?"

"Yeah... I mean, yes, it does. Thanks, man, I was running a little low."

"Crash, I need you to take off your stupid-goggles and listen for a few seconds. Alright? So, yeah, I'm drunk. But I didn't know you were arriving today. This place is... it's temporary; in fact, I'm moving out tomorrow. Look"—I pointed to the corner of the room where my bags were—"my bags are already packed. What I said back at Caltech was real. This is not a joke. I'm not messing with you."

"Oh, really," he said, stuffing the cash in his pocket. "Then what the fuck did you just do to me?"

"I was preventing you from making a bad decision." I grabbed the bottle of whiskey, the notes on the gravity shield, and said, "C'mon, let's go to the office. You're driving."

CHAPTER 39

Crash drove a black Chrysler Cordoba. The same model car that had recently flooded the television networks with advertisements featuring a B-list celebrity by the name of Ricardo Montalbán.

"Nice seat," I said in an attempt at humor. "Is this real leather? Rich Corinthian leather?"

Crash turned a grin as he massaged the back of his neck. "According to that Spanish dude on TV, it is. But hey man, don't be fucking with my neck anymore. OK?"

"Sorry about that."

When we got to the office, I opened the door and said, "Welcome to InEvitech—the home of inevitable technology."

Crash shook his head. "We're gonna launch satellites from *here*?"

"Well, no. We'll probably need a launching pad for that; but it's a start. So, what do you think—do you like it?"

"It's nice. Looks new."

"It is."

I showed him the office, then grabbed two glasses from the cabinet, poured a shot of whiskey into each of them, and sat Crash down at the kitchen table.

"Listen, Crash"—I handed him a glass—"you're a smart guy, and I've got big dreams. I need those smarts of yours so I can put stuff into space cheaper than the other guys." It had occurred to me, sometime back, that launching satellites into space would be a great cover for launching spaceships. Plus, launching satellites into space could bring in a substantial amount of money. I continued, "In exchange, I can help you with whatever it is you need help with. So you tell me. What do you want—really want?"

"To be an astronaut. That's what I always thought I'd be. But that's not going to happen. Oh, and by the way, I'm pretty sure launching *stuff* into space is against the law."

"Well, let's not sweat the small stuff. Tell you what. You help me put things into space and I'll make you an astronaut. You got a pen?"

He fished one out of his coat and handed it to me. On a construction invoice, I wrote out an I-O-U for a million dollars and handed it to him.

"That is a post-dated legal document. If I fail to get you into space within a year, you can collect on it. Also, if I *do* get you into space within a year, you can collect on it. Crash, I need to know you're not going to run out on me the second I walk out that door."

His facial tells and aggressive head-scratching told me he was both skeptical and intrigued.

I continued, "As far as your job, I've arranged through an accounting firm to have your paycheck, five hundred dollars... no, one thousand dollars a week sent here. A company credit card is on its way, and you're welcome to live here if you choose to—"

"Wait a minute," he said. "What exactly is my job?"

"You're the lead engineer and project manager for this company. Our company. I need you to design a manned spacecraft that can deploy satellites."

"You mean like NASA's shuttle program?"

"Well, it doesn't have to be that, but sure, why not."

"I knew it!" he said, jumping up from his chair. "You're crazy! That's impossible."

"Sit down! You're not listening. Here"—I handed him six grand, the remaining bulk of my walking-around money—"this is a six-week advance."

Crash leaned in. "Jeez, you're serious about this, right?"

"Listen—there was a time in the not-so-distant past when people believed the Earth was flat. Recently, the Wright brothers showed us how to fly. Now, people like you make it possible for people like me to walk on the moon."

"Seth. Startup costs for any launch system, theoretical or not, will be in the tens of millions. And that's just a guess."

"Don't worry about the money, that's my job. What do you say?" I asked, holding up the glass of whiskey "Do we have a deal?"

He clinked my glass with his. "Deal."

"Good choice." I removed the gravity shield notes from my suit pocket and laid them on the table. "I want you to go over these notes, see if you can make heads or tails out of them. But first, I need you to give me a ride home."

CHAPTER 40

Crash dropped me off at the Starlite and I went to bed. Then, someone was knocking on my metal skull... no, that wasn't it. Someone was knocking on the door. Just as I sat up, Marisol let herself in.

"Ooo... Lo siento. I think you out." She had a master key in one hand and the handle of a vacuum cleaner in the other.

I shifted my feet onto the floor. "Good morning, Marisol. It's nice to see you. I haven't seen you around for a few days."

"Sí, Mr. Seth. I am very much busy. It is good to see you." She pocketed her master key, parked the vacuum off to the side, and began removing the trash can liners.

When she went back to her maid's cart, I slipped into my slacks and wondered if I had the gumption to ask her out to dinner. Thing was, it had been decades since I had been attracted to someone. The thought of rejection weighed heavy on my mind. She continued to go about her room-cleaning procedures as I got ready for the day. I was going for my bags when I realized there was a strong possibility that I might never get another chance like this.

"Well, I've got to head out," I said loudly. "It was really nice to see you again." Don't be a fucking pussy, Seth; ask her out, right now. As I bent down to grab my bags, I stopped and said, "You know, Marisol, I was wondering if—"

She pulled a plastic bag from her waistband and snapped it open and looked at me.

It was now or never.

"Hey, Marisol, I'm going to a dinner party tonight, and I was wondering if you would, you know, like to go with me?"

"Now you remember our kiss?"

"Yes. Yes, I do. It was very enjoyable."

"You checking out of Starlite?"

"Yeah... I got an apartment." I pointed to the credenza. "There's a tip for you in the envelope."

"What is time for this dinner?"

"Six-thirty. I could pick you up here or at your place."

"Sí, I go with you to dinner. You pick me up here at that time."

"OK. Well, I'll see you then." Beads of sweat glistened from her upper lip, beckoning me. I almost gave her another kiss but didn't want to risk screwing things up.

CHAPTER 41

After checking out, I got in the Maserati and thought, that went better than expected. I fueled up at a nearby 7-Eleven, bought some coffee and pastries, then drove to the InEvitech office. When I got there, the blinds were closed tight and Crash was asleep at his desk. I set the refreshments down and said, "Good Morning, Vietnam!" in a loud Robin Williams imitation.

Crash jumped from his chair and into a defensive crouch. He shook his head a few times then relaxed. His sudden alertness surprised me.

"These equations," he growled, grabbing at some papers from the desk. "Where did you get them?"

"Ahh, you liked them, didn't you."

"I know you're a fucked-up crazy fuck," he yelled, "but this shit is dangerous."

"Hold your horses there, Gunpowder," I said. "I can explain."

He appeared to be on the verge of either punching the wall or my face. I handed him a coffee and left the proximity of his fists.

"Fuck!" he said, after burning himself while removing the hot drink's lid. He tossed the cup into the kitchen sink and said, "We're dead men. You know that, right?" He cooled his hand under the tap. "This is government property—*stolen* government property. They're probably outside right now, watching us through sniper scopes."

"Nope, already checked on my way in—there's a few jaywalkers out there, but no snipers. Now listen, Crash. Those equations, they're not stolen; they belonged to my grandfather... Hold on. Are you saying *it* works? Anti-gravity?"

He snuck up to the window, lifted one of the slats in the blinds, and peeked out. "Your grandfather?"

"Yeah, my grandfather."

"Yes," he said, making his way back to the kitchen. "It works—in theory. Simple electronics... so fucking simple, and obvious too. I can't believe I didn't think of it myself. Your grandfather, Seth—it's important that I talk to him, right away!"

"You can't; he... he recently passed."

"That's unfortunate. Sorry. But Seth, this"—he waved the equations in my face—"it's a goddamn game changer. War, commerce, space exploration..." He slicked his brown hippy-length hair backward and began to pace around the kitchen. "Seth, this is *everything*! It's a spaceship, a space station. Shit, it's a fucking ticket to Mars! Do you understand what I'm saying... the implications? Why the hell didn't you tell me about this before? We'll need protection. Everyone's going to want this. Everyone!"

"Doughnut?" I asked, opening the box of pastries.

"Sure," he said, removing a Bavarian cream éclair.

"So," I said. "You gonna stick around and build it, or do I have to kill you?"

He stopped chewing for a moment, grinned and said, "Fuck yeah! I'm in."

"Excellent choice, because in addition to becoming the world's leading authority on anti-gravity technology, you just became a 20% owner of InEvitech, the world's only anti-gravity device manufacturer. How's your memory?"

"Photographic."

"Good. Commit those equations to memory, then burn 'em. Your silence is our safety."

"You got it, boss."

My mind opened up to the good news. I started toward the door, then turned and said, "I need you to look into purchasing a larger base of operations, preferably in the desert, lots of land: a square mile at least. It's going to need an airstrip and some hangars. Margie—she works a few doors down at the real estate place—she can help. And get a floor safe installed, here in the office, ASAP."

"Sure. Where are you going?"

"I'm gonna go get us some protection."

After removing a couple stacks of walking-around money from my safe deposit box at the Sands, I drove to my new apartment at Fort Banks. Skip the concierge helped me with my bags. He was personable and, strangely enough, he wore two dress shirts—one right on top of the other. While showing me how to program new combinations for the door and safe, he gave me the run-down of Fort Banks: it had twenty-six units, was built five years ago, and was designed for tenants with a need for both privacy and security. Also, I was the first and only tenant. I thanked him with a fifty and began unpacking my gear.

I stored the Box in the safe, then went out and bought two cases of beer and a full complement of top-shelf booze and a load of basic food necessities. On my return trip, I stopped off at Mohamed's Middle Eastern Food Cart where I ordered a falafel plate from Ahmed. I asked him about Mohamed's health.

Ahmed set down the meal he was preparing and nodded me close. "You are Seth, yes? How is it you say... not good looking. Doctors, they say, very bad pneumonia, insides shutting down. Only Allah knows now."

"Jeez—that's bad. What hospital is he in?"

"Valley Hospital, on Shadow Lane. You see him, let him know food cart is well. Yes?"

Mohamed was in intensive care, but a bribe of two hundred dollars got me to his side. He was unresponsive. Tubes and beeping machines surrounded him. He was one of the first kind souls I had met in this city. I wondered where his family was. Why was he alone? I held his hand.

"Mohamed, don't worry about the food cart. Ahmed is doing a great job. Try to get better; I miss our little talks."

The machines began to *beep* alarmingly. Nurses flew in like flighty ghosts and attended to prescribed protocols. Then it was over—Mohamed was over.

I got in my car and drove. The city and its streets merged into halftone colored cartoons; I had to get out lest I become one. I drove on, into the desert where I found a happy place and powered down. The absence of human contamination was reassuring. I rolled down both windows, adjusted the seat backward, and listened to the song of the desert, performed by critters and trees and bushes and wind and temperature differentials, all interacting together to produce music that only I could hear. Surprisingly, the song's melody, intensity, and movement were readily manipulated by my own perceptions of its existence. After I added a choir and a reed section, the music evolved into a concert of memorable proportions. After the finale, brought on by a temperature shift in the wind, I got out and fired five rounds through my .38. The last round was a dead-on shot through a desert reed swaying in the wind.

On my trip home, glare from the sun impeded my vision. I worried about the food in the backseat and saw things on the road that probably weren't even there. It didn't matter; these things happened from time to time. Who was I to judge such events?

At Fort Banks, I unpacked my supplies, then took a shower. I thought about the Box and its implications, the impending Soul Breaker Virus, and I thought about Marisol, and I thought about Mohamed. I dried off and looked in the mirror. I was thin and a bit awkward in the face. *Never measure yourself using others as a ruler.* That's what Master Poe would have said. I got dressed and I mentally prepared myself for my dinner date with Marisol and the Lees.

CHAPTER 42

Marisol stood quietly under the carport of the Starlite Motel. She was wearing a brightly colored tunic that had been adorned with geometric shapes, and her face had been hennaed with tribal symbols. Behind her, the lobby's flickering neon sign oscillated an otherworldly glow. Damn, she looked good. I hurried over to greet her.

"Good evening, Marisol. I'm really glad you made it. You look beautiful." I opened the passenger door and helped her into my car's low-slung seat. I fastened her seat belt, then gently closed the door. As I nudged the car into traffic, I said, "You look so different. In a good way though."

She placed her hands on her lap and offered up a polite smile. "Gracias, Señor Bridges. Gracias. You make glub?"

For a moment I thought she was asking me if I *made love*, but quickly remembered our previous conversation and the funny way she pronounced the word club. "Yes, I did, thank you. Maybe we could go there after dinner? How does that sound?"

"It is good that you join club."

Well, I thought, at least she can pronounce her C's now. Either that or she was just messing with me. We drove to the MGM without further discussion.

As we entered the casino's lobby, I spotted Adamit and his family in an alcove. Just as we got within speaking distance, both Adamit and Katya dropped to one knee and bowed their heads.

"Hey guys," I said. "What's up? Someone lose a contact?" I looked to Jacob and Becky for answers, but then, they too knelt. "Come on, you guys," I said. "Get up. I want to introduce you to Marisol; she's joining us for dinner."

Adamit, with his head still lowered, said, "Your Majesty."

"OK, you guys, you're starting to piss me off. You better start showing a little respect, or it's going to be an early night—for everyone."

Marisol, who had taken cover behind me, came forward and said, "Gracias. Por favor, levantense."

"Have you guys been drinking?" I asked as they stood.

Becky went to Marisol, hugged her, and said, "We are so pleased to meet you, Marisol." She motioned to her family. "This is my sister Katya and my brothers, Jacob and Adamit."

We exchanged nods and smiles. Becky took Marisol's hand and led us all into the elevator.

A Muzak version of the theme song from *M.A.S.H.* joined us for the ride up. Katya and Adamit stared at the ceiling in a failed attempt to ward off tears. Had someone died? Did they know about Mohamed? Did they even know him? It would probably make things worse if I said anything. I placed my hands on the back of Marisol's shoulders in an attempt to reassure her that my oddly behaving friends meant no harm. A sense of relief washed over us when the doors slid open. A middle-aged woman with a warm smile greeted us.

"Saluto! I am Constance. Welcome to Le Bistro Le Boli. Please, follow me."

The restaurant's decor was Old-World Italian, juxtaposed with modernistic wall-sized windows that offered up outstanding panoramic views of the city. The staff was immaculate in both appearance and competence. We were seated at an ancient wooden table that held an impressive place setting for six. Apparently, the Jericho Sims people had rented out the place for our exclusive use.

As we ate, I brought everybody up to speed. I spoke of my coerced meet-and-greet with Cyrus, a few select snippets from some of my recent visions, my encounter—minus the deadly details—with the Shifter James Jamerson, my recent relocation to Fort Banks, and, finally, my plans to begin launching space-bound satellites into low-earth orbit within a year. They listened patiently and without interruption. Marisol appeared to be completely enthralled, although I doubted she understood much of what I was saying.

"What about you guys?" I asked after we had eaten the main course. "How is everything going for you? Work... life?"

Katya spoke briefly about her job and its nuances. Adamit was nonchalant about his state of affairs. Becky and Jacob were discussing their current unemployment status when Marisol enthusiastically interjected, "Our time is now. Yes?"

The statement incited a round-robin of questioning nods and shoulder shrugs between all of us. I was proud of her, that she had the confidence to speak at a table full of strangers.

After some small talk, and as coffee and dessert were being served, I stood up and said, "Everyone, please, may I have your attention. I'd like to thank you all for coming tonight. Truth is, I invited you to dinner because I have a proposal for all of you to consider. My business partner Crash and I have secured proprietary knowledge that will, among other things, put a reusable manned spacecraft into the Earth's orbit and have it return safely. Thing is"—I looked around the table—"I'm going to need your help. I know this is asking a lot, but I need you—all of you. I've already asked Dean, and he's onboard."

"Mr. Bridges," Jacob said in a formal tone. "How do your visions match up with these plans?"

"Well, suffice to say, I've seen you all up on the moon, on a base we built there. It is called Moonbase Virgil, and you all loved the view." That last bit about the moonbase seemed to have piqued their interest. "And Becky"—I went to her, leaned down, and whispered—"Your future-self told me to tell you: it's OK to love Izumi."

Becky smiled and nodded briefly, then she began to hold back tears.

I walked back to my chair and continued, "Adamit, I want to put you in charge of physical and intellectual security. It's going to be a big job, so I figure Becky and Jacob could help. Katya, I was hoping you could head-up public relations, acquisitions, investors, front-of-house stuff. Starting pay is a thousand dollars a week. So, what do you guys think? I mean... I don't need an answer right now. Just think about it... OK?"

I sat down and looked at my tablemates. The room quieted. Marisol looked around. The tensions I felt on the elevator ride up now returned and filled the room. Adamit broke the silence.

"Seth, it's a tempting offer; we're all in a holding pattern right now, and well..." He steepled his huge fingers in front of his pursed lips. Katya took a sip of her coffee. Becky adjusted herself in her improvised booster chair, then reached out and took hold of Jacob's hand. Adamit turned to Marisol. "Your Majesty," he said, with a measured tone. "May I inquire as to your considerations on these matters?"

Fuck. There he went with that stupid talk again. I was about to say something when Marisol stood, threw her hands in the air and said, "Sí, we will be able to fly. Seth is the way. I join too!"

Hmm... I liked that. Adamit rose, held up a glass, and said, "Mr. Bridges, we are honored to accept your offer. A toast. To our future."

Their swift decision to join up caught me by surprise. No one, in my entire life, had ever taken me or any of my ideas seriously. I collected myself as best I could.

During the elevator ride down, I glimpsed Marisol looking at Adamit and Katya. She was holding her finger close to her lips—perpendicular, like she was asking them to keep a secret. Probably just an itch?

The brisk evening air greeted us as we said our goodnights. Marisol took hold of my arm as if we were a romantic couple. We walked slowly into the night.

"Sure is nice out," I said. "Hey, would you like to go to the club now? But we don't have to. I mean, we could go for a drive, grab a drink. I don't know... get some cookies? Your choice."

"Sí, club is good, but other time. Now you take me home."

Marisol's directions home consisted of her pointing at upcoming street signs and saying, "here," and "there." Shortly after we pulled into an industrial park, she held out her hand and said, "Parar." Most of the street lights in the area were broken, and the whole place looked shady—criminally and literally. A dog barked in the distance. Marisol kissed my cheek, opened her door and said, "Buenas noches, Mr. Bridges. I clean la casa Tuesday."

"Marisol, wait!"

I sure as hell wasn't going to let her walk alone in this seedy neighborhood. By the time I'd gotten out of the car, she had disappeared beyond the light and into the darkness. I looked for her down some blind alleys and up a few broken stairwells.

"Marisol!" I yelled. "Come back! I'll walk you to your door. Come back, Marisol! Come back... please."

CHAPTER 43

Marisol ran through the shadows to a dilapidated sign-making factory that had closed a decade before. She opened a side door and went in. The empty building was quiet except for the usual sounds of pigeons and rodents adjusting to her presence. She could hear Seth calling out her name. It felt good. It had been such a long time since she'd felt it: the stirring in the back of her stomach, and the desire upfront in her mind.

She went to the basement and opened the thick door that protected her sanctuary. The small, ancient stone chamber was lit by a single bulb that hung from the ceiling. Opposite the wall-mounted sink and toilet was a small metal cot that held a thin mattress, a wool blanket, and a blood-stained pillow. She secured the door and sat on her bunk. She remembered seeing Seth when he had first arrived in Vegas. He was exactly what she had envisioned. Yes, she thought, there is enough time for love without failure. She removed an ornate ceremonial knife from beneath the pillow, ran her fingertips along its serrated, razor-thin edge, and chanted, "We can be like them. We can be like them."

Then, she cut into the tortured memories of her past.

CHAPTER 44

Mun Taizu hovered in a stationary position in her laboratory, studying Chronospool data in her HUD's readout display, waiting for a communiqué. It had been a full minute, she thought, since the consciousness of Octavius 4 had been sent back: more than enough time for history to have righted itself. Had she been deceived? These guards were pathetic, and these scientists were idiot malefactors. She nodded to herself. A personnel change was in order. She checked the continuity of the lab's secreted audio feed, then floated over to the door that led to her sanctum.

"Doctor," she said as she opened the door. "Continue with the next one."

"Yes, Mun," said Doctor Heisenberg. "Your will is our command."

Mun monitored the lab on her HUD. She saw Doctor Heisenberg and his associate Temporalogists bring out Octavius 5. They gagged the boy's frantic high-pitched screams, cleared the tank, and began the process of loading him into the machine. Then, Mun turned up the gain on the lab's audio feed and heard Captain Tighzon talking to his squad.

"Guardians of the Realm," he said in hushed conspiratorial tones, "I have misled you. This—what we're doing here—it's wrong on a catastrophic scale. If these experiments succeed, even partially, everything we know and love will cease to exist. We, together, can refuse orders that violate Clause 1, Section 7 of the Mind Corp Imperatives Act of 2047. Join me, comrades, and let us stop this madness while there are still tomorrows to be had."

Mun shook her head in disgust. She had known when she hired this bunch, there might be Cause loyalists in their ranks. She entered a prearranged code into her HUD, then flew back into the lab with her contingency plan: six mercenaries.

"Traitors!" Mun screamed at Captain Tighzon. "You're all traitors!" She smiled as she activated the lab's Electro Hold: a paralyzing, room-sized, electro-sonic death grip that held the lab's occupants motionless. "You think you can defy me?" She made a cutting motion with her hand and smiled as the mercs, armed with harmonic katanas, systematically beheaded Captain Tighzon and his squad.

"Doctor Heisenberg," Mun said in her calm voice. "You will continue with the transfer?"

He kneeled submissively in an expanding puddle of warm blood. "Yes, Mun. I will continue with your glory."

She went to the tank and said to the boy, who Doctor Heisenberg had named Octavius 5, "Find a man called Dings at the Las Vegas Independent Cab Co-op. Tell him this: The New York State Lotto numbers for 02/11/1980 are: 7, 16, 44, 47, 51, 59. And remember, Dings is the answer. Find Dings and give him this information." Then, she turned back to the doctor and said, "Well then, doctor, proceed."

Heisenberg got to his feet, entered the coordinates into the TSQEC, and sent the mind of Octavius 5 back in time and into the mind of Colton Hill.

CHAPTER 45

Colton Hill grinned as he walked out of the Las Vegas County lockup, confidant his purpose in life—to exploit all the stupid people around him—was on track. A block later, he used his good arm to fling his bag of belongings into the middle of the street.

Fuck it, he thought. That fucking prick Seth had broken his arm, and yesterday, his cheap-ass stepmom had told him not to bother coming home. Said she was done with him and thrown all of his shit into the garbage. Said he had to straighten out his life or he would end up like his stupid dad. Tough love: yeah, that's what she called it. What a stupid concept. He didn't think Dad would appreciate those two words being put together. Bitch Stepper Bitch Mom was as stupid as the stupid shrink she had stolen the phrase from. I should call Dad at Rikers, he thought, but it's so fucking expensive. He didn't have shit for cash, just the twenty, and he'd need that for other stuff. Maybe he could steal a car and go pay him a visit...? First things first. Buy some booze, get a little action, and find a place to crash. Thank you, Stupid Bitch Mom, for leaving me homeless. She'd get hers. The culvert would have to do for now.

Colton was stalking an inebriated transvestite, weaving down Fremont street, when he felt something go painfully wrong in his head. He dropped to his knees in pain, and blood drooled from his eyes, and his ears, and his nose. He heard a new voice, inside his head, and it wanted him to kill somebody named Sethco The Destroyer.

Twenty minutes later, Colton was loaded into an ambulance and brought to the emergency room at Centennial Hills Hospital. Two hours after that, he escaped from the hospital's psych ward—or, depending on who you asked, was just allowed out.

As soon as he got back to the strip, Colton told the new voice in his head, "OK, Octav. You are the newest member of The Colton Bunch. We are a gang of ruthless criminals, and we do as we please. I'm not only the leader of this gang, but I'm also the Captain, head honcho, and El Presidente. Do you understand? Hey, Octav, you in there?"

"Yes, sir. I am here. It is important that we find a person called Dings. He works at Las Vegas Independent Cab Co-Op. He will assist us in our mission."

"I just told you: I give the orders around here."

"No," said Octavius 5, "I do."

"Ahh!" Colton screamed in pain. "Stop! OK, OK."

"You must help me with my mission."

"I will. But I need stuff, too. And I already know this guy Dings."

"You do?

"Yes. I met him a few days ago. That's how I got this busted up arm."

"What is it that you need?"

"Not much. Come on I'll show you."

Colton marched into Fanny's Liquor Store. He grabbed a large plastic bottle of Vegas Best Vodka and went up to the register. He pulled the twenty-dollar bill from his pocket and thought: what kind of criminal pays for stuff? He pulled his shirt over his face, whacked the cashier over the head with the bottle, and ran out of the store.

They took refuge on the fringes of Vegas inside a cracked storm-drain culvert that a developer had abandoned years ago. Colton opened the can of Sterno he had stashed there on a previous outing, and strained the liquid part of the fuel into the bottle of vodka. He lit a cigarette, then the remaining Sterno. The flame cast flickering shadows on the curved walls of the culvert. Colton peered into the darkness, took in the full moon, then shifted his gaze to the colored lights of the city and howled.

"We did good, Octav, we did good. I think we have the makings of a strong criminal organization. Like the mafia. My dad is in the mafia. But those guys will be nothing compared to us. We're going to run this town. That's my dream, Octav, to run this town. Everyone will come to us asking for favors: Oh, Colton, can you help me? Colton, I need a loan. Colton, I'm in a real jam, can you help me out? You see, Octav, that's how they do it. Somebody needs a favor, you give it to them: then, you make it so they can never pay it off. That way you own them for life. It's kinda like slavery... but different. Actually, if you think about it, it's better because you don't have to feed 'em and stuff... What do you think about calling ourselves the Vegas Hill Gang, or the Coltoneers? Octav, are you listening to me?"

"Yes, I am listening. You must honor your agreement to help me find and kill Sethco the Destroyer. Is that understood?"

"Of course, I'm a man of my word. I'm not like my dad—you know he turned state evidence against his bosses? I'm better than him. He's weak, and I think he killed my mom—my real mom..."

Colton took a swig of the fortified vodka and a drag of his cigarette. "Check this out, Octav." He pulled a red Sharpie from his pants and drew a crude swastika on his forehead. "Now I look like Manson. People will respect this kind of devotion. I know I would." He pocketed the Sharpie and stared into an area of Vegas where the lights of the city bumped into the walls of darkness. "Hey, Octav, come to think of it, I know a guy named Seth Bridges; you think he could be this Sethco guy you're looking for?"

CHAPTER 46

After losing Marisol in the alleyway, I went back to the car, rolled down the windows, and listened for her. Where had she gone? She was a strange one, and what was with that weird way Adamit and his family had treated her—what the hell was that all about? After half an hour of waiting, I drove home and retrieved Grandpa's Box from the safe.

I activated the Box and began reading about the hazards of space travel: radiation, gravity differentials, speeding meteoroids, and all manner of life-ending unknowables that waited for anyone who dared to enter it. I located a placeholder from my last session and read: *8/25/1980: InEvitech, a private aerospace company (believed to be the birthplace of the Sethco Alliance), located in Las Vegas, NV, successfully exited the Earth's atmosphere in their three-man spacecraft, Penelope One. After deployment of a small communication satellite, InEvitech's three-man crew safely returned to Earth. This flight was the first documented use of a GRD (Grav-Resistant Drive.) The historic journey is considered by many as the New Dawn of Mankind.*

I fucking did it! Or we did it—or would do it. I poured another drink, stepped out onto the deck, and looked out over the desert. The dark stillness helped to organize my thoughts. In less than nine months we were going to launch a three-man spacecraft named *Penelope One*. A stupid name for sure. And what was with the Sethco Alliance angle? At some point, I'd have to figure that out—probably a company I was going to start in the future; and, oh yeah, somehow the Box had updated itself and referred to our gravity shield as a GRD...? Worry about that later. The fact was, we were going to do it, and it was not all that difficult. All we needed was a miniature submarine-type shell. We would dress it up with wings, equip it with a GRD, slap on some maneuvering thrusters, install a VHF radio, throw in some bagged lunches and canned air, and voilà, a manned, satellite-launching spacecraft. Out in the distance, I heard a coyote howl.

That night I slept well: no dreams, no visions, just restful sleep. In the morning, I went to the Sands looking for Adamit. He wasn't around, so I took a stroll around the casino—soaking up the sights and sounds. My walk was interrupted by some increasingly distressing internal cramps. I realized right then and there, my aversion to sit-downs on public toilets would not be avoided.

The restroom attendant, who could have been a doppelgänger for Scatman Crothers, greeted me with a welcoming smile.

A few minutes later, while washing my hands, he came over and said, "Good sir." His deep and resonant voice bellowed off the blue ceramic wall tiles. "May I offer you a towel?"

"Thank you," I said as I took the towel. "You have a real nice facility here: clean, good ventilation, both forgiving *and* forgetful."

He proffered his hand. "Most folks call me Reggie or TP, but my God-given name is Reginald T. Piedmont the First."

I set the towel down and shook his hand. "Seth Bridges. Toilets, in my opinion—one of man's greatest inventions."

"Indeed," Reggie said. "Indeed they are." I placed a hundred-dollar bill in the wicker basket on the counter and left. "Good sir! Mr. Seth! You forgot this."

Reggie was holding my .38 in his upturned palms. Fuck. I doubled back. As Reggie carefully slid the revolver back into my holster, he said, "Reckon you'll be needing that, with the devil after you and all."

"Reggie"—I tried to remember his ridiculously long name—"P. Clevius. How'd you do that? With the gun, and what devil are you talking about?"

"I'm a proud member of the Bathroom Security Councilmen of America."

"OK...?"

"Ha, ha. Just jiving with ya, Mr. Bridges. It's a parlor trick," he said, proudly adjusting his waistband. "I call it the hand-shaking gun grab. Misdirection, smoke and mirrors—mostly mirrors. Houdini taught it to me, so I can't tell its workings; but I can tell you this: this morning, there was a devil here; a*nd* he was aski*ng* me ab*out* you. I reckon it has something to do with that Sunday paper advertisement, the one offering a reward for information on you? You know, the reward nobody ever seems to get?"

We went back inside the restroom. Reggie pointed to a urinal. "Psycho took a urination right there: had the Lost in his eyes, and a red swastika tattooed on his forehead. Your age, I reckon, white, medium build, alone, but acting all crazy—and talking to people that weren't there."

Paranoid walked in and pretended to take a leak in the urinal. It sounded like the not-so-bright assassins from the future were up to their old tricks. I thanked Reggie with another hundred-dollar bill, then headed over to the Landing Lounge.

CHAPTER 47

Just as I was about to chomp down on a hot slice of pizza, Vinny, from the pizza joint, came over and sat on the stool next to mine.

"Is that all you ever eat?"

"No. I eat lots of stuff. You here on business?"

"Thing is, I was looking for you, and someone told me you like this casino. So ahh, I thought you'd be interested in knowing there's another guy in town after you."

"Go on."

"He's legit, a real whack-job psycho killer. For a hundred large I can make him disappear—tonight."

"You can do that?"

"Me? No, I'll source it out."

"A hundred is a little steep, isn't it? And how do I know you're not just ripping me off?"

"You don't. But I've got a reputation to protect. Half the money now, the other half afterwards. You'll get a Polaroid of the mook when the deed is done. Do we have a deal?"

"First of all, I don't want you killing anyone. Second, that's way too much money. I'll pay you twenty grand to make him take a long vacation. Maybe ship him off to Mexico or somewhere like that. You could leave him there, shoeless and destitute. But no killing."

"Seventy-five."

"Thirty-five?"

Just then Adamit came over and he had his angry face on. "Seth, are you sure about this?"

Vinny cleared his throat. "Mr. Bridges, there must be some misunderstanding. My services, my pizza, are always free for you and your friends." He lowered his head and scurried away.

Adamit shook his head. "What's going on, Seth? Why were you about to give that sand shark money?"

I told Adamit about my restroom conversation with Reggie and my growing paranoia and concern for the future.

"Listen up," he said. "You're done with guys like that. I quit my job this morning. The Lee's are now working for you, full time. After our dinner last night, I had Becky and Jacob follow you around—part of your new 24-hour security detail. You will be protected. So no more Vinnys. OK?"

"Thanks, man," I said with a nod. "That means a lot. I've been so busy lately... everything is moving so fast."

Adamit smiled, slapped my shoulder, and said, "So what's next, boss?"

"Well, for starters, you don't have to call me boss. But since you're on the clock, come on, let me show you our office."

Paranoid appeared, hiked up his pants, and gave me the thumbs up sign. As we headed out of the casino, my new head of security fell into his natural state of projecting hallucinogenic fear into those who dared look in our direction.

The sky was clear, the temperature was around seventy degrees, and my Maserati sagged to one side as I drove Adamit to the office. Crash was working at a drafting table when we walked in.

"Hey, Crash," I said. "This is your new co-worker, Adamit Lee. He's heading up our security." I turned to Adamit. "Mr. Lee, this is Crash. He's the brains of our outfit."

Crash seemed unsure of his next move.

"C'mon," I said, "Shake Mr. Lee's hand before he gets mad."

"Pleased to make your acquaintance," Crash said as they shook hands.

"Likewise," said Adamit.

I nodded at Crash. "Mr. Lee will be working with his brother Jacob, and his sisters Becky and Katya. I hired the whole family. How're things moving along here?"

"Ahh... great. Margie has some property for us to look at. It's an airfield just outside the city limits. We're supposed to look at it tomorrow morning, around nine."

"Good stuff," I said. "We'll all meet back here in the morning and check out the property."

CHAPTER 48

I drove Adamit back to the Sands and handed him eight grand. "This is for you and your family," I said. "It's two weeks' pay. I'll get you on the official payroll ASAP."

"Seth, we're not doing this for money. We're doing it because it's right, and more importantly, it's our *purpose*."

"Purpose?"

"Yes, that's why they exist."

"They?"

"Purposes. Seth, everyone has a purpose, whether they know it or not."

"Purpose-smurfess—two hours ago you saved me thirty grand. I'm gonna pay you whether you like it or not."

He opened the car door and maneuvered his way out of the bucket seat.

"Hey, Adamit," I called out. "Change of plans. Get in your car and follow me to my place. I want to show you something."

"Nice place," Adamit said once we'd made it to my apartment. I retrieved the Box from the safe and asked him to put his finger on the control ball. Nothing happened.

"OK," he said.

"Watch." I said as I placed my fingertip on the control ball. The holographic display hovered above the Box. "This thing holds all the information that will ever be. Everything, technology, future events. Everything! And it updates itself. *This* is what we are building our company around."

He looked at me stone-faced and said, "So, what do you think about heading over to Purgatorium, maybe grabbing some grub?"

Purgatorium's bomb-sniffing dogs were on patrol, and the staff was busy preparing for the night shift. We grabbed a large booth and ordered food—a lot of food. Adamit ate and ate—I'd never seen anything like it. He was polishing-off a Boston cream pie when Dean and his chorus of geishas showed up and joined us.

Adamit stood up, belched a satisfying burp, patted his stomach and said, "I need to rest. Seth, I'll see you in the morning. Becky is on watch tonight. Goodnight, fellas." He bowed to the geishas and said, "Oyasumi no josei."

They returned his bow—giggling.

Dean gave me a Cheshire-cat grin, shook my shoulders, and said, "Man, I knew I'd find you here. What's shaking, brother?"

"Ahh, you know, just a bunch of Shifting stuff. How're things with you"—I tried to remember the geisha's names—"and the ladies?"

"Couldn't be better. You remember Asuka, Izumi, and Yoshimi? They're always asking about you. Tell you the truth, I'm a little jealous."

"You should be jealous, they're beautiful," I said. "How long do you plan on keeping them all to yourself?"

Asuka filled the bowl of a hookah. Izumi stood by with a flame. Yoshimi set out two glasses and filled them with vodka. I took a hit from the hookah. It was a smooth-tasting blend of tobacco, marijuana, and hash. I held it for a moment, trying to decide if this was the right time to firm up my previous job offer with Dean. When I looked over at him, his hands were balled-up and pressed into his temples: most likely reviewing five-minute scenarios of the future. On my exhale, Dean jumped up and said, "Whoa! I can't believe I just did that."

"What?" I asked. "What'd you do?"

"Oh, you'll see," he said. "And I'll get back to you on that other thing, but for now... better buckle up your seatbelts, everybody; it's about to get real up in here!"

I took another hit from the hookah and held it for as long as I could. As I exhaled, Cyrus the Effing Willhammer and Penelope Purple Eyes, flanked by the two gargolian hyenas and an entourage of fifteen or twenty henchmen, made an entrance. The whole lot of them looked suspicious. What were they doing here?

Up on the stage, some roadies did a quick soundcheck, and a group of musicians took their respective places. Dean leapt onto the stage, clutched a live microphone, and announced, "Ladies and gentlemen, Agents of Fortune... BLUE OYSTER CULT!"

A familiar cowbell and guitar riff introduced their song "(Don't Fear) The Reaper." I downed the shot of vodka and thought, why was this band here, now, playing that song? Were they the house band that played for the early bird dinner crowd? Everything appeared to be randomly connected, like I was in some crazy-ass existential nexus. Or... maybe whatever was in that hookah bowl was just a tad too potent. Penelope and Cyrus caught me looking at them. Multi-century relationships must be tough. But here they were, keeping their love alive.

When the greatest one-song concert in the world ended, Penelope and Cyrus headed for the exit. Penelope looked back at me and called out, "Hey, mista! Don't forget me."

A cold chill ran through my body. Dean scooted in next to me and said, "Agents of Fortune, baby. Agents of Fortune. That's us. That's who we are." He gulped the remainder of his drink, slammed the glass down, and said, "So, when do I start my new job?"

I told him he would be the physical plant manager for a yet-to-be determined property. "More importantly," I said, "I need you to guide us through the development of our satellite deployment vehicle."

"I'm a waiter, not a rocket scientist," he said. "What makes you think I can do this job?"

I paused for a second. "You're, what... like sixty, sixty-one years old? You're strong, intelligent, our shift cycles are in sync, and in your previous lifetime you wired the planet. I trust you."

He scrutinized my face for a moment. "Do you mean that? The part about trusting me?"

"Yes, Dean. I do."

He stood up, pulled me close, and said, "I won't let you down, brother."

I handed him a napkin with the office address on it. "Meet us here, tomorrow morning at 8:30. Pay is a thousand a week."

He raised his glass. "Agents of Fortune, baby, Agents of Fortune."

The geishas and I joined in, "Agents of Fortune!"

The band's vocalist walked by, held up a drink, and said, "I'll drink to that."

CHAPTER 49

In the morning, I opened my eyes and thought: I feel good, eight hours rest, no visions, and I had a worthwhile day ahead. What more could someone want? Love got out of bed, stood up and, if I'm not mistaken, passed some gas and started complaining about things I didn't understand. Thankfully, I had the ability to ignore such outbursts and continued on with my day.

I arrived at the office a half-hour before our scheduled meeting with Margie. Hand tools, busted-up radios, electronic testing-meters, and food cartons were strewn about. Crash looked up from an improvised workbench.

"I've done it!" he said with a wide-eyed grin. "It's incredible!"

His voice had me worried. "What… exactly have you done?"

"Come here," said the pot-smoking, beer-guzzling genius from Caltech. "You're gonna want to see this."

He carefully separated a brass sphere, which measured three inches in diameter, into two parts. The bottom half was filled with thin wires, diodes, a small circuit board, and a nine-volt battery.

"Yeah," I said. "Go on."

"Seth! It's a working prototype of your grandfather's equations. I bought most of the parts down the street at the Radio Shack. Get this: it operates by reversing the compositional frequencies of whatever it's attached to—in this case, the bottom half of this globe I scarfed from the brass bed in my room; hope you don't mind. Seth, it's so fucking cool, and simple." He screwed the top half of the sphere to the bottom, then clipped the loose end of a three-foot nylon tether to a fastening cleat at the bottom of the sphere. "Watch this," he said, turning a small pentameter dial located on the underside of the sphere. Like magic, the globe rose above the workbench and leveled off under the anchor of the tether. "Go ahead, push it down!" he said. "With your hand, push on it!"

I pushed down on the sphere. It put up a few pounds of resistance, but I was able to force it to the workbench and hold it there for a few moments. As I slowly reduced pressure, it returned to its previous position above the table.

"Not bad, huh?" Crash said. "I call it the Gravity Reverse Drive, or GRD. That dial"—he pointed to the underside of the sphere—"is at one right now, but it goes to ten."

Hmm... that was what the Box had called it too: a GRD.

"Crash," I said. "This is really incredible. And the name, what do you call it? A GRD? That's got a real nice ring to it."

"Thanks, boss, but there are some problems that we have to talk about. If this gets out—"

"I know," I said. "We're dead men walking if anyone gets wind of this."

"Yeah, that's what I was thinking. It's way cool and everything, but I'm not ready to die."

"Don't worry. Neither of us are dying, at least not anytime soon. Disassemble it right now, and give me all your notes... and any receipts for parts. I'm going to burn 'em. For now, this is our secret. Agreed?"

"Agreed."

"Did you get a safe installed yet?"

"They're installing one today—behind the dogs-playing-poker picture in the big bedroom."

He disassembled the sphere while I collected related receipts and paperwork, then burned them in a metal wastebasket near an open window. We organized the office and returned it to its former state. The sphere was now completely disassembled into innocuous parts, its paper trail nonexistent.

"Looks good," I said, giving the office the once-over. I heard some music outside. It was Dean and the gang. I went outside to greet them.

Adamit and his family were hanging around Dean's very hip '68 Ford Mustang GT Fastback, which was cranking out the Boomtown Rats song "I Don't Like Mondays."

Dean shut off the stereo and said to Jacob, "You know it, brother. I went with the Alpine set-up—a hundred and fifty watts of sonic goodness."

Margie pulled up and we followed her into her office. "Good morning, everyone," she said. "For those who don't know me, my name is Margie Ledue. I'm a real estate agent. Today we'll be looking at a property just off of Interstate 160 West. You can follow me; I'll be in the beige LeSabre. Are there any questions?"

CHAPTER 50

Thirty minutes later our caravan pulled into a decommissioned Air Force training facility. The property had two hangars, a control tower, a two-thousand-foot tarmac runway, and a three-story main building that held a mess hall and sleeping quarters.

After a twenty-minute tour, I asked Margie, "How much?"

She looked down at her file. "Two hundred thousand. Ten percent down; the owner is open to financing."

I took in a deep breath and exhaled as I surveyed the property. There was no denying it: the place had everything I needed.

"Margie," I said as I stuck out my hand, "I'll take it."

"And the down payment?" Margie asked as she shook my hand.

"I'll drop it off tomorrow, at your office."

"Alright, then. We have a deal."

I was feeling so good I put my hand on her shoulder and said, "You ever think about a career change? I'm asking this because I'd like to hire you. The job pays a thousand dollars a week, and you only have to work part-time—that is until you can join us full time. Give it some thought. OK?" She hugged her file tight and gave me a skeptical look.

I found Dean in one of the hangars. "What do you think? I hope it's good, 'cause I just bought the place."

"I can work with this," he said. "They don't build like this anymore. Gov spec."

"That's reassuring. You think you could get me a quick inventory of the buildings and the mechanical systems by tomorrow? We've got to get this place up and running within the month."

He nodded. "Not a problem. Love this shit."

I invited everybody to take a seat at some old picnic tables near the main building. The sky was clear, the sun was high, and the heat of the desert had begun to tighten its grip.

"This is it guys," I said. "Our new home. The place where we build a no-frills, satellite-launching manned spacecraft, and then put it into outer space. And we're going to do it within eight months. We'll keep the other office for now, but this will be our new base of operations. We'll call this place the base, and our in-town location the office."

"Mr. Bridges," Margie said. "Do you have any concept of what you just said? I may only be a realtor, but even I know that's impossible. Eight months, to get into space? That's ridiculous."

I felt a hand on my arm. Marisol? As I turned to look, I realized it was just the desert-heat playing tricks with my mind.

"Actually," Crash said, "we can do it. We have the technology. Won't be easy, but it can be done."

"Jumping Jehoshaphat," Katya said. "If Seth says we're going to space and launching satellites, then the only thing left to do is get busy helping him."

"Look out, NASA," Jacob yelled. "We're coming for *you*."

"Here, here," added Becky.

Adamit nodded as Dean punched the sky and let out an emphatic, "Yes!"

Wow. Everyone's support threw me for a loop. Margie was right to be skeptical, and I knew explanations would be necessary in due time.

"Alright," I said. "This is my proposal. We meet at the in-town office every morning at nine. We'll talk, and together, we'll get this whole base up and running before you know it. Katya, I'm going to need you to do public relations, secure investors, and help with acquisitions and business stuff. Do you mind?"

"Sounds delightful. I love a challenge."

"Dean, you'll be in charge of the physical plant. Crash, could you design a ship that can go into space with a three-man crew, launches a satellite, and come back safely?"

He held up his hands and gave me an exasperated look. "Yeah, yes… but we're going to need some technical help, a lot of it."

"Jacob, I need you and Becky to work with Adamit and protect us from danger. We're dealing with valuable technology. People will kill for it."

Becky grabbed my shirt, pulled me down, and hugged me. "Don't you worry, brother; we won't let you down."

"Thanks, Becky. I'm not going to let you guys down either."

CHAPTER 51

Adamit gathered his family and laid out preliminary plans for base security. When he'd finished, I waved him over to my car, and we headed back to the city—the Maserati sagging under his mass.

At a traffic light, I downshifted, then turned to him and asked, "So, how'd I do?"

"I think it went well," he said with a shrug. "And that airfield—it just might fit the bill."

We stopped off at Vinny's, ordered lunch, and sat at a table. Vinny came over and asked, "May I sit?"

Adamit nodded and said, "Is he dead?"

Vinny pulled up a chair and sat. "Well... uh, we sort of lost track of him, but I got this." His hand trembled as he gave Adamit a grainy black-and-white photograph. "This is your man. His name is Colton Hill. He's a real psychopath, sociopath, one of those paths. He's got mafia connections, and he takes crazy-people drugs."

Adamit studied the photograph for a moment before handing it to me. The face in the photo was Colton, alright.

"Where and when," Adamit asked, "was that taken?"

Vinny wiped his brow with a napkin. "Two days ago, at the Tropicana. This mook was causing major problems. I got a guy there, works video surveillance."

Adamit dismissed Vinny with a wave.

"I know this guy," I said.

"Do tell," replied Adamit.

"He's an old classmate of mine. He tried to rob me, and ah... I broke his arm. Now he's got it in for me."

As we left Vinny's, Adamit asked, "Do you mind if I drive?"

I tossed him the keys and said, "What do you think about an armored car? You know, the kind that looks like a regular car but has armor."

He got into the driver's seat, adjusted the seat, mirror, and headrest. "Sure, armored car. Where to?"

"What day is it?"

"It's Tuesday, the twelfth. You alright?"

"Shit, the Olympics. I almost missed it."

After emptying out my safe deposit box at the Sands, we drove over to the sportsbook at Caesars. Cagey was working the window. I asked him if Mr. Anastasio was around.

"You still after those Olympic lines?" he said.

"That's right."

"Hold on, I'll get him."

"Good afternoon," I said as Mr. Anastasio came up to the window. "I'd like to place a bet on the US Olympic hockey team please."

He gave me a scrutinizing once-over. "Why are you carrying that piece, kid? Is someone after you?"

"No, it's just, well, it makes me feel like a man."

"Alright, alright," he said, stubbing out a cigarette. "Enough of the horseshit; this is the deal. I'll take your action, one game at a time." He pulled out a clipboard with a stat-sheet on it, looked at it and repeatedly clicked his pen. "Let's see... the first game is Sweden versus the USA. It starts in five hours. I'll give you even odds. What's your action?"

I retrieved ten ten-thousand-dollar bundles from my pockets and piled them up on his desk. He groaned as he handed me a receipt.

We left Caesars and drove off.

"Do we medal in hockey?" Adamit asked as he drove.

"We win the gold, believe it or not."

"I love this country. So, where to?"

"Just ahh—" I pointed at the windshield—"drive through the Hive."

A few miles later, Adamit said, "Is that what you call downtown, the *Hive*?"

He had me and my fondness for derogatory descriptions of things on the line. I parried. "I haven't had any foreboding episodes with Colton. We're probably safe for now. Why don't you just drop yourself off at your house? We'll call it a day."

He snorted a chuckle. "No can do, amigo. Until my relief arrives, we're like Siamese twins."

"Well... in that case, let's go to my place."

When we pulled into the driveway at the Fort Banks apartment complex, Adamit put the car in neutral, scratched at the side of his face, let out an exasperated sigh, and said, "The real hive is a state of mind. Some people get up every morning, ignoring the choices life offers them. Eventually, those choices wither away, and that's when people behave like bees in a hive or ants in a colony—too busy to care about a world that exists beyond the boundaries of their own shadows."

"Really? You know you sound like my old sensei Master Poe."

He turned to me. "You know Master Poe?"

"I sure do. He taught me budo philosophy: 'Seek nothing, and all will be revealed.'"

Adamit laughed a bit and said, "How about, 'The most expensive things in life are free.'"

"Or," I said. "'One must abscond with happiness whenever encountered.'"

Adamit smiled. "I always liked that one."

"Yeah, me too." I pointed to a spot near the entrance. "You can park over there; I'm the only tenant."

Once we were inside my place, I asked Adamit if he wanted a drink.

He briefly inspected the apartment before heading into the kitchen. "Did you notice that your concierge was wearing three dress shirts, one on top of the other?"

"Yeah, I know. His name is Skip. He was wearing two when I first met him."

Adamit removed a platter of food from the fridge, set it on the kitchen table, and handed me a note. "I think this is for you."

The note had two penciled-in smiley faces. Marisol must have started her weekly cleanings. I smiled at the thought of her, here, cleaning, making dinner, and—

Adamit crunched into a cold taco near my ear. "Do you mind if I have some of this?" he asked.

"Didn't you just eat?" I grabbed a bottle of rum, two glasses, and went into the living room, and flicked on the TV.

The opening ceremonies for the Olympics were underway and the US hockey team would be playing Sweden in a few hours. After finishing another taco, Adamit said, "Hey boss? What do you think about guard dogs on the property?"

"Have a seat," I said, nodding to a nearby chair.

He hung his sport coat on a peg near the door, then eased himself into the chair. Holstered under his arms were two semi-automatic pistols.

"Drink?" I asked, pouring him a shot and one for myself. He waved it off. "Go ahead," I said. "Have a drink. I insist."

We both finished our drinks in one gulp. He refilled the glasses.

"Admit," I said, "you're the head of security; if you want ten dogs or two dogs, mastiffs or chihuahuas, that's your call. Thing is, I'm curious about Marisol. I mean... the other night, you and Katya—hell, your whole family acted strangely around her. Do you know her?"

He downed his drink and scratched vigorously at the scar on his face. "She's beautiful and you like her. There's not much more I can say on the subject."

I had hoped for more, but I wasn't going to press. I downed my drink, refilled the glasses, and said, "Are those .45s?"

He pulled out one of the .45s, removed the ammo clip, cleared its breech, and handed it to me. "They're Colt .45s, model 1911."

The grip had been customized with ivory and the trigger with gunsmith holes.

"Nice." I handed the gun back. "Do you have a lot of experience with this sort of thing? You know, guns and protection?"

He slapped the clip back in place, chambered a round, set the safety, and slid the gun back into its holster. "I kept Tesla from being assassinated—well, not the first time, but the second."

"Tesla? That's who my grandfather got the Box from."

He nodded.

"So, tell me," I said. "What's it like jumping fifty years into the future?"

"You'll find out," he said. "But I warn you, it's just your mind. Your body is different—same-gender, but it's someone else's. I wasn't always this big, and Katya—well, let's just say she wasn't always so pretty."

We bullshitted and drank into the night. After informing him we had at least eight years before the Soul Breaker Virus hit, I offered him the use of the spare bedroom, and I passed out in mine.

CHAPTER 52

It was a gun battle—outside Caesars Palace. How had I gotten here? It must have been a vision... inside a dream? Was I asleep? I performed my dream test and tried to fly. Nope, couldn't fly—not a dream. It must be a vision.

I was with Adamit in the main parking lot at Caesars Palace. We were crouched behind the engine compartment of my car, taking cover from some gunmen shooting at us. My heart was racing and I was covered in sweat. Adamit was ghost white. Blood occasionally spurted from his chest.

He slumped, dropped his weapon, and gurgled, "Sorry boss."

I wondered what Master Poe would do in this scenario. Then, I rushed at the enemy, my .38 in one hand and one of Adamit's 1911's in the other. I kept my head low, zigzagged around a fire hydrant, and attempted a flanking maneuver. Bullets whizzed by my head: the heat from a few of them brushed my skin. A sudden updraft swirled some tattered-up escort-service flyers in its wake. Oddly enough, I wondered if the flyers were all from the same printing company, and if the girls in the photographs knew each other. I refocused, squinted into snake-eye vision, aimed at one of the assailants, and unleashed a volley from both weapons. Then, I took cover behind a banged-up Dodge Dart. My flanking gambit worked. I spied two assailants. One was slumped down and motionless: the other was fumbling about, attempting to reload his handgun with one arm.

Nearby, a public-transit bus worked its way through some gear changes and pulled away. From behind its fume-clouded windows, faces stared back at me, their eyes shifting between myself and the shooters. I straightened up and ran at the enemy, firing, emptying both of my weapons. Then it was quiet, except for the ringing in my ears. The two bad guys were sprawled out on the sidewalk, both dead.

One of them was Colton. What a fucking loser, I thought. The other was Dings, an even bigger loser.

I snatched a New York state lottery ticket from the top of Dings' filthy sock. A towline of consciousness pulled me away from the blood and carnage, away from Dings, Colton Hill, and away from Adamit, my friend and protector.

I woke to clanging sounds coming from the kitchen. Breakfast was in the air. I was covered in cold sweat. The thought of Adamit's crumpled body and his blood-gurgled last words had left me both worried and horrified. And Dings—what a jerk. Even so, I felt sorry for the guy. Damn. With visions like that, who needed tomorrow?

After jotting the event in my journal, I took a piss, a dry heave, then ambled into the kitchen. Becky was standing on a chair cooking over the stove. Jacob was in the living room, on the couch, drawing something. Adamit must have switched watches with those two sometime last night. I wasn't sure what kind of protection they could offer; what if a bunch of killers kicked in the door right now? Though, I had to confess, it was comforting to have them around.

Becky eased herself down from the chair and handed me a cup of coffee. "Good morning."

I took the cup and forced a smile. "Thank you, Becky, and good morning to you. Hey, how's the big guy?"

"Fine as wine, left a few hours ago. Why? Is something wrong? Should I call him?"

"No, I'll talk to him at the meeting What time do you have?"

She held out her wrist. "Seven-thirty."

"Morning, Jacob," I said as I went to turn on the TV.

"It was a tie," he said. "The hockey game with Sweden. Two to two."

A tie? I thought. My head throbbed. Crap. Of course, it was. I should have remembered that. Well, at least the timeline was still stable. I joined him on the couch and watched him sketch out some technical drawings of our new airfield. Becky brought over breakfast.

CHAPTER 53

"Mr. Bridges," Margie said, as our first formal meeting at the office got underway. "Congratulations. The base is yours."

After we finished the paperwork, she handed me two large sets of keys.

"So, Margie," I said. "Have you considered my offer? We could use your talents."

"I have, and the answer is yes—part-time for now."

"Excellent! Everyone, let's welcome Margie to the team."

She took a playful bow as we gave her a round of applause.

"Well," I said, "now that you're on the team, could you look into having the base's water, electricity, and phones turned on?"

"Already been taken care of."

"Boy, you're good. Let's see—we're going to need some bookkeeping and payroll systems put in place. Here"—I handed her the checkbook for my account at the Vegas Trust Bank—"Use these funds to get things up and rolling. There are more deposits on the way. OK, who's next?"

Dean gave a report on the airbase's condition.

"That's not too bad," I said. "Why don't you go ahead and begin repairs and add a reception area to the front of the barracks. Oh yeah, we'll need a machine shop, along with a bunker-styled vault installed in one of the hangars."

Dean took notes and nodded as if he'd been doing this sort of work his entire life.

"I've started on a logo and an investor query," said Katya, "But I'll need more information on what we're doing."

"I understand," I said. "Tomorrow I'll show you—all of you—the technology we're working with. In the meantime, Katya, I need you to begin a search for a DC-4."

"Are you asking me to buy a DC-4? As in a big old airplane?"

"Yes, but make sure it's in good condition. Here, take this"—I wrote down the number for Jericho Sims and handed it to her—"these guys can help you."

Adamit said, "I've decided to have Jacob head-up base security. Becky and I will stay focused on keeping you alive."

Jacob unrolled his plans for the base and laid them out on the table. He pointed to them as he spoke. "Double fences here, security lighting here and here. The front gate will be here. We'll have armed personnel, closed-circuit cameras throughout the property, and dogs."

"Excellent. Thank you, Jacob." I turned to Crash. "Our spacecraft should be around thirty feet long, hold three people, and look like this." I sketched a scaled-down version of *Penelope One*, the space-shuttle-looking plane I'd seen in Grandpa's Box. "I was hoping you could find somebody back at Caltech that could help with the design and construction. Well, guys, I guess that's it for now. Thanks."

I pulled Crash in close and said, "Can you assemble the Sphere? I'll need it for tomorrow's meeting."

He brought me into his bedroom, removed the dogs-playing-poker picture from the wall, opened the safe, and handed me the sphere. "I kinda already put it back together."

"Good. Keep it locked up."

"Where to?" Adamit asked as I headed over to my car.

"I'm running low on funds and I'm hungry; let's go grab some lunch and then head over to Caesars."

He tucked himself in behind the steering wheel and started the engine.

"Hey," I said, "where did you get the keys?"

He flashed me a pie-eating grin. "I made a copy of them."

During lunch, I told him the details of my most recent vision—including his demise. "You took a bullet for me, Adamit. I'm pretty sure you died. Anyway... now that we know about it, we can prevent it, right? I suggest we kill Colton Hill and tell Dings to go back to Brooklyn. The sooner, the better."

"I've never had to kill anyone before," he said. "There was the war, of course, but I couldn't say for a fact I actually killed anyone. I never really aimed to kill."

"Wait, you were in Nam?"

"Nooo. WWI. I'm an old fart, remember?"

"Oh, yeah. But hey, you don't have to kill anyone, I was just blue-skying it: talking out loud. Let's just get 'em first. Then we can figure out what to do with them. Alright?"

Cagey was manning his station at Caesars Sportsbook. He gave us a nod and I handed him my betting receipt.

"Yeah," he said, inspecting it. "This was a push. Do you want your money back, or do you want to let it ride?"

"What are the odds for tomorrow's game? Czech hockey versus the USA?"

He grabbed a clipboard and gave it a look. "For you, even odds."

Adamit stepped up to the window and had a private talk with Cagey. A minute later he turned to me and said, "I got your odds up to 2:1."

"Is my credit still good?" I asked Cagey.

"You have a hundred thousand credit on the push, plus a two hundred and twenty-thousand-dollar line of house credit."

"Well then, that's my bet. All of it—"

"Seth, wait!" interrupted Adamit. "Are you sure? Remember what I said about things changing?"

I pulled him aside. "I have to make these bets before this timeline gets all screwy." I confirmed the bet with Cagey, turned to Adamit, and said, "Well, I'm done for the day: what about you?"

He nudged me forward. "For starters, let's get you out of here." We were both on full alert, and for good reason: just outside the casino's doors was the parking lot where Colton and Dings would try to kill us.

CHAPTER 54

"Boy am I glad you're on our team," I told Adamit after we got in the car. "Do you know how intimidating you are?"

"What do you think about a lion for the base?" he asked as he started the car. "He could run patrol between the double fences. Jacob would take care of him."

"Are you messing with me? A lion?"

"No, I'm serious. His name is Virgil. Virgil Caine. Would you like to go see him?"

Hmm, wasn't our base on the moon named Virgil? "Ahh... sure, why not? Yeah, let's go see this Virgil Caine of yours."

Forty minutes later we arrived at St. Francis Exotic Animal Rescue.

Falling apart and in need of repair, the rescue itself was on its last legs. A feeble old man struggled to open a creaky entrance gate. The noise triggered a frenzied chorus of screeching monkeys, birds and other wild things. That was, until the thunderous roar of a lion quieted the cacophony.

"Hello, who goes there?" said the old man. His voice was low on air. "Be you animal-friend or animal-foe?"

The old man held a thin walking stick, and his eyes were sealed shut with cataracts.

"Lucien, it's me," said Adamit, as we walked over to the Sammy-Davis-lookalike. "I'm with a friend. We've come to see Virgil."

From under his tattered poncho, the old man reached out a bony hand and felt the bulk of Adamit.

"Adamit!" he said excitedly. "Come in, come in. Thank heavens you got my message."

"Lucien," said Adamit. "This is Seth. I'm working for him now. He's going to save Man from the darkness."

The old man surveyed my face. "I save dangerous animals, and you save a malicious species—how extraordinary."

After some talk concerning the well-being of Katya, Becky, and Jacob, Lucien brought us into a menagerie of animals he'd saved from imminent death. There were at least fifty cages of varying sizes. Most were empty, but here and there a cage contained an odd assortment of critters: a dirt-soiled peacock, a troop of hyper-curious spider monkeys, a one-armed sloth, an angry warthog, and a wingless eagle.

"This," Lucien said, as we made our way over to the largest of the cages, "is Mr. Virgil Caine."

The African lion was gaunt, had mange, and was despondent. Adamit opened the metal door, went in, and knelt down next to the lion. He spoke a few encouraging words, then began scratching an area behind the cat's ears.

Lucien let out a weak laugh, then coughed into a bloody handkerchief a few times.

"Angel or Devil be callin' for me directly," he said. "Doctors say I've got the cancer. Sure be grateful iffin' you folks could help old Virgil out. He's royalty, Mr. Bridges. His father was Leo the MGM movie lion." Lucien continued, his voice becoming labored. "Most all the other animals have new homes; the SPCA and friends are helping out. They say they can't take Virgil. Iffin' they do, they'll have to put him down." He began to tremble. "Lord knows I can't die with that on my conscience."

Adamit waved me over. "C'mon in and say hello. Don't worry; he likes people—except for the bastard that had his claws and balls removed."

I knelt down, next to Virgil and Adamit, in a shit-and-straw-filled cage. The cat was under-weight and his eyes were glazed over with some kind of big-cat respiratory infection. I scratched behind his ears while he purred for his life.

"Alright," I said. "Now what?"

"Well, you're going to stay here and keep him calm. I'm going to get a sedative from Lucien's trailer and inject it into our hairy friend. Then, we put him in the back of your car and take him to my place. Jacob should have his pen set up at the base by morning."

This had been the plan all along. Save Virgil Caine. I liked it: everything about it seemed so right.

We loaded the exiled King of Beasts into the back of the Maserati. When it was time for our final goodbyes, Lucien sobbed into Adamit's chest.

"People and animals must learn to love one another," he said. "Then they can fight the darkness together."

The added weight of the stinky snoring lion bottomed out the car's suspension—exaggerating every crack in the road. On the outskirts of Vegas, Adamit bought fifty pounds of meat from a butcher shop. At the Lees', and with the assistance of Jacob and Becky, we dragged and hefted the groggy Mr. Caine into the Lee's living room.

Then, I drove home: Becky rode shotgun.

CHAPTER 55

"Payroll's been set up, and your paychecks will be issued on the first of every month," said Margie, getting our morning meeting off to a pleasant start. Just then, everyone turned toward the sound of the front door opening and closing.

"Sí. I trabajo too?"

It was Marisol. Dean dropped to his knees. Dammit! Now *he* was acting weird. Adamit stood and bowed.

Katya went to Marisol and said, "Buenos dias, Marisol. Bienvenido."

I was both surprised and relieved to see Marisol. I thought I had hired her the other night at dinner—but in what capacity?

"Marisol, how are you?" I said as I got up and gave her a slight embrace. "I was worried about you. You left so quickly the other night." Before she could answer, I turned to our team. "For those of you who are not familiar, this is Marisol. She'll be working with us."

Marisol offered everyone a polite smile, released Adamit's bow with a nod, then laid a hand on Dean's shoulder. Dean returned to his chair and rubbed at his eyes. Marisol spoke a continuous stream of Spanish.

Katya interpreted: "Marisol says she is feeling first-rate this morning. She would like to know if this is the place where she'll be working? Also, she wants you to know that she is a skilled cleaner and a flavorful cook."

Becky hopped off her chair and ushered Marisol into the seat next to mine. Marisol sat, smiled, and said, "We work now?"

I nodded with a grin. "Yes, Marisol, we work now."

Margie picked up where she'd left off. "If you have any questions for me, I'll be in the real estate office a few doors down." She turned to Marisol. "It was very nice to meet you." As Margie left, she came over and whispered in my ear, "You need to fill that bank account of yours."

Jacob stood on his chair and gave his report, then added, "We have acquired Mr. Virgil Caine, a ten-year-old African lion that will be part of our security team at the base—he's there now."

Dean jutted his fist into the air. "Right on, brother-man!"

Jacob continued, "Virgil will patrol the base's perimeter with four dogs that arrived yesterday. They're puppies right now, but I'm going to train them—"

Marisol jumped to her feet and exclaimed, "I help Jacob!"

"That would be fantastic," said Jacob. "But for now, I have to get back to the base. Mr. Bridges, would it be OK if I moved into the barracks? With so much work, it would be easier if I just lived there."

"Sure," I said, "that sounds—"

"I too," said Marisol, waving her hand in the air.

"Yeah. OK, sure," I said, nodding to both of them. "That'd be great."

They left together, holding hands—like children.

Marisol was such a strange one. How had she gotten here? Had she just said she was going to live at the base?

"Hey, Dean," I said, "what's with the kneeling crap?"

He nodded at Katya.

"Alright. Katya," I said. "Your turn. Tell me, what do you know about Marisol?"

"Seth," she said, pushing my mind with her words. "All you have to do is ask her."

It seemed logical. Just ask her. Yeah, that's what I would do—I'd ask her. "OK," I said. "Who's next?"

"Should we do the demo now?" asked Crash.

That was when it hit me. He was the real genius here. He had built the GRD—made it work. Sure, it wasn't his idea, but it was his design. I gave him a nod.

"People," I said. "Crash, one of the most brilliant minds on the planet, will now demonstrate our proprietary advantage."

There was a smattering of applause as he cleared the tabletop and tethered the sphere to it.

"OK, everyone," he said, "if you don't mind, I need you to stand back." He made a few adjustments to the sphere's tether, then started in on a prepared speech. "Ahem... um... Seth's grandfather devoted his life to untangling the compositional fabric of gravity itself—a force that, up until now, eluded all who sought to enslave it. I say up until now because he—Seth's grandfather—succeeded in divining the true nature of gravity. And what I'm about to show you is the result of a life spent doing what it was meant to. Ladies and gentlemen, I present to you... oh... hold on, just give me a sec." He adjusted a dial at the base of the sphere. "OK, here we go." Nothing happened. He opened up the sphere and tweaked some inner workings. "OK, it should work now." He turned the dial. Again, nothing happened.

Katya took hold of his hand and ushered him into the spare bedroom. She must have used her Shifter magic on him, because when they returned a minute later, Crash made a correction to one of the wires and said, "Ladies and gentlemen, I present to you the one and only Gravity Resist Drive—or, as I like to call it, the GRD."

The sphere rose up from his hand, tightened up on the tether, and floated two feet above the tabletop. Crash proudly said, "Welcome to the future!"

Everyone teetered between clapping and incomprehension. Crash lowered the sphere, untethered it, and handed it to me. The office slipped into silence—except for the muffled sounds of the outside world, a world that would, undoubtedly, and in short order, demand entry.

Dean slammed his fists on the table and yelled, "Whoo-hoo! We're gonna eat cheese and crackers on the moon!"

"I know some people that can help us," Katya said.

"OK guys," I said. "What you just saw is proprietary. You cannot discuss it with anyone."

After the meeting ended, I took hold of Crash's shoulders and said, "You did it!"

"Thanks, boss. Sorry I doubted you earlier."

"No problem: great work. Go ahead and take the weekend off, see the sights. But lock up the sphere first."

CHAPTER 56

Adamit drove me to the base; it was alive with electricians, painters, plumbers, and roofers—all pounding repairs into the property. We went over to Jacob and Marisol, who were at a newly erected cage; they were draping puppies over Virgil our lion. The big cat licked the rambunctious pups with motherly affection. Someone had bathed him and he appeared to smile as he looked up at us.

"Aren't they terrific?" Jacob said. He pointed to a Labrador mix. "That's General Lee, and that one over there," he said, pointing to a scrawny short-legged runt of a dog, "that's Double Lee. He's a Corsican rat hound. The cutie next to him, that's Dixie. She's a tree-walking coonhound. And that last one," he said, nodding to an awkward looking red pup that was licking Marisol's ankles, "that one is Heidi. I haven't figured her out yet."

I kneeled down and gave the pup a soft pat. "So you're Heidi."

Marisol, who was barefoot and wore a tunic dress, came over, scooped up the big-pawed puppy, and kissed it. "I work hard, help Jacob. Sí?"

"Do you *really* want to live here?" I asked.

"Sí, Mr. Seth. I cook, clean, help Jacob with animals. I have dinero for rental."

"No, no. That's not what I meant... Are you happy here?"

"Yes, Mr. Bridges. Muy happily."

I just looked at her—amazed, trapping her image in my mind. She released the pup and walked away.

"Hey Jacob," I asked, watching Marisol walk away. "What's with the names?"

He jutted his chin out. "General Robert E. Lee was our great grandpappy. These dogs will remind us who we are... where we came from."

Adamit came over and said, "She's keeping you at bay. Slow down and enjoy it: you can't rush these things. A candle that burns from both ends burns half as long."

"Now, I know that corny-ass trite didn't come from Master Poe. Come on, let's go see if Vinny has any new info."

Vinny wasn't around at the pizza place—probably hiding in the back—but we were happy to partake in his *free food for life* offer.

Toward the end of lunch, Adamit wiped his face and said, "Let me get this straight: you're a Shifter with the gift of visions, and you have a box containing information from the future. Am I leaving anything out?"

I slurped the last of my soda. "Well, sometimes I call myself from the future—you know, on the telephone."

He cocked an eyebrow and scrutinized my face. "You don't say?"

I thought about a scene from the movie *Bill and Ted's Excellent Adventure*: in the scene, Bill and Ted have traveled forward in time and need keys to get into a building. So they agreed that when they went back in time, they would hide the keys behind the bush. Then, they looked behind the bush and the keys were there.

"Hey Adamit," I said. "Let's try something. Give me a random word, any word."

"Olive."

"Good word. Now, watch this." I looked at the clock and the sign with the phone number for take-out, then wrote on a napkin: *On 2/14/80, at 12:05 P.M. PST, call Vinny's New York Style Pizza, tel#702-555-6959. Ask for Adamit Lee and say the word OLIVE.*

I covered the note with my other hand and wrote: *Also, have present-day Adamit tell me about Marisol.* I put the napkin in my breast pocket, and somewhere in the back, a phone rang.

One of the cooks called out, "Phone call for Mr. Adamit Lee."

Adamit went to the counter, then returned a minute later.

"So," I said. "Do you have something to tell me?"

He gave me a poker-faced, "No."

"Who was it?" I asked.

"It was me, calling myself from the future. Very enlightening."

"What'd you say? I mean to yourself?"

Adamit polished off the last of his drink, crushed a few ice cubes in the back of his mouth and said, "He—or rather *me*, in the future—said the word *olive* and that today would be the best day of my life." He stood up. "Let's get outta here; you're starting to give me the heebie-jeebies."

"Yeah, well, welcome to my world."

On the way out of Vinny's I spotted a payphone. Thoughts of Marisol were vexing me—I couldn't get her out of my mind, and Love had begun to project her face onto reflective surfaces. Fortunately, it was Valentine's Day, a perfect excuse to let my intentions be known. I dropped a few coins into its coin slot and called Jericho Sims.

"Jericho Sims," said a pleasant voice at the end of the line. "What is it that we can get for you today, Mr. Bridges?"

"Yes, I would like to order—for delivery—a large commercial refrigerator, a week's worth of fresh food for two, and a butchered cow."

"Understood. And the address?" Huh, that was easy enough. I gave the operator the address for the base and told him to put the delivery on the first floor of the barracks building. "Will there be anything else?" he asked.

"Yeah—I want a heart-shaped box filled with fine chocolates and a large bouquet of flowers sent to the same location. Put on the card: For Marisol, Happy Valentine's Day. From: Seth. How do I pay for this?"

Adamit shook his head with a grin. After a short pause, the operator said, "This account is paid by the Las Vegas Player's Complementary Network; is there anything else I can help you with today?"

"No. That'll do it, thanks."

"What?" I said to Adamit as I hung up. "What's so damn funny?"

He shook his huge head and said, "You're one messed-upped sad sack of a Shifter."

"Ha, ha, ha, very funny. Come on, let's go."

Just then, Cyrus Willhammer's black-cherry Rolls Royce pulled up alongside us. Kogo—the exotic hottie who had saved me in my visions, as well as kidnapped me for Cyrus—rolled her window down and said, "Master Willhammer invite you for tea."

Adamit appeared to be enchanted with Kogo. He fixed his eyes on her, and he said, "What's your name?"

"My name Kogo," she snorted with indignation.

"Why does your master wish to see us?" Adamit continued.

"Master see Seth only." Her obsidian eyes unnervingly accented her jet-black, perfectly even, eyelid-length bangs. In a blink, she was out of the Rolls and striding a confident beeline toward me. Adamit hefted himself like a charging rhinoceros in an attempt to intercept her. She tacked, and in a blur, straddled his back and held a thin blade to his throat.

"We no die today comrade Shifter," she said. "Today, we live!" She bit into his earlobe, slapped his bottom, and backed away with a bemusing, "Ha, ha, ha."

I climbed into the back seat of the Rolls. "C'mon, Adamit, get in. That's Lieutenant Musashi, and she's on our side. She just doesn't know it yet."

Adamit grabbed at his injured earlobe, looked for some blood, then joined me in the back seat.

Kogo drove us to Cyrus's private entrance at the Stardust Casino.

CHAPTER 57

We took the elevator up to the top floor. When the doors slid open, Cyrus greeted us with a hearty, "Welcome my children. Welcome."

He was seated at the end of the long, carpeted runway, on a high-backed chair that resembled a throne. Three-foot-tall vases that contained huge bouquets of brightly colored flowers paralleled the carpeted walkway. At his side sat Penelope, in a chair similar to his, but more feminine. She wore a silky red gown with a severely flared white collar that exaggerated her comic-book-villainess persona. The hyenas were there—one on Cyrus's left, the other to the right of Penelope.

Things were different this time. We were allowed to keep our weapons, and the mood was less confrontational.

Kogo cleared her throat, stomped one foot, and stated, "Now you bow before your masters."

We just stood there—defiant. Cyrus waved Kogo off and said, "I would not expect anything less from the two of you.Please, come closer. I have a proposition."

As we got close, Cyrus opened his arms in a grand gesture and said, "Sit. Please." Shadow servants placed two chairs at the end of the walkway. "I mean you no harm," Cyrus continued. "Are we not all friends here?"

The hyenas tugged at their chains and vocalized their excitement with high-pitched giggles—that was, until Adamit shot them a glance. Then, they just cowered and whimpered. We sat. I could hear movement from the darkened areas of the room—probably sharpshooters waiting for provocation.

I wasn't sure how these two old Shifters fit into the scheme of things, but it didn't matter. I was fed up with all the theater and drama, and something inside grew angry. I stood up, kicked my chair backward and yelled, "Why are we here?" Mechanical clicking sounds and hyena whines squeaked into the air.

Penelope leapt to her feet. "Stop! Seth, I'm sorry. It's just... This is how we do things. Please, sit down. We like you. And Mr. Lee, don't take any of this personally; you know how much we respect you."

Adamit righted my chair, and we both sat back down.

"Mr. Bridges," Cyrus said, his voice calm. "You now sit before me, having escaped your fate. I have misjudged you—a mistake I shall not repeat. As you have probably garnered, I am an extraordinarily wealthy man with equally expensive tastes. It's not easy to find a beneficence for someone you love." He picked and released a rogue thread from his trousers. "Have you ever been in *love*...?" Before I could answer, he continued. "You see Mr. Bridges, Penelope and I have shared centuries together. Today is Valentine's Day—our anniversary." He turned to Penelope and gave her an affectionate smile. "I wish to demonstrate my love for her, let her know how much she means to me. And most of all, how I'd be lost without her."

He snapped his thumb and finger together. A henchman lumped over a duffel bag, unzipped it, and revealed its contents: bundles and bundles of hundred-dollar bills.

"Mr. Bridges," Cyrus said. "Do you mind if I call you Seth?"

"Sure... I mean, go ahead."

"Well, Seth, I understand the wheels of progress have begun to turn for you. I'd like to help, and in return, I was hoping you could assist me. You see, I wish to purchase a vision from you and give it to Penelope, my one true love." He turned to Penelope, gave her a Tiger Woods *yeah, I just sunk that birdie* nodding grimace. "I suppose," he continued, turning back to me. "I could take it from you, but now that we are all friends..." He gestured to the cash. "You will be paid five million dollars for the vision. You do believe in love... don't you?"

I looked at Adamit. He appeared calm, but his breathing rate had increased, and there was sweat beading up on his forehead. It was a tempting deal: I needed the money, and Cyrus wanted to show off for his really-old girlfriend.

"Mr. Willhammer," I said. "Do you mind if I call you Cyrus?"

He opened and closed his gloved fingers a few times, then offered a tolerant nod.

"Well, *Cyrus*," I said. "I can't *just* have a vision. It doesn't work that way."

He snapped his fingers. Shadow people placed a small table next to me. On it was a shot glass filled with the same stinky, syrupy liquid he had me drink the last time I was here.

"Your drink," Cyrus said, "contains a mild sedative and an agent that should induce a vision. Do we have a deal?"

I nodded and downed the stinky, soy-sauce-flavored concoction before Adamit could protest.

A stringed quartet, tucked-in behind the shadows, began playing a hypnotic melody—construction music for my subconscious. As I closed my eyelids and entered the time-stretching, unbalanced-washing-machine consciousness teleporter, Cyrus and Penelope each placed a hand on my forehead.

I found myself looking out into the void of space, my face inches from the safer side of a polycarbonate viewport. Outside, various-sized spacecraft were in the process of arriving or departing. An info-burst spilled-out from my Cog-Link: This was the Suo Gan Space Station, I was an Artificial, a captain, and I was about to undertake the most important mission of my life. I looked down at the dock and saw the largest and fastest transport ship in the sector, the *Kogo Maru,* the only fleet ship equipped with an Algeronian slip drive. She was taking on supplies. A familiar melody caught my attention. To my left, Cyrus was behind a piano and playing the song "The Moon is a Harsh Mistress." Penelope sat atop the piano and sang the lyrics, but she was no Linda Ronstadt.

Like a memory inside a dream, it felt real—more real than Chicago playing "25 or 6 to 4" in a club called Purgatorium, in a time that now seemed like a memory.

I had no time for reminiscing. Today is a special day, I thought, an important day. Images of my crew, mingling in the alcove behind me, reflected off the viewport. I smiled with pride. Four women, three men. All of them were outfitted with state-of-the-art implants and upgrades. They were the best Modern Cause crewmen I'd ever served with, and they'd been chosen because they had nothing left to lose—at least in this time period.

I turned to them. "Good morning, people. I take it you've managed to violate all shore-leave protocols?"

Chief Petty Officer Anna Milken stood straight and performed a brisk salute to her swollen, black-and-blue eye socket, and said, "Sir, yes sir!"

I returned her salute. "At ease, Chief."

Quartermaster Moko "Gasman" Madrid stuck his head into a waste bin, which he'd tucked between his knees, and threw up. Just then, my trusted companion Heidissa, who was our Flight Surgeon and an ART, skipped on in, looking as fresh as a spring flower on a warm Iconium day. She looked back to the gate where her beefed-up man-toy waved an unsure goodbye.

"Don't take any wooden nickels," she said, loud enough for all of us to hear.

"You're late, Doc," I said.

She gave me a confident smile, went to Gasman, and began massaging a nerve bundle at the base of his skull.

"Star-humping-tastic," I said. "Now please, everyone, I need your full attention; there have been some critical developments we need to discuss. As most of you know, Project Appleseed has been near and dear to my heart for as long as I can remember."

Our chrono navigator and astro-pilot—who was also the younger sister of our chief petty officer—downed a nipple of Teater juice and said, "You ain't got no heart, Cappy."

"I was speaking metaphorically. And Milli," I said, eyeing the empty nip, "shore leave is over."

She pulled another from her vest, opened it, and said, "Chrono says I got ten more tics." She downed it and let out a satisfied burp. Then, after drop-kicking the empty nips in the direction of Cyrus's tip bowl, she gave me a crisp salute and said, "CyNav-pilot Commander Alyssa Milken reporting for duty. *Sir!*"

I waved off her salute. "Please Milli, just sit down, will you? I'm trying to tell you something. Now, as I was saying—ahh, screw it. We're replacing the command crew on the *Kogo Maru*. Project Appleseed is ours. I don't need to remind you that we're not coming back, at least to this time period. You have one hour to get your affairs in order."

The space station began to vibrate with a rumble: slow at first, then faster. The consciousness of future-me exchanged places with present-me. Then, I was back in the lair of Cyrus Willhammer.

The two hyenas were looking at me curiously—their heads tilted. Cyrus and Penelope removed their hands from my forehead.

The string quartet quieted as Penelope clapped her hands and shrieked, "Magnificent!"

One of the shadow people scurried over, misted Cyrus's hand with a solution from a spray bottle, and wiped it dry.

"Was that one of your visions?" Cyrus asked as he put his glove on.

I longed to rejoin my crew on that space station. After dragging my sleeve across my forehead in an attempt to wipe away any of Cyrus's lingering hand-germs, I said, "How do you get into my visions?"

"I ask you again," he said in a not-so-friendly tone. "Was that a vision of the future?"

"Yeah, sure. That was the future, alright."

He began to goose-step around the room. His voice cracked as he said, "This changes everything. Mother will be so pleased." He turned to me and Adamit. "You must go now. I will summon you shortly."

He gestured to someone in the back of the room, and twenty nubile humans, costumed in the attire of different time-periods, emerged from the shadows and began to perform in the light of their master.

CHAPTER 58

Adamit stuffed the bundles of cash back into the duffle bag, hauled it up over his shoulder, then herded Kogo and myself into the elevator.

Ram Jam's hit song "Black Betty" shouted down from the elevator's speakers.

"Four-point-two billion people are going to die an early death," I said, fascinated by the elevators' indicator lights. I was loopy from whatever had been in that shot glass. "Or maybe it's four-point-four? Anyway, after that we are going to plant human colonies all around the universe. Hey Adamit, do you think Cyrus and Penelope are going to bump uglies all night?"

Adamit shook his head.

"Hey," I said, "Cheer up! Today is the best day of your life. Remember?" I turned to Kogo, who was holding me up. "And you, Musashi." I planted a sloppy kiss on her cheek. "Adamit, I insist you hire this glorious creature, right now."

The elevator doors opened. We went outside; a town car waited for us. Kogo helped me get settled into the back seat. Adamit put the duffel bag of cash next to me, then went to Kogo and said, "Come with us."

"I cannot," she said. "Timing is wrong. Go. Soon we meet again."

Adamit got in, closed the door, and looked at Kogo through the glass.

"Hey," I said. "You're not going to leave her here, are you?"

He growled with determination as he opened the door and pulled Kogo inside. I wasn't sure what had happened between Kogo and Adamit while I was sauced-up and on that Suo Gan Space Station, but the back of the town car was now the scene of two schooners colliding in the fog. It was fascinating to watch. When Kogo ripped her shirt open and pressed her breasts into his scarred face, I crawled past the divider, got into the front seat, and told the driver to take us back to Vinny's.

When we got there, I grabbed the duffle bag, stashed it in the back of my car, and began to drive off.

Adamit, who had managed to untangle himself from Kogo's rigging, shouted, "Seth. Stop! Hold on!"

"I'll be at my place," I hollered. "I'll be fine. Take a break. And remember, this is the best day of your life."

I pulled onto the main boulevard and punched the accelerator. What the...? Love sat in the passenger seat. He tilted its head and smiled.

"Hey!" I said. "I'm doing the best I can. And anyway, I'm not so sure I can handle you and Marisol. I mean, I'm very, very, busy. And you're so... You're so needy." I pulled into the right-hand lane, turned to Love, and said, "You know what? You're like an animal in heat: it's disgusting. And furthermore, you should take a good look at yourself in the mirror. Ask yourself who you really are—and I mean the real you."

He nodded his head.

"Good," I said. "Now get in the backseat and behave yourself." He did as I wished.

In addition to the antics of Love, and the voices that sounded like whispers swimming through fan blades in my head, horns were honking, traffic lights were changing, and I had to avoid the fuzzy blurry things that were flying about my peripherals. It seemed Cyrus's stinky soy sauce was still swirling in my brain. Vegas and the people it contained were all out of sync—like an acid trip. Dean had once warned me about taking hallucinogens. Fuck! Had I just been a captain on a starship? Yeah, Seth, you were...

I made it to my apartment and stuffed the bundles of cash into the apartment's safe. In an attempt to get back to normal, I took a long shower. *Seek nothing and all will be revealed:* Master Poe's words of wisdom rained out of the showerhead with comfort and calm. The philosophy was corny and simplistic, but at the moment, it made perfect sense. With my eyes closed and the warm water pulsing down, I was able to see glimpses of the big picture, the kit and caboodle of the universe, comprehending the incomprehensible. The stuff that made up the more-realer-than-real.

I was drying off when I saw, from the edge of the mirror, something move. Damn it, I thought. I had left my gun in the living room. I wrapped a towel around my waist, turned sideways and slowly peered into the bedroom. It was Marisol; she smiled.

"Marisol!" I said. "What are you doing here?"

Her hands were cupped in front of her chest. "I know St. Valentine," she said. "He was good man. You too good man. Thank you for flowers." Then, she un-cupped her hands and gently blew a red, heart-shaped orb of glowing fog at me. "Happy Valentine's Day, Señor Bridges."

The fog swarmed me, invigorating my senses. Marisol shrugged her shoulders and let her tunic fall to the floor. And except for her necklace, she stood naked before me.

She placed her arms around my waist, released my towel, and whispered, "I bet on you."

Her touch felt natural, as if we had been together for our entire lives. She eased me backward and onto the bed. I attempted to slow her down, let her know that I didn't want to take advantage of her. But she would have none of it. She kissed me and I knew Love had been right. Marisol and I were right. The fear of losing myself vanished, because it was ridiculous. I kissed her back. And as I paid nature's toll, something remarkable happened: I left my body and was transported, along with Marisol, to another world.

The futuristic world was chrome and glass, and tall and rounded, and had clean features that were hard to define. And it was void of people—just orbs of energy interacting with each other. As I turned to reassure Marisol that no harm would come to her, we were suddenly somewhere else: in a dank noisy jungle. We were standing outside a burrow that had been dug into an earthen mound. Three jaguars played cautiously in the opening. I took hold of Marisol's hand and things turned dark. I tried to perform my dream test and somehow get us out of there, but it didn't work. Then, images of death and war played out before us, over and over. It was hard to discern time, and I wasn't sure if we'd been transporting around for moments, minutes, or hours.

I remembered telling Marisol, "Don't be afraid, Marisol, I'll protect you."

CHAPTER 59

The morning sun slipped through a gap in the curtains and found me in bed—alone. Sounds from the kitchen called me in. Becky, who stood on a chair in front of the stove, was cooking breakfast. I looked around, but no Marisol. Had last night been just another dream? Becky climbed down from the chair and handed me a cup of coffee.

"Marisol left with Jacob," she said, studying my underwear with a scrunched-up face. "They went to the base. Oh, and you won your bet last night. The Americans beat the Czechs seven to three."

I took a seat and attempted to recall the events of the previous day. Becky put a plate of pancakes in front of me and said, "Long day, huh? Yesterday?"

"Yeah. Hey, Becky, what time did Marisol leave last night?"

"Virgil had some problems around midnight—trouble breathing. Jacob thought Marisol could help."

I set my fork down. "Why would Jacob think Marisol could help Virgil?"

I remembered the ball of fog she had blown at me last night, and that strange dream I had had with her in it... had it been a dream? Had I performed a dream test? It didn't matter: I felt content enough to scrap all my plans and run away with her. Just me and Marisol, getting back to the basics, like normal people.

"Well," Becky said, pouring me a glass of orange juice, "Marisol's more than she appears to be. A whole lot more."

"Yeah. You can say that again."

Crash, Margie, and Marisol were no-shows for our morning meeting. Dean gave us an update on the renovations, then Katya told us she had located a DC-4 transport plane.

I finished the meeting by saying, "People, we *are* going to outer space. Yesterday I had one of my little episodes, and guess what? We did it. We conquered space."

With the meeting adjourned, Adamit and I drove to Caesars.

It was in the parking lot, near the fountains, that Adamit shut the car down and said, "What's up, boss? You seem kind of quiet. Did I do something wrong?"

"No, no," I answered. Thoughts of Marisol wracked my mind. I felt empty inside—lost. "It's Marisol. I think I'm falling for her."

He chuckled a bit. "That makes two of us. Kogo, that girl you want me to hire. Well, she went all ninja on my ass last night—for six hours. Best day of my life, even if I do say so myself."

"Did you hire her?"

"Working on it."

"Don't take no for an answer."

At the sportsbook, I let my winnings from the Czech USA game ride on 2:1 odds that, tonight, team USA would beat Norway.

We were on full guard mode as we left Caesars and headed over to the base.

When we arrived, Virgil leaped onto the car's hood and roared an enthusiastic welcome right into the windshield. Jacob and Marisol helped him down. I looked at Marisol. It had been six or seven hours since we'd been together, but it felt like years.

Jacob slung himself over Virgil's back. "Look, Seth. He's all better. Marisol made him better."

Sounds of compressors pumping air and hammers hitting nails echoed throughout the property.

I turned to Adamit, handed him a stack of cash, and said, "Do me a favor. Give each of the workers a couple grand; I'm gonna go talk with Marisol."

He gave me a nod, exited the car, and headed toward the sounds of progress. I went to Marisol. I wanted to ask her if she'd had the same dream. But when I reached for her, she pulled back.

"Mr. Bridges," she said, "I work now." Then, she walked away as if I had offended her.

I stood there in the hot morning sun, next to my stupid Maserati Ghibli SS Coupe. Heidi—the puppy that was so ugly it was cute—looked up at me and squeaked out a bark.

I kneeled, pulled her close, and said, "Aren't you the lucky one. Did you know I'm fifty-eight years old, and I still don't understand women?" She licked my face a few times, and I released her.

For no fathomable reason, I drove into the desert, pulled out my .38, and began shooting up a squadron of abandoned mailboxes. Then it came to me: go home, and open Grandpa's Box. It might have info on Marisol and her heart-shaped orbs of fog.

I chased mental images of Marisol back to my apartment, wolfed down some leftovers, poured a drink, and started my query. I looked for hours but could not find any mention of her in the Box. Although, I did learn a lot of other interesting stuff:

our first spacecraft, *Penelope One,* would have a single chemical propellant engine that provided maneuverability through a series of mechanically controlled thrusters. In addition to providing vertical lift, the Gravity Resist Drive would, upon re-entry, decrease our rate of descent and minimize frictional heat buildup. Our navigation systems were rudimentary and would consist of a compass, an altimeter, and a homing beacon tracker, but mostly line-of-sight. Communications would be a side-band/ham radio and a standard wide-band avionics unit. Temperature-controlled pressure suits and redundant oxygen supply systems would keep us alive and breathing. Our first voyage into space would last one minute and forty-seven seconds. I wrote it all down, then returned the Box to the safe.

The sun was about to set when I heard someone enter the apartment; it was Becky. She held her .410-bore sawed-off shotgun at her side.

"Just me boss. You OK?"

She laid the gun on the coffee table and turned on the TV. Life had dealt her a crap hand, but she was more composed than any other woman I've known. I poured her a drink and set it next to her. A rerun of *All in the Family* played on the screen. Archie was yelling at Meathead, Gloria was crying, and Edith, while drying her hands with her apron, shrieked, "Everything is fine."

I kissed Becky goodnight and went to bed.

CHAPTER 60

"Good morning everyone," I said to the whole InEvitech crew, now crowded around the office's kitchen table—so crowded that a few people spilled into the adjoining rooms. Margie began to say something, but I held her off with a wave. I grabbed a half-gallon orange juice container from the trash and held it up horizontally.

"People, *this* is our new DC-4 transport." With my free hand, I held a crumpled-up paper coffee cup. "And *this* is our yet to be built spacecraft." I brought the cup to the underside of the orange juice container. "We will fasten our spacecraft to the belly of the DC-4." I lifted the half-gallon container and crumpled-up coffee-cup higher. "At thirty-thousand feet, the DC-4 will release the spacecraft and remain airborne to monitor the spacecraft's progress." I handed the OJ container to Dean while keeping hold of the coffee cup. "The spacecraft will engage our Gravity Resist Drive, rise vertically into near-earth space, and deploy a communications satellite." I stood on my chair, lifted the coffee cup higher, tore-off a piece of the cup, and tossed it upwards. "After the satellite deployment, we will maneuver our spacecraft back into Earth's atmosphere." I stepped down from the chair. "From there, we just glide her on home and land." I lowered the cup, made some engine noises, and set it down on an open section of the kitchen table.

"Sí. Is good plan," said Marisol, as she raised her hand. "You call ship *One Hope*."

Marisol had given me a new perspective on life, but Grandpa's Box had indicated the craft would be named *Penelope One*, not *One Hope*. Adamit and Katya immediately seconded Marisol's motion. This would be interesting, I thought: changing the history contained within the Box.

I gave Marisol a nod. "Very well, the name of our first spaceship will be *One Hop*. Now, who's next?"

"The DC-4 is landing today," Katya said. "I'll need a check for 375k." She handed everyone a small box. "I've taken the liberty to design business cards for each of you. I hope you like them."

"Now that's progress," I said.

"Excuse me for interrupting, Mr. Bridges," said Margie. "But I want to let you—all of you—know that I'm on board full time now."

Becky lifted her coffee cup and loudly said, "To Margie."

We all cheered, "To Margie."

"Well, that's good news," I said, "because I've already added your name to this account"—I handed her a four-million-dollar bank deposit receipt—"You're cleared to write that check for the DC-4. And while you're at it, go ahead and pay off the remaining balance on the base and any outstanding bills. OK. Who's next?"

"The bulk of the renovations should be wrapped up in three days," said Dean. "I'm flying in some specialists to go over the tower's electronics. They're hitching a ride on the DC-4 and should be arriving sometime this morning."

"Excellent," I said. "How's the..."

After the meeting ended, I had Adamit drive me to my apartment. I retrieved the Box from the safe.

"Watch this," I said as I pulled up the first flight of InEvitech on the holographic display.

The change had happened! Our first flight into space would be on a ship named *One Hope*. Not *Penelope One*. My mind whirled with the implications. The Box was adaptive, organic... alive.

"Adamit," I said. "Yesterday this said that our spaceship would be called *Penelope One*, and now it says our ship will be called *One Hope*; do you know what that means?"

"Yes. I do," he said. His unflappable demeanor remaining true. "You and the Transdifferentiational Probability Matrix Attenuator seem to be working well together."

I closed the Box. "Transdifferentiational Probability Matrix Attenuator? Huh... You hungry?" I asked as I returned the Box to the safe.

CHAPTER 61

We grabbed a booth at an almost empty Purgatorium.

"Tonight's the night Colton makes his move," Adamit said after our meals arrived.

"Caesars Palace, after the hockey game." I nodded in agreement.

A disturbance at the door caught our attention.

Penelope and Cyrus were demanding an exception to the no firearm's policy. After relenting to house rules, they and their entourage of twelve bodyguards and two hyenas headed in our direction. Adamit put his fork down, wiped his face, and stood up. He seemed to grow bigger, meaner, barely recognizable. I stood but found myself becoming weak in the knees—fearful of my comrade. Half of Cyrus's goons held back, unable to move. Probably frozen in fear at the sight of Adamit—who now projected a terrifying, monster-like appearance. The hyenas cowered and had to be dragged over.

Cyrus, who had shaved off his mustache, slid a sheet of paper onto our table.

"Mr. Bridges," he said as if to convey a matter of routine. "You will sign this document. It gives me fifty-one percent ownership of InEvitech, and it gives you the startup money you need: twenty million—cash." He gestured to his staff as three military-green duffle bags were brought over and unzipped. Bundles and bundles of hundred-dollar bills were exposed.

"Seth, darling," said Penelope. "We're offering you twenty million. Everybody wins. Sign the papers. It's the only sensible option."

That was about the time Cyrus's guards removed retractable batons from their belts and circled in on us. "Mr. Bridges," Cyrus said calmly. "We don't want to hurt you *or* you Mr. Lee."

We stood our ground—implacable. Cyrus barked, "Sign the papers, Mr. Bridges, or all your hopes and dreams will vanish! Here, today!"

One of the thugs handed me a feather pen. "The hell with them," said Adamit, through clenched teeth, "I can take 'em. You just give me the word."

Just then, Kogo threaded through the pack of goons, kissed Adamit, turned to me and said, "I wish to work for you alone, Mr. Bridges. You my new master."

"Absolutely," I said. "Welcome aboard, lieutenant. And, by the way—nice timing."

She positioned herself in front of Adamit, spit on the floor, and beckoned the truncheon goons with a Bruce Lee *let's get it on* hand call.

Some noise at the club's main entrance caught everyone's attention. It was Marisol, Jacob, Becky, Mr. Virgil Caine, and all four puppies: sauntering on in as if they owned the place. Cyrus's guards bristled as they stiffened up their unprotected flanks.

Marisol, whose face shifted with the iridescent patterns of a chameleon running over a pool of Skittles, walked over to my side, slipped her hand into mine and murmured, "Ah, Howard having bad day."

Virgil released a spine-shivering roar. The goons ducked for cover. Cyrus and Penelope dropped to their knees and bowed their heads. Marisol glided over to Cyrus and stood before him.

"Mother," he said. "A humble tribute to you."

He curtly motioned to his minions as they dumped the cash from the duffle bags onto the floor. Marisol placed her hand on Cyrus's forehead and spoke calming Germanic words. When she finished, Cyrus, Penelope, and their entourage scrambled for the exit, leaving the hyenas behind.

Jacob went over to the hyenas, petted them cautiously, then unclasped their silver shackles. The puppies joined in and welcomed the hyenas with excited snorts, sniffs, and wagging butts.

I looked at Marisol. She gave me an uneasy smile—like she was scared or had done something wrong—then she just left. Jacob followed her, as did Becky and the animals. The club was quiet.

I turned to Kogo. "Thanks for the help."

"It OK I move into base?" she asked.

"Sounds fantastic."

Adamit kissed her, then kicked one of the duffle bags in my direction. "Well boss, it looks like you just got a little more capital."

I looked at the cash. "That's not ours."

"No, it's yours. Marisol just gave it to you. Come on, give me a hand loading these bags up. I'll go find a hand truck."

CHAPTER 62

We loaded the duffle bags into my car and drove to my apartment. Skip the concierge, who now wore four dress shirts, helped us bring the bags of money up. After thanking him with one of the bills, I went to the kitchen, poured some drinks and set them, along with the bottle, on the kitchen table. The cracking of expanding ice helped to move the moment forward.

"So," I said to Adamit, "is this what you signed up for?"

He downed his drink in one gulp and said, "It's time I told you about Marisol."

"Oh, really?" I said. "Why now?"

He gave me a look that involved the raising of one eyebrow and said, "She gave permission." He refilled his glass. "We—by *we* I mean us Shifters—call her the Progenitor, but she has many names. The Mayans called her Akna Ah Puch, which, loosely translated, means the Goddess of Life and Death. The Greeks called her Enyo, and the Celts and Druids called her Rhiannon. Hindus, they called her Kali, and the French named her Joan of Arc. And you... what was it again? Oh yeah, *my maid.*" He took a sip of his drink. "Seth, she created us. She is the first, the original Shifter. This place, Vegas? It's all hers. She bought the land in 1905 from the Pacific Railroad, then instructed the Mormons to build it out. She's been receiving a percentage of all the profits since the place opened. Marisol is the wealthiest person in the world."

He finished his drink, poured another, then began to pace around the apartment.

"She doesn't look that old," I said flippantly, regretting the words as they left my mouth.

Adamit whirled and lifted me up to the ceiling with one hand while casually taking a sip of his drink with his other. "Your maid is well over a thousand years old, probably two," he said in an even tone. "She's not even from this planet. She is the alien that we serve. A shapeshifting alien from another planet. Do you understand what I'm telling you?" He set me down, navigated around the duffel bags, and lay on the couch. "The first time I met her was in a muddy trench, in a town called Verdun. It was World War I. I met her again fourteen years ago when she pulled Katya and me from that plane wreck. You know the one I told you about." He sat up and ran a finger along the scar on his face. "None of this is a coincidence: everything she designs has long-term implications."

"So," I said, "she's an alien? What does she want with us?"

"She's as close to a god as you, us, or they"—he pointed towards the window—"will ever know. She wants us to have wars so we can hasten technology, advance it to the point where we can build her a spaceship to go home in. And you, my friend—you are smack dab in the middle of those plans. That Box of yours? It's another gift from Marisol. Seth, you're the one that's going to take her home."

I thought of the dream I'd had with her the other night—all the death and violence.

"Me?"

"Yes, you."

"How did she get here?"

"Don't know, exactly. Spaceship, most likely? What's important is that she's here, and we owe her our lives; and whether we like it or not, we're going to help her get home. Besides, we don't have a choice in the matter."

I grabbed the bottle, joined him in the living room, and filled our glasses.

He brought his drink to his mouth, hesitated, then said, "They say her *gift* is equal to the combined gifts of every Shifter that ever lived. She can strike down legions of men with just a thought, and then, on a lark, she can bring them back to life. Think about that... Some say the strain of existence has taken a toll on her sanity. That's probably why she acts that way; you know, the whole innocent maid routine." He downed the drink, got up, and kicked one of the duffle bags. "This money was meant for you, even before it was printed. You're the key. Cyrus, Penelope, or any other Shifter with half a brain won't get in your way. Not if they want to live. I owe her my life, but still"—he shook his head—"she scares the bejeezus out of me." He picked up the phone, dialed some numbers, said a few words, then hung up. "Can I borrow the car?"

"Yeah, sure, go ahead."

"Don't leave the apartment," he said. "I'm sending Becky over. Your buddy Colton is out there, so do me a favor, just stay in tonight—protect the money."

He had a point, twenty million dollars needed to be watched. "No problem," I said, patting my .38.

As I refilled my glass, I thought about what he'd said. It seemed so far-fetched—Marisol was about as dangerous as Bambi slipping around an icy pond. If she was so powerful, why couldn't she stop these assassins from the future? Perhaps Adamit was the one losing his sanity. Tonight's bet seemed insignificant next to the twenty million that was bagged up at my feet. Win or lose, I was done tempting fate, at least for the time being.

CHAPTER 63

After her encounter with Cyrus at Purgatorium, Marisol joined Jacob, Becky, and the puppies upfront in Jacob's pickup truck. Virgil rode in the back with the hyenas.

"Jacob," Marisol said as he began to drive. "Can you take me to the industrial park?"

"Of course." He followed her directions to the abandoned sign factory. "Are you coming back to the base tonight?" he asked as Marisol exited the truck.

"No. Soon, but not now." She handed Becky a puppy. "Please give Heidi to Seth; they are meant to be." Then, she padded away, into the growing shadows of the dilapidated building that had once been the home of the Las Vegas Electric Light & Sign Company.

After the sounds of her newest family faded, she went below, to her cell. It had taken centuries, but her plans to return to Algeron were coming to fruition sooner than expected, closing in on the entropomorphic singularity she had composed. The unforeseen variables from the future had only served to accelerate the exponential nature of her architecture. She did not like to reveal her identity, but today had been the point of no return. Seth, she thought, would bring her home before her light darkens.

She gripped her knife and began to slice into the flesh of her thighs.

"We can be like them; we can be like them."

The knife scraped and chipped bone. Blood and pain eased down her leg and into the floor drain. She healed the wounds and thought of Algeron and the spirits that were her people. She recalled the crash and how she had roamed this planet for too long. She reminded herself that it was the ship's malfunction that had left her stranded on this primitive world.

She remembered transforming herself from an Algeronian Magnitude 7 Scout into the closest, most acceptable life form. She remembered breathing in and exhaling; her new brothers, Hunahpu and Tbalanque; and how they had all fought for the milk food. She remembered the dark place where they had huddled and how it had protected them with dirt walls and plant roots. She recalled how her new mother had warned them to remain quiet and not leave the den, and how her new brothers had explored the entrance anyway, walking into the light, daring each other to go further, and how Mother would return and slap them with her paw.

She remembered the day her brothers had left the safety of the den: how mighty they were, and how they had ruled the forest together, and how she had remained behind for two seasons, with Mother, learning the ways of the jungle. She remembered her mother's determined yellow eyes, pitch-black fur, and muscular body. She remembered the day a new male had decorated the territory with his scent, and how Mother had swiped at her before disappearing into the forest. She remembered how alone she had felt, waiting for Mother to return. And she remembered, very clearly, the last time she had seen her Earth mother.

One day, while spying on a clan of painted-skin monkeys, she saw them stringing Mother's fur between two palm trees. They were eating her. That night, she killed the clan of skin monkeys, save for one. And, after transforming into that one, she had marched through the jungle on two legs, into the next village, chanting, "We can be like them..." in the Algeron tongue.

Marisol wiped the tears from her face, turned on the light, and willed herself from her human body. She flew outside and gazed down on Vegas, the money machine that was helping her get home. Then, she went about tidying up some loose ends and variables from the future.

CHAPTER 64

The sun was blushing off the last of its pink evening hues when Becky let herself into my apartment. She carried her sawed-off shotgun in one hand and a rambunctious puppy in the other.

After setting the weapon on the table and the puppy on the floor, she said, "Isn't she wonderful!"

The reddish, so-ugly-she's-cute puppy trotted around the apartment with a clumsy gait. Her head and paws were oversized in comparison with its body and its eyes were dissimilar in color.

"That's Heidi," Becky said. "Marisol thinks she should be your new companion." Just then, the puppy squatted on the carpet and peed. "Jacob didn't want to give her up," Becky continued, "but he knows you'll treat her like the terrific bunch of wonderfulness she is. You're a wonderful girl, aren't you, huh?"

Heidi yelped, gave Becky a curious head tilt, then, if I wasn't mistaken—smiled.

I came in from the deck. The pup was a mastiff of some sort, probably the same breed as Hooch in the movie *Turner and Hooch*, starring Tom Hanks.

"What do you want for dinner?" Becky asked.

"Anything you can cook up will be fine." After filling a mixing bowl with water and setting it down in a corner of the kitchen, I put some newspaper in a cardboard box, cut down the sides, and hoped the puppy would use it as needed. I brought the little bundle of ugly over to the couch and set her down next to me. "Do you know, in the future, I have a wife named Heidissa and she has also heterochromia?"

"Are you talking to Heidi or me?" asked Becky.

"Both of you, I guess. So Marisol thinks I need a puppy, eh? She is cute."

"Who? Heidi or Marisol?"

"Both."

Heidi nodded off and began to snore. After dinner, we retired to the living room and watched ABC's coverage of the Olympics.

"Do you really think we can win the gold?" Becky asked. "In hockey? It seems improbable, the Russians and all."

Heidi jumped on the floor and started to squat. I picked her up and placed her in the cardboard box. She did her business then rejoined us on the couch.

"She's a smart cookie," Becky said, scratching the pup's head.

"She sure is." I said as I gave the puppy a gentle pat. "And yes, Becky, we're going to win the gold, one game at a time."

We dozed a bit while the TV kept us semi-conscious. At some point, Heidi leaped from the couch and yelped at the door with all the volume she could muster. It was Adamit and Kogo.

"Relax," Adamit slurred as he waved his arms. "It's just us."

Becky scooped up Heidi and held her close. Adamit weaved his way into the kitchen and grabbed a bottle from the liquor cabinet.

"Colton Hill and your rat-faced cabbie friend Dings—they're dead." He took a swig from the bottle. "Oh yeah, we found this." He handed me a New York State lottery ticket. Then, he passed the bottle to Kogo, kissed her, waved his finger in the air and said, "And your girlfriend... oh, correction, your maid—you know, the one that's over a thousand years old and cleans up after you? Well, she just stole their hearts. Wait! How do I say this better? Hmm... let's see: there are two bodies in the parking lot of Caesars Palace with gaping holes in their chests. They're literally missing their hearts." He let out an exclamatory burp. "We went to kill them, but they were already dead when we got there." He pointed at Heidi. "Dogue de Bordeaux, excellent choice."

The lovers stumbled into the spare bedroom and closed the door.

CHAPTER 65

It was morning when Heidi began to lick my face and wake me. The aroma of coffee and breakfast had me strolling into the kitchen where Becky was busy serving pancakes to Kogo and a hung-over Adamit.

"Top of the morning to you, Mr. Bridges," Becky said, cheerfully pulling a chair out for me. "You hungry?" she asked as she poured me a cup of coffee.

"Famished." I sat down, gave my two sullen table-mates a nodding smile, and took a sip of the brew.

Adamit's eyes were bloodshot. His huge head hung a little lower than usual, and his hands trembled as he drank from a glass of water. Kogo returned my good morning nod with an expressionless stare. She was hard to read and looked ridiculously dangerous.

I put my cup down, offered Kogo another reassuring smile, and said, "So, how's everyone on this fine Sunday morning?"

Heidi tried to bark out an answer but only managed a series of high-pitched yelps.

"I ran out and checked that lottery ticket from last night," Becky said. "It's a winner, fifty grand—if you can get to New York, that is."

"Keep it," I said. "Split it with Jacob. I'm pretty sure Dings would agree."

"Well," she said, "we'll figure something out."

"Oh and by the way, Becky," I said as she served me up breakfast. "I would like to thank you for being a magnificent cook, a sexy lady, and a top-notch security agent."

She gave me a surprised grin, then picked up Heidi and went to the living room. Adamit lifted his head. "About last night—I'm not sure what got into me."

"You weren't hitting that Teater juice, were you?" I said. "That stuff is green death if you ask me."

He let out a labored chuckle. "No."

I took a slurp of coffee. "Don't sweat the small stuff. Hell, it was probably a bad ice cube. These things happen from time to time."

"Thanks, boss. It's just the whole Marisol, Colton, and Octavius situation—it kinda threw me for a loop."

"See," Kogo said, reaching for his hand. "I tell you, it OK."

I took a few bites of toast. "So, Kogo, what's your story?"

Adamit perked up and said, "She's a Shifter, boss, on her second shift. She's studied both sides of the martial arts for decades; plus, she is an excellent driver."

"Whoa!" I said, "Hold your horses there, big guy. I just want to hear her talk."

Kogo stood up as if this was a formal request. Her beauty was juxtaposed with a killer's veneer. "I orphan from China: study, then teach at Chinese Opera. I shift, spend next life working in the Imperial Guard protecting emperor. Then, I shift forward, become rōnin, corporate ninja for Mitsubishi. Cyrus buy my contract. Now I here, work for you."

"That is one impressive resume if I do say so myself. Kogo, you are a lifesaver." I stood and bowed. "My life is in your hands." I held up my cup. "To you, Kogo."

Heidi scampered into the kitchen and yelped with excitement. Becky came over, hugged Kogo, and said, "Welcome, sister."

Kogo's hard exterior softened ever so slightly with the hint of a smile. "Thank you. I swear my life to protect you all."

Adamit and Kogo headed out on some errand shortly thereafter. I spent the next three hours surfing the Box. Just before lunch, I called Jericho Sims.

On the second ring, a woman said, "Jericho Sims. This is Juliet. What is it we can get for you today Mr. Bridges?"

"Yeah, hi. I need an armored car. Is that something you guys do?"

"Please hold."

Thirty seconds later a man came on the line. "Mr. Bridges. My name is Pinknie—S. E. Pinknie. I'm an agent for the Jericho Sims Corporation. Our purpose is to provide anything you may need in a prompt, professional manner. We are a French company, incorporated in 1898, by our founder Jeanne Arc. Currently, we have offices in twenty-nine countries. Our credo is, 'If it exists, we can get it.' Am I to understand you are in need of an armored vehicle?"

"Actually, I'd like to buy one. A GMC Suburban-type truck, you know, a 4×4, and I'd like it delivered, if possible."

"I understand, Mr. Bridges. Could you please hold?"

"Yeah, sure."

A minute later, S.E came back on the line. "I have a black, 1978 threat-level-three suburban. It's a rare British 7.4-liter diesel with fifteen-thousand miles. The price is $78,000."

With assassins from the future trying to kill me and so much cash lying about, the price seemed more than reasonable. I gave him my address and said, "Just get it here. I'll pay cash."

After lunch, Becky and I ended up on the couch watching the television game show *Let's Make a Deal*. I held Heidi close to my chest and occasionally gave her kisses. She returned my affection with puppy kisses and snuggles. She was ugly and awkward but I knew she'd soon grow into a beautiful dog—and, if my visions were correct, a lot more.

Around dinner time my desire to be with Marisol got the better of me. Why was I so pathetic?

I threw on my suit coat and made a beeline for the door. Becky and Heidi held me at bay.

"Where do you think you're going?" said Becky.

"I have to see Marisol."

"No! You have to stay here and help me protect the money."

She was right, but I didn't care. I eased my way past her, and just as I was opening the door, Adamit walked in. We exchanged nods.

"If you're looking for Marisol," he said, "you won't find her. She's gone. Jacob dropped her off around midtown yesterday, and she hasn't come back to the base since."

"Where exactly did Jacob drop her off at?"

"Seth," he said, shaking his head. "I don't think you understand. Let's go inside; we can talk about it."

"C'mon," Becky said, pulling on my suit. "You're not going to find Marisol if she doesn't want to be found."

Heidi tugged on my pant cuff, coaxing me back inside. Maybe they were right. Becky pushed me onto the couch.

Adamit brought over some drinks and said, "Listen up, Seth. She just gave you twenty-million dollars. What, that's not enough? You need more? Let me guess, you want to be close to her at all times? Well, welcome to the club. There are a thousand Shifters that feel the same. We're programmed that way. And Marisol? She'll do what she wants, whenever she wants, and there's not a damn thing *you* or anyone else can do about it. She has plans for you—for us." He eased out of his shoes, unholstered his .45s, and laid them on the table. "Just be thankful she's on our side. Listen, you want to go to space and save humanity, that's great—but remember, Marisol's plans come first. By the way, we beat Norway five zip. Is that how you remembered it?"

"I don't think we blanked any team..."

Adamit took a sip of his drink. "You can't step in the same river twice."

"Master Poe?"

"No, Heraclitus said that in 500 BC"

"Really? With a name like that he should have said: you can't—"

"Seth!" Becky yelled from the kitchen. "Don't say it!"

I watched Heidi tugging at Adamit's socks, eventually removing them.

"Why me?" I downed my drink. "I mean... why am I in love with her?"

"Maybe," Becky called out, "you two were meant to be with each other, in love." Heidi let loose what could have been her first real bark and pranced around the living room like a show dog on parade. I turned to Adamit.

"What about you? Kogo seems like ah—well, like a nice girl."

He beamed a conspiratorial grin and said, "I also think we were meant to be."

CHAPTER 66

The next morning, Becky knocked on my bedroom door and said, "Seth, there's a man here with a delivery."

I put on my pants, went to the kitchen, and greeted a lanky Black man: the same man I had seen on Moonbase Virgil. He had a calm demeanor and a disarming smile, wore an expensive-looking suit, and looked a lot like Nat King Cole.

He extended his hand. "S. E. Pinknie, Jericho Sims Corporation," he said through a baritone rasp. "We talked on the phone yesterday. I have your vehicle as requested."

"Fantastic," I said, shaking his hand. I pegged him as a Shifter, knocked on the spare bedroom door, and said, "Hey, Adamit, the armored car is here." I turned to S. E. "Could I interest you in some coffee?"

Becky ushered us over to the kitchen table and began serving up some joe.

"So, S. E.," I said. "How long have you been with Jericho Sims?"

"Let's see... be going on thirty-something years now. Joined the firm the day I graduated from Brigham Young. I suppose you could say I inherited the job from my father..."

As Adamit came in, I introduced him to our guest who—surprisingly—was not put off by Adamit's intimidating exterior. I surmised they probably knew each other. We discussed, over a breakfast served up by Becky, the GMC Suburban and all its bells and whistles. S. E. explained that he didn't make deliveries as a rule, but that he'd heard about our run-in with Cyrus at the club and wanted to meet the guy that had put Willhammer in his place.

"That pompous ass has bamboozled our company more than once, and each time we had no recourse. How'd you do it, Mr. Bridges?"

"Yeah," chuckled Adamit. "Tell us how you did it."

Heidi pranced around the table and started in with her newly developed bark. I grabbed 78k out of one of the duffle bags and handed it to S. E. He gave me the GMC's keys, title, and registration.

"The plates are temporary, good for seven days," he said. "Shall we go down and look at it?"

"No, that's OK. Do you need a ride back to your office?"

"No, thank you. My assistant is downstairs waiting for me. Well, I guess I'll be on my way."

I paused him. "One more thing. I want to give you a retainer of one million dollars." I nodded to Adamit, who counted out ten 100k bundles and placed them in brown paper shopping bags.

S. E. wrote out a receipt. "Thank you, Mr. Bridges. The Jericho Sims Corporation looks forward to helping you with all of your needs."

"Hey, how do you guys know it's me when I call?"

"You're the only one that has that number."

After S. E. left, we loaded the duffle bags of cash into our new machine-gun-black GMC Suburban. Adamit got behind the wheel. Becky joined him up front. I sat in the back with Heidi. The truck's large turbo-diesel knocked with torque. Its stiff suspension and thick exterior offered a sense of security. A few minutes into our drive, I noticed the Vaseline skyline of Vegas appeared to be losing some of its lusters.

"What do you think?" I asked.

"Are you kidding?" Adamit said, stomping on the accelerator. "It's perfect. A regular war wagon."

"Nice."

CHAPTER 67

We deposited most of our newly acquired twenty million into the InEvitech account at Vegas Trust, then drove back to the office and got the meeting underway.

Marisol was a no-show, but there was a new guy in the room. He was Asian, around 35, and looked and sounded like the guy that had played Sulu on the original *Star Trek* series.

Crash took the reins. "Ahem… Welcome, and good morning—"

"Crash, hold up," I said. "Hey," I asked the room, "has anyone seen Marisol?" I looked around, seeing only shrugs and questioning faces. "Sorry. Please, continue."

"OK," Crash said. "We have been fortunate enough to secure Doctor Eiichiro Kobayashi." Crash nodded toward the new guy. "He's an aerospace engineer that will be helping us design and build our spacecraft. And he's a licensed pilot."

"Damn straight," said Dean. "We got Sulu on our team."

I grabbed my coffee cup and held it up. "Good work. Cheers, to Doctor Eiichiro Kobayashi."

Everybody followed my cue and welcomed our new shipbuilder.

He stood up, bowed, smiled, and said, "Call me Eiichiro. We will be needing a high-altitude jet for parts. And thanks for the job."

"Understood," I said as he sat down. "OK, gang, before we go any further, I would like to introduce Kogo. She's working security."

Kogo, who was wearing her plaid dress chauffeur's outfit, stood, offered up a quick snort, then sat back down. Almost everyone stared at her with bewilderment. Heidi ran around the table and started barking.

Adamit said, "Cheers, to Kogo."

Everyone lifted their cups and welcomed her.

"Alright," said Dean as he began his report. "The base is coming along, and the offices are ready for furniture. I've had new air conditioning and heating systems installed, and the main kitchen and mess hall are complete. The radar dish is undergoing inspection as we speak. That's about it, except, I'll need more information on the bunker: size, and how secure?"

Damn, this guy knew his stuff. He had worked right through the weekend.

"Excellent work, Dean," I said. "Put the bunker under the machine shop, make it thirty feet by thirty feet with a vault or large safe inside. The more secure, the better." I thought about the deposit I'd just made. "And Dean, I need it completed ASAP."

Dean, who was taking notes, looked up and nodded.

Margie handed out credit cards. "They've got a ten-thousand-dollar limit," she said to everyone. "Try to keep the charges business related."

I handed her the GMC's title and registration. "I was hoping you could get the offices furnished and register this vehicle?"

"No problem," she said, glancing at the papers.

Jacob stood on his chair. "Cyrus's two hyenas are doing quite well back at the base. I've named them Buffy and Jody. And contrary to their appearance, they're quite tame."

I had forgotten about them. Two days ago, Cyrus had lost—to us—twenty-million dollars, his hyenas, and Kogo his chauffeur. He had to be pissed about that.

"What do you want me to do?" Katya said. "I'm feeling kinda left out."

"I need you to buy a high-altitude jet for the doctor. Talk to the Jericho Sims people you got the DC-4 from. And by the way—you and everyone in this room are invaluable. We're doing important work here. I know that sounds pretentious, but it's true, and I can't do it by myself. I need all of your help, and then some." An upwelling of pride took me by surprise. Heidi started barking as I walked around the room. "This planet. What do you see? Peace, love, understanding? No—this rock is too small for those words to have real meaning. I'll tell you what I see: a doomed planet: it's just a matter of time. Space"—I pointed up—"that's the answer! And that's where we're going! Are you with me?"

Dean yelled, "We're with you, brother."

Heidi let out a howl and, as if on cue, everyone stood up and cheered.

I had never believed in karma, but generosity—that was a whole different matter. I dumped a million dollars on the table. "That's a bonus. Everyone gets an even share."

I scooped up Heidi and joined Kogo and Adamit in our new truck. I wanted to look for Marisol, but there was business to be taken care of.

"Kogo, Caesars Palace, please."

My original plan was to let my winnings ride, but things had changed: I no longer wanted to mess with fate unnecessarily. At Caesars Sportsbook, Cagey took my betting receipt.

"OK, guys," he said, adjusting his ponytail, "give me a second and I'll get your money together."

He had us meet him in the small room located at the end of the counter. He counted out 1.9 million, the money we'd won on the Norway game, and put it into large money bags.

"You want action on tonight's hockey game? Romania versus Team USA. I'll give you even odds."

I looked at Adamit and shrugged. "I'm done for now, but you're welcome to bet some of this money if you want. Your call?"

"Why don't we bet half a mill, see if the future is what it used to be."

"Cool."

Just as we were getting into the Suburban, Heidi began barking at me frantically. That's when a nightmare of a vision hit me—hard and fast.

I was with Adamit and Kogo, and we were running through an alleyway in the Industrial District. I wasn't sure of the time, or day, but I knew something was wrong. We stopped in front of a rusted door on the side of an abandoned warehouse. Something behind the door was terribly important. We busted through the door and ran inside. Startled birds took to flight; their wings flapped loudly in the warehouse's still interior.

"There!" I yelled, pointing to the staircase that led below.

We scrambled down the stairs. At the bottom, just off to the right, was another door: a reinforced walk-in cooler type. I pulled on the handle. It was locked from the inside and wouldn't budge.

"Marisol!" I screamed.

Adamit joined me and together we pulled on the handle, but still the door wouldn't budge.

"Use this," said Kogo, tossing a length of iron pipe toward Adamit. He dug the end of the pipe between the door and its frame, and the three of us pulled on the improvised lever. The lock snapped and the door flung open. A single bulb, hanging from the ceiling, cast a dim light on the horror show within.

Marisol lay motionless on the floor: both her thighs had deep slashing wounds. It was as if someone had tried to cut her legs off. Blood pooled around the stone chamber's floor drain.

CHAPTER 68

When I came to, I was lying on the backseat of the Suburban, and Heidi was licking my face.

"Welcome back," Adamit said.

"Adamit... what the...?" I sat up. "Marisol!" I yelled. "I think she's in trouble. We have to save her. Hurry, Kogo, drive to the Industrial District. Go as fast as you can. She needs our help. She could be dying!"

Kogo floored the accelerator. She clipped two cars and ran all the stoplights as I gave directions on the fly to the alley where last week Marisol had me drop her off.

"That's the place there!" I said, pointing to one of the abandoned buildings. Things began to happen as if we were in my vision. But this time it was all real. We got out of the GMC and ran over to the warehouse. Kogo opened the side door. Startled pigeons took flight. I hustled over to the staircase.

"Kogo," I said, as we ran down the stairs. "We're gonna need a pry bar."

We rounded the corner and faced a locked walk-in cooler door. The same door from my vision. Adamit and I pulled on the handle. It wouldn't budge.

I calmed myself and said, "When we get inside, she's gonna need medical attention. We'll have to get her to the hospital—fast."

Kogo tossed Adamit a length of iron pipe, and we began to pry the door open. When its internal lock snapped, the door swung open. Kogo brought her hand to her mouth and gasped.

Marisol lay on the bloodied stone floor. Her legs were almost severed from her body. Adamit rushed in and placed two fingers on her neck.

"She's alive," he said, as he tore his shirt into lengths of cloth and used them as tourniquets on her upper thighs. With the bleeding slowed, he scooped her up, and we ran back to the truck. Kogo drove faster than the heavily armored Suburban was meant to go.

"Is that you... Adamit, my brave?" Marisol said.

"Yes, Your Majesty. Please, don't talk, you've lost a lot of blood."

"Kogo Musashi, my dove, is that you? Are you here?"

"Yes, Your Majesty, we take you to hospital. You get better soon."

"Do you make each other happy?"

"Yes," Kogo and Adamit said in unison.

"Mr. Bridges," Marisol said, her words barely audible. "You came for me. You all came for me. I cook, I clean... I help Jacob with the animals."

"Faster, Kogo!" I screamed. "Drive faster!"

With Marisol in his arms, a bloody and bare-chested Adamit stormed the emergency room. "I need a doctor!" An orderly wheeled over a gurney and carted Marisol away. My mind flooded with anger. What kind of sicko could do this to another person?

A short time later, a doctor approached us.

"She's stable," he said nervously. "But both legs need to be amputated—the sooner, the better."

I ran past the doctor and found Marisol in the intensive care unit. She was unconscious and connected to tubes and beeping machines. I brushed her blood-crusted hair aside and kissed her.

"Come on, Marisol. I need you. Someone has to clean up after me."

She opened her eyes. I reached for her hand and gently squeezed it. She smiled ever so slightly and whispered, "Do you love me?"

I kissed her hand. "Yes! Yes, I love you. I'm your man."

She began to glow and her eyes filled with kaleidoscopic starburst patterns. Her skin became fur, short black fur, and, as unbelievable as it sounds, she morphed into a jaguar. An amulet dangled from her neck. She, or it, scratched a hole in a nearby screened window and leapt out.

I walked back to the emergency-room lobby like a zombie—my mind slipping around the edge of grip. Adamit and Kogo rushed to me.

"Let's go," I said flatly.

Adamit shook me. "What's going on? How is she? Why are we leaving?"

"She just turned into a jaguar and jumped out the window."

As we rolled down the highway, the desert wind whipped sand against the Suburban's bullet-proof windows. Was she out there, sprinting down a service road or running a ridgeline? Maybe if I looked closely, I could see a dust cloud she'd kicked up or some sort of sign—

"You alright?" Adamit asked. "You don't look so good."

I shook my head and began to gag. "Pull over." I wretched whatever was in my stomach onto the dusty roadside. Then, as I dry-heaved bile, I fought off a panic attack with the words of Master Poe: "Even in chaos, a pattern emerges..." No, that didn't apply... "If you desire happiness, be happy." Yeah, I'd run with that for now.

"Better?" asked Adamit as he helped me back into the truck.

I wiped my face with my shirtsleeve. "I'm ready to go home now."

Underneath the safety and comfort of the war wagon's seats, its tires turned out a reassuring melody. A few miles later, the zombie-like fog in my brain cleared.

"Kogo," I said. "Turn around, we need to go to the base."

CHAPTER 69

Dust billowed from the wheel wells as we pulled under the base's carport. Dean came over and opened the passenger door. "Boss"—he unfurled a roll of blueprints—"do you have a minute to look at these plans? Whoa! Is that blood?"

Margie pulled up in a golf cart. "Seth, we need to talk about some zoning issues."

"Not now!" I mumbled. "Please, everybody, just leave me alone."

I walked over to Virgil's cage. He was lying down, his head up, alert. A muscular black jaguar had taken cover behind him. I opened the cage door and cautiously approached the two. Virgil rose to his haunches, issued a warning growl and swiped his paw at me. Moving slowly, I circuitously made my way over to the jaguar and knelt. It was wearing Marisol's necklace. It laid its head on my lap, purred for a few moments, then transformed back into the Marisol I knew. I draped my suit jacket over her and walked her out of the enclosure. All the while the crew watched in silence. I brought Marisol up to her room. She sat down on her bed.

"I'm sorry," she said in perfect, unaffected English. "Sometimes I go too far, but I had to know."

"Know what?" I asked as I wrapped a blanket around her. She smiled. I didn't care who or what she was. The world could go fuck itself; I didn't care. I had everything I needed right here. Becky knocked twice, came in, and set down a tray containing a few cans of ginger ale and a plate of saltine crackers, then left. Heidi jumped onto the bed, nuzzled Marisol, and licked her face. The wind blew a gentle breeze through the room's open windows, fluttering the curtains.

I sat on the bed next to her. Marisol took hold of my hand, and we both lay back. A wave of vertigo swept over me; my stomach lurched as if we were in a plane dropping out of the sky. The sensation of falling stopped as I entered what I believed to be Marisol's mind. And like a dream, we were flying, traveling backward in time, returning to her first memories on Earth. We set down in a rainforest. It was hot, dark, and smothering.

"I am from Algeron," Marisol said as we walked down a thin jungle pathway. "It is a small planet that exists in another galaxy. Algeron is unique in that it has never been exposed to an extinction event. Unlike your world, and others, my species has been evolving uninterrupted since our abiogenesis: the beginning."

We rounded a small hill and walked down a contour line.

"As a result," she continued, "we have evolved into pure energy: the essence of being, without the physical limitation of form. We conquered space and the speed of light around the time your predecessors decided it was time to come down from the trees and walk upright through the grasslands." Marisol held a branch up as I ducked under it. "Although we do not have a physical form, we still require protection from space and its dangers."

She paused for a moment, pushed aside a large fern that was blocking our view, and showed me her spaceship. As it had been, just after the crash. I reminded myself I was in her consciousness.

"That is me," she said, pointing to a glittering iridescent orb that was three feet tall and a foot across. It was Algeronian Marisol as she had looked two thousand years ago. She was in a truck-sized spacecraft that had an insect-like appearance. "Long ago, when I first arrived on this planet, I feared that I would never see home again. Failure for us is barely a concept."

She walked me over to a nearby earthen mound and pointed to a burrow at its base. There were three baby jaguars inside.

"Look," she said, as Algeronian Marisol flew from the crashed ship and into the smallest of the baby jaguars. My Marisol, who was still holding my hand, turned to me and said, "You see clear now?"

CHAPTER 70

Heidi woke me just as the sun was preparing to rise. I gave Marisol, who was asleep, a kiss, then draped a blanket over my shoulders and went down to the picnic table in front of the barracks. Heidi followed me. I picked her up and held her close under the blanket. I lit a smoke from a pack of Marlboros somebody had left behind.

A gentle stillness had settled over the base. High overhead, the sonic thrum of jet planes rumbled. An emerging band of orange light peeked out from under the violet sky. I pulled the blanket tight and surveyed the property. Huh... Last month this place had been dead and forgotten, and now it was breathing again. Two crows flew overhead and cawed. Somebody was cooking breakfast in the mess hall. My stomach grumbled. Adamit and Kogo came over and joined me.

Kogo pointed to a small white dot in the sky. "Light is Cygnus, place forgotten souls are reborn."

"Do you know much about the stars?" I asked.

"I study astronomy—Huazhong Institute in China."

"What's the plan for today?" Adamit asked.

I put the cigarette out, took a deep breath, and said, "Let's just keep on doing what we're doing; it seems to be working. Hey, what are you two doing up so early?"

Kogo took an aggressive tone and asked, "Why you call me lieutenant when we first meet?"

"When I first met you, in the future, that was your rank—lieutenant."

"You no joke with me?"

"Nope. That's your rank, at least in the future."

"You Sethco Alliance?"

"OK, Kogo," said Adamit, intervening, "that's enough."

She gave me a bow. "I sorry, Master."

Jeez, it never ended. I started back inside, stopped, then turned and said, "Kogo, I'm not your master, but believe me when I tell you, we, all of us, are on the same team."

I went back to Marisol's room. She was in her tunic and standing next to her bed. She looked healthy, and her legs seemed fine. I got dressed, took her hand, and we walked downstairs to the mess hall. As soon as we got there, she left to join Becky who was busy in the kitchen cooking up breakfast. Dean came in, gave me a friendly slap on my back, and said, "I love this place. I love *you* man. I'm so happy; I got me a happiness high."

Nobody mentioned Marisol's transformation, and for the next half hour, I stuffed my face and nodded along to the conversations at hand. Among other things, Katya, Becky, and Adamit had decided to move into the base.

Dean was talking about moving some of his personal items into a vacant room when Jacob came in and said, "We beat Romania, 7-2."

After breakfast Kogo drove Adamit and myself over to the office for our morning meeting.

"OK, everybody," I said as I poured myself a cup of coffee, "let's get started." I put Heidi, who had somehow gotten on the table, on the floor, and then I took a seat. "Things happened yesterday. Some of them believable, and some not so believable. Get used to it. I have; so can you." I took a sip from my cup. "Marisol is fine. I suspect things will be back to normal later today, or tomorrow. Margie, Crash, Doctor Eiichiro, it's time you know what Becky and Jacob already know. We—that is Katya, Kogo, Adamit, Dean, and myself—are involuntary time travelers. We get extra time in life by traveling back and forward in time. This extra time gives us the advantage of experience. We're just like you, only older. Me? I'm fifty-eight years old. Dean is about the same age. We both lived this time-period once before, but are new at this time travel stuff. These guys"—I nodded at Katya, Adamit, and Kogo—"are older, and have more experience."

As I spoke, no one freaked out or anything, so I continued. "As far as Marisol is concerned, well, she's something of a mystery. But we are all interconnected. You, me, Marisol, we were all put together so we could, among other things, save man from his dark side." I wanted to tell them about the Soul Breaker Virus, but I didn't think they could handle it. "Now, I'm sure you all have a ton of questions, and I promise you'll get those answers, but right now, we've got work to do."

Katya stood up and glamored our new Short-Timers. "What Seth is saying is true. We are all friends here, so there is no cause for concern."

Heidi let out a squeaking bark of agreement. Crash and Eiichiro exchanged whispers, head shakes, and facial agreements.

Margie crossed her arms, snapped some gum she was chewing, and said, "Time travelers? That makes perfect sense. Why didn't you tell us that before?

Though it does beg the question—what are you doing here? Shouldn't you be out saving Kennedy or something... making the world a better place for all of us? Hell, just think what you could do if you joined up with Superman; you could solve all kinds of crimes, and who knows, you could save cats stuck in trees, help little old ladies cross the road and—"

"It doesn't work that way," I said. "But I can assure you, what we're doing here is more important than crime fighting and chasing ghosts in the past. We're getting off this planet before a bug called the Soul Breaker Virus takes humanity out to the dumpster." That was easy, I thought.

"Whatever," said Margie as she placed a packet on the table. "Here's the new truck registration. Oh, if you don't mind, I have to leave—non-time-traveling problems and such."

"Margie," I said. "And this goes for everyone. From now on, our morning meetings will be held at the base." I was pretty sure she wasn't going to quit; hell, yesterday I had given her one-hundred-thousand reasons to stick around—in cash. "OK, gang, that's it for now. Crash, Eiichiro, I need to talk to you two."

When the office had cleared out, I said, "Crash, get the sphere and give Eiichiro the rundown."

Adamit and I hung back as Crash told Eiichiro about the Gravity Resist Drive and how it would be used as the primary lift engine for our spacecraft. Eiichiro's jaw slackened as Crash activated the sphere and had it hover over the table.

"Hai, brilliant!" Eiichiro exclaimed. "I can help you sell it to NASA."

Crash tried to catch Eiichiro's words, but it was too late. Adamit came over and gave the doctor a look from hell. Eiichiro took a deep gulp.

"Doctor Kobayashi," I said. "We're not selling this to anyone. In fact, I plan on giving it to the world, but I want to test it first. That's why I need *you* to build a spacecraft around it."

Eiichiro offered a rigid salute and bowed obediently. "Hai," he barked out. "Understood."

Crash helped settle him back into a chair.

I told Eiichiro my ideas for the spacecraft: a simple scaled-down version of NASA's space shuttle. The craft would have to have quick-release mounting brackets located on its topside so it could be fastened and deployed from the undercarriage of our DC-4. It must be able to maneuver in outer space as well as in Earth's atmosphere. It would need a reasonably sized cockpit for three, as well as a payload area for a satellite. And it would need to be flying inside seven months.

"Crash," I said as Eiichiro digested my ideas. "I need you to build the ship's GRDs and head up the entire project. Store anything spaceship-related in the base's new bunker. Eiichiro, you are not to inquire how the Gravity Resist Drive works, just build the ship around it. Do you understand?"

"Hai, I understand." He stood, bowed twice, and sat back down.

CHAPTER 71

After the meeting, Kogo drove Adamit and I over to see Cagey at Caesars. From behind the glass, Cagey looked up and gave us a groaning, "Hello." He took our betting slip and counted out our winnings.

"You guys are killing me," he said, rubbing the back of his neck. "Listen, if you let this ride, I'll give you 2:1 odds on tomorrow's game with West Germany."

Adamit chuckled. "West Germany! Hockey's their national sport. We want 4:1."

Cagey threw up his hands. "I can't do it."

Adamit shrugged. "Then give us the cash."

As we were leaving, Adamit lowered his voice and asked me, "Are we still betting?"

"Well," I said with a shrug. "We won this game in the past. It's your experiment: you make the call."

"Hey guys, hold up," Cagey said, as he hustled-out from behind the cage and caught up to us. "I may have been mistaken. The odds have improved to 3:1, provided you bet the whole million."

Adamit gave me a wink and took the action.

We had an early lunch at the Tumblin' Dice Diner, then drove to the base. Jacob and the four puppies met us under the base's car park.

"Watch this," Jacob said as he bent his elbow up at a ninety-degree angle and made a fist.

Cyrus' former hyenas bore down on our position—slobbering mucus with every stride. Jacob opened his hand. The hyenas skidded to a halt, sat down, and panted.

"Marisol helped me with the commands," Jacob continued. "They're brother and sister. The larger one, there on the left, that's Buffy; the smaller one is Jody. Pretty cool, eh? Anyway, I wanted to let you know the base is secure: CCTV cameras are rolling, there's a constant perimeter patrol, and there is armed personnel at key entry points. Got her locked down tighter than a crab's ass at low tide."

I thanked him for his prose and his dedication, then headed over to the main building with Kogo and Adamit to check out our new front office.

The office lobby was more elegant than I had expected. It was smooth, without corners, and modern and functional. Margie was behind a round reception desk, fidgeting with some electrical cords when she noticed us.

"Oh, hello," she said. "Welcome to InEvitech; would you like to book a trip to the moon?"

I hustled over to Margie and kissed her. "I knew you were special the moment I met you." I threw up my arms and hollered, "This, ladies and gentlemen, is a lobby."

Margie held out her palm like a presenter on a game show. "C'mon, I'll give you guys a tour."

She showed us the remodeled mess hall kitchen, the new conference room, and six smaller individual offices. Upstairs, the two floors of bedrooms and common areas upstairs remained in their original government-spec condition. After the tour, Adamit stayed behind with Kogo, in her room.

I went outside into the midday heat, walked over to Virgil's enclosure, and interlaced my fingers through the cage's fencing. Virgil fixed his eyes on mine. Marisol appeared from behind him. She was barefoot and the sun shimmered iridescent colors across her skin. She opened the cage door, held my hand, and led me in. I nodded at Virgil and offered him an awkward wave. His piercing yellow eyes, sharp incisors, and hot breath had me nudging behind Marisol for safety. She laughed.

"Mr. Caine thanks you for saving his life." She kissed the beast.

"My pleasure, Mr. Caine," I said. "Glad to have you around."

Marisol brought me back to the barracks and led me up to her room. We lay down on the adjoining twin beds—hand in hand. Then, once again, we became ghosts, traveling backward in time, touring Man's history of weaponized technology.

CHAPTER 72

Our first stop was high in the sky, as passengers in Marisol's mind, beyond Earth's atmosphere, and over to an area where a half dozen satellites were being placed as a foundation for something much larger.

"The future is constructed from the past," Marisol said in unaffected English. "War, always war with your kind. I do not judge your species' violent core: I merely use it. Perpetual conflict advances weapons, communications, medical procedures, and the building of great cities. All byproducts of Man's insatiable desire to accumulate more power. See that?" She pointed to the baseball-diamond-sized triangle of satellites. "It is the beginning of a missile defense grid in space. They are up there now building it."

I nodded in agreement and thought, that's weird; I'm in space and I can breathe and everything seems normal. We drifted down into clouds that hung over Southeast Asia, and we saw a squadron of American B-52 bombers dropping napalm bombs onto 1968's Vietnam.

Marisol said, "The Domino Theory justification."

Then, we went further back in time, to World War II, just in time to witness a nuclear bomb named *Little Boy* explode over Hiroshima.

"The nuclear age," said Marisol with a nod.

"Yup," I said as we suddenly found ourselves in a muddy trench.

Dead men and those with the color of death lay scattered about without concern. They were American doughboy soldiers, and if my history served me correctly, we were in France, in the middle of a battle, on the Western Front of WWI. Artillery shells and aerial bombs rained down on our position. The stench of rotting flesh, cordite, and diesel clung to the air and nostrils.

A line of German soldiers, equipped with flamethrowers, gasmasks, and bayonet-tipped long arms were bearing down on our position. A yellow gas clung to the dystopian landscape, and in the sky, bi-planes buzzed like flies. I saw a man that looked like Adamit, but not as big. He was slumped down in the mud and bleeding out. I went to help him, but once again I found myself in a new location. I was high in the sky, aloft in a basket with Marisol, under a balloon, over a naval battlefield. Below us was Charleston Harbor, the same harbor I had sailed through two years ago on my high school training vessel, *Tabor Boy*. The smoke of cannons and wooden ships burning filled the air, as did the shouts and screams of men fighting for their lives.

Marisol pointed at something that skimmed just under the water's surface and said, "That is the *Hunley*, the first battle-tested submarine. War is the mother of innovation."

The tour continued. Sometime after the implementation of hand cannons and chariots, I found myself, along with Marisol, at the base of a cross. A Roman soldier stuck a spear into the man that hung from it. Jesus? Marisol caressed the dying man's feet. He smiled at her knowingly, then closed his eyes.

Our trip ended as we nudged forward to the seventh century. I found myself seated across from Marisol, drinking tea in a pagoda, high atop a stone structure. I was dressed in a regal, bleached-white, four-panel ancient Chinese dress that was quite comfortable. Marisol was in a Chinese tunic and skirt combo that had dramatic colors and stunning details around the collar, sleeves, and hem. Dean's geishas—Yoshimi, Asuka, and Izumi—were there, tending to our table. Below us, tens of thousands of workers were busy as bees constructing the Great Wall of China.

We were in mid-conversation, and everything appeared to be routine. I set my tea down.

"But Marisol... people from the future are trying to kill me."

"Yes, that is true."

"Why?"

"They fear you."

"Why do they fear me?"

She shook her head disappointingly. "You are the one who does not fear the seasons. You *are* their reaper." She tapped her finger on my forehead and said, "Now, go reap."

Suddenly, I was transported forward: into the future. It was oddly proportionate, remembering things that had yet to happen; and like a moment of déjà vu, I wasn't sure what type of reality I was in. In front of me, two steel doors stood between me and the reason I was here.

I accessed my Cog-Link and scanned the entry for weaknesses. Satisfied with my telemetry, I ran at the doors while firing gradient-8 plasma bolts from my wrists. By the time I reached the doors, it was a simple matter of kicking them inward. Inside was a laboratory filled with high-tech machines, military personnel, and a pile of headless corpses. A man in a blood-splattered lab coat stood next to a boy that was strapped down on a table. An old lady tooled around on a floating throne. She looked as if she was about to explode with indignation.

My Cog-Link confirmed that the location was that of the Taizu lab. The same lab that had been sending Octaviuses back in time to kill me.

My force field auto-engaged just as the old lady—whom my Cog-Link identified as Mun Taizu—shrieked, "IT'S HIM! HE'S HERE! KILL HIM! KILL HIM NOW!"

From the top of my wrists, I let slip a volley of self-targeting mind-flow fléchettes. The guards slumped to the floor, dead.

I saw a large clear cylindrical tank with pink liquid in it—it must have been their Wayback Machine. Cog-Link recognized the man standing next to the table as Doctor Heisenberg.

"What number is he?" I asked.

"Are you going to kill him?"

"No, Doctor," I said, removing the restraints. "I'm here to save him."

The doctor nodded. "He's number eight, the last of the clones."

Above us, Mun Taizu whirled about on her floating throne, shrieking like a stuck-loop Robotron. I fired a bolt through her chair's guidance system and grounded her.

"She's all yours," I said to the doctor. "But be quick about it: my ship is going to vape this dump in five minutes. You're welcome to join us if you like." I cradled the unconscious Octavius 8 in my arms and headed out of the lab.

Just as I was about to leave, I turned and saw the doctor grab a harmonic saber from one of the fallen guards. He ran up to Mun and cut her head off. He kicked it—I suppose for good measure—tore off his lab coat, and called out, "Galahad, it's time to go. We're free!"

CHAPTER 73

It was 6:00 a.m. when a rooster's *cock-a-doodle-doo* woke me. Heidi nudged my leg with her nose. I gave her a pat and kissed Marisol, who was still asleep. After collecting my thoughts and writing them down, I went outside with Heidi. The sky was the color of wet cement that someone needed to pour. We climbed into the front seat of the suburban. Kogo got behind the steering wheel.

We drove to the Tumblin' Dice Diner. Once there, Heidi barked friendly hellos to the waitress, hostess, and busboy. She was a good girl, growing in size and smarts every day. In the morning paper, I spotted what I was looking for: we had beat West Germany 4-2.

"Kogo," I said, once we were back in the truck. "What do you say we go to Caesars and get our money?"

She started up the diesel and gave me a queer, almost seductive smile. "Me love money. Long, long time."

I couldn't resist the opportunity to give her a jab. "Hey Kogo, how long do you love money?"

She put the truck in gear. "Long, long time."

"How long?"

"Long, long time."

We both cracked up at our exchange. Heidi yawned and snuggled up in the space between us.

"Well," I said, "what are we waiting for? Let's go get Caesars' money."

When I presented my betting slip, the cashier shook her head and said, "Just a moment."

I looked at Kogo, who was holding Heidi, and shrugged my shoulders. A pudgy, mean-looking blue-haired woman stood behind the window and waved our betting slip.

"*This* is an illegal bet," she said briskly. "We're not going to honor it. Furthermore, you are banned from this casino, and any other casino if I have anything to say about it. Now leave and don't come back."

"No," I said. "You owe me three million. Is that something I should forget about, walk away from? Where's Cagey or Mr. Anastasio?"

The fish-faced functionary yelled into the slot under the window, "You should be giving *us* money. We're supposed to win; you're supposed to lose."

A posse of security personnel conveniently appeared. Kogo handed Heidi off to a nearby waitress. Just then, a drunk guy shoulder-bumped me from behind.

"Cheater," he slurred. "You're supposed to lose, just like the rest of us."

I ducked as he threw a sloppy punch at me. His momentum carried him toward Kogo. She put him down with a lightning-fast front kick into his sternum. Security closed in. Kogo held her hands up in mock surrender. Then, ever so slowly, she reached down, grabbed a crease from the leading edge of her plaid dress, lifted it and revealed that she wore no underwear. "You likey like?" she asked in her version of a Hello Kitty voice.

Those of us who had witnessed this turn of events became frozen with surprise. What Kogo showed us was, well, perfectly stimulating. She smiled at her admirers for what seemed like an eternity. Then, she began to whirl forward—closing in on the security personnel with the staccato motion of a hummingbird dodging the first drops of a summer shower. And like a fight scene from a Bruce Lee movie, her choreographed kicks, punches, and elbows melded into a flurried ballet of comic ferocity. After pivoting off a support column and delivering a controlled hammer punch to the last of the guards, she smiled and took a few playful bows. She was poetry in motion—probably lived for moments like these.

"Hey," shouted a voice. It was Mr. Anastasio. He held up his hands apologetically and faced Kogo. "Please, there's been a misunderstanding. We're a little short on cash right now. Come back later; you'll get your money."

Heidi, who had managed to get into the action, stood her ground and growled at the fallen. The drunken straw man who had thrown the first punch was carried away amidst the confounded groans and painful whimpers of the security staff. Kogo gave Mr. Anastasio a hard look, spit a spray of Japanese leaden indignation onto the carpet, then walked us out.

The dry heat of the morning felt good.

"Wow," I said, Kogo's victory filling me with pride. "You're good. I bet you weren't even trying back there, were you?"

She tilted her head and shrugged her shoulders. "I enjoy fight. No hurt people bad. Just send message."

We made it back to the base and into our new conference room just as the first official meeting at the base was beginning. Marisol was serving coffee and pastries when Crash stood up. He tucked in his shirt and slicked back his hair.

"Yeah, uh, well, Eiichiro and I would like to express some concerns."

Heidi started barking at his feet and pulling at his shoelaces. I looked down at our conference table. It was wood, oval, and it felt exotic. Repurposed old growth? The finish still allowed my fingertips to discern the lifelines of what must have been a magnificent tree.

"What I'm trying to say is," Crash said, interrupting my big-tree thoughts. "Well, what's the deal with that Soul Breaker Virus thing you mentioned yesterday? It sounds bad."

Shit, I thought. How was I going to tell them this world was going to end? Just do it. Wasn't that what Nike said?

"Crash," I said. "Eiichiro, and those of you who don't know. Your world is ending in seven years. It didn't happen in my world, but it's going to happen here. Ninety-nine percent of the world's population is going to be wiped out and there's not much I can do about it. Apparently, I tried to stop this virus one hundred and thirty-two times and failed. I suppose you could try to stop it, but my path is clear. I'm going to ride the virus out with a base on the moon. Obviously, you and your families are all welcome to come along with me. In fact, I've seen you all there, on the moon, riding the Virus out. So, your call."

"Hai," said Eiichiro. He stood up and bowed. "I understand." Then, he sat back down.

Crash relented with a shoulder shrug and said, "OK, but if we are going to build a spacecraft, it's gonna take money. A ton of money, and workers."

"I agree," said Dean. "We have a machine shop, so we can build just about anything, but still, we're going to need help: machinists, fabricators, and craftsmen. The good news is the bunker is in place"

Katya rose with a curtsy and said, "I've located a high-altitude British Electric Lightning jet. The doctor agrees it'll be great for parts. Should I buy it?"

"Yes," I said. "Buy it. Margie can help with the paperwork. Hey, everyone— money is not a problem. I got thirty-five, maybe forty million just waiting to be spent. And there's more on the way. So I don't want to hear about money anymore. I want to hear about progress. If you have problems money can solve, then solve them. Any questions? Good. From now on we meet here, 8:00 a.m., Monday through Friday, weekends as needed. That's it. Now let's go get some work done."

I went to Marisol who was clearing the kitchen table. "Would you like to go for a ride? Maybe get some lunch or something?"

She turned to me. "I too busy Mr. Bridges." Then, as if to escape from sexual harassment in the workplace, she left the room.

Kogo probably had revenge on her mind when she said, "We go get long-long money?"

I gave her and Adamit a nod. It was a good thing we were in the war wagon because on the drive over to Caesars, a sudden downpour literally flooded the streets.

Cagey was at the sportsbook, waiting for us. He had our winnings bundled and ready for bagging. He apologized for the earlier confusion and added, "I can give you guys 5:1 odds on tomorrow's hockey game, Soviets versus USA."

The *big game*, I thought. The effing Miracle on Ice. The 5:1 odds seemed way too low, but still, that was a huge payday. That kind of cash could go a long way at the base.

"We'll take 10:1," Adamit countered. "Especially when you know it should be 15:1."

Cagey did a side-to-side doubletake and said quietly, "They're not going to pay if you win. Just take your winnings and leave. It's over."

"This thing is going south," I confided to Adamit. "What do you think?"

He took a deep breath, paused for a moment, and said, "I'm not sure he's telling the truth. Maybe he's just protecting his end-of-the-month bonus. If they accept our action, they're going to have to honor it."

I turned to Cagey. "We'll bet a million on the game and take the rest with us."

Outside, the sky had cleared. Ozone molecules and sun rays greeted us like long-lost friends.

CHAPTER 74

We drove back to the base. Jacob's half-grown puppies welcomed us; they were rambunctious and seemed to be everywhere at once.

"Adamit," I said. "Go ahead and give twenty grand to each of the construction workers; they've earned it. And have Dean stash whatever is left in the bunker. I'm going back to my apartment."

I joined Kogo upfront in the suburban. After a few miles she said, "Mr. Bridges, you can fight, yes?"

It dawned on me that I could fight, or at least defend myself. "I'm not a fighter, Kogo, but I have studied wrestling, boxing, and jiu-jitsu, mostly for self-defense. And I'm a good shot with a gun; plus, I've got you."

"You know *jiu-jitsu*?" she asked through a laugh. She was beautiful, impossibly rare, completely dangerous, and she had just laughed.

We went to my place. After she cleared all the rooms, I said, "I'll be fine, Kogo. Come back tomorrow morning." She went to the living room, turned on the TV, and sat down on the couch.

I put on some clothes, grabbed a bottle of rum, two glasses full of ice, and joined Kogo on the couch. I poured a little rum into the glasses and offered one to Kogo. She waved her hand and shook her head with a, "No." I downed both drinks and settled into the couch.

On the television, Walter Cronkite recited the news of the day. One of the stories was on Iran and their ransom demand of twenty-four billion dollars for the release of the fifty-two American hostages they held. Another story told of the Soviet Army and how they had dug deep into the mountains of Afghanistan... A human-interest story about a new company called TorwardAll Pharmaceuticals grabbed my attention. They had just received FDM—the Federal Drug Monitoring branch of the FDA—approval to begin trials on "Stasis Telomereis," their experimental life-extension drug for dogs. I took a mental note of the story.

During the Center for Disease Control's report on this year's flu epidemic, Kogo filled one of the glasses halfway up with rum and drank it. Then, she leaned back, crossed her arms, and slumped her head.

"Hey, Kogo, I said. "What's up?"

She looked up at me, then clenched her teeth and quietly growled.

I refilled the glasses and said, "Come on, you can tell me anything."

"Why?" Kogo said, jumping at the chance to confront me. "Why can I tell you such things? You are a bad man. You Sethco the Destroyer... You kill, destroy future."

"What the hell are you talking about? I didn't kill anyone... except for that guy that was trying to kill me. But that was in self-defense, and I didn't actually pull the trigger. Although I would have. And what's up with that Sethco crap you keep laying on me? Why do you keep saying that? *Why?*"

She straightened out her posture and looked at me. "Sethco kill billions. Future folklore, prophecy from *Book of Jamerson*. It say: Sethco not one person, not one thing. Is more like... blame for past. Scapegoat to hide badness of Man. My master say: humanity need hero with face of villain. I no think you are hero."

I still didn't understand, but knew I would never create a company, call it Sethco, and destroy things. Sure, I was a jaded fuck, but I cared—at least to some degree.

"Where did you read this Jamerson prophecy?"

"My first master, Su Sung. He was Old Shifter and scribe for *Book of Jamerson*."

"Let me tell you something, Kogo. Folklore or prophecy, the future is not guaranteed. I know this because Jamerson himself showed me how to change the past. Kogo, you don't know it yet, but in the future, you help me change the past. It's not easy, but it can be done. But something tells me that's not what's bugging you; is it? Why don't you tell me what's really wrong?"

"Today is day of my birth."

"Oh, that's great. Happy birthday, Kogo." I held up my glass. "Cheers." Kogo went to take hold of her glass but stopped. I set my glass back down. "Do you mind me asking how old you are?"

"I was born in Year of Monkey, one hundred and twenty-one years ago."

"That's... incredible. My God, you must have seen and done so many things. What is it like having so many memories?"

"Many bad things cloud out good things."

"Do you remember everything, or do you—"

"I remember all. Memories are most painful thing in long life. You cannot hide from what lives inside you. I born in Chinese internment camp. This day sad for me. I never know parents."

"Jeez, that's terrible. I'm sorry you had to go through that."

"Is OK now. The past make me strong. They bring me to Peking Opera School, isolate me, beat me, train me to be perfect student. When I become more than teacher, I escape, kill many bad people."

I stood, held up my glass, and said, "To space and a life well lived."

She stood, as if to accept my proclamation, then vanished. I felt a tapping on the back of my head. I turned, saw a blur, then realized she was back in front of me. Her breathing rate had increased and perspiration beaded on her forehead.

"Hey, Kogo, that's your thing, isn't it? Your gift. Speed."

"Yes, Mr. Bridges, but time, not speed. I slow time: a second, maybe two. It OK I go to space with you?"

"Of course," I said. "I wouldn't go there without you. You're my guardian, my savior. Let me tell you something. In the future, I end up floating around in space for three years, almost dead, and you, Lieutenant Kogo Musashi, you come and rescue me. And by the way"—I stood up, opened my arms, and gave her a careful hug—"happy birthday, Kogo Musashi."

She stuck her face into my chest, trembled, then began to sob.

"Oh Kogo," I said. "Things will work out, I promise."

"Musashi greatest swordsman ever. I orphan, no Musashi."

"No, you are Kogo Musashi, the greatest *fighter* that ever lived. Didn't Marisol call you Kogo Musashi, her dove? She is the Progenitor. So that must mean something, right? Hold on; I just remembered something."

I went to my bedroom and located the one book I owned, *the Book of Five Rings,* a gift from Master Poe. I skimmed through its pages until I found the illustration I was looking for: a close-up illustration of Miyamoto Musashi's hands gripping a sword.

"Look, Kogo," I said as I returned to the living room. "His little finger on his right hand is only half-grown—just like yours. Don't you see? It's a genetic trait."

She looked at the picture. "Oh... his finger look like mine. You think we are family?"

"Yes, I do, because you are."

"Thank you, Mr. Bridges," she said quietly.

She seemed OK, but still, being stuck here with me, on her birthday, watching Walter Cronkite? Hell, she had probably never had a real birthday party. My plans for staying in for the night changed into doing all I could to make Kogo's birthday special.

"Cheer up," I said. "We're going out on the town, my treat."

"No, it OK," she said, looking away. "I fine now."

She was so alone. How had Adamit let this slip?

"Kogo, I'm taking you to dinner. And don't try to stop me. I don't want to have to use my jiu-jitsu on you."

She smiled. "Oh no, not jiu-jitsu."

Just then, somebody banged on the door. In an instant, Kogo was there—her blade at the ready.

CHAPTER 75

"Who there!" Kogo yelled.

"Land Shark," answered a flat and disguised voice.

Kogo looked at me and shook her head questioningly. Apparently, she wasn't familiar with the *Saturday Night Live* reference. I peered through the peephole and saw Adamit. I opened the door.

"Sorry for not giving you a heads up," Adamit said as he rushed past me, "but I didn't want to risk the surprise factor." He lifted Kogo into his arms and gave her a big kiss. "Happy birthday, darling."

Thirty minutes later we entered the club. Most of the InEvitech crew were there. Jacob had even brought along Mr. Virgil Caine, Buffy and Jody, and all the puppies. The guards ignored our weapons and waved us on in. As we took our seats in a room aside from the main hall, a twelve-piece Chinese orchestra began playing the intricate melodies of a bygone era. Lighting interacted with the music and gave the room a swaying motion. Mr. Virgil Caine plopped himself down in front of the musicians and took a snooze. The half-grown pups competitively ran about the room, locating as many new odors as possible. The hyenas took up guard positions near the entrance. I have to admit it was an epic dinner party, but something was off. I couldn't identify what it was, but it was inside me and it wanted out.

"Hey man," said Crash. "Eiichiro and I want to thank you for that bonus money, and ahh... I'd like to apologize for our rough start. This whole Vegas trip has been a real mind bender. I wasn't prepared—mentally that is."

I patted his shoulder. "That makes two of us. We've come a long way in a short time. Hell, you're gonna be on the moon in a few years so let's just keep looking forward, not back. OK?"

He gestured with an understanding nod and two thumbs up.

That was when Marisol came over, faced me, and placed her arms around my shoulders. She gave me a satisfying kiss and said, "I go now."

Where the hell had she come from? I got up and tried to stop her, but it was no use. She was already gone. Had she ever been here? Had I imagined her? Fuck! That girl would be the death of me.

My heart pounded. I wanted to punch something *or* somebody. Why was she doing this to me? Was I some sort of plaything? Did she think she was better than me? No, Seth, she's a fricking god from another planet. She is better than you in every way. I supposed I could do worse... Yeah, come to think about it, it's wasn't such a bad deal. She's beautiful and smart, she has a sense of humor, and she likes to cook and clean... The only thing missing is a bunch of bambinos. Can aliens have babies? She'd make a great mom. Why was I complaining? I was just being stupid and selfish. I couldn't see the good things that were right in front of me. I had to snap out of it before I fucked this up.

After dinner, I joined Dean and the geishas in the main hall. "Dean, I need blow, booze, weed, and... and titties!"

"Already on it, boss."

Asuka, Izumi, and Yoshimi took turns rubbing calmness into my shoulders. In between gobs of coke, I drank a bunch of rum drinks and smoked hash from a hookah.

Purgatorium's main hall was packed with Short-Timers. On the stage, an East Coast punk-rock band called the Freeze was grinding out gnarled tones into an overloaded PA. The frenetic music spawned chaotic slam-dancing and an edgy vibe. When they ended their current composition, a song about broken bones, roadies prepped the stage for another band. A thick fluorescent-green fog rolled in and settled over the lower half of Purgatorium's interior. Multi-colored laser lights speared through the room and stabbed ever so briefly into people, the walls, the ceiling, and floor. A full horn section emerged from the stage's shadows. They simultaneously brought their instruments to their lips and blew the opening bars of "The Night They Drove Old Dixie Down." On stage was Robbie Robertson and his aptly named band: the Band. I had thought they had retired the year before with their "Last Waltz" tour, but here they were. Levon Helm, the band's drummer, began to sing the lyrics to their song "The Night They Drove Old Dixie Down." A song about the tribulations of a Confederate soldier named Virgil Caine.

An hour later, my frustration with Marisol had taken a turn onto ugly street. I left Purgatorium for the casino above.

I walked alone, down the pathways of deception, past the slot machines, over the disturbingly pretty patterns on the carpet, anger ringing in my mind. I wanted to hurt strangers. Where did anger come from? Was it stored away in some distant cosmos, waiting to be injected into those who desired it? Is there a planet called Hate in this cosmos? Bells rang and people walked by. Why does everyone wear jeans? It's not like they are comfortable. I guess they give people a sense of individuality—be yourself and dress like everyone else. Oh wait, that guy is not wearing jeans. He's OK.

"Would you care for a cocktail?" asked a waitress.

I remembered thinking: she was young, gorgeous, and probably had no inkling of the pain and hardship this cruel world had in store for her.

"Yes, I want rum and lots of it. Better yet"—I handed her a wad of hundreds—"bring me the whole bottle and some ice. Please."

I settled in front of a five-cent slot machine. Becky, who was on security detail, watched me from the corner aisle. I shooed her away and told her to leave, but she just hid her watchful eyes further back in the casino. I pulled on the slot machine's stupid lever and kept drinking.

Who the hell did Marisol think she was? What, I was a bird, and she was… a jet plane?

At some point, I started snorting cocaine from the slot machine's faceplate. It was late, and I had forgotten about the casino's security cameras. I was up 500 nickels when the floor manager came over and said, "Sir, it's time for you to go home."

I collected my coins, and, with the help of Becky, stumbled out of the casino. Outside, the morning sun smiled a hello. I wanted more alcohol but knew I was too far gone. My pocket-sized female protector poured me into a cab and sat quietly next to me. The taxi's tires hummed the melody of a well-traveled road. At Fort Banks, Becky grabbed a wheelchair from behind the concierge desk and, with Skip's assistance, wheeled me into the lobby.

During the elevator ride up to my apartment, I slurred, "I love you, Becky."

She entered the combination for the door lock, steered me into my room, and pushed me onto the bed.

My world churned. I remembered how painful love could be. I bet Marisol had instructed that Cupid fucker to shoot an arrow right through my nuts… Bastards.

Goodnight, Exon.

CHAPTER 76

My head ached and my stomach roiled. I wasn't sure what time it was, but the sun was high in the sky. I freshened up as best I could and readied for another day. Nickels were scattered about the carpet. Tears, which fought to soothe my dehydrated eyeballs, distorted the fallen coins, giving them the appearance of two armadas of tallships, from the kingdoms of Heads and Tails, engaged in a high-seas battle. I went into the living room, sat on the couch, and brushed the sticky wooden-nickel ships from the soles of my feet. Becky brought over a tray of hangover helpers: water, ginger ale, coffee, and three aspirin.

"Good afternoon, Mr. Bridges. How are we feeling today?"

I paused her by holding up my index finger, then scrambled into the bathroom and prayed for air as I expunged the previous night's indulgences into the toilet. They must have served me the cheap stuff last night, I thought. No... I had bought a top-shelf bottle; this was what happened when you drank too much, period. Try to remember that for next time. Maybe you should quit, I told myself. I had important things to do. Alright, I'd give it a try. Did I have to go to work? No, I was the boss, and it was Saturday. I could sleep in.

I cleaned myself up and returned to Comfy Couch City.

"We're feeling much better now," I said to Becky. "Thank you for asking." I sipped alternately from the three glasses of hangover helpers and downed the aspirin. "Hey, Becky, what's the damage? How much trouble am I in? And where's Heidi?"

She brought over some toast. "Relax, boss, you're fine, no trouble. Marisol took Heidi after you left the dinner party."

Becky gave me a quick synopsis of my post-memory casino activities, then went back to the kitchen where she was preparing some food. To get at things beyond her reach, she kept moving a chair around and standing on it. It didn't seem to bother her, but it bothered me. I needed to get some sort of bench or stair system, so she would be more at ease. Dean could build it. She was confident, though. I had to give her props for that, and her positive attitude—that was a godsend.

"Hey, Becky, I don't want to pry or anything, but—what's it like? Being, you know, a small person?"

She marched over and stood in front of me. "I'm just like everyone else, just shorter. Oh, and by the way, I invested that lottery ticket you got from Dings on the Americans to beat the Russians today."

"Well, good luck. Say, do you know when the game starts?"

Knock. Knock. Knock.

I saw Dean through the peephole. As I opened the door, he backed-on in, dragging a table-sized folded-up satellite dish.

"Hey, boss," he said, "could I get a hand here?"

I grabbed the back of the contraption. "Sure, what's going on?"

"You've got action on the big game, so I figured you might want to see it in real time. Not that tape delay sh... Oh, hey Becky. How yeh doing?"

"Fine, Dean. Thank you for asking."

"Here"—he handed me a scrambler box and a coil of coaxial cable—"put the box on the TV and run the cable out to the deck. That's where I'm going to set the dish up."

Twenty minutes later, Channel 3 was airing a pregame show with a countdown clock that indicated it would be twenty-nine minutes until a bunch of improbable American college kids would play and beat the best hockey team in the universe. I had millions riding on the game, but when the broadcast announcers began explaining the true nature and significance of the contest, the money seemed insignificant in comparison.

The Soviets had won eight of the previous nine Olympic hockey gold medals and were on a twenty-one-game winning streak. Sure, they were the best, but tonight, communism would fail to capitalist exceptionalism. Flickers of the game from forty years ago flashed through my mind...

There was another knock on the door. It was Adamit, Kogo, Yoshimi, Asuka, and Izumi. Becky welcomed them all with hugs. Judging by the amount of food coming out of the kitchen, Becky had probably planned for this day well in advance. We were talking about the game when there was another knock on the door. Katya, Margie, Crash, and Eiichiro filed into the apartment. The place was getting so filled up, I had to pass out pillows for seats. It was hard to hear the TV over the chatter, but from what I could gather, the puck would be dropped in ten minutes.

Skip the concierge stuck his head through the half-open front door and asked, "Is everything alright?"

Becky pulled on one of the dress shirts he was wearing. "Come on in, sweetie, take a seat. We're going to beat the Russians!"

He gave the room a half-hearted wave, found a spot in front of the TV, and sat down crossed-legged on a pillow. When I had first gotten this apartment, I had figured it could be my own secret-squirrel hideout, but now, it felt right to be entertaining and have people stop on by. The only thing missing was Marisol and Heidi. I took a deep breath and realized my hangover was gone.

CHAPTER 77

As the puck dropped and the game began, the announcers kept up the patriotic hype and speculated on the possibility of an upset. After the first period, the game was tied 2-2. Excited voices filled the apartment. Speculation on why the Russians had replaced their goalie for the start of the second period was postponed when Marisol, Mr. Virgil Caine, and Heidi joined the party. Heidi ran over, jumped into my lap and gave my face a few licks. She was growing bigger every day, and her breath smelled like flowers in a meadow.

Marisol went straight to the kitchen. My heart quickened. Virgil growled a "Hello," commandeered a spot directly in front of the TV, and passed a dose of pungent lion gas. Skip stood up to protest, but then he gathered himself, sat back down, and tossed out accommodating smiles to those that cared. Wait, I thought, who was watching the base? Must have been Jacob. He was a good man, plus he had the assistance of Buffy and Jody.

By the end of the second period, the Russians were ahead 3-2. Eight minutes into the third, a high sticking penalty gave our side a power play. Dean turned up the TV's volume just as the tying goal rang out. Whoops and screams filled the room. A few minutes later we scored again, giving us a 4-3 lead. The next ten minutes pushed my faith in the past to the limit. We joined in with the TV announcer Al Michaels and counted down the final seconds.

At the end of the count, Dean yelled, "Do you believe in miracles?"

The room exploded with cheers as the Americans took the victory. Dean uncorked a bottle of champagne and sprayed everyone in the room. Virgil stood up and roared.

Marisol came over, kissed me, and said, "All our times are now." Then, she turned and began cleaning up.

As the party began to break up, we exchanged goodnights and I went to my room. Then, out of nowhere, I was sucked into an unbalanced, future-casting, liquid-metal vortex.

CHAPTER 78

"Captain...?" said CyNav-pilot Commander Alyssa Millken. I was sitting in a captain's chair, overlooking the bridge of an enormous spaceship. My Cog-Link filled me in: I was an Artificial and the captain of this ship—the *Kogo Maru*. Our mission, Project Appleseed, was to plant seven colonies of Modern Cause humans on seven Kepler-3-Goldilock-target planets. A warning icon alerted me to a flaming red ball heading right at us.

"You in there, Cappy?" asked the commander, with a couple of knocks to my Iconium-clad skull. "We got company."

"Helmsman, report!" I said with instinctual brevity.

"I'm not sure, captain... it looks like a Hypervelocity Star."

"Threat level?"

"Imminent danger, sir."

"Solutions... anybody?"

"Captain," said the commander, "grav waves are increasing. Warping is inevitable. Our best option is to engage slip drive and proceed to our next planting."

"I concur. Enter the coordinates. Helmsman, engage emergency-drive protocol alpha in four... three... two... one."

Our Algeronian slip drive enveloped us into a distemporal furl. And for the next half a minute—as antimatter was injected into our Heinlein III Donkeys—we were propelled at twenty-eight light-years per second.

We unfurled above a planet called Pitcairn. *One Hope 8*, the last of our colony plant ships, was dispatched to the planet's surface to begin colonization-deployment procedures. *One Hope 8* had a complement of ten male and thirty female Modern Cause humans. And like all our plant ships, *One Hope 8* was fortified with indefinite-life power converters, six years' worth of food, and specialized colonization supplies. Protocol dictated that we remain in orbit for the next three weeks.

I went to my quarters, sat on the bunk, and prepared for three weeks of Sleeporg mode. I could hear some of the crew arguing about a misplaced HHP (Happy Holo Patch) of Old Earth. I chuckled knowing my brain was chock-full of the real thing.

Overall, we'd done well: Project Appleseed was a success, and I'd made good on my second chance.

As I leaned onto my bunk, a cosmic rubber band slung me back to my bedroom at Fort Banks. And believe you me, returning from the future was disconcerting.

CHAPTER 79

I entered my recent exploits in space into my journal and got ready for another day. Somewhere between a piss and making a pot of coffee, I surmised that the malfunction rate for humans was around eighty-six percent. Heidi jawed at the improvised rope handle on the front door, then trotted down the hallway. She had figured out that pawing at the elevator's lobby button would open the doors, and pawing at the down button would take her to the lobby; once there, Skip would let her out. I was pouring some food into her bowl when I noticed two duffel bags in the living room. They were filled with bundles of hundred-dollar bills. I opened the envelope that rested between them.

Seth,
This is the money from the hockey game.

Adamit

PS. We are banned from Caesars; the rest of the casinos will follow suit.

Kogo bounced into the kitchen wearing pink flower-patterned underwear and a sleeveless tee-shirt. Nip-slippage, undulating ass, and her Cooterville-covering panties vied for my attention. I supposed I looked in all the wrong places for too long because, all of a sudden, my legs went out from under me. And before I knew what was happening, Kogo had straddled my chest.

She leaned back, pointed a finger at me, and laughed her childish, "Ha, ha, ha!"

I used an old-school elevator reversal and placed her in a dangerous invisible neck hold—a move I'd learned from Master Poe. Kogo effortlessly shifted my left arm down, locked her legs around my neck, and, right before she choked me out with a jiu-jitsu sleeper triangle, I noticed the flower patterns on her panties were in fact daisies.

When I came to, I took a mental note not to stare at Kogo when she was wearing only underwear. She helped me up and asked, "So, what we do today?"

I looked around the kitchen for my dignity. "We can start by taking that money to the base."

She gave me the once-over. "First you take shower, put on fresh suit, brush teeth."

We drove to the base and made our way over to the mess hall. It was Sunday, InEvitech's official day off. Dean and the Lee family were seated around the dining-room table and having a grand old time. I dragged in the duffle bags of money, set them in a corner, then took a seat. A hand reached around my midsection. It was Marisol. Fuck!

She brought her lips close to my ear and whispered, "We live, Seth. We live."

More of her obvious nonsense. I wanted to throw her on the table, rip her clothes off, and take her right there, but she'd already disappeared into the kitchen. Double fuck!

Jacob, who was listening to a radio via an earpiece, shouted, "We just beat Finland two to four. We won the gold!"

We all cheered at the news.

"Boss," Jacob said. "When you said we were going to win the gold. I mean, that was out there, man. I thought you were full of it."

"Think about it," I said. "Those Russian hockey players probably wanted to lose. I mean, what good is being the best at something if you live in a prison. Hey Dean, I've got a deposit for the bunker."

"Check this out," he said. "It leads to the bunker." He went over to the water cooler, moved it aside, and pushed on the wall to reveal a hidden passageway: a four-by-six-foot tunnel. "This was here all along. Spotted it on the original plans. Cool, right?"

"Very cool," I said. We worked our way down a short stairway, then traveled in a straight line to the other end of the tunnel, dragging the duffle bags behind us. The tunnel was lit by incandescent bulbs centered on every other ceiling slab. Along the way, I noticed folded-up cots, water storage tanks, and expired foodstuffs. We worked our way up another staircase and came to the exit door, which had a Farrah Fawcett poster taped to it. We opened the door and found ourselves in Hangar 2. Dean showed me the electronic lock combination and led me into the bunker. "Excellent," I said as I set a duffle bag down, sat on it, and promptly fell into one of my unbalanced-washing-machine episodes.

"Captain," said Quartermaster Moko Madrid. "Observation protocols have been fulfilled. The last planting has successfully taken root. What are your orders?"

Dean, the bunker at the base, and Vegas itself were pushed to a less busy section of my mind. I instinctively understood my reality: I was the captain of the *Kogo*

Maru, and we had just completed Project Appleseed: our mission of planting colony ships on seven Kepler-3-Goldilocks-target planets. I thought about the quartermaster's question and realized I had been contemplating it for the last three weeks. Our antimatter fuel was all but exhausted, so we couldn't go back to Earth. Even if we could, the Earth we knew was gone, replaced by a world that was two-hundred-seventy time-dilated years older. I knew there were six tics left on our slip drive because I had planned it that way. Six tics was sufficient to take us to any one of a thousand habitable planets.

"OK, everybody, listen up, this is your captain," I said in broadcast mode. "We've made it this far and we're still alive: we have a few tics left so the choice is yours. We can find a new home and settle down, or, if you want, we can do some exploring? Either way, it's up to you."

A few moments later, I looked to my crew who had gathered around me.

"Captain," said Chief Petty Officer Anna Millken. "We want *you* to make that decision for us."

They'd been waiting for this moment ever since we had received Project Appleseed. I looked at my crew. They all nodded. "Well," I said, "according to my calculations, it's time we settled down a spell."

We went to the bridge and took our respective positions. I looked at our CyNav-pilot and said, "Pick us a winner, Milli."

The last of the anti-time matter allowed us to travel to the star Pilar. It held six planets in its grip. We settled on the second and called it Kalesh. In a way, this was the eighth plant of our mission. It was a beautiful planet, mostly water, with Earth-like features including mountainous regions, jungles, deserts, and polar ice caps.

"Well, captain," said Flight Surgeon Heidissa as we took our first steps on the planet. "Was this what you envisioned?"

She had been my dearest companion since the beginning. I was pulled away before I could answer. Then, I was back in the bunker. Dean had his hands on my shoulders and a grin on his face.

"Was it a good one?" he asked. "Can you tell me about it?"

CHAPTER 80

Las Vegas
June 07, 1980

The months passed quickly: The puppies were full-grown, Paranoid and Lonely were more like Facebook friends now, and, as far as Love was concerned, he just hid within the confines of Marisol's shadow. My alcohol consumption was a thing of the past, probably because I was already in the place I wanted to escape to and everything I needed was here, plus I was happy. Adamit and Kogo, Becky and Izumi, and Doctor Eiichiro and Margie had paired up as romantic couples. We'd hired a pilot—Russo Albarosso, a Jericho Sims recommendation—who Katya had taken a liking to, and more importantly, our spacecraft *One Hope* had begun to take shape and was ready for testing.

We had outsourced *One Hope*'s main body panels and structural systems to third-party fabricators. Avionics and manual flight controls had been scavenged from the Electric Lightning jet we had acquired, and Crash had hired six craftsmen who had assembled our thirty-two-foot-long *One Hope* with the love and dedication a parent shows for a newborn child.

Katya had secured our first payload, a communication satellite contracted by AT&T. Its timely deployment was insured with a million-dollar bond held in escrow. I wondered how NASA and the governments of the world would react to our mission. Would they try to shut us down? Would they even know? I was pretty sure I'd taken care of Octavius 8, but Octavius 7 was still out there—somewhere. He could throw a wrench in the works. I feared for the worst and began drawing up contingency plans and fallback positions.

I was in my bedroom at Fort Banks perusing the Box and occasionally proffering up some time-traveling conundrums and suppositions with Heidi, when Becky popped her head in and said, "Hey, boss, sorry to bother you, but Skip and some guys from the government are here. Should I let them in?"

I shut down the Box and went out front. Heidi began sniffing at the gap under the front entrance. Becky opened the door. Skip, who now wore five dress shirts, one on top of each other, knelt and gave Heidi's ears a good waggling.

"Good girl," he said. "Who's the best girl in the world?" He gave her a kiss, stood up, apologized for the intrusion, and nodded with a sideways thumb action at the government worker on his left.

The man held out a badge. "Merrick Fife. I'm here on ba-ba-behalf of the state of Nevada."

The poor bastard had a stutter and looked like a goat. I tried to introduce myself, but he ignored me and tacked a cease & desist order on the door.

"Wha-workman's compensation insurance has not been pa-paid," he stammered. "You must sta-stop all business activities. The-tha-this is your only warning. Fa-fa-failure to comply will result in pa-penalties of one-tho-thousand dollars a day."

He peered past the doorway, stuck his head into the apartment, and began sniffing loudly—as if to locate a particular odor. Heidi backed up a few feet, bowed playfully, then lunged at the man and tackled him onto the hallway floor. She wagged her tail enthusiastically as she repeatedly licked his face. Surprisingly, the downed government guy began to vocalize encouraging chuff-like sounds as he returned Heidi's kisses with a few of his own. Skip covered his mouth with feigned concern, but the opiate-addled-smirk on his face indicated otherwise.

"Jeepers creepers," said Becky, pulling Heidi off the bureaucrat. "Are you OK, mister?"

I helped Merrick get to his feet. "Sorry about that."

"My, my," he said. "She sure is a rambunctious girl."

"Mr. Fife," I said, "do you like your job?"

"Fa-king sucks tu-turkey turds!" He turned toward Becky. "Begging your pardon, ma'am, for the la-language."

She offered him a forgiving nod.

"Listen," I said. "How would you like to come work for us? Pay is a thousand dollars a week, plus housing if needed."

He bent down and gave Heidi a pet on her side. "What kind of work?" he asked without stammer.

"Well, this here is Becky. I'm not sure you two have been properly introduced." They shook hands, and I continued, "Becky's brother Jacob—he has his hands full with my base security and taking care of a bunch of animals that live there. I was thinking maybe you could help him out with the animals: feeding, cleaning up after them, talking to them, that sort of thing. Do you like animals, Mr. Fife?"

He paused for a few seconds, then bent down and hugged Heidi. "I love animals; how did you know? Taking care of animals is all I've ever wanted to do. Holy cow, I'll take it—yessiree. Thank you."

I untacked the cease and desist order. "Don't thank me. Heidi's the one who hired you."

He looked into Heidi's eyes as tears trickled from his. Then, as if he were on some off-Broadway production, he began to sing, *"I love you, pretty girl; you are so pretty girl. I love you pretty girl, I love, love, you..."*

We were days away from drastically altering mankind's timetable for space travel. Was Merrick Fife the first of the bureau-crobes that would plague my world with spurious legal and moral authority? I couldn't hire them all, though I suspected most had achieved some semblance of bureaucratic complacency or were so bored with their stations in life that they didn't care about mine. Nevertheless, the encounter only strengthened my resolve to create fallback positions.

CHAPTER 81

The base's Tuesday morning meeting got underway, and although we had all been consumed by the logistical demands of the project, everyone seemed to be in good spirits.

During the discussion of the next week's flight trials, Marisol came in from the service door, tidied up, and refreshed our drinks. She had all the answers. She was making me work, keeping me independent.

Jacob's walkie-talkie pinged a tone. He unholstered it and said, "Go ahead. This is S-1."

"Security officer Kesleuogh. Sorry to disturb you, boss, but there's a bunch of people from the government out here at the front gate. Some guy named Nettles is flashing a badge and demanding to see whoever's in charge."

So it began. We'd show them everything, I thought. Well, almost everything. Paranoid decided it was a good time to make an appearance. He walked in a tight circle, then stopped, threw up his arms in disgust, and disappeared into the wall. Thanks for the help, buddy.

I gave Jacob a nod. He pressed the radio's transmit button and said, "Tell 'em we'll be there when we're good and ready."

"Understood," replied security.

"Dean," I said. "You and Crash go secure the GRDs, any related paperwork, and put it in the bunker. Margie, call your brother and get him here, *now*. Everyone else, let's put our best face forward and welcome our guests."

"Best face?" Adamit asked.

Kogo slapped him hard. "Yes. That one," she said. "That your best face."

He scowled a grin, lifted her up, and kissed her.

We went outside to greet the uninvited. Adamit took the lead as we walked over to the assemblage of government employees. There were ten of them, and I'd bet my oldest brother's next girlfriend, each of them believed they were more important than the other. A middle-aged man who appeared to be the head malfunctionary flashed his badge in a well-practiced one-handed maneuver.

"Special Agent Bill Nettles. I'm the representative liaison for the state, local, and federal governments. We're here to help you. Now, which one of you is in charge?" His dull eyes complemented his cheap grey suit and he held a suspicious-looking briefcase at his side.

Katya took hold of Nettles' badge for a moment, studied it, then slipped it into his front pants pocket. "My name is Katya; I'm a special agent myself."

He shook off her Shifter glamour and spit out a diatribe of complaints and violations that needed to be *immediately* addressed: exotic animal permits had not been secured, union representation had not been documented, an EPA impact study was required whenever change-of-use government land had been sold, and the IRS needed to verify the existence of our corporation.

Despite a temperature of 101° Fahrenheit, the ruse was amusing. I stepped forward and introduced myself as the owner of the property. Five minutes later the government contingent began their investigation with the understanding they could go anywhere on the property as long as base employees accompanied them.

Margie ushered a bald, bespectacled, middle-aged IRS agent into her air-conditioned office. Katya, Kogo, and Becky introduced themselves to a group of our new *friends* from the EPA and gave them access to what they needed. Jacob and Merrick helped out with the exotic animal minions, while Doctor Eiichiro, Crash, and our new pilot Russo helped out escorting the remaining inspectors.

With Adamit on my right and Heidi on my left, we gave Nettles—in my opinion, a poorly manufactured wrench of a man—the grand tour of the base. By the time we had made it over to Hangar 2, Nettles was sweating profusely.

He slung his suit jacket over his shoulder, pointed at the padlock on the hangar's door, and barked, "Why is that door locked?"

"Dean," I said, "one of my employees, he's got the key. He should be here shortly."

Heidi, who was now a hundred-thirty pounds of muscle with a head the size of a mailbox, gave Nettles a woof that triggered a thunderous roar from Mr. Virgil Caine.

Nettles dropped into a defensive crouch and yelled, "What the fuck was that!?"

We led him over to an area near Virgil's cage. The five-hundred-pound King of Beasts nudged his cage door open and trotted over to greet us. Nettles' face twitched and his eyes bulged. Then, he turned and quickly walked back to his car, occasionally looking over his shoulder to see if we were following him—which we were.

He opened the front door of his government-issued K-car, turned around, and yelled, "You haven't heard the last of me. I will return!" The front tires of his car spun pebbles into the wheel wells, and dust billowed as he sped away.

A brand-new red Corvette slid to a stop at the entrance. Our lawyer got out of the car and hollered, "Don't say a word."

The rest of the government workers must have decided the show was over, because they too got into their vehicles and drove away. I highly doubted our troubles were over; in fact, it was just the opposite. We were now a blip on the government's radar. And now that blip, a composition of wires, electricity, and human ingenuity, was a cancer feeding on our future. I gave Bruce a million-dollar retainer, and he promised to make all our legal troubles disappear.

CHAPTER 82

Two months before, during the celebration of DARPA Special Agent Bill Nettle's third divorce, an escort named Victoria jumped out of his divorce cake and captured his heart. He had known right then: she would be the new Mrs. Nettles. Unfortunately, Nettle's plans for love and light had become derailed: it was last weekend, during a drug and alcohol-fueled rampage, that Victoria had called him a *boring dick* and left him for a biker named Big Rip. And if that hadn't been enough, just yesterday, during a performance review, his new supervisor, Deputy Director Galen Fox, had ridden his ass about action-oriented results. And now, he thought as he drove away from the base, some fucking lion and a group of weirdos had made him foul his pants. He reminded himself never to eat leftover Mexican for breakfast—*stick to American; that's what his mother would say.*

Sweat poured down his face as he removed his soiled underwear and tossed them into some nearby bushes. He was proud of his ability to stand in line without complaint or humiliation, but this was different: those hippies, or whatever they were, had made it personal. Adrenaline surged courage through Nettle's veins. He turned his Detroit disposable around, stomped the accelerator, and headed back to the scene of his most recent indignity.

At the gate, he locked up the brakes, grabbed his suitcase, and faced his tormentors. A thin film of dust settled on his polished black shoes. The owner, the ugly dog, and that quiet Frankenstein-ish guy just stared at him. Nothing to fear, he told himself: just a bunch of potheads, commies, and war-dodging hippies.

"I need to get into that locked building," he yelled. "You know the one I'm talking about. No more games. This is official government business!"

Dean drove over in a golf cart and said, "Hangar 2 is open." Then, he mimicked Jim Carrey's character Ace Ventura, and said, "Go ahead, look around."

Once inside, Nettles pointed at our Learjet 35—another Jericho Sims acquisition I'd bought as part of my fallback plans. "I know what that is, but"—he pointed at *One Hope*, now docked on a workaround jig in the center of the hangar—"what the hell is that supposed to be?"

I walked over to our spacecraft and patted her. "This is the reason you're here. It's a machine I'm building."

"You're building a machine?"

"That's right."

"What kind of machine is it?"

"It's the kind of machine I want to build."

"Oh, so you're a wise ass. Well, let me tell you something, Mr. Wise Ass, you're not building anything without my say so. I've got purview over all government sub-contractors in Clark County, so you better start giving me some straight answers. And you better start doing it mighty quick, because I'm not in the mood for any of your hippy-dippy games."

"I'm not a sub-contractor for anyone. I'm an independent agent, and this is private property."

"That's irrelevant." He pointed at *One Hope* and said, "What is it? Some kind of spacecraft or something?"

"That's right."

Inspector Stinky Pants walked around *One Hope*. His right index finger, repeatedly and noticeably, was triggering a shutter-release button located on the underside of the briefcase handle.

"Why does it have windows and seats?"

"That's for us."

He pulled on his lower lip and narrowed his gaze. "Oh, right. Just checking."

Marisol came over, took Nettle's hand, and ushered him back to his car.

Special Agent Nettles drove away from the base feeling euphoric. He smiled and fantasized about the lengthy report that he would write, and about that brown-skinned girl who had helped him back to his car. Probably an illegal alien, he thought. But it didn't matter; she made things simple, less chaotic. He could fix her, make her the next Mrs. Nettles. He decided it would be best, for everyone involved, to use the bureau's resources to investigate her.

CHAPTER 83

The following night, our first real flight test began. Our new aviator Russo sat in *One Hope's* pilot seat and took hold of the flight controls. Crash sat directly behind Russo and operated the Gravity Resist Drives. I sat behind Crash and took in the whole operation. Officially, I was the payload specialist, a fancy title for the guy that pulled the satellite deployment lever.

Jacob had the ground crew open the hangar doors, then waved us out with an *all clear* sign. Dean removed his fists from his temples, came close to *One Hope's* canopy, and shouted, "Crash, the battery-selector switch is shunting into a cross-feed; keep it on *One* or *Two*, but not *All*."

Crash gave Dean the thumbs-up sign, made the adjustment, and lifted us five feet into the air. Russo incrementally pushed the thrusters forward. It was 12:15 a.m. and the crisp moonless night seemed to call out to us.

"Nice and easy," Russo's voice reported through our headsets. "Just like we planned: hold this altitude to the end of the runway, then we're going to turn her around and head back."

"Roger," Crash and I acknowledged simultaneously.

The thrusters pushed us forward at fifteen knots, and the GRD held our altitude at five feet above the ground. At the end of the airstrip, Russo screwed up the turnaround, and on the return leg, had us zig-zagging between the runway and the dirt shoulder.

"Alright," he said when we were back in the hangar. "Let's set her down and put her to bed. On my count, three... two... one..."

Crash lowered *One Hope* onto her docking-cradle with an intuitively soft touch.

The ground crew secured the hangar's doors. We went through a quick series of switch-flipping and dial-turning shutdown procedures before uncoupling our suits' umbilical cords. Adamit and Doctor Eiichiro helped us out of the ship.

Heidi barked excitedly as we all gave each other hugs and slaps on the back.

Becky took a picture of us standing next to *One Hope*.

Dean removed the craft's GRD modules and locked them in the bunker.

We hung up our gear, left the hangar, and headed over to the barracks.

Marisol emerged from the darkness. She gave each of us a kiss, said, "Thank you," then faded back into the early morning shadows.

After a short post-flight meeting, I went to one of the spare bedrooms and lay down. Tomorrow we were going to attempt to hover at five thousand feet, then glide back to the base. It should be OK. Just then, the bed began to wobble... Oh shit, here we go.

I traveled, or at least my mind traveled, through the wobbling liquid metal vortex that was my vision transport system. Then, I was somewhere else.

I found myself on an odd-shaped couch. Cog-Link filled me in: I was living on a planet called Kalesh, I was a thousand years old, had used up all my shifts, and had just spore-sourced my journals to anyone with a Glax-net receiver. My worries about our upcoming glide test faded, replaced by the current thoughts of my future mind. I remembered how I, along with the crew of the *Kogo Maru*, had completed Project Appleseed, how we had landed on this planet, how we had built a settlement, how the crew joined up and had children, and how, within sixty years, our population had grown to four hundred Modern Cause Kaleshin humans. I remembered how we heeded the advice in our *Algeronian Guide to Existence*—standard issue with all Appleseed colony plants—and how it had kept us spiritually and politically fulfilled. I also remembered that I had used up all my shifts and that I was a crippled-up old man.

With the help of my antique glider, I went outside and found my favorite spot on the shore of Green Ghost Lake. After easing my-rickety-self off the glider, I leaned back on an imported bristlecone tree and surveyed the lake: to my left, a blue moon was rising over the calm waters; to my right, a green sun was gently setting into the horizon.

I used a stimstem to shoot a lethal dose of Tedium in my neck: an act I'd always been prepared to do. With a feeling of release and contentment, I continued my journey down memory lane: I'd been a king, a pauper, and a robot. I'd surfed the Outer Rings of Valkyrie, harnessed Orkanian fog, danced through subspace, and made Man an intergalactic species in the process. I'd died more times than I wished to remember, and all along the way, I'd made the best of friends. Huh—not bad for a plumber. And to think it had all started back on Earth, on a beach called Herring Cove. Damn, we'd had some good times. Now look at me—a feeble old man, the oldest born human in all the worlds. I'd seen too much, traveled too far, and lived way too long. An internal *beep* confirmed my journals had been successfully spore-sourced to whomever cared. Finally, I was ready to make peace with my makers. I shut down my Cog-Link, closed my eyes, and murmured, "Now I lay my soul to sleep, take me home before I wake—"

"Woof!"

I sat up. A black dog and a child were standing next to me.

"Exon!" I said.

"It's Exeon," said the child. "Remember?"

"Yes, of course it is," I said, scruffing up the pooch's chest hair. "Exeon, you dog-brained, mangy-haired robot. And you, young lady?" I said, turning to the child.

"Grandpoppy! It's me, Sabita. Have you been taking your medicine?"

"Sabita! Of course, my number one greatest granddaughter. I'm just fooling with you, child. Come close, let me look at you."

She smiled and laid a hand on my forearm. "Grandpa, why do you like this place so much?"

"It reminds me of home."

"But this *is* home—"

"Granddaughter," said a familiar-sounding female voice, "come here, quickly!"

The woman was an Artificial, had dissimilar colored eyes, and looked like a compilation of all the women I'd ever shared fond memories with. I struggled to remember her name. Heidissa?

"Husband," she said, "what foolishness are you up to?"

I smiled, realizing I could never hide anything from her. "Heidissa, have I told you recently how much I love you?"

"Old man, what have you done?" She looked down at the stimstem that had fallen from my hand. "No!" she howled.

A temporal band pulled me away: past the green sun and its solar system, past other galaxies and their worlds. It pulled me into a Sparticle-Trap—a place where time stood relatively still and where the connective moments that created the trap revealed themselves. I saw the City of the Dead: then, I saw the domes of ART Command. After that, it was the laboratory where that old lady sat in a flying throne, and then, I saw a three-man spaceship hovering over a desert. Finally, I saw Death— he was playing checkers with me.

Then, I was back in a spare bedroom at the barracks.

CHAPTER 84

Heidi nudged me into the present. Twelve lifetimes of future memories lingered in my mind... I ached to go back to Kalesh, to at least to say goodbye to my friends and family. But I couldn't, so I did the next best thing: I attempted to hold onto the recollections of my future family and fellow Kaleshins. But they were too numerous, and the more I tried, the more they faded away.

After jotting down the highlights of my most recent vision, I freshened up and followed the sounds and smells of breakfast down to the mess hall.

Marisol, Becky, and Yoshimi were busy serving up breakfast to a full table of InEvitech employees.

"We're having a Sunday brunch," Becky said, handing me a cup of coffee. "I know it's Monday, but we couldn't do it yesterday, and, well... here we are."

Marisol added some sugar and cream to my coffee. Kogo and Adamit exchanged endearing glances. Eiichiro and Margie sat next to each other—probably playing footsies all morning. Russo, who was seated next to Katya, had just said something that made her blush. Dean was all smiles as he engaged Asuka and Izumi in lively conversation.

Becky continued, "Seth, we understand yesterday was important. But... I've been volunteered to ask... What I'm trying to say is, I know it's Monday, but can we pretend it's Sunday? You know, just hanging out, eating? No work, just relaxing with food, friends, family. What'd you say?"

I was mentally drained from my time on Kalesh and a break was exactly what I needed. "I'm going to have a granddaughter named Sabita," I said. "So, it's fine by me. We'll call today an un-day and postpone the glide test until tomorrow. How does that sound?"

They cheered with *hoorays* and a few *yeehaws*.

After my second plate of pancakes, I asked Russo how he felt about the glide test.

He shrugged his shoulders and squinted his face a bit. "The new wing-tip extensions should give us the horizontal stability we need—as long as the GRD is dialed in proportionally."

Our Gravity Resist Drive technology trumped the laws of aerodynamics, rendering them inconsequential to our endeavors. The use of wings on *One Hope* was for gliding back down, a deception to mask our technology. Sure, we would use them when the cameras were rolling, but we didn't really need them. And we didn't need a DC-4 to bring our ship to altitude either, but we did need to keep our technology secret. Eventually our charade would be exposed, but for now, our dog and pony show should buy us time.

"All's quiet on the Western Front," Jacob said as he and the pack of dogs came in and joined the feast.

Yoshimi came over and filled his coffee cup. I stood, clinked my glass with a spoon, and said, "May I have your attention, please? We had a great day yesterday, an important day; one of many milestones. We did it together, and I can't stress this enough—you're the people that made it possible. *You* are the pioneers and visionaries the future will speak of. Without you, this—all of this—would just exist as a story in my mind. Hell, us, together, we *are* the future." I lifted my glass. "Cheers. Now, go and enjoy your un-day." I grabbed a bottle of Perrier water and headed over to Hangar 2.

One Hope sat in her cradle. Her clad, stainless steel and titanium hull were three quarters of an inch thick. Her bifurcated windshield and canopy had been fabricated from three-quarter-inch laminated ballistic glass. I smiled, opened the canopy, folded Crash's GRD seat off to the side, and clambered over to my seat in the stern. I strapped myself in, pretended I was in space, and took a few gulps from the bottle. The tight quarters of the ship felt safe. Outside, the mid-morning sun cast an orange glow inside the hangar, accentuating dust motes drifting in and out of its beams. I leaned back and smiled, knowing that someday I would have a granddaughter. My thoughts drifted to the Box and some technology I'd seen in it: robotics, human augmentation, cold-fusion shields, kaku boilers, Algeronian slip drives, procedures for harvesting antimatter from the sun's corona, and the math used for the temporal chronorhythm filters the Box used to predict the future.

Most of the technology in the Box was beyond today's science, but it certainly illuminated the paths that needed forging. It was like monkeys and typewriters. You couldn't give typewriters to monkeys and expect them to compose. No, first the monkeys would need the capacity to understand what the symbols were and what they meant. They would need to understand how groupings of specific letters make words, and how groupings of certain words made sentences, and how sentences could transfer and preserve ideas and so on. Of course, before any of this could happen, the monkeys would have to understand their own mortality and want to preserve ideas for the benefit of their descendants.

Some squeaking sounds from up front caught my attention. Outside, on the portable staircase, Marisol was spraying blue cleaning solution onto the windshield, then wiping it down with a tattered face cloth. I waved to her.

She smiled, then mouthed the words, "You see clear now?"

I unbuckled my harness, stuck my head out of the canopy, and said, "Yes, Marisol. I can see clear now."

Maybe she wanted to spend more time with me? I helped her maneuver the staircase over to *One Hope's* canopy and brought her inside. She sat in the pilot's seat, smelling like lilacs and Windex. I sat in the seat behind her and offered up some water. She downed the remaining half bottle in one long gulp, turned to me, and said, "Are you well?'

"Yeah, of course."

"Why you spend your time alone?"

"Ha. Well, I'd like to spend more time with you, but we both know that's not going to happen."

"Does that make you sad?"

"I'm not sad. I'm happy."

"You no look happy."

"I'm happy... Well, maybe I'm not super happy. You know we never talk. I mean, we talk, but not *talk*, talk. You know what I mean?"

She stared at me as a therapist might do.

"Marisol, we're supposed to be in a relationship, but you never really talk to me—just those cryptic sayings you're so fond of. *And*, you're always cooking and cleaning. You never spend any time with me, and when you do, like right now, for example, you pretend to be someone that you're not. That's not how relationships should be."

She placed her hand on mine and said, in perfect English, "I'm sorry, but this is how it must be." Then, she smiled, reverted to her innocent maid voice, and asked, "You take me on date now?"

"You're kidding, right?"

She shook her head, kissed me, and said, "Please."

CHAPTER 85

A low flying jet woke me. It was morning and I was in my bed at Fort Banks. Marisol was gone. The clock radio next to my bed clicked and the *Brady Bunch* song "Sunshine Day" played at a quiet volume. I recalled my date with Marisol and a smile crept across my lips: we'd seen *Caddyshack* and laughed through most of it. We'd had an early dinner at some hole-in-the-wall restaurant that served, according to Marisol, the best tasting food in all of Vegas. After that, we had gone to see Siegfried & Roy at the Mirage Casino. And then we'd spent the night doing what couples in love are supposed to do. It had been, by all accounts, a perfect date. I got out of bed, prepared for another day, and headed over to the base.

By evening, final preparations for our glide test were wrapping up. Dean had the ground crew tow us onto the tarmac. After a five-minute scan into the future, he gave us the *all-clear* sign. Crash and Russo completed the preflight checklist and waited for clearance from Eiichiro and Becky who were overseeing the test from the control tower.

Tonight's mission was simple: under cover of darkness, we would use the GRDs to shoot *One Hope* straight up, hover at five thousand feet for ten seconds, glide back to the base, secure the ship, have a post-flight debriefing, and then maybe a late-night snack.

Lift-off went according to plan, but low-hanging clouds played havoc with our navigation. Crosswinds at three thousand feet had Crash sparring with the more delicate aspects of gravity and momentum. At five thousand feet, Russo had to deviate from the flight plan and engage the thrusters to keep us stable. After what seemed an eternity, Russo said, "That's ten seconds. Now we glide home. Hang on!"

Our swift descent had the ship's air-control systems grappling with the buffeting atmosphere; butterflies swooned in my stomach. My pressure suit was too tight and my safety harness cut into my groin. As we headed down, Russo aligned the nose of the ship with the runway lights and began his approach, but we were coming in too hot. At the last second, he pulled up on the controls, just missing the runway. He banked hard to his port, engaged the GRD override control, simultaneously fired the thrusters, spun us 360 degrees, and then set us down on the runway with a *thunk*.

"That was *fun*," he said.

The ground crew towed us into the hangar on a wheeled sled. Eiichiro bowed as we disembarked. Becky, who had elected herself as the head of Flight Safety and Planning, led us to a debriefing room, questioned us, and wrote a log of the event. Afterward, we walked into the mess hall and were showered with cheers and congratulations from our colleagues. When things settled, we enjoyed some food and discussed tomorrow's daytime test: releasing *One Hope* from the belly of our DC-4 during flight.

Marisol picked up a few dirty plates, walked to the front of the table, and said, "Soon I show you my world. The way has been prepared."

"On that note," I said. "Let's get some sleep, gang. We've got a big day tomorrow."

I stayed and helped Becky and Marisol with the cleanup. After Becky left, Marisol stood close to me—nose to nose. She crossed her arms and cracked a mischievous smile. I could see starburst patterns flickering from deep inside her dark eyes, inviting me in. Her intoxicating aroma triggered a desire that could only be satiated by—

She kissed me and said, in a non-accented voice, "Come on, let's go upstairs."

Like before, she had me lie in the bed next to her. She took hold of my hand and gave me another journey into the past. Back to the time she had spent with her adopted children, the Maya. We were ghosts, walking among the Maya unnoticed. Marisol led me to her crashed ship, which the Maya had built a temple around.

"After the crash, I was lost," she said. "I decided to stay with these people. They became my children. They took care of me while I orchestrated my plan to return to Algeron. You see there?"

We walked around a section of the stone temple and over to the other side of Marisol's spacecraft. We saw Past-Marisol working on an advanced-looking, multi-layered holographic spreadsheet of some kind. It was small and manageable in some places and extremely large in other places. From what I could make of things, it was a timeline of events that had yet to happen.

"I had to devise a way to get home," Marisol said.

"What did you come up with?"

"I sent an SOS, but that exhausted the ship's remaining power. I was forced into plan B."

"Plan B?"

"Yes, that is what brought you and I together."

"So it wasn't my charming personality and dashing good looks?'

She held the small stone on her necklace. "This is the Interfector: it is the soul of my ship. I used it to navigate a line, through an infinite number of quantum-based matrices and transmutations that could aggregate and foretell probable continuums that would conclude with me returning to Algeron."

"Sounds like a lot of work."

"It took decades, but Seth, I never finished. It was too much for the Interfector. Then, the drought came. I could only forestall the inevitable, not prevent it. The resulting sadness impeded my mission."

Marisol led me out of the temple and into the village. Tens of thousands of Maya were dead, while thousands of others were just malnourished moving skeletons. "It was my second failure. Then, I was alone again."

Marisol took my hand, and we began to travel the world, meeting people and inciting conflicts. Time became immeasurably relative: minutes, hours, days blended into each other. We went to the areas of the world where Man was repressed and conflicted: Asia, Europe, and Africa. Marisol encouraged innovation through wars. She would tell groups of people how their lives mattered, and how it was wrong to let the many be controlled the few. This was her plan. Kingdom against kingdom, religion against religion, brother against brother: fomenting wars that would create the technology that would eventually bring her home.

CHAPTER 86

It was early when I woke. I found some loose paper, went to the bench out front, and jotted down my adventures in Marisol Land. Above me, the haze of the Milky Way was making way for the morning's first light. A slight breeze folded over the desert. It was going to be a hot one—probably over a hundred degrees. Just as I was finishing up my recollections, Marisol came up behind me and placed her hands over my eyes.

"Guess who?" she asked.

Her welcome touch put things into perspective: an alien suffering through millennia, on a strange planet filled with strange creatures.

"Nanu nanu," I said in my Robin Williams *Mork from Ork* voice.

"No," she said playfully. "It's me, Marisol!" She kissed me and took my hand. "Come, come. You have a lot of work today. I'll cook you breakfast."

For the next hour, Marisol cooked and served breakfast to myself and the staff. As we ate, we discussed this morning's upcoming glide test: a test that would confirm whether the DC-4's release system worked at altitude and whether our deception was plausible.

Eiichiro would captain our DC-4, which we named *Mother*. Dean would act as co-pilot, and Adamit would be on board to operate the release mechanism that would deploy *One Hope* at altitude. Jacob would be in charge of the ground crew. Becky and Katya would coordinate the test from the tower. All the while, Margie and Kogo would be standing by for the unexpected.

Then it came time to perform the test.

"You guys ready?" Russo said over *One Hope's* communication channel.

I coupled my suit's umbilical cord into *One Hope*. "Ready as I'll ever be."

Crash said, "To go where eagles dare. Well, not exactly true but yeah, I'm ready. Let's go."

After we completed our preflight punch list, Russo called Becky, "Tower, we have a go. Do you copy?"

"Tower to *One Hope*. Roger, we have a green board. Standby, confirming with Ground." Becky relayed the green light to both the ground crew and the DC-4s flight crew. I couldn't calculate all the variables that could go wrong and kill us, but Crash could. He was my hedge. He had designed and built *One Hope*, and sure as shit, he wasn't going on any suicide missions.

The takeoff was shaky but thankfully free of complications. From the captain's chair of *One Hope*, Russo relayed basic telemetry to the tower at sixty-second intervals. For ten minutes we climbed high into the sky—safely fastened to the underside of the DC-4.

"*Mother* to *One Hope*," Dean said over the comm. "We're holding steady at ten thousand. The next five minutes are *entirely* clear. Repeat *entirely* clear. Are you ready for drop sequence?"

"Roger, *Mother*," Russo replied. "Standing by on your count. Over."

We braced ourselves as Adamit came over the comm. "Five... four... three... two... one..."

We disengaged from *Mother's* belly as if we were an iron duck born from the imagination of a hungover steelworker. We wobbled, and just as we were about to enter a downward-spiraling cartwheel of doom, Russo, who was breathing loud enough to trigger the threshold gate on his microphone open, jockeyed the shuddering flight controls, then powered up the thrusters to stabilize us.

"Piece of cake," he said over our local comm. "You guys OK?"

"I'm good," I said.

"Me too," said Crash.

"I was just thinking..." Russo said as he entered us into a slow banking loop. "You guys want to stick with the plan, or go up a little further? Get a better view. Astronaut style?"

The question had caught me by surprise, but I swirled it around in my brain for a few moments. "It's up to you guys," I said. "Dean cleared us for five minutes. I'm game if you are." I poked Crash's shoulder. "It's your call."

He let out a groan, re-adjusted the calibration nut on the GRD's cable control, and said, "Might as well get it over with."

Russo slowed our airspeed to forty knots. Through the canopy, I could see the DC-4 roll left.

"*Mother* to *One Hope*," Eiichiro said over the comm. "You guys OK? Come back. Over."

It was uncanny how much Eiichiro's microphoned voice sounded like Sulu from the original Star Trek franchise.

"*Mother*," Russo said. "We're taking a detour. No worries, five by five."

Becky broke in, "Ground Control to *One Hope*—what is your status? Over."

"Roger, Ground Control," I said. "Flight plan has been amended to include scenic route via low-Earth-orbit insertion. Over."

"That's a negative!" Becky yelled, her voice so loud it distorted the transmission. "Return to base. Return to base! Do you understand? This is not the time for a joyride. Get back here! Right now. That's an order!"

"Well, she's pissed," I said over the ship's local comm channel. "We might as well get our money's worth."

We climbed swiftly as Crash dialed-in proportional power to the Gravity Resist Drive. Two minutes later, we entered the thin layer that separates Earth from the rest of the galaxy. We floated through a slow rolling tumble. I was finally in space—we were finally in space.

"Hey, Crash," I said. "Do you remember that time when I said I'd get you into space?"

"No, Suit-Man. You said you'd make me an astronaut."

"Well, I did it. Burt."

Cold crept in.

Crash said, "We should install a heater."

"Alright. That's enough," Russo said. "I'm taking us back." He engaged the thrusters and followed the base's radio signal back home. As the gravity of Earth pulled us increasingly faster, atmospheric friction built up on our hull. Crash was well-prepared for this and slowed our descent with the use of our GRDs.

After we landed, the ground crew towed us into the hangar. The portable staircase was placed alongside the canopy, and Russo led the way down. Just as he got to the bottom, Becky seized him by the groin—I couldn't tell if she had him by his junk or just his flight suit, but she was angry. She walked him out of the hangar before releasing her grip.

"Follow me!" she yelled as she led us into the barracks. Heidi trotted behind us.

Once we were inside the debriefing room, Becky slammed the door shut. She waited for us to remove our helmets before saying, "Nincompoops!" Then, she kicked Crash in the shin. She continued, circling us like a frustrated mom who had just found her lost kids in a mall. "You almost got yourselves killed! What were you thinking? I'm very, very disappointed." She knuckle punched my right thigh. "And you! You know better. Why would you risk everything? It doesn't make sense. I'm not sure I can work under these conditions."

Heidi let out a howl.

"See what you've done?" Becky continued, pointing to Heidi. "You've even upset her!"

"It was my idea," I said. "Don't blame them—"

"Save it!" She opened the door, turned to us, and said, "That's it. All flight tests are canceled. You're all grounded!" Then she stormed off.

I stepped out of my flight suit and slung it over my shoulder. Heidi nudged her head under my hand. I bent down and gave her chest a rub. Becky was right: it had been a stupid move, but hell, we had just gone into space. Simultaneously, the three of us jumped into a celebratory group hug.

"We did it!" Russo said. "We did it!" Heidi barked and joined us in our impromptu Lucky-Charms-leprechaun dance.

We walked into the mess hall as conquerors, but the room was empty. Where was everyone? Marisol brought out a large bowl of spaghetti topped with tomato sauce.

"Food," she said, sprinkling grated cheese over the spaghetti. She handed out some plates and forks. "Eat."

The three of us ate while Marisol looked on, her arms were crossed and her face expressionless. The spaghetti was excellent, the best I'd ever had.

I'd eaten a half a plate of food when Becky came in, looked up at me and said, "Alright, rule breaker. I'm on Seth-watch tonight. So guess what? You're stuck with me."

It had been months since the last attempt on my life. I was reasonably sure I'd dealt with Octavius 8 and his creator, that old-hag Mun Taizu, but Octavius 7 had been sent back in time, presumably to the here and now. He was out there—most likely making plans for my demise at this very moment.

Kogo drove Becky and me to Fort Banks. I went straight to my room, lay down, and pondered things like Grandpa's Box, and how the hell are we were supposed to launch a satellite into space, in four days, if I was still grounded. I could override Becky's orders, but I didn't want to take the risk of losing her and her entire family. Shit, tomorrow we had that trip out of the country to find a secondary base of operations.

I slowed my mind with some Master-Poe-breathing exercises and fell asleep.

CHAPTER 87

"Seth, my friend, how have you been?" said Mohamed as he worked the grill. "Did you enjoy the ba'lawa?"

"Yes, it was delicious; will you thank your sister for me?"

"But of course."

"Mohamed, do you mind if I ask you a question?"

"Ask away, my friend."

"Well, what I'd like to know is: how much does the world weigh?"

"That is an easy one. My sister Kali once told me the world weighs exactly one heart."

"Oh... Well, that's rather cryptic. Wait... Mohamed... Aren't you dead?"

He smiled.

I woke to Heidi's big mug inches from my face. Could dogs read minds? Did they dream like us? I remembered the numerous articles I'd read dealing with such questions and decided they were all wrong and that the world could, during the course of certain events, weigh exactly one heart.

I packed an overnight bag and joined Becky and Heidi in the kitchen.

"Good morning," Becky said, pouring me some coffee. "My, my, you're looking particularly dapper this morning. How about a kiss for your sister?"

I bent down and gave her a wet one on the lips. "Morning. So, hmm, I take it you're not mad at me anymore?"

Her face flushed as she adjusted the hem of her blouse over her hips. "No, I'm not mad—just don't do it again."

"You got it. And thank you, Becky."

As I took a seat at the table, Izumi came in from the spare bedroom. She bowed at me, then bent down and kissed Becky like a familiar lover. Becky said something in Japanese, and they both laughed. Heidi placed her muzzle in my lap.

"She wants you to walk her," said Becky.

Heidi and I took the elevator down to the lobby. Skip greeted us when the doors slid open.

"Morning Skip," I said. "Hey, do you ever go home?"

"This *is* my home, Mr. Bridges. And if you don't mind me saying, that girl of yours has grown into a beautiful woman."

Heidi offered up a few muffled woofs and an excited sneeze, then went over and pawed at the glass door entrance. I opened the doors, and she bolted onto the manicured lawn, did her business, then playfully challenged me to a game of dog tag. I tried to play along, grabbing at her face and tail, but she was faster than a Jupiter 2 protection drone.

"Everybody, listen up," I said as our morning meeting at the base got underway. "Thanks to you and your hard work, we're on schedule to launch our first satellite in four days." There was a smattering of clapping and some cheers. "But today, now that Becky has ungrounded us, we're going on a scouting trip: Adamit, Katya, Dean, Russo, and Eiichiro, pack your gear and passports, and meet up on the tarmac in an hour. Pack for at least a day, maybe two. Jacob, you're in charge while we're gone. Becky, could you file a flight plan? Everyone else, I need you to stay focused on the launch."

Becky placed her hands on her hips and said, "Ahem, I could if I knew where you were going!" She grabbed my hand and led me into the debriefing room. She pulled a step-up close to a large table, stood on it, and popped open some chart tubes. "These are the possible base locations you asked me to look for. Each one has the pros and cons listed on the title page. There's more detailed information included in the appendix." She rolled the charts open and flipped through them. "Let's see. We have Haiti, Saint Vincent and the Grenadines, as well as Costa Rica. There are some secondary loca—"

"Which one do you recommend?" I asked.

"It's a hike, but I'd go with Saint Vincent."

"Saint Vincent it is. Now you can file a flight plan, and see if you can contact a commercial real estate agent that can show us some properties when we land."

Forty minutes later, we climbed into the cool interior of our Learjet 35. Russo would be at the helm and Eiichiro would be the co-pilot.

Adamit secured the hatch and sat next to Katya. I wondered about the time they had survived a plane crash together—

"Hey, Seth," said Katya. "Did you hear? There's this company out of San Francisco: TorwardAll, I think it's called. Anyway, I saw it on the news the other day—they're developing this drug that will extend a dog's life by thirty years or something like that. Swell, right? It's still in the prelims, but I bet you could snooker some for Heidi."

Yeah, I thought, I'd seen the story, but I'd been scared to give it further deliberation. Was this development the beginning of the end? Morgan had said something about a Puppy Pox... What if people misused the drug: instead of giving it to their dogs, they took it to extend their own lives? What if that was what started the pandemic? No, who's kidding who. That is *exactly* what started it. Who could blame them though? Hell, who wants to get old and die. I've done it and it sucks. This drug though, it's the goddamn fountain of youth. Death is gonna be pissed. How could TorwardAll not see this? I supposed I could try to warn people, but who would believe me? Probably just make it worse. Wait, maybe I could buy the company, keep some drugs for Heidi and destroy the rest. The Box had mentioned something about a vaccine made from horseshoe crab blood... No. Morgan had said I must allow the Soul Breaker Virus to infect the planet. And that mankind's existence depended on it. And that I had already tried one hundred and thirty-two times to stop the Soul Breaker Virus? Didn't I already debate this? Yeah, Seth, you did. Right. Probably best to let nature run its course. I nodded at Katya, then took a big swig of ginger ale. Its fizzy bite felt refreshing.

As Russo increased the RPM's on the Learjet's engine, there was a muffled knocking on the hatch's exterior. Adamit groaned and unbuckled his safety strap; then, he told Russo to hold position, and opened the hatch.

I heard Marisol say, "Buenos días, Señor Adamit. Cómo está usted?" Heidi bounded down the aisle and slobbered up on me. Marisol spent a few minutes in the cockpit, then came aft and sat beside me. She wore colorful tribal clothes and her face undulated with shifting colors. She buckled up, placed her hands on her lap, smiled at me and said, "I think it's time you see my family—in Guatemala."

"OK," I said with a shrug.

Russo taxied us to the end of the runway, braked, then throttled up to take-off RPM. The jet shuddered as the brakes were released, then we wheeled down the runway and took flight. Four and a half hours later we landed and refueled in Guatemala City. A customs agent did a cursory check as I walked Heidi on the tarmac. She did her business, and we got back in the plane.

We were cleared for take-off with a warning that a severe storm had stalled in our flight path. Twenty minutes later, we entered the warning's reason: a black storm wall. Lightning flashed, and thunder cracked, and turbulence shook us. Then, we were in the eye of the storm and it was calm. Below us was the green of the jungle. Russo banked the plane into a slow downward approach. When the landing strip became visible, he lined us up for our landing. He pulled the controlling surfaces up and skimmed the jungle canopy as he aligned the nose of the Learjet with the runway. Despite the raging tempest on either side of us, we landed safe and sound, deep inside a valley, surrounded by mountainous jungle. I loved it.

CHAPTER 88

Adamit opened the hatch and lowered the Learjet's collapsible stairway. Dank humidity and exotic odors filled the cabin. Heidi sniffed her way down the staircase with a cautious nose. We followed her lead and stepped onto the tarmac as strangers in an extraordinary land. Around one hundred and fifty brown skinned villagers of different ages and genders welcomed us with smiling faces—more stood behind them. They were short, had black hair, and wore little clothing.

A compact man with an inviting smile stepped forward. Unlike the others, he wore khaki shorts, an Izod short-sleeved shirt, Sperry Top-Siders, and appeared to be in charge.

"Greetings," he said. "I am Geronimo. Please, call me G-Moe." He made a grand gesture with his arms and said, "Welcome to Sethco Proper."

Heidi politely sniffed G-Moe's backside, then pranced back to our group. Just then, Marisol stepped onto the collapsible stairway. Her skin shimmered with an iridescence that gave the impression she was glowing.

Our reception committee fell to their knees and began chanting and sobbing, "Akna Ah puch Quetzal, Akna Ah Puch Quetzal..."

Heidi leaped into the air and played tag with a butterfly. Sweat trickled down the curve of my back. Had that G-Moe guy just said, *Welcome to Sethco Proper?* Fuck it! It was still Earth, wasn't it?

Marisol walked among the villagers, releasing them from their subservient positions with kind words and a gentle touch. Animals chattered in the distance. A flock of parrots flew overhead. I took in the property. Larger than our base in Las Vegas, it was more of a town than an airport. Off to one side of the freshly-painted runway was a thick green tree line that appeared impenetrable as rock. Past the main buildings and the control tower was a new two-lane paved road that led to a grouping of dozens of ranch-style homes. Each home had a front lawn, a white-picket fence, and, at the end of a driveway, a mailbox. And, if I wasn't mistaken, further down the road were signs indicating the presence of a Kmart and an A&P shopping center. To the right of this improbable neighborhood was a large jungle village, complete with open-fire pits, butchered forest animals, and wooden huts with thatched roofs. In the distance, dark clouds that flashed with lightning surrounded the perimeter of the property. Yet, where we stood, it was sunny and calm, almost as if the storm was protecting us and the village from the ravages of the outside world.

"Mr. Bridges," said G-Moe, gesturing to one of the large buildings across the runway. "Would you and your associate's care for some refreshments in our lounge?"

I felt the fickle finger of fate push me forward, as a cog on Marisol's wheel. I nodded. Russo and Eiichiro stayed with our plane as a ground crew began servicing it. The rest of us followed G-Moe into the modern building.

Chilly air brushed our faces. Air conditioning seemed out of place in the jungle, but damn, it felt good. A sign above the dining room entrance read—Landing Lounge Bar & Grill. I could smell food, and the place looked exactly like the Landing Lounge back at the Sands Casino.

G-Moe led us to one of the tables in the empty lounge. A lovely girl, outfitted in a Sands Casino uniform, brought over a cart containing bottles of cold beer, pitchers of ice water, and a bowl for Heidi. I pulled out a chair for Marisol.

"Excuse me," I asked the waitress whose name tag read *Trinidad*. "Is the water safe to drink? I mean, we're not from around here."

"Of course, Mr. Bridges," she said. "We have a distillery for drinking water. Now, what can I get you folks from the kitchen?"

I shrugged my shoulders. "Um, do you have any menus?"

Maybe it was the presence of Marisol, or maybe it was her first time taking an order, but the poor girl began to shake. And judging by her facial cues, she was about to have a breakdown. I should have read the situation more clearly, been more sensitive to my surroundings.

Marisol got up, kissed the waitress on the forehead, and spoke the words of an understanding mother.

The waitress wiped a tear from her face. "I'll be right back with your menus."

G-Moe placed some papers in front of me. "Mr. Bridges, if I could get you to sign at the bottom, the transfer will be legal."

I passed the papers to Katya and looked at G-Moe. "What transfer?"

He poured himself a glass of water and downed half of it. "Mr. Bridges, I can attest to the fact that all of your specifications and requirements for the property have been met. The six billion in cash and bearer bonds, as well as the twenty-one tons of gold, has been assessed by Lloyds of London and are secure in the underground vault. I assure you, with my life, everything is as it should be."

I looked around, threw up my hands and said, "What property? What gold?"

Marisol laughed. "This is your new base, silly; I built it for you."

Heidi started barking at me. I looked at Marisol. "I don't understand. When did you—"

"We have to help each other, Seth," she said. "Everything you and your team needs is here. The path has been cleared."

She was right. And the best part of her plan was that there was no government overwatch.

"Boss," said Dean. "This place is perfect."

Just then, Russo came hustling in. "Mr. Bridges. Jacob called me on the Learjet's radio. He said there is an emergency back at our base. They're threatening to jail everyone and close the base down unless you get back there and answer some questions."

"Who is *they*?"

"Sorry, boss. Some guy named Galen Fox. Works for DARPA. He's threatening to arrest our people. Jacob says we have to get back there ASAP or we are finished."

"Motherfuckers," I said. "Marisol, I accept your offer and thank you. Katya, let me have that paper." I signed the document and got up. "Well, I guess we're heading back to Vegas."

"You want me to stay here and get things organized for when you return?" asked Dean.

"No, I think you'd better come with us. We might need your five-minute skills back home. What about you, Marisol? Do you want to stay or come back with us?"

She was holding the small rock that dangled from her neck. Strangely enough, she rolled her eyes backward as if she was about to go into a seizure, then looked at me.

"No, no, no," she whispered to herself.

"What is it, Marisol?"

"We must go at once."

"What's wrong, Marisol?"

"My plan has been interrupted. We must adapt." Then, without another word, she ran back to our jet.

We followed her lead, got in our Learjet, and took off for Vegas. During the flight home, I tried to talk to Marisol a few times, but she had retreated inward and would have no part of my interactions.

CHAPTER 89

It was late in the night when we landed. Adamit led us down the Learjet's collapsible stairway. I felt exposed. Had it been our glide test, I wondered, that had triggered this action? Maybe it was the base inspection? Or was it something more nefarious?

"Boss," said Jacob. He along with Kogo and a few of the other staff members were waiting for us as we disembarked. "They look serious," he continued. "They won't leave until they talk to you."

I dropped to one knee. "Where are they?"

"The lobby. Margie's watching 'em. What's going on, boss? Trouble?"

"Yeah, you could say that. What do you have on these guys?"

"There's two of them: a Mr. Charles Burns who seems OK and the other guy. He's mean and calls himself Galen Fox. They're from DARPA. We checked them for weapons, and they're clean. Oh, and our cameras have picked up a lot of movement just beyond the property boundaries. The dogs are howling at something out there. I sent some guys out earlier, to check it out, but they haven't returned."

Dean, who had been engaging in continuous five-minute scans of the future for the last twenty minutes, lowered his fists from his temples and said, "Still clear boss. But something is off."

"What do you mean?"

"I can't explain. It's just... it's not changing the way it normally does. Just echoes."

"Keep on it, and let me know if there is a change."

Master Poe had preached: *The element of surprise is more powerful than the blinding glare of the sun.* Unfortunately, I couldn't think of any surprises at the moment. I needed more mental training. It would help me think more clearly when situations like this happened. I looked around for Marisol. Damn it, she'd gone off somewhere.

I waved everyone over to the barracks.

As we entered the lobby, the two government agents remained in their seats.

"Which of you is Galen Fox?" I asked.

One of the men rose and said, "That would be me."

He wore glasses, looked around fifty-five, and was outfitted with a standard issue off-the-rack suit. He extended his right arm toward me. The other guy was a few years younger, had a disheveled appearance, and swayed his head side to side.

"Wait Seth," Dean said. "Something is wrong."

Adamit stepped forward, but he didn't seem all that scary.

Katya went close to Fox and said, "What do you want?"

"We want the Box that Mr. Bridges possesses, and then we want to kill every last one of you."

Jacob and Adamit quickly unholstered their sidearms and aimed at the two government men. Kogo tacked to the side of the men; but her movements seemed groggy.

"Dean," I said as I reached for my revolver. "Give me a report."

"I got nothing boss. My thing, it's not working."

Burns smiled to himself.

"So?" I said to Fox. "You're just going to take our property and kill us? Is that your plan? Don't you want to put us in some sort of inescapable deathtrap, like a James Bond movie. You know, the kind of scenario where we have at least a chance to survive?"

Fox surveyed the room and said, "Nature abhors a vacuum." Then he raised his eyebrows and nodded his head.

It was then that I noticed dozens of green laser beams reflecting off his glasses. I looked to my crew—they were all lit up with stuttering green dots. We had been set up. Why hadn't Dean seen this coming?

Katya said, "Mr. Fox, you do not want to kill us. You like us."

"That's not true," Fox said. "Mun has sent me here to kill all of you. Oh, nice try with the suggestive statements." He nodded towards Burns. "My associate is a nullifier—a gift nullifier that is." Fox touched his ear for a moment, then said, "Understood." He looked at his watch and said, "Mr. Sethco, we have just secured the Box from your apartment. The future is now safe. All that's left now is the messy part."

"Wait," I said. "Your mission is flawed. If you kill us, all will be—"

Fox yelled, "Victory!" into his wristwatch.

CHAPTER 90

The lobby's windows disintegrated as a squad of snipers simultaneously let loose a volley of rounds on each of our positions. My .38 flew from my hand. A second round caught me in my left shoulder. As I grabbed my wound, time decelerated. Everything seemed disjointed, loopy, and reminded me of a word I had once heard—koyaanisqatsi: the humiliation of a world out of balance. I saw my people slump to the floor, and I saw Fox and Burns casually walk out of the room. At that moment, the strange word made sense.

The sound of whomping helicopter blades had those of us that were still alive ducking as we looked up at the ceiling. Suddenly, large-caliber rounds rained down, shredding the room into slivers of glass, wood, and metal. The concrete floor trembled as explosions reverberated from the courtyard.

We never stood a chance.

Then it stopped. It was hard to breathe, hard to do anything. There was blood and dust everywhere. My mouth was dry and chalky, and my hearing was compromised with silence. I saw a watch. Its second-hand kept ticking, defiant of the severed wrist it was attached to. It was a diver's watch. Must have been Russo's—he being a pilot and all.

Someone lifted me up and cradled me in their arms. It was Adamit. He looked like an angel—an angry, avenging angel of war. He kicked the water cooler aside and carried me into the emergency tunnel.

Blood blurred my vision, but I could still make out light bulbs as they flashed by. *Let me help you:* those were the first words Adamit had ever said to me. His kindness truly belied his appearance. That seemed so long ago. I tried to count the lines between the ceiling's cement slabs. One, two, four, seven, three... Hadn't he said his adopted parents had met on the set of the *Wizard of OZ*? No, Katya had said that... More bright bulbs. One, two, four. And that he had once been a bodyguard for Tesla?

—Wait, that was a half a slab; didn't count as a whole. Should I have been counting light bulbs instead of slabs? I remembered when he had said: *You should've seen Kogo go all ninja on me last night.* Yeah, that had been funny. He had just been trying to be normal. I had to respect him trying. He wasn't a monster: just looked like one, that's all.

We busted through the door at the end of the tunnel. Dust-choking air, spent cordite, and moonbeams filtered down through the tattered remnants of Hangar 2's roof. Adamit shifted my weight in his arms, entered a code into the bunker's security keypad, and brought me inside. I had taken four hits: my right leg was shattered at the knee, the top part of my shoulder was missing, there was a hole in my belly, and some shrapnel had run clean through my left eye socket.

I still had a few moments. Nothing was as I had imagined it: no real pain, just flashes of what had been, and thoughts of what could have been. I could taste blood in my mouth, and I was cold and thirsty—very thirsty. Perhaps if I entered the number of ceiling tiles into the water-cooler cup-dispenser, I could get a drink, and then everything would revert to the way it was. I didn't want to die. Life was good, and I had things to do, and I had a family on Kalesh, and I had to save Man from his dark side.

Adamit set me down.

A voice crackled from the bunker's intercom, "Mr. Sethco, Octavius 7 would like a word with you before you die. Will you open the door, or do we have to blow it?"

Ha, the dumbasses from the future had finally gotten their act together. Good for them.

Adamit, who had taken a few rounds, winced a questioning nod in my direction.

"Go ahead," I slurred. "Open it."

Within the darkened corridors of harsh spotlights, I saw a pile of lifeless bodies—all InEvitech employees. The decapitated head of Virgil Caine was propped up on the hood of an assault vehicle—his eyes still prideful. As Adamit raised his arms in surrender, I wondered how Marisol could have let this happen. Then, I saw her. She was holding the rock that dangled from her necklace in one hand, and was walking towards Fox and his men. She stopped, casually twirled a lock of her hair, then looked at me and smiled.

All of a sudden, the heads of Fox and his men started popping—not literally, but it was what I imagined was happening to them. I say this because they all began to scream and grab at their heads. Blood oozed out of their eyes, ears, and mouths as they fell to the ground—lifeless. It appeared that she had increased the cranial pressure in their heads to such a degree that their capillaries were just bursting. Whatever it was, I was glad they were dying. She came over and held me.

I managed to ask, "Why did you let this happen?"

She supported my head. "We have to be like them. Do you understand?"

"Yeah. I get it."

"Good. Now I want to tell you something." She gave me a kiss. "Seth Bridges, I do love you."

I felt hope, but it wasn't enough. I started to fall down a tunnel. But it wasn't the unbalanced-washing-machine vision-generating tunnel I was hoping for: it was the scary tunnel I'd fallen in back at Herring Cove Beach—back on the day this had all begun. It was cold: not temperature cold, rather the alone type of cold. There was no wind or pull of gravity, and it was more of a cerebral tunnel, and it had my very being descending into the empty dark nothingness below. I kept falling and falling, faster and faster. Then, Death joined me. He, or it, grabbed at me, but his bony hands went right through me. He seemed angry at not being able to catch me. I knew it was over, and I knew I was supposed to give in and let nature take back what it had given, but I couldn't: I had too much to live for. I calmed myself and thought of where I should go.

CHAPTER 91

A cosmic bungee cord took hold of me and slowed my descent. Then, the omniscient fog surrounded me. I could see shadows within the fog: people moving in slow motion. Then, the fog cleared, and the shadows morphed into guards that were dressed in sharkskin zoot suits. They were floating me down a white hallway. *Yes*, I thought. I was back in San Francisco. And I was still in the game. Wait, James is here. All I had to do was get a warning message to him, and he could deliver it to me before the attack happened. It was a simple plan, but there were problems: I was strapped down to a hand truck and being moved around like a piece of garbage, and as far as I knew, James was back in the cell and stuck to a Velcro wall.

The guards were now perp-floating me through a glass tunnel. Hordes of angry, ugly people banged and yelled at me from the other side of the transparent panels. Paranoid walked beside me.

"Boy, are they mad at you," he said.

He seemed to be enjoying himself. Which was odd, because that wasn't really in his nature. It was then that I noticed he had brought along a friend. It was Vengeance.

The zoot suits brought me into a large, amphitheater-style hall—which erupted like a commercial-break tea*ser for a Jerry* Springer Father's Day reunion show. All the while I kept thinking: I have to get back to James. They transferred me onto a tilted table that faced a raised judge's bench. A bouquet of assorted colored flags served as a backdrop.

A tall man in a Beefeater guard costume banged a scepter on the floor four times, then effeminately yelled, "Order! Order in the court! The 'Do the Right Thing Court' is now in session. The Honorable Judge Robert George Steinem III presiding."

As the hall quieted, Paranoid said, "I don't think they like you."

Vengeance, who bore a distinct likeness to Liam Neeson, gave me a confident wink.

The judge was costumed in a barrister's gown and had the face of a reptilianized babushka.

He rapped his gavel a few times, adjusted his powdered wig, and said, "Let us begin. You, Seth T. Bridges, AKA Sethco the Destroyer, along with the Sethco

Alliance and all of its subsidiaries, have been charged with our newest ordinance: Crimes Against the Collective. How do you plead?"

Shit, I thought. I'm in the middle of a real-life version of the Crucible. I could work with this.

"With all due disrespect, your vomitiousness," I said. "I plead guilty."

"You cannot plead guilty," yelled the judge, while repeatedly banging his gavel over the noise of the court. "You are guilty. You have to plead not guilty." The hall of bobble-headed mobbers hooted and hissed with group-anger. "I warn you," continued the judge, "do not tamper with my patience *or* the authority of this court." He flicked his tongue over his lips a few times while the hall settled. "The specific charges against you are sedition, hearsay, withholding intellectual promise, and failure to prevent the deaths of four and a half billion people. Now, answer me. How do you plead?"

The last time I had been here, James had said something about a plan. Hell, I probably owned most of the tech in this room.

Just then, the hovering Jupiter-2-looking drone I'd seen in my previous visit to this place appeared before me. My HUD filled me in: the miniature spacecraft was an InEvitech Hellhawk Stealth Sentinel. It had been following me this whole time—cloaked and waiting for instructions. The rigid jailor overalls I wore were actually made of a non-Newtonian fiber, and were developed by Sethco Industries for instantaneous protection during collisions—not restraint. And, to draw me out, these people had dog-napped a Heidi look-alike, which was actually Heidi's granddaughter. Originally, I had been here under the guise of a prisoner swap, but now... *A lot is riding on this one, Seth.*

I linked up with the Hellhawk Sentinel, then tapped out the release code for my jailor suit. As soon as the suit released its grip, I reached down to the backside of the tilted table and picked up a key fob and two grapefruit-sized, hand-held, plasma-bolt-firing HOGS. I activated the key fob, which surrounded me in a threat-level-9 personal-defense shield. Paranoid beamed with joy. Vengeance gave me a subtle nod. The Hellhawk Sentinel hovered to my left, confirmed impending action, then initiated the offensive.

After taking out the authoritative functionaries with deadly force, I detuned the HOGS's self-targeting plasma bolts to a non-lethal power setting. Almost everyone took a shot.

I rushed back to James's cell, released him, and said, "James, they came to our base and killed us all. It was assassins from the future. I need you to warn us. Can you do it?"

"Give me the specifics."

"Ahh..." I thought about Becky's brunch the Monday before. "James, come on Monday, June 8, 1980. Tell me this: Priority Exon. Base is in peril from Galen Fox, a rogue agent at DARPA. Do not engage. Evacuate immediately to Marisol's new base in Guatemala. End message. Can you get it there in time?"

"Time is my thing. It will be done."

The fog returned, and I felt ill.

CHAPTER 92

Heidi nudged me awake. I was in one of the spare bedrooms at the base and had had the strangest dream. Perhaps it had been a vision. It was about a family I had in the future, on a distant planet called Kalesh. I couldn't remember all the details, but I knew I had a granddaughter, and I knew that everybody was in danger. Then, I felt ill with dread. I shook it off, freshened up, and followed the sounds and smells of breakfast down to the mess hall.

Marisol, Becky, and Yoshimi were busy serving up breakfast to a full table of InEvitech employees.

"We're having a Sunday brunch," Becky said, handing me a cup of coffee. "I know it's Monday, but we couldn't do it yesterday, and well... here we are."

Marisol added some sugar and cream to my coffee, then gave me a wavering smile. The dread returned as if a bad case of déja vu had flooded my senses. Something was wrong. My employees seemed unaffected by my anamnesis, although Paranoid, who now sat in the empty chair next to me, appeared very concerned. A wave of nausea washed over me. My heart quickened.

"Seth," Becky continued. "We understand yesterday's test was very important. But, well, I've been volunteered to ask... What I'm trying to say is, can we pretend it's Sunday? You know, just hanging out, eating? No work, just relaxing with food, friends, family. What do you say?"

"Sure, sure... We'll call today an un-day. Hey, does anyone feel like we've done this before?" Dean put his hands to his temples for a few seconds, then said, "Uh, oh."

"What is it?" I asked.

Dean turned and pointed at the entrance of the mess hall: James Jamerson walked in with one of the base's security guards.

"James," I said.

"Sorry for the intrusion, Mr. Bridges, but it couldn't be helped. I'm here on the most urgent of matters."

Everybody in the room turned their attention towards our guest.

"Please," I said, "Take a seat. Coffee?"

He nodded as Becky, who was at the ready, poured him a cup. "Mr. Bridges," he said, "your life is in danger. All of your lives are in danger. I have a message for you. It's from you, in the future. The message is as follows: Priority Exon. Base is in peril from Galen Fox, a rogue agent at DARPA. Do not engage. Evacuate immediately to Marisol's new base in Guatemala. That's the message, Mr. Bridges." Just then, use-to-be agent James Jamerson reverted back to Motown's greatest musician, funk brother James Jamerson.

"How in the hell did I get here?" he asked.

"Katya," I said, "Could you explain to Mr. Jamerson, in your own special way, how he got here? And could we arrange for his travel to wherever he would like to go?"

"I'd love to," she said, leading him out to the lobby.

"Marisol," I called out.

She stood before me. There was sweat on her upper lip and her nostrils flared ever so briefly as she inhaled and exhaled.

"Is that true?" I asked.

"Yes, I have been constructing a base for you for some time now," she said, in perfect, unaffected English. Everyone stared at her as she continued. "It has everything you need to get into space. I recommend you heed the warning and take immediate action."

Priority Exon, I thought. What the hell did that mean? Was it some sort of verification code from my future-self to my present-self? I had probably rebooted, like that time at the Circle of Willis Lounge. Shit, that meant I had died again. Fuck... OK, we'd get the hell out of here. We'd need a plan though. I should eat these pancakes: it was going to be a long day.

"Everyone," I said. "May I have your attention? We will have an emergency meeting in the conference room in one hour. Until then, I suggest you eat up. It looks like we're going on a trip."

CHAPTER 93

An hour later, I entered the conference room and faced my InEvitech crew. "Listen guys, I'm sorry things turned out like this. I don't have all the specifics, but as far as I can tell, there are people in high places that want us and this project *terminated*. Thing is, we can't fight them. They have the full force of the government backing them. For that reason, we have to get off this base today—before they get here and start terminating."

Becky brought over a pot of coffee and a stack of paper cups and set them on the table. I poured myself some coffee and paced around the table. "As some of you know, assassins from the future have been trying to kill me ever since I arrived in Vegas. Somehow, the minds of these assassins are sent back in time, then infused into the consciousness of selected people from this timeline. I think Galen Fox is one of these selected people. James, the gentleman who was here earlier—he is an agent from the future sent here to warn me of impending attacks. He saved me from one of these assassins before, and I believe him now when he says we are all in danger. And now that we are leaving, I've decided it's time to give the Gravity Resist Drive technology to the world. My hope is, if we give it to the world, they won't come after us." I set my coffee on the table. "What you don't know is that I have access to a device; I call it the Box. This Box holds technical knowledge from the future—"

"Is that where the GRD came from?" asked Crash.

I nodded. "Yes. Nikola Tesla gave the Box to my grandfather, and then my grandfather gave it to me. That thing holds schematics for stuff that is essential for space travel. It's a lot more dangerous than the GRD, and I'm pretty sure you could use the info in it to conquer the universe. So, there's that. Hmm, additionally, for those of you who don't know, I have visions of the future. I know that sounds preposterous, but it's true. And in those visions, I've been to other worlds. And believe me when I tell you, those worlds are as real as the ground you're standing on, and as numerous as grains of sand on a beach. They're out there, just waiting for us. The information in that box will get us to those worlds. Now, if that's not enough motivation, there's that Soul Breaker Virus I mentioned before. In seven and a half years, it's going to kill just about everyone on this planet. Full disclosure: in my timeline, in the future I come from, this plague never happened. Now, I don't make the rules, and

I don't pretend to understand them, but believe me, when that virus makes its debut, the safest place"—I pointed at the ceiling—"is going to be up there."

I stopped pacing and stood at the head of the table. "Apparently, Marisol has built us a new base of operations in Guatemala, and it's ready for us to move in."

Marisol stood up and said, "I have built a base for you. It is a state-of-the-art facility. And there are houses there for all of you. Modern houses, like the kind you live in now. I've added a Kmart, a Stop & Shop, and a few restaurants to help you feel at home." She turned to me and said, "I must go now," and left.

"Why was she talking like that?" asked Margie.

"Well, the truth is," I said. "That woman is an alien who has been stranded on this planet for two thousand years."

That last bit of information slackened more than a few jaws.

"Please, bear with me," I continued. "Marisol is neither an angel nor a demon. Sure, she has her agenda and personal problems, but hey, don't we all? She's helping us because she believes, over time, we can get her back to Algeron: that's her home planet. Thing is, it is no coincidence that we're all here, in this room, right now. You were meant to be here." I started to walk around the conference room again. "The future has chosen you. We are, as Dean so aptly puts it, the Agents of Fortune. And let me tell you, this future of ours—it holds a tremendous amount of opportunity for us, as well as every man and woman that is not held back by fear of the unknown. God has given us the most precious thing in the entire universe—life. This is *our* time. And if we're to be more than the decadence of our advantage, we have to justify our existence with exceptionalism."

"So, let me see if I got this right," said Margie. "If I pack my bags and leave with you today, you and your shifting friends get to fly around in spaceships and give Marisol a ride home?"

"Yup," I said. "That's pretty much the gist of things. But you should know, we're going to have a lot of fun doing it. Listen, I'm not going to think less of anyone who remains behind. In fact, you can use our company lawyer, gratis. But Margie, you should know, I need you *and* your skepticism. Heck, you can have a spaceship of your own, or at least one named after you. Would that help?"

Eiichiro whispered something in her ear.

Jacob stood on his chair. "Seth, we're in, and I'm pretty sure we'll follow you to the gates of hell, but you're asking us to leave everything behind. You're sure about this, right?"

I paused for a moment. "Can anyone ever be sure of anything? Listen, in two years we are going to have an autonomous ship, the size of the Boston Garden, in geosynchronous orbit around the Earth." I had just made that up. "In six years, we'll have a base on the moon." Well, that was true. "OK, it's not gonna be fun and games all the time, but this is a decision you will have to have faith in. Not the watered-down kind of faith you can never touch, but tangible faith, illuminated by your intelligence, your creativity, and the compass that is your mortal coil—you know, that genetic conductor that has spent the last couple of million years getting *you*, getting *us*, to this very moment."

There were no debates as I shifted from explaining things to giving orders. "We should be out of here by five tonight. My plan is to put our animals and essential tech onto *Mother* and strap *One Hope* to her belly. Russo will pilot *Mother* to our new base in Guatemala. Eiichiro will follow in our Learjet. Crash, I need you to give the GRD equations to Katya and Margie. You ladies will send, mail, or phone or fax them to every major newswire, newspaper, and TV station as soon as possible. Jacob, have the planes fueled up, and load everything from the bunker and all of our technology into *Mother*. Merrick, get the animals ready for travel. Dean, could you run continuous five-minute checks on the future?"

"What about my security guards?" Jacob asked, "And their families—are they invited?"

"Absolutely," I said. "Double their pay and give them a 50k bonus. Margie can write the checks for you. Cancel that—you know what? We'll pay in cash. Probably be a good idea, for everyone's safety, to go dark: no personal phone calls. Becky, I need you to file a flight plan—"

"It won't work," said Eiichiro.

"What do you mean?" I said. "What won't work?"

"*One Hope* weighs a ridiculous twelve thousand pounds," he said. "That's the maximum load capacity of a DC-4. If we add people, animals, and equipment, in addition to *One Hope*, she'll never get off the ground."

Fuck, I thought. Maybe I should have consulted the Box. Just then, the conference-room phone rang. I picked it up. "Hello?"

"Hey, what the fuck are you doing?"

"Who is this?"

"Oh, I thought you might recognize the voice. Listen, the Nothingness, it's begun. People, ships, cities, they're disappearing. Seth, there's a lot on the line. You'd better get this right."

"Really. Like what? What's on the line?"

"Well, for starters, there's your life, the lives of your family, your friends, and co-workers. Let's see—oh, yeah, there's Sabita, your Granddaughter on Kalesh. There's the human race and there's—"

"OK, OK. I get the point."

"Good. You must launch that satellite today. Everything is dependent on that causality. So don't screw it up. Got it?"

"Yeah, I got it."

"Good. Later, alligator."

There was static, a few clicks, and then an operator said, "Chronospool trace receipt 004. Sethco time derivative unknown." *Click—dial tone.*

Dammit. I wasn't sure I was cut out for this stuff. "Change of plan," I said. "Eiichiro, you'll fly *Mother*, with our animals and equipment, to Guatemala. Russo, you will pilot *One Hope* and launch the satellite with Crash and me."

"I hope you're joking," said Becky, "because there is no way in God's green earth I would let you guys go up in an untested spacecraft. I forbid it."

"She's right," said Eiichiro. "You can't take *One Hope* into space. It would be suicide."

That was about the time that Dean's three geishas came into the conference room.

"Dean," I said, "could you fill the ladies in? Becky, I need you and Russo to come up with a flight solution that has *One Hope* launching the satellite and then flying to our new base in Guatemala."

"But Seth—"

"Eiichiro," I said. "Could you find some rubber, like inner-tube rubber, and glue as much of it as you can to the exterior of *One Hope*? It's for radar stealth."

"Hai!"

"Everyone else," I continued, "help out where you can. And *please*, keep your eyes open for trouble. Kogo, Adamit, you're with me. Where the hell is Heidi?"

CHAPTER 94

The mid-morning sun greeted me as I got into the backseat of the suburban with Heidi; Kogo and Adamit got into the front. I wondered if the government had eyes on us as we scrambled to and fro. Our first stop was the Vegas Trust Bank. Twenty minutes later the owner arrived, opened the vault, and handed us all their cash: fifteen million—nine million short of what they owed me.

After emptying the safe at our in-town office, we headed over to Fort Banks. Adamit and I went up to my apartment. Kogo and Heidi waited for us under the front entrance portico. As Adamit stuffed the money from the bedroom safe into paper shopping bags, I grabbed Grandpa's Box, my suitcase, and my journal. We hustled down to the truck and jumped in. Skip, who wore six white dress shirts, one on top of another, and carried a blue hard-shell Samsonite suitcase, smiled a shit-eating grin and joined us inside the truck. Adamit snatched the blue suitcase, probably thinking it was a bomb or something, and flung it out of the window. Then, he pulled Skip out and dragged him onto the lawn. Kogo emptied the contents of the suitcase onto the wet grass: toiletries, underwear and a few mementos.

"What are you up to, Skip?" Adamit said.

"Hold on," I said, and got out of the truck.

Heidi came over, jumped up, and placed her paws on Skip's shoulders. The two began to dance. "That's my girl," he said.

"Hey!" I said, as I pulled Heidi off of Skip. "That's my girl you're dancing with. Now, what's your deal?"

He put on a serious face, straightened out his array of shirt collars, and spoke in a rehearsed manner. "I've got twenty-eight years of flying under my belt. I'm your third pilot for tonight's bug out."

How had he known? Hell, I thought, I didn't even know most of the details. He was right though; we still needed a pilot for our Learjet. Skip picked up his belongings and stuffed them back into his suitcase.

"I've spent three hundred years roaming the planet looking for a purpose. Today is the day I find it. Anyway, Marisol promised."

"Well," I said, "C'mon then. I hope you're a better pilot than you are a dancer."

Kogo drove on, heading back toward the base. I pushed Skip to the far side of the GMC's back seat and confided in Grandpa's Box. It confirmed that, tonight, we would successfully launch *One Hope*, wait for a single rotation of the Earth, deploy our satellite, and then glide back down to our new base in Guatemala. I closed the Box.

"Hey, Adamit, I'm going to need you to guard this box while I'm up in *One Hope*."

"No problem, boss. I'll take good care of it."

We were on the outskirts of town, in a slight valley: visibility was poor due to a pocket of late-morning fog. Suddenly, Kogo slammed on the brakes, pointed at the road, and said, "Apparition."

An awkward looking woman stood in the middle of the road. It was Madame Deux Vox Fantastico. She was holding a suitcase. As Adamit opened his door, Heidi leaped out, mouthed the singer's suitcase by its handle and brought it back to the truck. Adamit helped the vocalist into the back seat. Madame Fantastico patted Heidi with a trembling hand.

"Mr. Bridges, Rhiannon said you would free me from Cyrus. Is this true?" Her words were melodic and bird-like. "Please, I can't go back. He will do bad things to me—or worse."

"Rhiannon?" I said. "Who the hell is Rhiannon?"

"Marisol, boss," said Adamit. "Rhiannon *is* Marisol."

"Oh. Right."

Heidi licked the tears from the vocalist's face.

I faced the singer and said, "Madame Deux Vox Fantastico. We would be honored if you would join us."

She lowered her head and quietly sobbed into Heidi's neck.

CHAPTER 95

We packed our gear and loaded up our people without a hitch. The sun was still high in the sky as Crash, Russo, and myself watched Eiichiro taxi our DC-4 to the end of the runway, complete a textbook take off, and head upwards. Skip, who was piloting our Learjet, followed suit. Except for the fading thrum of *Mother* and our Learjet heading south, the base became very quiet. Russo used his flight-suit-covered elbow to wipe a smudge of grease off of *One Hope's* starboard wing.

"She's as ready as she'll ever be."

Crash offered us all a smoke and lit one for himself. "So," he said. "I guess this is it?"

I wondered where Marisol was. She hadn't been seen since this morning, and I was worried about her. The telephone in our hangar began ringing.

Who the fuck could that be? I went over and answered it. "Hello?"

"Hey, what the fuck are you still doing on the ground? Hurry up! The Nothingness, it's closing in. The edges of our universe, your future universe, they're folding inward, disappearing—"

"OK. What am I supposed to do with that information?"

"You just need to get up there and launch that satellite. ASAP! That means now. And by the way, when you see Jesus Morgan Freeman, tell him to *king* me."

"What the hell is that supposed to mean?"

"Shit! The CyComm is disappearing. One last thing. You have to do something. It's going to hurt, and you're going to bust a lung doing it, but you have—"

There was static, a few clicks, and then an operator said, "Chronospool trace receipt 005. Sethco time derivative unknown." *Click—dial tone.*

I walked back to *One Hope*. Crash gave me a nod. "Who was that?"

"C'mon," I said. "We better get going."

We climbed into *One Hope,* plugged our suits in, and ran through the lift-off punch list. Everything was a green light go. Today, we would head straight up, launch the satellite, and hopefully fly back down and land at our new base in Guatemala.

"Alright amigos," Russo said as he fired up the stabilizer thrusters. "This is it. All systems are a go. Crash, you have the honors."

"Roger," Crash said as he initiated the GRD. "This might get a little squirrely."

I looked out of the porthole and saw Marisol. She looked up at me and smiled. She'll be the death of me, I thought. Just as I waved to her, Crash increased power to the GRD and we zoomed straight up in a stiff vertical climb. That's when two mean-looking fighter jets bore in on us.

"Crash," I said. "We got bogies on our ass. We need more juice. More juice! Fuck! They're shooting at us!"

"OK," he replied. "Hang on!"

Four more jets flew by. Then, they turned, adjusted their flight paths, and followed us up in a steep vertical climb. Russo broadcast their warnings for us to land into my headset.

"What do we do?" he asked. "They want us to return to base. They say they're gonna shoot us down."

I could hear bullets pinging off our hull. "Keep going," I said.

"Are you joking? There shooting at us."

"If you want to live, go up," I said.

Crash didn't wait for Russo to respond; he just increased power to the GRD.

The G-forces of our gravity drive had me pinned to my seat. I could barely move. Then, just as we were leaving the atmosphere, we took a big hit.

CHAPTER 96

What the fuck, I thought. How long had we been out here? I remembered a thud and then some loud whooshing sounds. Yeah, now it was coming back. There had been that violent spin: the fuel tanks had probably gotten shot, ignited, and spun us up here like a twirling firework. The G-forces must have rendered us unconscious. I slapped my hands together. Damn, it was cold.

"Hey, guys," I said in my comm. "Do you copy? Wake up. We've got problems. Crash, Russo. Do you copy? Come back. Somebody say something."

"Arghhh..."

I shook the seat in front of me. "Hey, wake up!" It was dark in the cabin, and bits and pieces of the ship drifted about. I rotated the battery-selector switch to backup. Beeping sounds and dials, from a half-dozen locations, sprung to life and reported our condition.

"Whoa," Russo said, as he knuckled a few of the gauges. "What happened?"

"We got hit with something," I said. "Must've ignited the fuel canisters and pushed us up here. You OK?"

"Yeah, fine. Hey, I'm reading sixty minutes of air. What's the status on the backup?"

"Roger, let's see... Battery's showing two hours power at this level."

"Backup air. Seth. What's the status?"

"Air? Shit, I'm not sure."

"Seth, where are the backup air tanks located?"

"The last time I looked they were strapped to the undercarriage."

"*Brrrr*, it's cold in here." Crash said through chattering teeth. "Hey man, turn on the heat. I'm freezing my ass off."

"Good to hear from you," I said. "Listen, the fuel tank for the thrusters got punctured—shot us into space. We have an hour's worth of air, two hours left on the batteries, and we're sitting dead in the water. Well, dead in space. Figure out how to get us home. I'm gonna release the satellite."

"Wait! Just hold on. Let me think for a second... Alright. Whatever you do, don't release the satellite. It's got nitrogen thrusters; maybe we could use them somehow."

"How long would it take to remove them?" I asked.

"Hold on, just give me a sec. I gotta check out the systems. Let's see, GRDs, guidance and local comms are functioning—"

"Hey guys," Russo said. "We got a problem. We're losing air. In the last sixty seconds, we used up two minutes of air."

"Crash," I said, "where exactly are the emergency air tanks?"

"They're outside, under the cargo bay."

"Russo," I said, "how much air do we have left?"

He rapped the gauge. "At this rate, thirty minutes."

"So, Crash," I said, "are we on backup air now?"

He hesitated a moment. "Yeah, the tanks switch over automatically."

"Well, next time do you think you might be able to engineer room for some backup air inside the ship? You know, so they don't get shot up and stuff." That was stupid; I shouldn't have said that. It wasn't even his fault. Eiichiro had been the chief engineer for *One Hope*. Hell, I had approved the design. None of it mattered now.

I tried to remember what had happened: fighter jets had been bearing in on us, Crash had been pushing us up with the GRD. Oh shit... now I remembered. There had been those white flashes. And then, when I had looked down, there had been two mushroom clouds over Vegas. The bastards had really done it this time. There must have been thousands of dead on the ground. Damn, we had gotten out of there with no time to spare—or had we?

"Ideas?" I asked. "Anyone?"

"Stupid air tanks," Crash mumbled.

I put my hand on his shoulder. "Sorry for snapping at you. But Crash, right now, I need you to clear your mind and think."

"Ahh... I could plumb the backup air directly into the thruster array and use that to get us back to the atmosphere. The problem is, we can't hold our breath that long. Not enough air, damn it. If we could locate the leak, maybe we could clamp it off. There's just no access to the tanks, though... Fuck."

"Hey, you guys," Russo said. "Look up, off the starboard at two o'clock. See that? It's the goddamn Skylab. Those jokers told everyone it was decommissioned, said it fell to Earth."

"Whoo, hoo!" hollered Crash. "They got O2 scrubbers and spare air canisters for sure."

That was one hell of a coincidence, I thought. Shifter shit... definitely.

"Rangefinder says there's a mile between us," said Russo, "and we're closing the gap. The problem is, we're going in opposite directions."

"Can you contact them on the radio?" I asked.

"Not sure," Russo said, adjusting the radio's controls. "We'd have to get lucky—thousands of frequencies. Give me a second. I'll see what I can do."

It occurred to me that if we could get a hold of someone on the ground, they could call the Jericho Sims Corporation. Sims could contact Skylab and have them toss us over some air canisters. It was a completely ridiculous long shot, but the clock was ticking.

"What'd you got for air?" I asked.

Russo rapped the gauge. "Twenty-three minutes."

"Roger. Hey, can you access ham-radio frequencies on our gear?"

"Sure, that's an easy one."

"Alright, this is the plan. Get a hold of someone who speaks English on the ham radio. Tell them it's an emergency and have them call Jericho Sims. If anyone can help us, it's them. Their motto is, *If it exists, we can get it*. Let me know when you've got someone. Crash, if we get some air canisters, could we plumb them into our thruster array?"

"No problem," he said, still looking around for the leak. "They'll need three-quarter-inch standard male threads or equivalent adaptors. Forty pounders will fit the bill. All we have to do is bypass the thruster fuel tank with those ball-valves"—he pointed to an area below Russo's seat—"and connect the new tanks here." He pointed to a manifold near my seat. "Do you really think these Jericho Sims people can help?" he asked as he unbuckled his harness, turned, and faced me.

"They're miracle workers," I said. "Hell, I've seen them catch five-legged Boggles on the planet Pissiru. And they don't even have Boggles on that planet. So, when they say, *If it exists, we can get it,* they're not bragging. They really can."

Crash shook his head. "There's no planet Pisseru, is there?"

"Sure there is."

"I'm cold," he said. "Are you guys cold?"

"Wiggle your toes and fingers," I said, "that will help. Just keep doing it, and chin up. One way or another, we're going home."

Russo, whose speech was beginning to shiver and slur, said, "Seth, I got someone. Patching it through."

"Hello, is anyone there? Hello?" The distant voice sounded familiar.

"Yes, I can hear you," I said. My heart quickened as the radio squelched out some interference. "Can you hear me? Over."

"Yes." The voice said. "Who is this? Over."

I took a deep breath of stale air. "My name is Seth Bridges, and this is an emergency. I'm with two friends on a boat out of Vegas. We need you to place a phone call. Can you do that for us? Over."

"I reckon, but long-distance calls are mighty expensi—Hold up. Is this, *the* Seth Bridges? The one from the Sunday personals? The one that tipped me two hundred dollars a spell back—that Seth Bridges? Over."

I still couldn't place the voice, but apparently my penchant for over-tipping was finally paying off. "Roger, that's me. Over."

"Heavens to Murgatroyd. It's me, Mr. Bridges. Reggie. You know, Reginald T. Piedmont, from the men's room at the Sands Casino. Are you folks out in Lake Mead? Hey, you ever track down that Nazi fella? Over."

The chances of us contacting someone I knew were so remote that I had to conclude that additional Shifter-shit was in play. Probably a good thing considering our situation. How the hell had he survived a nuclear bomb? "Hey Reg, good to hear your voice again. Listen, we're in a bind up here, but more importantly, what's the situation on the ground?"

"Situation? Right as rain—better be, it's my day off. Got me some beer, nice and cold, go down *good*. Say, where you folks at again? Over."

"Reggie, we saw explosions over Vegas."

"Oh, that. The idiot-box says the Air Force had a mid-air smash up during one of them training exercises. One of the jets plowed straight into the top floor of the MGM. And now the whole building is on fire. Godawful stuff. Then there's that A-Rab apartment building, the other plane flew into that. I'll tell you what. My money says it's the commies. Been hearing damn sirens all afternoon. Hold up, let me look out this here window—"

"Reggie wait!"

Cold and desolation crept into my pressure suit while Reginald T Piedmont surveyed his world. After a few moments and a click, he was back. "I can see the smoke. Reckon it's just like the TV said: MGM Grand's on fire. Godawful. Hope those folks made it out in time. Over."

Hmm... maybe things weren't as bad as I thought. "Reg, this is important. I need you to call this number right now: 555-867-5309. And patch it to this channel. Can you do that? Right now? Over."

"That's what I do, Mr. Bridges, helping people in distress. Hold up, callin' as we speak."

Ten seconds later I heard the most incredible voice: "Jericho Sims. This is S. E. What is it I can get for you today, Mr. Bridges?"

Are you shittin' me? Reggie had done it; he had actually done it! I decided to lay it all out on the line and hope S. E. would get the gist of things in one take.

"Hey, S. E., I'm in a real bind. Currently, I'm above the Earth in a homemade spacecraft. I'm being patched through to you from my friend Reggie's ham radio. I have two crew members with me, and we're dead in the water—so to speak. We have about... fifteen minutes of air left. The good news is we're sharing an orbit with Skylab. We need you to contact those Skylab astronauts, rather, ahh, cosmonauts, and see if they can spare some forty-pound canisters of air. The canisters need to have three-quarter-inch standard thread male connectors or equivalent adaptors. We're thinking they could tether the air canisters together with a twenty-foot line, then push them out. With any luck, we can snag the rig and have enough air to work things out. Over."

"Understood," S. E. said. "What is your current position relative to Skylab? Over."

I waited a few seconds for *One Hope* to complete a tumble, then looked out of the canopy and got a visual. "Roger. Skylab is approximately one-quarter of a mile in front of us, though it's hard to tell exactly, and let's see... about two-hundred feet above us. It looks like we're traveling a smidge faster than they are, and we're closing the distance. Over."

"Roger, understood. Standby for instructions. Over."

In the background, I could hear the hushed and encouraging sounds of crisis management. "Mr. Bridges," Reggie cut in. "I surely am sorry. Didn't understand the fix you folks were in. What else can I do to help? Over."

"Reg, you're doing a great job. Just keep these lines open. OK?"

"Will do. Over."

"Crash, Russo, you guys still with me?"

Crash shivered out, "Roger."

"What's the plan?" Russo slurred, his teeth chattering.

A better question would have been: why hadn't I seen this disaster coming; and where the hell was Marisol when I needed her? She had been on the ground when we left. Yeah, she must have taken out the jets. That's where she had been, exactly where she needed to be.

"OK, guys," I said. "This is the plan: we get air canisters from that Skylab over there, Crash and I plumb them into our thruster manifold, and then we'll descend into the atmosphere and engage the GRD to keep us from burning up. After that, we'll glide down to safety. *That's* the plan. Any questions?"

There was a sputtering of snipes and protestations that consumed six seconds of air. Then silence. From the corner of my eye, I saw the glowing face of a Reaper flash past the port windshield. What was he doing here? Probing the ship, looking for weakness? He wouldn't find any. *One Hope* had thick walls and bulwarks designed to protect us from danger. In retrospect, she could have been bigger. A larger ship would have been able to fit the backup air inside the cabin.

CHAPTER 97

"Russo," I said, my voice slurring. "What do we got for air?"

"Fourteen minutes."

He rattled it off as if we were at a sports bar and it was the fourth quarter. Some nerve pain in one of my molars flared up. I wondered how Pablo, my old roommate from Tabor, was making out in dental school. Probably acing all his classes. He'd make a great dentist; he had the gift of nodding and saying, "Ah-uh," even when he wasn't paying attention.

"*One Hope. One Hope.* This is S. E. Do you copy? S. E. to Mr. Bridges. Come back. Over."

"Go ahead, S. E.," I replied. "This is *One Hope*. Over."

"Roger. Mr. Bridges, please, listen carefully. Commander Svetlana Gagarin is the sole occupant of the officially non-existent Skylab. Unofficially, she thinks your plan might have a chance. She's rigging two compressed-air canisters with a twenty-foot tether. When the time is right, she's going to set the canisters adrift. She estimates you'll be underneath her in four to five minutes, so be ready. Over."

"Roger. Understood. Four minutes. Good work, S. E. Please, thank the commander for us. We owe you guys—big time. *One Hope*, standing by this channel. Over."

"Godspeed, *One Hope*. S. E. standing by."

"God bless you," chimed in Reggie. "God bless you all. Over."

"Thanks, Reg."

Emboldened by our fortuitous opportunity to get air and live, I spat out orders: "Crash, I need you to come back here and get in my seat. Also, do we have any line onboard?"

It took us forty seconds to shift our seat assignments. "Alright, Seth," Russo said. "What's the plan? The actual plan. We need to know, right now!"

I looked at the air tank gauge. "This says twenty-four minutes. Half of that is twelve. Is that our total air supply: twelve minutes?"

He looked at the gauge. "That's the generous estimate."

"Alright, guys, here's what we're going to do. In three minutes, I'm going out there and snagging those canisters. Then, I'm gonna bring them back, so we can plumb them into the thruster array. Now, help me open these canopy turnbuckles. Shit, I need some line to tether me. Crash, did you find any line?"

"Seth!" Crash said, his voice so loud it distorted my headphones. "These are pressure suits. Not space suits. There's no fucking air in them. You do know that, right?"

Yeah, I knew it; but I had to do something. And according to future-me, this was it. I gulped down a few deep breaths and performed math in my head: twenty seconds to get out of *One Hope*, one minute to snag the air canisters, and one minute to dance with the Devil and get back here. Seemed simple enough, except for the part where I left the ship, snagged the canisters and then got back here on one breath of air. It wasn't going to work, and I knew it. If I were tied off and had a hook to snag the canister rig, I'd stand a better chance. The problem was time, and we were running out of it.

"Yes, Crash," I said. "I do know what this suit is capable of. What about a rope or some line? Do we have any?"

He held up a roll of duct tape. "No line, but I can unroll this and twist this into one. It's better than nothing. But your plan, Seth—it's suicide."

"Well, hurry up then. I need you to tie me off, toss me at the canisters, then haul me back after I grab them. OK? ...Do we have a hook or something I can snag the rig with?"

Russo turned and said, "Hey, guys, the commander lady is deploying the package off Skylab's stern. This is it!"

The green-faced Reaper billowed past the canopy's windshield.

"The cans are headed our way," said Russo, giving the play-by-play. "She's good. Fifty yards and closing. Looks a tad high, though."

"OK," I said. "Secure yourselves; I'm opening the canopy."

"Hold on," Crash said, unrolling the duct tape as fast as he could. "I haven't tied you off."

"There's no time. I'll use the valves on the compressed-air tanks to jet me back." I nodded to Russo as he turned the forward latches of the canopy open.

"Wait," said Crash. He floated a small chemical fire extinguisher at me. "Take this. At least you'll have a chance. And try to remember Newton's third law of physics—especially out there."

I removed the extinguisher's safety pin and secured my feet under a section of steel rail. The rig of air canisters was fifty feet above us and a good hundred feet away. We would converge vertically in about a minute.

"Crash," I said. "Whatever happens, make sure the satellite gets launched. Do you understand?"

"Let me tie you off!" he said.

"The satellite, Crash. Make sure it gets launched."

I took a deep breath, held it for a few seconds, then exhaled and took another deep inhale. Then, I disconnected my umbilical cord, secured its cover plate, opened the turnbuckle nearest me, slid the canopy open, and pushed off.

Images of wildebeests leaping into crocodile-infested rivers flashed in the back of my mind. This was not going to work. I remembered how I had almost drowned when I was ten, and how running out of air was really, really, awful. People took air for granted: it was all around us until it wasn't, and then...

Damn! Space was cold. I gave the handle on the extinguisher a quick squeeze. The propellant spun me backward and had me clunking my head into the nose of *One Hope*. *Fuck!* And just as I stabilized myself for another attempt, a Reaper streamed over and inspected my suit for weakness, or possibly craftsmanship—I wasn't sure. I kicked at him, then squeezed off a series of quick shots that got me moving in the right direction. A few minor corrections had me lined up with the canister's tether.

My lungs demanded attention. *Bust a lung:* wasn't that what future-me had said? Was he playing me for a fool? Just then, Paranoid showed up. He looked scared but willing to stand his ground and fight off the Reaper. Wait! What if future-me was an impostor: like an Octavius of some kind? Fuck. What if this was a trap? Paranoid pointed at *One Hope*. I looked back at the ship. Crash and Russo signaled me with thumbs up. Focus, Seth. You do want to live, don't you? I feathered a final adjustment with the fire extinguisher, then snared the tether and wrapped it around my forearm. With the hard work completed, all I had to do was get back to *One Hope*.

My lungs screamed for air. Surprisingly, I was able to squeeze a second breath out of the suit. I fired the extinguisher and headed back to the ship. My trajectory was dead on, but I was coming in too hot. Russo gestured his hands back and forth, trying to get me to slow down. And as Crash wrapped his hands around his helmet in an attempt to avoid an impending demonstration of Physics 101, I ran out of air. My vision faded into pinpricks of white light.

And then I was running.

The faster I ran, the less distance I covered.

I turned and saw the Reaper—mounted on a pale nag of a horse, heading my way.

He snatched me up by the back of my pressure suit.

I remembered Master Poe had once said, *A dead man has nothing to fear.*

CHAPTER 98

The next thing I knew, I was seated on a cushioned high-back chair in a room as boundless as the imagination. My helmet rested beside me on a floor that was gummy-bear squishy. Above, in the interdimensional miasma, there was a red glow that shone down on a small round table in front of me. Occasionally a musical note, soft but distinguishable, would flitter down from above. Other drawn-out notes would join in and, collectively, it sounded like circus music played slowly. On the table, a game of checkers was in progress. The Reaper, who had snatched me, sat opposite me. He leaned forward. A purple velvet robe, tailored from tens of thousands of tiny moving organisms, covered most of his skeletal frame. His neon-green holographic face was recessed into the robe's hood, and his eyes looked like mini-Earths that had been ravished by time and extremely cold weather.

"Have no fear," he said, in a voice reminiscent of James Earl Jones. "For I am SiSu, the lord of the realm that exists between hope and despair." He gestured his withered holographic hand at the checkers board. "Go ahead; it's your move." Then, he steepled his fingers. "You genuinely disappointed me. Going into space in a homemade wing-and-a-prayer deathtrap. What do you kids call that Fancy Nancy hero crap these days? Never mind, I don't want to know." His robe shifted through subtle color changes as the tiny organisms that it was composed of scrambled about. "I had plans for you. Unlike the others, you showed promise. You remind me of myself—in younger days. And now you go and do this?" He swiveled side to side and shook his skull disapprovingly. "That last move of yours was dangerous, foolish, and a flagrant violation of the agreed-upon terms." Like an octopus trying to adapt to a multitude of colored surfaces, his robe appeared desperate to console its master.

What terms? Who the fuck was this guy? Probably a hallucination brought on by oxygen deprivation. I had to stay focused and get the air canisters back to Crash and Russo. I shook my head in an attempt to snap out of it.

SiSu chuckled. "Those techniques are useless here. Tell me. Are you ungrateful? I just brought you in from the cold emptiness that was your life. A game of checkers—is that too much to ask of an old friend?" He smiled. "Have you forgotten how the game is played?"

He leaned forward. "Young man, are you aware that of all the creatures on Earth, it is only humans and their forebears that fear death? In a way it was you, Man, that created me."

"That's just terrific, Mr. SiSu," I said. "I'm very happy for you *and* my forebears. What about fearing life? Is there one of you for that?"

"I don't follow."

"Forget it. Just tell me, what do you want?"

"What do I want? I want so many things, but right now, I want you to be grateful. Think about it. I, the great and magnificent SiSu, while on vacation, just happened to spot your desperate soul flailing about. You are very fortunate indeed."

I looked around for an exit. "Oh, so you're lonely and you want some company. I should warn you, I didn't bring any lube."

"Ha, ha, ha. I do miss this type of spirited banter. You know, most of those I meet are defeated and boring. But you, you still have zest. I'm impressed. Hmm... you might even be worthy of a contract renegotiation."

I looked around for an exit. What was out there? Where would I go? Below me, on the checkerboard, I spotted a game-winning double-jump to a king.

"A contract?" I said. "I'm willing to negotiate."

Reaper SiSu chortled an evil-sounding laugh and said, "Oh you misunderstand—this contract is not with you; it's a prior contract with another entity—it shouldn't take too long. I'll tell you what, until then, and in honor of your wise-assery, I've arranged for a few visitors."

He pulled his hood backward and his face began to spin into a blur. Then, his spinning face slowed to a stop and morphed into the face of a boy.

"Hello, Mr. Bridges. My name is Octavius 1 Sun Taizu. On behalf of all who bear my name, I apologize. They sent us to kill you. We were children; we didn't know any better."

"Don't worry about it, kid," I said. "The world is a screwed-up place. But hey, at least you tried. Most people don't even do that."

The boy's face spun around like the vertical wheel of a slot machine, and then it slowed and reformed into the face of Dings, the cab driver who had set me up.

"Hey man," he said, "Just when I hit it big, you went ahead and had me killed. It was a grand-prize lottery ticket. Yeh know what I could've done with that kind of loot? Now they've banned me from hell. How's that for a how-do-you-do? Said I was screwing up their system. What kind of system is that? Anyway, I'm in limbo right now. You think maybe you could give me a ride outta here?"

Like a haywire slot machine in jackpot mode, the faces continued. Next was Colton Hill. A tear slid down his cheek.

"Hey Seth. I knew you would find me. That's what friends are for, right? Hey, have you seen my heart? It's around here somewhere. What do you say we find it, then you and I get the hell out of here?"

Before I could respond, Colton Hill's face transposed into Mohamed, my friend from the Middle Eastern food cart. "Seth, I see Allah has plans for you. Have you prepared your way?"

I got up to leave. Where to? I wasn't sure.

"Whoa, whoa. Hold on, son," said a voice I recognized as Morgan Freeman.

Fuck, why was he here? Was he going to explain everything? I sat down out of curiosity. Morgan was now in Reaper SiSu's chair. He had a long white beard and wore a flowing white robe. His monochromatic appearance exuded a robust Jesus vibe.

"We were just finishing up the details of a wager renegotiation," he said. "It would surely be appreciated if you could hold on for a few more moments—you understand."

I shrugged. Who was I to argue with Jesus Morgan Freeman? I wondered if he was related to the Morgan Freeman who had spoken to me on the ship above the planet Varuka 5. Wait! I was supposed to tell him something. What was it again…?

As I sat down, I heard, "We're so proud of you son." I looked up and saw Jesus Morgan Freeman transform into my mother from my original timeline: the one where I was a fifty-year-old misanthropic plumber, counting down time with beer, cigarettes, and chambered rounds. Mom looked eighty. She wore glasses, her favorite chemo wig, and seemed quite concerned with my present situation.

I had forgotten about this version of my mom. It seemed so long ago. By all accounts, I had been a lousy son. I wanted to tell her how sorry I was, but before I had a chance to, she morphed into my grandfather.

He looked me in the eyes and gave me a stern command. "Make them hear your voice. Let them know who you are. Who *we* are!"

Then my grandfather barked out, "Arooo, arooo," as he morphed into Exon, the best dog in the world. She wagged her tail, spun in a circle, chuffed a hello, and just as she got ready to get closer, she changed back into Jesus Morgan Freeman.

"We're almost there, young man," Morgan said. "How are you feeling?"

I shook my head. "Star-fucking-tastic. What's with these mind games? Why can't you just get to the point? I've got things to do. Wait! I've got to tell you something. I just need to remember..."

Freeman offered up a sympathetic smile. "I understand. We're all busy with something or another. That's what we do, right? Although I must admit, sometimes we get so busy we don't even know what we're doing, or, for that matter, *why*. Tell me, son, have you ever asked yourself *why*?"

I leaned forward. "Are you the same Morgan Freeman from the spaceship above Varuka 5?"

"I'm a ubiquitous avatar. Now, Mr. Bridges, I ask you, *why*? That's the question I mull every day. We have some time, so indulge me: why are you here?"

I shrugged. "Um? I ran out of air, and this is my subconscious messing with me?"

"OK. Why did you run out of air?"

"Because I screwed up."

"Why did you screw up?"

"I don't know. Because I'm human?"

"Why are you human?" He asked as if I had a choice in the matter, but before I could respond, he continued, "Perhaps the question should be, why do anything? You answer that one, and you'll be further ahead in the game."

"What game?"

Freemen continued, "Are you familiar with quantum mechanics?"

"Not really," I said, trying to figure out his angle. "I got people, though. They know all about that kinda stuff."

"Tell me, have you ever heard of Schrödinger's cat?"

"Sure—an experiment with a cat in a box or something like that. Right?"

"Yes, that's part of it. But more importantly, it is an experiment that demonstrates the possibility of alternate universes. What you do is: take a cat, put it in a box, close the box off, then introduce a substance that has an equal chance of killing or not killing the cat. Until the box is opened, that cat could be considered, by some, as both dead and alive. Some believe that the universe splits in two when the box is opened. One universe for the dead cat, and one universe for the cat that lives. Son, right now, *you're* that cat. Fortunately for you, my friends and I have just installed an escape door for that box you're in."

Oh great, so now I was a cat. Marisol was gonna be all over me now.

Morgan raised a finger and mouthed the words, "Hold on." Apparently, he was receiving an incoming message. "Yes. Yes. I understand. Very good." He turned to me. "Good news—your soul particles, the information that is you, has been re-collated, and, additionally, contract negotiations have concluded." He politely clasped his hands. "Spooky action at a distance: impressive stuff, even for me." He offered me his best Hollywood smile and said, "Well, then, everything appears to be in order. I do wish you the best of luck. Choose well, Mr. Bridges."

"Wait!" I yelled, just as he morphed into a familiar looking young girl.

"Grandpoppy," she said. "We miss you." I remembered her name was Sabita, and she was my future granddaughter from Kalesh. "When are you coming home?" she said, as her face flickered away.

I so desperately wanted to talk to her, but she was gone. I looked down, took hold of the correct game piece, and double jumped my way to a game-winning king. Then, I upturned the table and hollered, "KING ME MOTHERFUCKERS!"

Submarine klaxons blared from all quarters. Bright lights flashed red with warning. From the outward expanse, Crash and Russo appeared—small at first, and then they grew larger. They were flying right at me. They hoisted me up by my armpits and flew me away.

CHAPTER 99

"Here. Help me! Grab his arms." It was Crash. I could tell by his voice. "Forget the canisters," he continued. "They're gone. It's too late. Quick, strap him in a seat. Is he breathing?"

I tried to open my eyelids, to let Russo and Crash know I was alive, but my eyelids were not responding to my commands. I could hear someone locking down the canopy turnbuckles. Then, someone was pushing up and down on my chest. It didn't hurt.

"I can't believe we lost the air canisters," said Crash. "Is he alive?"

"Hold on," Russo gasped. "I've got him connected to the ship's air. Doesn't look too bad. He's not blue or anything. Hey, ahh, are we gonna die up here?"

It was quiet for a few moments. I figured Crash was sorting out the incoming flashes of brilliance that danced in his mind. I was so glad I'd hired him. He was a truly brilliant man. I had once read that geniuses have two peaks in their lifetimes: the first happens when they are between twenty and twenty-four years old and is due to ambition and blatant disregard of established rules. Their second peak of insight happens when they are around fifty, when they are semi-retired and have a chance to absorb the wisdom of their experiences and apply it to—

"Fucking A!" I heard Crash yell. "I can't believe I didn't think of this earlier."

"What do you got?" Russo asked as he doled out evenly timed chest compressions on my chest. "Let me guess. Knock on Spacelab's door and hope they let us in before we're dead?"

"Forget that sardine can," Crash said. "The answer to all our problems has been right here all along."

I heard him slap something hard.

"All we have to do," he said, "is reverse the poles on the GRD's battery connection. The Gravity Resist Drive will become a *Gravity Increase Drive*. The mass of the Earth will suck us back like a tractor beam. We'll have to reverse the poles again, on re-entry... No, all we have to do, once we hit the atmosphere, is switch over to the backup GRD; that will slow us down. Yeah, that'll work. Fucking brilliant, if I don't say so myself. You ready to go home?"

"Fuck, yes." said Russo. "Tell me what to do!"

It was at that moment I understood what Master Poe had meant when he said, *The world will provide anything to anyone who seeks it.*

"Open that toolbox," I heard Crash say. He was probably pointing to the toolkit fastened to the sidewall of the hull. Then he said, "I need the large Phillips head."

Russo stopped compressing my chest. I could hear him unfastening the toolbox, grabbing at the screwdriver, and saying, "Here it is," to Crash. Then, I felt Russo lift me up and strap me into a seat.

I wondered how Crash was managing the hand tools with his pressure suit on, and I thought I could use a few more chest compressions. I kinda felt like I was running out of air again, but it wasn't as painful.

"Find a new home for this," I heard Crash say. "And hand me the ten-mill box end."

I heard Russo wedge a piece of metal, probably the cover plate to the GRD, under his seat. Then he said, "Here."

I imagined he was handing the wrench to Crash. I wished I could ask Russo for more chest compressions. I could hear Crash swapping out the two battery cable leads. But I was fading—my very being was fading.

"OK, that's that," said Crash. "Russo, get back into the pilot's seat." I could hear Russo getting into his pilot's seat. Then Crash asked, "What do we have for air?"

"Four minutes," was the answer Russo gave him. It was hard to discern because now my hearing was failing me and I really needed that air.

Crash bumped into me as he made his way to the stern. There was a loud whoosh. I was sure he'd just released the satellite. Good, I thought. Launching that satellite was a causality that would shape the future.

"We don't need that anymore," Crash said as he strapped himself in. "OK, here we go," he continued. "We're gonna head straight down; it looks like Africa. You speak African?"

I tried to answer him but I couldn't. I was no longer on *One Hope*.

I was a ghost, outside, floating around, and looking down on *One Hope* from space. I got scared and quickly slipped back into the ship.

"Janbo," someone gasped.

I turned and saw Russo. He looked like he was in bad shape, but there was hope in his eyes.

"Russo," I said. "It's me, Seth."

He didn't respond. I was a ghost, I thought; he couldn't see or hear me.

I watched Crash as he switched the backup Gravity Resist Drive to standby and slowly increased power to his impromptu Gravity Increase Drive. The ship began to move, slowly at first, and then, gradually, it sped up—toward Earth.

"You did it!" Russo cheered as he looked out of the canopy. "We're going home! I love you, man."

I looked out of the canopy too; the Earth was growing larger. How long did I get to be a ghost for, I wondered.

The ship began to vibrate and hum as we buffeted Earth's outer atmosphere. I watched Crash dial-in the Gravity Resist Drive as he simultaneously reduced power to the Gravity Increase Drive. His gloves, which were part of his flight suit, made the task impossible. He took a deep breath, removed his helmet, stripped-off the top half of his pressure suit, and bare-handed both gravity drive control dials. As we pierced the atmosphere, he was able to keep us from burning up by synchronizing the drives and slowing our speed.

He'd better get this right, I thought.

Sixty seconds later, he equalized the drives and held us level, stationary, and in the middle of the sky.

"Good job," I said. But, of course, he couldn't hear me.

Then, he unfastened the canopy, slid it open, and sucked in the air.

I joined him.

"Yes!" he gasped. Then, he burned his hand on the outer hull, said, "Ouch," and looked out over the side of the ship.

We were over a desert. I remembered him saying something about Africa. What the fuck was I supposed to do with myself now?

Crash ducked back inside.

I followed him.

He gave Russo a few smacks on the shoulder. "We're holding position at three thousand feet above the west coast of North Africa."

Russo had removed his own helmet and was sucking in air when Crash said, "Here, help me with Seth's helmet."

Oh, now they were going to check on me.

Russo began to perform CPR on my body—my dead body.

"It's too late," I told them. They were scared: I could see it in their faces. "It's OK, guys," I said.

They kept up the CPR for a good two minutes. Finally, Russo, breathing heavily, looked up and said, "He's gone."

"He can't be!" said Crash. "Are you sure?"

Russo shook his head. "I've seen a lot of this before. Back in Nam. No pulse. I'm pretty sure... Sorry, man."

"I told you guys," I said. "It's OK. It was my fault, not yours."

"HEY. YOU UP THERE. COME ON DOWN!"

Wait, I knew that voice.

"Did you hear something?" said Crash as he looked at Russo. "I think it's coming from the ground."

"Come on, guys," I said. "Let's go see who it is."

We all stuck our heads out of the open canopy and looked down. A thermal upwelling carried the aroma of the Atlantic Ocean, the desert, and the distinct sound of a female voice.

"WHAT ARE YOU WAITING FOR? HURRY UP. GET DOWN HERE."

About a mile below, someone was flashing a signal at us.

Crash said, "Strap in, we're going down." We all got back inside and took our seats. Crash and Russo navigated us straight down and onto the side of a dune. I watched as they dragged my body out of *One Hope* and propped it up on the shady side of our craft. The stranger, who resembled a female version of Lawrence Of Arabia, walked over, pulled off a facial scarf, and gave us a reassuring smile.

It was Marisol. I knew it! That girl was always up to something. Hadn't Adamit said she could kill a legion of men with a thought and then bring them back to life on a lark? Maybe she could put *me* back into my body. I wondered if my brain still had enough oxygen in it, or had it begun to decay? How the hell had she gotten here anyway?

Seth—she was an advanced alien species; she could do all kinds of miraculous things.

"Hi, Marisol," I said with a wave.

She walked right past me on her way over Crash and Russo. "I've arranged for your transportation to Guatemala," she said. "Thank you both for being so brave."

In the distance, a dual-rotor Chinook helicopter was coming over a rise. I could read *Willhammer Salvage and Rescue* on its side. And, if I wasn't mistaken, the pilot was Dex, the cabbie who had picked me up in Vegas when I'd first arrived.

I turned back to my dead self and saw Marisol. She went over to my body, leaned down, and blew green fog into my mouth.

Suddenly, ghost-me was sucked away. I was a kid again, back in my original timeline, relieving my life over as if it were the first time. The years passed by in a flash, but each day was as long as a day, and each year as long as a year, and they were rich in detail and minutiae. I suffered through the indignities of growing up without knowledge of the future.

Then I was back in high school, working evenings and weekends, so I could have some cash and a girlfriend. Then, I was off to college. After that, I was back at my miserable job and my equally miserable life. I lived in my shack, drank a lot of alcohol, and watched the world turn from a chair in my backyard. One day when my efforts to drown out the noise of the world were no longer working, I found myself driving to Herring Cove Beach. It was early in the tourist season, and thank God the beach and its parking lot were almost empty. I smelled like shit from a job at work and I had a headache.

After downing a nip of vodka and a whole can of Budweiser, I flicked on the radio, pulled the .38 revolver from under the seat, and laid it on my lap. On the radio, an old geezer was boasting that the only regret he had in his entire life was not proposing to his *lovely* wife sooner. Bullshit, I thought.

Then, as the show's bumper music, "(Don't) Fear the Reaper" by Blue Oyster Cult, was leveled off, I saw her—down aways, along the shore. She was barefoot, wore a long white summer dress, and was skirting the line between the sand and sea. It was at that very moment that it all came back to me, everything: Vegas, the building of *One Hope*, walking on the moon, my life on Kalesh, everything... Then, the woman in the long white dress walked over and smiled at me.

It was Marisol. It had always been Marisol. I got out of my truck and faced her. She kissed me and said, "You see clear now."

"Yes, Marisol. I do."

Then, I was sent back into the Africa desert, and back into my body, which was propped up on the shady side of *One Hope*. Crash and Russo were staring at me.

I sucked-in a huge breath and yelled, "KING ME, MOTHERFUCKERS!"

The End